Louie G

Alan E Bailey

The Alexander Saga

For my nieces and nephews;
Angie, Mason, Jessica, Emily, Lindsey,
Kara, Brittney, Jeremy, Jaxon and Jordan
and my grandnieces and grandnephews;
Maddy, Nick, Caleb, Evangeline, Isabelle,
Kaylynn and Violet.
As my father always said,
Remember who you are.

With special thanks once again to Walter, Irene,
and Katherina for your input, corrections, suggestions,
revisions, and countless hours of proofreading,
and also to Mark,
for your unquestioning support.

Alan E Bailey

FOREWORD

This book is the second novel in *the Alexander Saga* series. Like the first book, *Myrtha*, it is fiction that is based on the true story. *Louie G* is a story of determination and of secrets kept, that was difficult to write and is sometimes disturbing to read, but shares the triumph of love and courage in our American family.

To understand the origin of this series I have to explain that my parents did not always have a happy marriage. In fact, about thirty years ago when I was living in another state, every time they called I thought they were going to tell me they had filed for divorce. Happily, they were able to reconcile, although their differences were always pronounced and many. They were from a generation that stuck it out, and I believe that their final years together were mostly happy ones.

My father died in April, 2005. My mother outlived him by seven months. They had both been ill a long time. We had a lot of time to prepare, however, we expected Mom to go first. It almost seemed like Dad died without warning.

Mom was always the organized planner of the marriage and while she had severe physical limitations, she dealt with living alone so much better than Dad ever would have. But, as time went by, she grew lonelier and less able to cope with the demands of daily living. I fell into a routine of spending Sunday afternoons with her. We would go through her mail and pay her bills, but mostly we spent those afternoons visiting. Her body was failing, but her mind was still active and clear as a bell.

That last Sunday of October, as I was beginning to gather my things to leave, a time that was always difficult and she delayed and prolonged as much as possible, she became increasingly agitated and near tears. I put down my things and sat down beside her again.

She said there was something she needed to tell me, something she had always wanted to tell her children, but Dad would never let her. I was not surprised. They were also from a generation that kept their secrets. She became more distressed, saying it was something about Dad's family. Something she thought we needed to know about ourselves. I could see it was something she had kept

3

bottled up for a long, long time. I waited for her to continue.

Then to help her, I said I thought I already knew what it was. The hints had always been there. Mom and I agreed to talk about it some other time. And that was it. Two weeks later, my mother had a massive stroke and died at home.

I have often wondered if I really knew what she was talking about that Sunday afternoon, or more specifically, if we were thinking about the same thing. I also know that if Mom had been the first one to go, that conversation would not have happened and my curiosity about the family might never have been raised. In fact, without that talk, this book and this series would not have been written.

After Mom's funeral, her seven children and their families went back to their homes and their lives. Before long, I realized that the rich verbal history her family passed down was not being shared with the next generation of my family. We are scattered farther than our parents could have ever imagined. I also realized those stories would die with me someday.

So, in 2009, I began a project of writing a series of letters to my nieces and nephews, documenting those stories. Over the next year I wrote twelve letters, sharing the stories as close to what I could remember being told to me.

Those letters became the inspiration for this fictional series, *the Alexander Saga*. The first book, *Myrtha,* focused solely on my mother's side of the family. As I fictionalized the letters into the novel, adding dialogue, characters, and the necessary bridges to link individual stories, I soon realized I would need to divide the stories into at least three books. The biggest challenge of the first book was selecting, cutting and condensing from the vast wealth of stories that the generations of women on that side of the family told.

All the time I was writing *Myrtha* I had the nagging realization that I knew virtually nothing of my father's family. He rarely spoke of his childhood; it was not a happy one and he left home at a very young age. While I saw Myrtha, my maternal grandmother, several times a week for the first twenty-six years of my life, I can count on one hand the number of times I saw Louie G, my father's mother, during my entire lifetime.

After finishing *Myrtha*, and thinking I already knew the secrets of my father's family, I began research for this novel. There are some wonderful websites and online tools for doing that. I was able to trace his mother's family through the American South and even further back to England in the late 1600s. I was amused that while my mother's family seemed to think she had married beneath her, I so readily uncovered that my father's mother was descended from, and carried the surname of, a titled English family. But after uncovering the basics, my research became more frustrating and even after driving across the South to Charleston, I found myself coming to one dead end after another.

4

Nothing I found clearly supported my theory of my father's heritage and, in fact, seemed to only raise more questions: Why did one branch of the family buy and sell large tracts of land in eastern Louisiana during the early 1800s? Why did their impoverished son file a claim for a 50-acre homestead only twenty years later? Were they really slave owners, so completely incongruent with what I thought I knew about them? And even more puzzling, what prompted them to leave their homes in the eastern states and migrate to the vast, wild and dangerous coastal flatlands of Texas in the 1840s and 1850s?

There is one person in this family tree who especially intrigued me, and still raises more questions than she provides answers.

In 1750, Mary Freeman seemingly appeared from nowhere, born to unnamed parents in the eastern wilds of the newly-opened Georgia colony. She remained unmarried until the age of twenty-eight, a serious old maid in those times, and then married the son of a prominent family who was also twenty-eight and from the same county. They were married in another state. They had only one child, born the same year they were married, and the couple apparently never lived together – or even lived in the same county. He lived to be seventy and she lived to be eighty-seven. In spite of her humble beginnings, she died a wealthy woman. I was simultaneously appalled and fascinated with what I found in the legal documents filed for the settlement of her estate.

The line from Mary Freeman extends down seven generations through my paternal grandmother Louie G to me. I believe this lineage is the answer to the question my mother raised that Sunday afternoon in October, 2005.

And this book is that story.

Alan E Bailey
Springfield, Missouri
November 1, 2013

For the reader's convenience, a list of characters by period is presented in family tree format at the end of the book.

PART ONE

MERCY

CHAPTER ONE

Charles Town
South Carolina Colony
1717 - 1734

Mary Freeman was white.

Her Great Aunt Charity saw to that a long time ago. Charity Wainwright simply claimed Mary's mother as her own and presented her to all of old Charles Town as her niece, which in fact she was. Charity's brother, Richard Wainwright, owned Mary's mother and he was Mary's grandfather.

Mary's mother was a quadroon, which meant she was one-quarter black. That one-fourth was from her grandmother. Old Bess worked in the kitchen on the Wainwright plantation, some twenty miles up the river from Charles Town. Old Bess came from Africa. No one really knew when Bess had been born there, but it was in 1690 and five years before the Old Massah himself was born in the Carolina colony.

She had an African name and, not long after she became a woman, she left her mother and became a man's wife. He was a strong man, good and handsome, but he could never subdue Bess. She was willful and strong and too smart for him. She bore him three sons before the hood was thrown over her head and her hands were held behind her back and tied together. She had stayed too late working in her garden outside the village. She fought wildly against her captors until they overpowered her. They were Igbo and from her grandmother she knew enough of their words to understand they would kill her instead of letting her go. She was taken to the coast and held with others who had been captured too. After many days they were chained together and taken to a ship that waited for them. And she said goodbye to Africa.

The *Cateret* was only a small part of "The Middle Passage." Every year hundreds of trading ships left England for the West African coast. In Africa the ships were emptied of their stores and were filled again with captive Africans. From Africa, those ships sailed directly west to South America and delivered those captives for sale in Brazil and then on up through the Caribbean to the colonies.

In Carolina, captives brought directly from Africa would be off-loaded at Sullivan's Island for "seasoning;" a process of making them ready for sale. At Sullivan's Island the ship would be refilled again with captives who were ready to be sold, that is they understood the basic commands for the work they would do, and had learned to fear the lash as punishment. When captives were ready for sale, they would make the brief, but final, voyage to Charles Town where they were sold and became slaves.

In Charles Town and on up the coast, the ships would be refillec livestock and goods from the colonies that were bound for Englε profitable trade. With good winds and good luck, a ship could cι triangular run twice in a year.

In 1717, Thomas Creed was captain of the *Cateret.* After selling off some of his African cargo in South America and the Caribbean, he refilled his ship with enough seasoned slaves from Barbados so that he could sail directly to Charles Town and by-pass Sullivan's Island. During all of the Yamasee War, almost no ships had landed in Charles Town, including slavers. Only one slave ship arrived in 1715 and none in 1716. The shortage of slaves caused by the cessation of supply was exacerbated by the Yamasee's kidnap of existing slaves from farms whose white owners they had killed or had fled to the safety of the town walls. In the Carolina forests, the Indians delivered those slaves to traders who likely took them north to Virginia and Maryland where they were sold into slavery again.

With the war settled and trade restored, the residents of South Carolina paid handsomely for anything the ships would bring them, especially slaves. In pursing that potential for profit, some captains pushed their crews to the point of mutiny, with the sailors as likely to feel the sting of the lash as the human cargo they transported.

Although Captain Creed recognized the profits awaiting him in Charles Town he was not as brutal with the crew of the *Cateret.* They had an early start on the Middle Passage's triangular route and were set to easily complete two full circuits before the winter storms set in. He maintained a firm hand, but he knew pushing his crew harder would not mean a third circuit.

He also was sick of the trade and of its stench and misery. He planned to retire from it at the end of the year. His men clearly understood their limits, and they also understood that the more captives they delivered alive to the Americas would mean more in their purse when they returned to England. But those limits did not mean they could not pleasure themselves sometimes with the female captives, especially when a fresh load was brought on board. Captain Creed tended to turn a blind eye to that.

As soon as she stepped onto the ship, Bess was pulled aside with some of the other women for the crew's pleasure. When the sailor who grabbed Bess was finished and pushed her roughly in front of him to join the others below deck, the man in charge of the ship - she would learn he was called The Captain - noticed her. Standing on his upper deck, Captain Creed saw the tall, strong and fine woman that Bess was. She saw him looking at her bared breasts. She had fed three sons from them and now she understood her life was in his hands. She looked directly at him with understanding and knowledge and he had her brought to his quarters. She became his comfort girl for the voyage.

...veling that way for the next three months, as the sole property and under the protection of The Captain, assured her survival. The old captain was not as demanding as her husband had been and Bess satisfied him easily. She prepared simple food for him and kept his cabin tidy. In exchange, she had a steady supply of food and even a dress in the style of the colonies that he produced from a trunk somewhere. It was the color of new grass on the savannah after the rains, and although she did not understand him, he said it favored her. Perhaps the dress had belonged to his real wife in England.

Bess set about learning his language. She made it a game, rewarding him as he revealed his language to her. Sometimes she caught him staring fondly down at her in the early morning when she awoke in his bed beside him, but when the ship arrived at the final port that was called Charles Town she was herded off the ship with the others and sold. The Captain could not return to England with her. Keeping only the dress he had given her, she was shackled and chained and taken off the ship with the others. As they were herded down the gangway one of the women who was brought up from below decks, grabbed at one of the sleeves of the dress, ripping it away at the shoulder. Then she hawked and spat at Bess, showing her contempt for The Captain's pet.

Bess arrived in this new land of Charles Town showing that she was pregnant. The child was most likely from the young sailor who took her the first day on the ship. The Captain was too old and fat to properly plant his seed within her, but when her belly began showing on the final few weeks of the voyage he still strutted around like the old village rooster.

In Charles Town, Bess was paraded along with the other captives before the crowd for inspection. Most of the captives were terrified but Bess had seen slaves sold in her village and knew what was happening to her. When she was taken aside and stripped naked for inspection by a white man about her age, instead of bowing her head and trying to cover herself in shame she looked directly at him, put her hand on her bare chest and said, "Bess." (It was the name The Captain had given her) and then rubbing her belly she said The Captain's word; "baby."

Even more surprised than he had been seeing Bess dressed in a white woman's gown, however tattered it was, Richard Wainwright was completely taken aback that she spoke to him in English, especially among the mass of cowed and terrified heathen Negroes on this shipment that was mostly fresh from Africa. They showed marks of the lash but she did not. From where had she come? He asked her a question but she only looked at him and he knew she did not understand what he asked. She had only been repeating words she had heard.

But she was healthy and her eyes were bright and her black skin glowed without the smell of blood that the traders rubbed on them to give a good color after the starvation of the voyage. He also saw that her face with the high cheek bones, thoughtful eyes set closely together under a high, defined brow, the long nose with its high bridge, thinner lips and narrow jaw, was more reflective of his own English profile than the others from the ship. He bid up the price for her and at the end of the day she was tethered behind his carriage with four others from the ship. They ran along behind as he was driven through the streets of Charles Town to his sister's house. He always boarded with his sister when he stayed in town.

When the others, all male, were chained together at their ankles and locked in the stable that night, Bess was locked alone in the windowless garden shed behind the house. When her new captain and his woman came out in the morning to unlock the shed, Bess was already up, dressed in her dress, and standing quietly in the middle of the shed with her hands folded and her head bowed.

"She's filthy Richard," Charity said after looking her over. "But that's to be expected after such a voyage. She looks young and healthy, and from those eyes I would say she looks more intelligent than most. You did well."

"Can you cook? Do you cook food? Food to eat?" Charity said loudly to Bess, bringing her hand to her mouth like she was eating an invisible biscuit. Richard laughed outright at that. "She's straight out of Africa, Char. She can't understand a damned word you're saying."

Bess answered the chief's woman with quiet and deliberate words, "Bess cook, Mam'selle. Bess good cook food captain."

One day when the ship was docked in the islands, The Captain took Bess off the boat and into town, thinking she may fetch him a fair price. She was tethered to him with an iron shackle around her wrist, but she walked proudly and obediently behind him so the tether was unnecessary. She took in everything, noticing others like her who walked behind their captain or captain's woman, carrying their bundles. She overheard that her untethered counterparts addressed their captain's woman as "Mam'selle," a word she remembered now and used with her new captain's woman to show her respect.

Charity smiled in approval at Bess and then turned with a triumphant and teasingly disdainful look at her elder brother. "Your new slave cooks Richard, and apparently she speaks some French, too. I will have Patience clean her up and she can help in the kitchen while you are here."

While Charity teased Richard, she kept a close eye on him. His young wife had died of the fever she contracted during the evacuation of the plantation to Charles Town at the beginning of the Yamasee War. The young Master, their son, was also sick with it but recovered only to die during the starvation of the siege. This purchase, sorely needed to replace the field workers kidnapped from the plantation, was the first sign of interest from her brother. When he was in Charles Town he typically spent his time drinking at the Globe Tavern until he had to be carried home by Charity's footman, Benjamin.

Charity's cook, Patience, was told to make a hot bath and clean up the new girl.

In the kitchen house, Patience assumed the new African knew nothing. She heated water while Bess watched and then poured it the bathing tub. She brought out a bath sponge and a cake of the soap she made every fall. Then she brought Bess to the side of tub and started to remove the dress. Bess pushed Patience away, which resulted in Patience giving Bess a good hard slap on the side of her face.

"Bess bath," Bess said with her hand to her stinging cheek and trying to hold back her anger at the woman – a woman without tribal markings but whose round and flattened face were from a people who had been subdued long ago by Bess's people. Although the woman was clearly in charge here, her people were still inferior in both strength and culture to the Yoruba and she would not undress Bess. The Captain had liked a bath on the ship, even though it was only sea water. He bathed often during the voyage. Bess always prepared his bath and after she vigorously rubbed him dry before the sea water dried to salt on his skin, she sometimes bathed in the tub after him. "Bess know bath."

"Well, take your own damned bath then, Missy," Patience huffed, throwing a wet sponge at Bess and soaking the front of the dress The Captain had given her. When Bess took the soap cake she could not help holding it to her nose as she breathed deeply. "That my good lavender soap, Missy," Patience explained. "Nothing but the finest for m'lady."

"Soap," Bess managed holding the cake to her nose again. It smelled wonderful. Almost too wonderful to waste in the bath water. She would eventually learn it was scented with lavender from Miss Charity's herb garden. Long ago, the lavender was brought from England by Charity's mother who planted and tended it carefully in the sandy loam of the plantation. When this house was built in town, a row was planted in the herb garden behind the kitchen house, solely for the purpose of scenting the soap Patience made and to fill the pomanders Charity sewed for her clothing and linen trunks. There were dried bundles of it hanging from the rafters of the kitchen. Charity's house smelled of lavender.

Since bathing the new girl was her responsibility, Patience watched. She would motion what Bess needed to do by pantomime, rubbing parts of her own body with an imaginary sponge. When she was satisfied Bess was clean she unfolded a large linen bath sheet and wrapped it around Bess as she stood naked in the tub. It was a wonder Bess had never experienced.

After the bath, Patience brought out new clothes for her to put on. "This dress for a whore," she said, wrinkling up her nose with disdain at the old dress Bess arrived in. And although Bess did not understand the word she stored it away as Patience dressed her in clothes Charity brought down from the house while Bess was in the tub. It was a simple layered ensemble almost exactly like the one Patience was wearing. It had been hastily put together from cast-offs Miss Charity had once worn for simple day wear.

"You gone do this by yourself next time, Missy, so you pay tenshun." Patience commanded, not sure if Bess understood. She was comforted that Bess was watching the process intently and seemed to understand. Bess looked from the loose garments to the clothing Patience was wearing for comparison.

As Bess stood naked in the kitchen, Patience showed her to lift her arms and then she slipped the white linen shift over her head. It was open in front at the neck and halfway down to her waist. The shift hung loosely from the shoulders and came just below her knees. Bess fought the urge to struggle against the feeling of being bound again as Patience tied the sleeves shut just below the elbows. She would learn later that everything, except the shift, came off again at night before she lay down in the bed beside Patience for sleep. The only time the shift came off was when Bess took her bath. Like Patience she would have two shifts so one could be washed each week. The rest of the clothing was never washed as long as Bess wore them. In fact, the outer clothes still had the smell of Miss Charity's perfume on them. They had not been washed after Miss Charity discarded them.

Bess would also learn that Miss Charity had four complete changes of clothing for her day dress at home, as well as two finer gowns and undergarments for when she went out. Most of the women in Charles Town owned only two sets of clothing. Her extended wardrobe showed that Miss Charity was indeed a wealthy woman. She would also learn that Miss Charity secretly bathed in the kitchen each week. It was excessive, to the point that it would seem odd if any of Miss Charity's friends knew of the practice. But Miss Charity felt a weekly bath was necessary, especially in the low country climate. Because of that, she also wanted Patience to bathe weekly. Instead of making another bath, Patience usually washed herself in Miss Charity's bath water, after Miss Charity was dressed and back in the house, of course. The fact that Bess had a fresh bath in the middle of the week that no one else had already bathed in was not lost on Patience.

With the shift in place, Patience took a long strip of light brown linen. She folded the cloth lengthwise and then lifted the cloth to put the middle at the back of Bess' neck. Bringing the ends of this kerchief to the front she fanned them out to cover Bess's bosom.

Then over the shift and the neck scarf went the most unusual thing Bess had ever seen. Patience called it "stays." It was a sort of jacket with no sleeves. Patience helped her put her arms through the arm holes and then while Bess held the jacket together in front, Patience laced a strong cord back and forth across the front to hold it closed. Then she pulled the cord so the stays were snug around Bess's middle section.

"Not too tight over that baby," Patience said. She slipped her hand underneath the bottom of the stays showing Bess it was still a little bit loose at the bottom.

Bess felt her breasts nearly flattened at first under the stays. Then they shifted upward and threatened to spill over the top. This was ridiculous. She wanted to laugh and it must have shown on her face because Patience laughed out loud.

"You a gen'rous woman, Bess," she laughed and patted her bosom, jiggling the décolletage showing over the top of the stays, but still mostly concealed by the scarf.

"Gen'rous, Bess repeated, and let herself laugh a little too.

"Might as well have this too," Patience said, holding up something from the pile Miss Charity had delivered. It looked like a goat bladder on a string, but it was made of cloth instead. "Pocket," she said and tied the string around Bess's waist. "Pocket," she said again and from the pile took a small cloth that Bess would use as a handkerchief and put it in the pocket. Bess understood. She could keep things in that bag hanging at her waist. "Pocket," she repeated.

"Us don' wear no stomachers like Miss Charity," Patience said next even though Bess did not understand. Bess would learn later that a "stomacher" was a solely decorative panel of the finest fabric that a lady wore like a breast plate over the lacing of the stays. Miss Charity only wore her stomacher when she was receiving guests or going outside the house. The extra layer was simply too hot in Charles Town and was absolutely too hot for kitchen work.

The final piece Bess would wear was the petticoat. It was a gathered skirt of darker brown linen that was gathered at the waist with its hem just above Bess' ankles. It was longer than the white shift. It tied around the waist and Patience yanked it around so the opening at the side would give Bess access to the pocket she wore underneath the petticoat.

It was all the same clothing Miss Charity wore, but Miss Charity's outfit had even more layers in addition to what Bess was now wearing.

Miss Charity always wore at least two petticoats of different colors, the one underneath always just a little longer so both colors would show. Then over her stomacher and petticoats Miss Charity wore a gown. The gown, also called a mantua, was made of fine fabric with wide sleeves that came below the elbows, leaving only a small amount of the shift's sleeve showing at the cuffs. The gown was also laced in front, over the stays, the kerchief, and the stomacher. The gown was laced with a fancy and decorative cord. The hem of the gown came almost to Miss Charity's ankles and the front of the gown gaped open the width of a man's hand from her waist to hemline to show the petticoats underneath. Miss Charity's best gowns also had an overskirt of complementary or even finer fabric that was gathered in folds at the back to form a bustle. When her finer gowns were worn in the evening, Miss Charity, and every other woman of her class who was under a certain age, would wear them without their kerchief, revealing bare décolletage above the top of the stays. There were strict rules for ladies to observe in leaving off the kerchief, and under no circumstance was that ever done before three o'clock in the afternoon. For those occasions she wore her finer gowns early in the day, Miss Charity had kerchiefs of the finest silk to appropriately cover herself and preserve her modesty and reputation.

And over it all Miss Charity wore a belt at her waist, with a pin ball and scissor clip hanging from the belt on her left side. Miss Charity's pin ball and scissor clip were ornately decorative and rarely used. She had servants to do those things for her when needed.

Day and night Miss Charity wore a ruffled white cap to hold and entirely cover her hair. Women washed their caps, sometimes called a mob cap, only when they were dirty. Miss Charity, who liked cleanliness, changed hers each morning. When she went out she had a selection of fine hats to wear directly over the white cap.

But there was no cap for Bess. Patience folded a square of cloth diagonally to make a triangle. The middle of the triangle went against the back of Bess' neck with the two long ends tied at her forehead. Then the loose third end was brought up and over her head and tucked under the knot so that all of Bess' hair was covered. It was hot and itched almost immediately. But Patience wore one so Bess was determined to wear hers too. She would have to get used to it.

Miss Charity also wore stockings and she wore shoes. Her cordwainer, or shoemaker, cobbled two sets of shoes for her each year; one sturdy pair and one fine pair. They were both sewn from cloth and had a wooden heel. The heels of the fine pair were covered with the same cloth as the shoe. Every year the cordwainer reminded her she was supposed to alternate the shoes each time she wore them, switching left to right, so they would wear evenly and keep their shape. But Charity preferred keeping the shoes solely for one foot, so they conformed to the foot and became more comfortable with wear. If they wore out too quickly she could always have the cordwainer cobble another pair.

When Patience was finished dressing Bess, every part of her was covered except for her face, her throat, the hint of décolletage peeking from the scarf above the stays, her arms from just below the elbows to her hands, and her bare ankles and feet. The frayed green silk gown she arrived in was taken away and burned.

Bess soon understood she was to help Patience with cooking the food. Patience would show her what she had to do, telling her in English Bess barely understood, it sounded so different from the words of The Captain. But Bess was soon tending the fire, much as she would have outside her own hut before she was captured, helping cook food that was both strange and familiar, and washing up after. In the kitchen they ate much the same food as they prepared for Miss Charity and her guests. Bess knew rice, okra, and yams, but other things Patience put on her plate were so strange Bess sometimes wondered who would have thought to eat them in the first place. Patience would rear back on her three legged stool and laugh heartily when Bess made a face after trying something new.

Patience would have resented Bess for catching on to things so quickly if she had not been bound for the Old Massah's plantation. Bess was no threat to Patience in her position as cook for Miss Charity. In fact, the more Bess knew the better it would look for Patience so she showed her as much as Bess could take in, and then a little more, talking all the while. Spices and fruit from around the world were plentiful in the sea port of Charles Town and Patience showed Bess how to use them. Patience loved to talk and it was a rare opportunity to have another woman in the kitchen who would listen.

Mistress Charity inspected her kitchen house each day and after a time she asked Patience how this new girl Bess was doing. "She a smart gal, Miss Charity," Patience replied when she was asked. "She learn fast and too smart a gal to work the field. Massah Richard need put her in his house, if I do say so." Bess stood and worked quietly at the table while they talked, as though she wasn't even there.

"Well, I don't know if he needs another kitchen girl and she's too black to be working in the big house, even way out there on the plantation, but I will have a talk with him. Thank you Patience," Charity said.

"I save you," Patience hissed at Bess as soon as they were alone. "I save you from the rice fields. Wear you out. Don' you forget Payshen."

"No mam'selle," Bess said. "Thank you, mam'selle."

"And stop saying that to me. You get us both trouble, gal. You call me Payshen, same as anyone. You hear?"

 Bess was realizing there were sounds in the English language that did not exist in Africa – or Af'ica as Patience told her was the place she and every other Negro came from. She struggled to form the sounds. She was beginning to be able to form the "th" sound so "this" and "them" were sounding more the way Patience and Miss Charity said them and less like "dis" and "dem," but the "sh" sound still eluded her – coming out more as a "sw" instead. She wanted to avoid words with an "sh." Patience was good about it but she also teased Bess sometimes that she talked like a field worker.

"Yes…Pay-sen," Bess replied carefully.

With Patience's suggestion, Charity remembered that her brother's cook was much older now, was slipping some, and would need to be replaced soon. Following that tack, and after it was agreed that Bess was destined for the plantation kitchen house, Charity persuaded her brother to leave Bess with her so she could train with Patience. If he would leave the girl until he came back in the fall after the next harvest, Bess would have the benefit of more months of kitchen training from Patience and would be more ready to take over his kitchen when the time came.

It was all explained to Bess, who seemed to grasp what Miss Charity was telling her to the point she actually smiled at the Mistress when she said, "Bess thank you, mam'selle."

All that summer, Patience kept her busy in the kitchen. When they had time, Bess went with Patience to the house and learned to do the household chores. Most of what she learned grew from skills she already knew from keeping her hut and tending to her husband and sons; organizing things together, sweeping. Patience showed her how to dust, polish wood, shake rugs, fluff cushions and even how to mix up the paste to polish Miss Charity's silver. She even showed Bess a new idea that some of the Charles Town households were using to make a paste from used tea leaves to polish finished wood. Wiped on and let dry, the remaining oil in the leaves left a soft luster and a pleasant aroma when the residue was buffed away.

Bess was in awe at the amount of food that was stored in the kitchen and the adjoining storehouse. It seemed more than they could ever use, but Patience explained that only two years earlier more than fifteen Indian tribes joined with the Yamasee in attacking settlers throughout the colony. They wanted to expel the colonists so farms and plantations were attacked with their white owners killed and slaves carried away to be sold to slave traders. Almost one in ten of the white population was killed in the raids. Those who could escaped and fled to safety of the walled city of Charles Town. Even though the walled town was under siege almost two years during the war, it was safer.

The family and personal servants from the Wainwright plantation crowded into Charity's house that year. Richard brought a wagon loaded with food and supplies along with them, but in the first months Charity felt obligated to share what they had with friends and neighbors who had less and were going hungry. As the siege continued, there were days when all they had to eat was rice, fish from the river when it was safe enough to fish, and whatever Patience could harvest from the dwindling garden. No ships dared to venture into their harbor. Then even the rice ran out and starvation set in.

The only thing that saved them was that in the winter of 1716 the Cherokees switched sides to join the colonists. That tipped the balance and by the time Bess arrived early in 1717, life in the countryside and within the walls was returning to normal. Ships sailed directly from England with emergency supplies and like everyone else, Charity quickly rebuilt her own stores. She vowed to never let them run low again.

As she trained Bess, the only thing that frustrated Patience was that Bess tended to put things she shouldn't in her pocket. In the house, if something was out of place and needed to be taken to another room, Bess would just slip it into her pocket for the time being. Patience knew what she was doing, but scolded Bess anyway, "Never put nothin' in your pocket not yours, Bess. If they see you, they think you steal it and it get you beaten."

Bess could not understand that. Private property had no meaning to her yet. And just what would she do with it if she kept it anyway? Everything in Miss Charity's house or kitchen belonged to Miss Charity, regardless where Bess may carry it. If she put something in her pocket and took it out to the kitchen house, the only other place she would ever be, it would still be in Miss Charity's kitchen house and it still belonged to Miss Charity. Everything Bess wore and even Bess herself belonged to Miss Charity, so anything she had in her pocket, even if it was tucked beneath her skirt, would naturally be Miss Charity's too. That was how it was, and had always been, with slaves. Anyone knew that.

As she scolded Bess about it another day, Patience put her hand in her own pocket and pulled out what she kept there and showed it to Bess; a few little treasures and her own handkerchief. And with that Bess understood. It was clear that the pocket was hers and hers alone. What went into her pocket belonged to Bess and only Bess. It thrilled her, that pocket. Anything that was not hers and hers alone should not go in that pocket, even while she walked from one room to another to put the thing back in its place. But anything that was hers and was in her pocket was hers to keep. It belonged only to Bess and no one else. For now the only thing in her pocket was the cloth she used as her handkerchief. Patience had put it there the first day. Bess had nothing else to put in her pocket, but she understood.

The day came when the Old Massah came back to Charles Town to sell his rice harvest. It was his first full harvest after the war. He would give a share of it directly to the Lords Governor for taxes, get gold or paper money for the rest, and then settle his debts. When his business was finished, he would take Bess with him to the plantation.

He brought three men with him. One drove Richard's carriage and two others drove wagons that followed. The rice harvest was being floated down the river to Charles Town on rafts. The three men with Richard would help the men on the rafts unload that rice and then they would all ride home in the wagons. Bess would be in one of the wagons for the ride home.

Those men slept in the shed at night where the four slaves had been chained the last time, but these men were not chained, nor was the door even locked. They seemed more like the Old Massah than slaves to Bess. Their dress was similar and they spoke English easily with Patience over dinner while Bess sat at the kitchen table with her head bowed, unsure of the few words she knew.

That night Patience told her those men had wives and children back on the plantation. They also had cabins of their own where they lived. Those cabins were built of brick and tabby just like the Old Massah's house. Some of those cabins even had two rooms. They, as well as their wives and the oldest children, worked each day for the Old Massah until their assigned tasks were complete, but then the rest of the day was their own until the next morning. In that free time they kept gardens and even raised small livestock for their own tables. They were trusted not to run and they were proud to be accompanying the Old Massah to Charles Town. While they were here they would take things they, and others, had made to the market to sell. And even better, they would keep the money. Coming to Charles Town was a reward and an adventure for them.

In the candle light, Patience even smirked and told Bess that the Old Massah was a slave too. He was a slave to the Lords Proprietor of the Carolinas. A portion of the rice the Old Massah grew on the plantation went to the Proprietors when harvest time came, just like the slaves had to give him a part of their time each day. And on top of that, some of the gold he got for selling the rice also had to go to the Lords Proprietor for taxes – taxes on his land and houses. It was the same for Miss Charity. Don't pay those taxes and they came and took you to prison until you paid. And then the governors were slaves to the king. Everybody in this world, except King George, was owned by somebody else. And even then, King George was owned by God. Patience laughed out loud at the thought of that.

The final night of his visit, after the Old Massah and his sister had gone to bed, Patience brought out a little cake she secretly made as a surprise for Bess, just for the two of them to enjoy. They pulled the kitchen's one real chair and a three legged stool to the table and sat down at the table Patience had set for their little party. Patience poured tea from the kitchen teapot into two mismatched tea cups that no longer were used at Miss Charity's table.

Patience said it wasn't really tea. Miss Charity and her friends were all wild for tea these days. Tea had been introduced in the colonies four years earlier and was considered very fashionable. Charles Town ladies would drink tea and feel the connection to the real Lords and Ladies who were also drinking tea at that moment from fine china tea cups in the manor houses of England. They sought to copy every detail they could learn about how tea was prepared and served, hoping to imitate the cultured aristocracy across the ocean. Tea was also very expensive and brought on ships from China. Miss Charity kept her tea locked up in a little chest that she carried around with her. Wherever Miss Charity was in the house, there would also be her little tea chest on the mantle of that room.

What Patience had actually brewed that night was the substitute that Miss Charity used when her real tea ran low or ran out. It was a mixture of sassafras, which grew in abundance in the woods, herbs from the garden and sometimes even the little red bead, or "hip," that formed on the rose bushes late in summer. Patience said this tea was almost as good as real tea, and actually she preferred it. Bess had never tasted either so she would not have known the difference. Bess was very careful to hold the cup the same way Patience was holding hers, to sip slowly from the golden rim and place the cup carefully back down on its saucer.

Then Patience glanced at the door to make sure no one was there and brought a small bag of sugar from her pocket and spooned some into the cups. Yes, it was real sugar. She took a little at a time from Miss Charity's bowl for her own tea. Miss Charity never missed it.

Bess felt honored and happy, but also felt like she might cry at any moment. In her time there, after that first slap, she had come to love Patience like another sister. Now it was time to leave her one friend.

They finished the little cake and Patience took her handkerchief from her pocket and wiped her eyes, then reached in her pocket again and brought out a little charm she had made for Bess. The little charm reminded Bess so much of home that the tears came in her eyes too and began running down her cheeks.

"I make this so you have something to carry in your pocket now too," Patience explained, smiling through her tears. "So you always remember Payshun."

* * * * *

Bess was barely settled on the plantation when her labor pains began. This was her fourth child, but her first in Carolina, which was what the Old Massah called this new land instead of Charles Town. She was working alongside the cook in the kitchen house when the familiar stabbing pain pierced her back, nearly doubling her over.

The weather had just started to cool. "Fall," they called it here, or sometimes the Old Massah called it "autumn." Something called "winter" would be coming soon and everyone worked furiously in preparation for it. The toothless old cook dreaded its coming. To explain it, she thrust Bess's hand into a bucket of water, just drawn from the river and said, "It col' like that, only worse." Bess was not quite sure what it was, but was eager to see this "winter."

The baby came easy in the kitchen house that fall of 1717. It was a girl, and she was lighter than any other baby Bess had seen. Not as light as The Captain, nor the sailor who raped her the first day she was on the ship, but lighter than Bess and any other slave on the Old Massah's plantation, or in Charles Town for that matter.

As soon as Bess was cleaned up the Old Massah came to the kitchen house to see her and the baby. She smiled up at him as she uncovered the new little thing. The baby's eyes were open and she looked up solemnly at the Old Massah, the man who owned her.

"Why, she's nearly white," he exclaimed, bending down to have a closer look. "Even though her color hasn't fully come up, I can tell she is white as a dove."

"Dove," Bess repeated. Bess knew doves and their mournful songs in the trees at the edge of the garden. The old cook told her those doves mated for life. One man and one woman together until they died. Maybe it would be like that for her baby, too, if her name was Dove. Bess nodded, "That nice."

"We will call her Dove," the Old Massah said, rubbing the baby's cheek softly with his finger. "Dove."

He went to his library that night and entered the name and date in his book where he recorded the purchase, birth, marriages and deaths of all his slaves. When he told Bess that Dove was entered in the book she felt proud and boldly asked if she could see it. Dove's name had been written in the book.

She had another year with the old cook, learning her ways before she died. It was another fall morning in her second year in the land of Carolina when Bess woke in the bed that she and Baby Dove shared with the old cook in the corner of the kitchen house. When she saw the old woman was gone she was glad she had escaped the coming winter she so dreaded. Bess became the cook for the big house. A young girl called Mintie who was light-skinned like Baby Dove was brought in from the fields to help Bess and to tend to the baby and keep her away from the fire while Bess was busy with the cooking.

Little Dove grew and she was a beautiful child. Unlike her mother, Dove's hair hung in long, glossy curls. The child refused to keep her cap on, and her hair was so beautiful that Bess did not make her keep it on as much as she should have.

Dove was exactly the same color as the Old Massah's coffee when he put cream in it in the morning, and he liked a lot of cream. Her bright, brown eyes with their thick lashes followed her mother and Mintie around the kitchen as they did their work. When the Old Massah came out to inspect the kitchen, she lifted her little arms up to him so that he laughed and picked her up. She laid her head against his shoulder while he carried her around and looked at the kitchen house. She fussed and cried when he had to leave. When he was gone, Mintie laughed and teased Dove that she was the Old Massah's little pet until Bess would make her stop it and comforted her daughter.

By the time she was six, Dove was showing an exceptional talent with a needle. To keep her occupied, Bess set her by the fireplace with a scrap of flax cloth and some red thread. Without being shown, Dove sewed the profile of a bird into the fabric, surprising Bess. With its wings extended in flight it looked so much like the embroidery the women in her village used to do that it brought tears to Bess's eyes.

After that Bess let Dove begin piecing squares of old fabric together to make a quilt for their bed. Because Dove did so well and did not need encouragement, Bess was critical of Dove's sewing, showing her where her stitches were not right and which ones were good. As time went on it was more and more difficult for Bess to find an errant stitch. After that, Bess showed Dove how to stitch together simple clothing. Together they made Dove a new shift from a length of the cloth Bess was allotted each year.

For Christmas the year after Dove's eighth birthday she secretly made her mother a mob cap, just like the one Old Massah's sister, Miss Charity, wore the last time she visited the plantation. Mintic had been sick with a cold that day, so Bess brought Dove to the dining room to help her serve the meal. Just seeing the cap on Miss Charity's head while she helped her mother serve, Dove figured out how it was made and sewed one for her mother to wear. Christmas morning Bess tried it on, right over the cloth she kept always kept tied around her head. She praised the work. Even without a lace edging it was still as pretty as Miss Charity's cap. Then Bess set it aside with the promise to Dove that she would wear it the next time Miss Charity came to visit.

As promised, when Bess served the next time Miss Charity visited, she wore the fine cap. Charity noticed almost immediately.

"Now, Bess. Wherever did you get that fine cap?" Charity asked in delight as soon as she noticed it on Bess' head.

"Dove make cap for Bess." Bess said proudly, yet quietly and with her eyes down as she was supposed to do in the house. "Dove make cap for Bess Christmas."

"Really? Dove made that? How on earth? Why Dove is only six years old isn't she?"

"She is eight years old now, Sister, last October." Richard Wainwright interjected impatiently while he leaned over his plate, inspecting and reforming the mound of rice on his dinner plate. His food always had to be just so on his plate before he would eat it.

"Eight! My goodness. Well, it's wonderful you are teaching her to sew, Bess. That is such a useful skill for any girl."

"No one show Dove sew cap. Dove just sew."

"Don't be takin' on so, Char," Richard said in a complaining tone and without looking up from his plate. Their dinner was getting cold.

"Now Richard, please do be quiet!" Charity scolded. "Bess, do you really mean to tell me that Dove just figured out how to make that cap without anyone showing her?"

"Yes, Mam'selle," Bess answered, in a withdrawing tone because the Old Massah was not wanting her to talk.

"Well, you tell her I said 'well done,' won't you now?" Charity replied.

"Yes Mam'selle. Bess tell Dove."

"I will tell her," Charity gently corrected.

Bess knew she would learn English so much better if Charity was around all the time. Old Massah barely spoke to anyone. But she remembered almost everything Miss Charity said. She went over it at night, every word Miss Charity said. When she was in her bed she spoke it aloud to Dove who was learning right along with her. She wished Miss Charity was here all the time so Dove would learn to talk like Miss Charity. It would help Dove in her condition.

"Yes, Mam'selle. I...tell...her." It was a good enough reply for Charity to let it go.

As the table was being cleared, Charity surprised them all by insisting, "Richard, you simply must let me take Dove back to Charles Town. I can use her to help with sewing the new portieres for the drawing room..."

"No!" Richard slammed his hand down on the table. Bess nearly dropped the plate she was scraping at the sideboard. "I want Dove here. Now stop meddling in all this, sister."

"But it would bring you another income, Richard. Ladies in Charles Town are paying a fair price for a seamstress these days. Why, I could even set up a service and hire out as a dressmaker." Richard was only silent in reply. Bess knew that meant he was thinking about it.

Bess was not ready to lose her daughter to Miss Charity, but she knew it would be an opportunity and it gave her hope for Dove. Any skill a slave girl could have in this land of Carolina would keep her off her back and out of the fields and would mean a better life. Maybe in time the Old Massah would agree and Dove could

23

go live with Miss Charity and sew for her. Bess remembered Miss Charity's house. Patience was still there too. It would be a good life for her daughter.

Eventually, when Dove was eleven years old, Miss Charity wore the Old Massah down and he gave his permission for Dove to go to Charles Town that summer to sew on Charity's wardrobe for the next season. She would also sew for the ladies among Charity's friends. As a secret with Dove, after setting aside a generous amount of Dove's earnings to give to Richard, she allowed Dove to keep the rest of what she earned from her sewing. Dove could spend the money as she liked for cloth for her own clothing and such, but Charity also encouraged her to save some of it back. Charity kept the money in secret compartment of the bureau bookcase in the drawing room. A little "dowry" fund for Dove, she called it

Dove came to love Charles Town. She arrived in late spring to begin the sewing for Charity's friends before they left town during the heat of summer. Charity always stayed in town all summer, preferring even the heat of Charles Town over the bucolic pace of life on the Wainwright plantation. Her upper gallery always had a pleasant breeze from the bay, even on the hottest days, and she preferred staying in her own home instead of being a guest elsewhere. Charity believed that heat was all a state of mind anyway. In August it was hot every place in South Carolina. She might as well stay home where she could leave off all but her shift if she decided to, and not have to be pleasant to other people.

When it came time for Dove to leave at the end of that summer, she nearly broke Charity's heart by begging the Old Massah's sister to buy her so she could stay with her forever. Charity considered it, knowing Richard would never agree to the sale, but she promised the girl she would see what she could do.

Richard Wainwright had never been the same after he became a widower the year before he brought Bess home. Bess arrived just as the Richard was starting to get his life back. From the old cook she learned the story and it made her understand the Old Massah better. He was lonely too, just as Bess was lonely. And in her mind and in that kinship she felt with him, she began thinking of herself as "Old Bess" just as he was "Old Massah" to all of the plantation. They had both lost children, his to the Yam'see war and her sons to the wide ocean that separated them. But she knew she had an easier time of it. The Old Massah's son, the Young Massah, was in the ground with his mother out in the family cemetery while Bess knew the women of her village were caring for her sons and that they would someday grow to be fine men, even if they forgot all about their mother.

Dove began spending the summers with Miss Charity in Charles Town. Each fall when she came home it seemed to Bess that her daughter had changed again. On her fourteenth birthday, Dove was given the cabin next to Bess for her sewing. She became the seamstress for the plantation, making shirts for the Old Massah and doing all the required stitching for his house. When that was complete she traded her services to make simple clothing for the other slaves. She was very young to have a cabin of her own, but it was necessary to keep the fabrics away from the fires and grease of the kitchen. Dove did not like sleeping there alone so she usually came to the kitchen house at bed time and slept there with her mother.

Also, with her status as seamstress, Dove was elevated to the rank of house servants who were allowed to address the Master as "Master Richard," "Master," or simply "Sir" when they spoke directly to him, although she still retained the title "Master Wainwright" when referring to him in conversation with everyone else, whether a guest of the house, another member of the master's family, or anyone else on the plantation. Old James, who still addressed the Old Massah as "Master Wainwright," even in private, frowned on anything less being used by the rest of the household. Dove found it hard not to giggle when she used that title with Miss Charity, and likewise when she referred to Miss Charity as Miss Wainwright on the plantation. Charity had steadfastly done away with the title of "Mistress" in her own household, preferring the more modern title of "Miss" instead.

Dove was also allowed to speak to the master without first being spoken to by him when the performance of her duties required it, although she was to do so quietly with bowed head and downcast eyes. Bess was afraid Dove had become entirely too relaxed in Miss Charity's household and carefully drilled her daughter on every possible application of this protocol until she was satisfied Dove knew her place and how to conduct herself in her new position.

Each evening, after the dinner dishes from the house were finished, Bess and Dove would prepare a simple supper to have together. Usually it was extra from what had been prepared for the Old Massah's dinner, so it was much better fare than the other slaves had in the quarters. Dove had learned to enjoy tea with Miss Charity so Bess always prepared some of her plantation tea, as she called it, for them to have after their dinner. She was amazed and proud that each time Dove came home from Charles Town she seemed more like Miss Charity than a slave girl. Her words sounded the way Miss Charity would say them and her posture and manners showed Miss Charity's training. Just the way Dove would hold her tea cup and gracefully sip her tea with her eyes downcast made Bess proud of her daughter. Dove always came home with new clothes too, unexplained although Bess suspected Miss Charity had at least provided the fabric. Dove always brought Bess a fine new petticoat or shift she had stitched up over the summer too.

But it also troubled Bess. There would be no place for Dove's fine clothes and manners on the plantation. None of the young men would ask for her if she was too high up. She would do better as a maid and companion to Miss Charity, perhaps married to a butler or a driver, but those people in town were even much lighter skinned than Dove. None of them would be impressed by her clothes and manners there. Bess began to be troubled over where her daughter was going to fit in.

Then there was an unexpected development during the spring of 1731. The Old Massah seemed to come out of himself, or at least the sadness and melancholy that had enveloped him since his wife and son died sixteen years before. Now he seemed reborn, with new energy. And it was soon explained.

The Sunday after Easter a carriage came up the drive. It was an older one and the horses were not matched, but it still pulled right up to the front door. Old James hurried to put on his jacket and open the front door, while the Old Massah came rushing past him down the stairs from his bed chamber where he had changed himself into his best breeches and newest jacket. He brushed past Old James, went down the steps and opened the door of the carriage before the driver could come down from his seat to do it.

It was the Widow Timsley, with her nearly-grown son Jonathan, coming to visit for the afternoon. Richard had invited her at church that morning. He had barely arrived home himself and had not had time to mention it to anyone. He turned to Old James and said, "Tell Bess there will be three for dinner today." It was the first any of the servants had heard of the visit.

Old James' sharp eyes did not miss the worn condition of the carriage, nor did it get by him as the Widow extended her hand and stepped forward that the slipper on her foot was frayed at the heel. This could only be trouble, and he told Bess as much when he delivered the news of the change in the dinner plans.

The Widow and her son were frequent visitors all that summer and fall. Then that Christmas the engagement was announced. Bess had already grown weary with the visits, with Mrs. Timsley ordering her about as she served in the dining room and that fat and lazy son of hers insolently slouching at the dinner table, his silk cravat askew, and disrespecting the Old Massah. He lounged in the drawing room after dinner, openly rubbing his belly while his half-closed eyes followed Bess when she was in the room, old enough to be his mama herself. She kept her eyes downcast at all times and answered politely, "Yes, ma'am" and "Yes, sir," to their commands.

From listening while she served in the dining room and stood in attendance in the drawing room after dinner until she was dismissed, she learned the Old Massah intended to name Jonathan as his heir after the marriage. The Widow Timsley clapped her hands and exclaimed that the two plantations would be combined as one property with the marriage. The Widow also observed that, with no other heirs, it would only make sense that it would all eventually pass to Jonathan.

When Dove had returned earlier that fall, Bess became fearful for her daughter's safety. When the Timsleys were in the house, which seemed to be almost all the time now, she made sure someone else came with her to help serve in the dining room. For a long time, Bess managed to keep Dove out of the Timsleys' way.

But eventually the day came when she had no one else to help her. Dove changed into a simple gray dress with a white apron. Before they left the kitchen house, Bess checked her over and tucked a few of the errant curls back under her white cap. She wanted Dove to look as plain and unnoticeable as possible.

But from the first moment Dove entered the dining room, carrying in the soup tureen behind Bess, Jonathan sat up straight and took notice. Then it seemed his eyes never left her. He leered at her, both coming and going, nearly slobbering after her as he slurped from his wine glass and his soup spoon.

It was not lost on the Widow Timsley. The Widow and her son had been invited to be house guests for Christmas. Now it was long after New Year's Day and they showed no sign of leaving. They seemed firmly ensconced in their guest rooms. The house servants speculated and grumbled among themselves that it was going to be that way until the wedding.

When Dove was sent back to the kitchen to bring the next course, the Widow announced, "I don't like that girl at all, Richard. You must get rid of her."

Bess, who was standing with her back to the room at the sideboard and carving the roast chicken to put on the plates, froze. Then she forced herself to continue what she was doing.

"What girl?" Richard asked, peering down the table at his fiancée.

"That slave. That serving girl. Oh…what is her name? Some kind of bird, I think. Wren?"

"Do you mean Dove?"

"Yes, that's it. You have to sell her. I don't like having her here," the Widow sniffed as though she was certain her wish would be obeyed and the matter was settled.

"Sell her?" Richard was amazed. "Why? What are you talking about?"

"Oh my dear," the Widow replied, suddenly coy. "Must you force me to be indelicate?"

Richard lifted his hands, his fork still in his right hand, signifying that he did not understand, "What do you mean?"

"A slut, my dear. I won't have a slut serving at my table."

In spite of herself, Bess clattered the lid down on the soup tureen. Jonathan took another lusty slurp from his wine glass that was now nearly empty.

Richard snorted and then laughed, "You are mistaken, my dear Mrs. Timsley. Dove has lived on this plantation her entire life. Oh – and with my sister Charity in Charles Town at times. She is only fourteen and I can assure you she is most definitely not what you say."

"But how do you know? Where did she come from any way?"

"She was born here. Bess is her mother."

"Bess? But Bess is black as night. How can this Dove be her daughter?"

"Bess was pregnant with Dove when she arrived here from Africa. I presume the father was one of the white slavers, but I assure you Bess has been nothing but virtuous since then. She is my cook, for God's sake."

The Widow blushed and hid herself behind her fan at the word 'pregnant.' It was not a word that was suited for dinner table conversation. "Well, that hardly makes her a virtuous woman. And she is still a slave, isn't she?"

"I will hear nothing more of this," Richard said firmly and without blinking, staring the Widow down as she sat at the other end of his dining room table. "I am not selling Dove."

She huffed and folded her fan, setting it on the table as Bess set the dinner plate before her. Jonathan smirked at his mother then raised his empty wine glass to Bess, indicating it needed to be refilled.

"And for God's sake, Jonathan, let the servants finish serving the course first," Richard scolded. "This is not a public house, even if you think it one."

Bess still kept her eyes down, but this time, if she had looked up they would have seen the delight and pride in her face at the Old Massah's words.

But that pride soon enough turned to terror later that night. Bess and Dove sat finishing their tea in the kitchen house. They had discussed the events of the evening. Dove suggested that she could send a message to Miss Charity in Charles Town, (revealing to her mother that Miss Charity had been teaching Dove to read and write among other things), asking if she might come back to stay there. Maybe, when she explained the situation, Miss Charity would even insist on buying her from Master Wainwright.

Bess had just opened her mouth to reply when the kitchen house door burst open. Dove gave a little cry of fright and as soon as Bess saw that it was the young Master Jonathan, she quickly stood from the table and positioned Dove behind her.

28

"Get out, you old nigger," Jonathan hissed at Bess.

"This <u>my</u> house." Bess said firmly, pushing Dove more behind her and positioning herself so the table was between them and the young master.

"Didn't you hear me, old woman? I said get out," he said, low and mean. Dove's breath was coming in frightened little gasps behind her. He was drunk. He had drunk even more wine after dinner and now stood swaying on his feet.

"I said, this my house. Until Massah Richard say different, I stays here."

He laughed and started around the table, "Then I will be takin' this gal with me, I guess."

"Not 'fore you ask Massah Richard, you ain't," Bess said, willing her voice to be strong. "She belong to Massah Richard, so you best be asking him before you do anything at all to her."

Dove was crying now in a soft whimper behind her mother. The implication was clear, but was not true. Bess was saying that Dove was Massah Richard's comfort girl. She was warning Jonathan against violating that and taking that which did not belong to him.

Jonathan, unsure, took another step forward, but Bess insisted. "You go on up to the house now and ask Massah Richard if you can have his girl. You go on now. Go on up there and ask him and bring him back with you to tell me. 'Cause I not gone believe it less I hear it straight from him."

"But 'til then..." Bess picked up the butcher knife and plunged at least two inches of the blade into the top of the kitchen table while looking directly at young Massah Johnathan with eyes that would kill, "...no one gone touch this gal."

Jonathan stumbled out of the kitchen house. She thought she heard him stumble on the steps, then retch and vomit on the path. As she went to close the door she saw him straighten up, wipe his mouth on his sleeve and stagger away toward the house. She shut the door and pushed the table in front of it. Then she sat with Dove on the side of the bed, hugging her and brushing back her hair until she was all cried out. Dove was embarrassed, and worried. What if her mother's lie was found out? But Bess said they would be safe for the night. In the morning she would speak to the Old Massah about it.

After she served Maser Richard his breakfast in the library the next morning she stood quietly by until he looked up at her.

"Yes?"

"I need to ask you something, Massah," Bess said quietly with her hands folded in front of her.

"What is it?"

"Young Massah Jonathan come to the kitchen house last night."

"What?"

"He want take Dove for his comfort. I tell him no."

"This is inexcusable," Richard blustered, throwing down his napkin and rising from his chair. "To take advantage of my hospitality in this way. It is unforgivable. Is Dove all right?"

"Yes, Massah. Nothin' happen."

"I'm sure you saw to that."

He quizzed Bess on the events until he was satisfied she was telling him the truth. Bess had never lied to him, so it did not take him long. If he had not been so appalled at his future stepson's conduct he surely would have laughed when Bess revealed that she had implied that Dove was already Richard's comfort girl.

"That was quick thinking, Bess. I am glad you could diffuse the situation like that." Bess was not sure what "diffuse" and "situation" meant, but she understood the Old Massah thought she had done the right thing.

"I will take care of this," Richard brusquely assured her. "You can tell Dove not to worry."

But Richard never had the chance. No sooner than Bess left the library, Richard's new solicitor, a young Frenchman from Charles Town named Jean Faure, arrived on horseback. He had been running the horse throughout the night to arrive as quickly as possible. At the door he handed the horse off to Old James to take to the stable and bounded up the steps. "I must speak to Master Wainwright at once," he told the housemaid and she showed him into the library where Richard had resumed his breakfast. The door closed and voices were raised.

Over the next hour, Monsieur Faure laid it out for him. In the interest of his client, and with the prospect of the upcoming marriage, he had ordered some investigations. The Timsley plantation was close to being seized by creditors for unpaid debts. Since the death of her husband, the Widow Timsley had not paid any of the shops in Charles Town where she had accounts. Her dressmakers, cordwainer and even her confectioner had stopped her credit, and were they all still in England, they would no doubt be in debtors' prison. On top of that, young Master Jonathan had a notorious reputation for fast living and playing cards. His gambling debts far exceeded the amount his father had placed in trust for him. It was obvious the two were fortune hunters and saw Richard Wainwright and his plantation as the answer to their financial troubles.

The Widow and her son were sent packing within the hour. She left the house in a huff, sloppily dressed with her shoes not properly buckled and her hat askance. Jonathan was still sleeping off the effects of his wine consumption the night before so Richard and Old James half-carried a moaning Jonathan down the stairs, still in his night shirt, and unceremoniously dumped him on the floor of his mother's carriage. The Widow leaned across her son and out the window to begin a half-whining complaint that there had been some kind of mistake. She was sure this was all a misunderstanding, if he would just let her explain. In reply Richard walked forward to where her mismatched horses were hitched and slapped the nearest one on the rump, sending the carriage clattering away and down the drive, and the Widow Timsley falling away from the window and back into the seat in a flurry of petticoats.

With that, Richard turned to Monsieur Faure, shook his hand, thanked him and asked if he would like to join him for a late breakfast.

Dove did not see Master Richard for several weeks. Typically she would not have anyway, but she wanted to thank him for his intervention with young Master Jonathan. No one except the solicitor knew the complete reason the Timsleys had been sent packing and Dove presumed it was because of young Master Timsley's misconduct. She was deeply grateful to Master Richard for his gallantry and his intervention.

One morning when they all thought Master Richard was out of the house, Dove was in the library repairing one of the drapery panels. The portieres were part of the flammables that had been packed all those years ago when Master Richard and his family evacuated the plantation house for Charles Town when they learned Port Royal was under attack by the Yamasees. Under the Mistress' instructions, those who stayed behind packed everything from the house that could easily be set fire and hid them in the woods by the swamp. When those things were unpacked after the war, one panel was too badly damaged by the damp to be reinstalled. The remaining sets, enough for the library, were transferred there and new portieres were made for the drawing room. Now, the fabric she was mending was worn through and shredding in the spot where the house servants grabbed the panels to throw them open in the morning or pull them closed at night. Dove was making a temporary repair and was nearly finished when Richard strode suddenly into the room, shut the door and sat at his desk before he saw her standing by the opposite window.

"Oh, Dove. Good Morning."

"I am sorry to disturb you, Sir, I thought you were out. I shall come back," she said demurely as she started to gather up her supplies.

"No, please stay. You are no bother. I forgot something and I will only be a moment."

Dove stood a moment, with downcast eyes. She wanted to thank the Master, but did not know how to begin.

"Dove, I am happy to find you alone. I wanted to say that I am sorry for the unfortunate conduct of the young Master Timsley. It is unforgivable that he behaved in such a way and in my own house."

"It's all right, Sir. I have wanted to thank you for what you did, in protecting us."

Richard looked at Dove, holding her sewing supplies and saw that she had been repairing the torn curtain. He came over to have a look at the curtain she had been mending. "I see it is almost worn through. These curtains have been there for a long time, since before my wife died, I think. I really should have Charity order some replacements."

"They are all right, sir. I am only mending them for now but when I have time I will put an edging of new fabric on them and they will be good as new. With your permission, of course."

"Oh, I am sure whatever you do will be fine, Dove. Just go ahead and do what you want to do with them."

"Yes, sir. Thank you."

Richard was thoughtful for a moment. "Dove, I really am sorry about what happened with Master Jonathan. I would hate to think that you thought you had to do something like that, or to think it was legitimate for him to even ask you, just because he was going to become my stepson."

"It's all right, sir. Nothing happened."

Richard's eyes crinkled slightly as he looked at her. "Nothing other than him frightening you and your mother half to death that is. I don't want you to ever feel like you have to do something like that when you don't want to. It won't happen again."

"I know it won't," Dove said softly. Then there was a long pause. She hesitated a moment, but he was standing so close. She looked up at him and said, "There is nothing you could ask me that I don't want to do for you, Master Richard."

Richard looked down at her, not sure if he understood. Dove was so young, just fourteen years old now, and although she had spent her summers in Charles Town she was still innocent to the world. She could not possibly understand the nuance of what she had just said to him. He smiled down at her, but could not find his words.

Without taking her eyes from his, she took his right hand and brought it to her side, just below her left breast, then moved it up closer, with nothing but her stays and the layers of cloth between them. "Nothing," she repeated in a whisper.

Richard was never sure who kissed whom, but he found himself with his arms around Dove and her lips eagerly seeking his. During that kiss she murmured, "I love you, Master Richard."

Then she broke away from him and turned away. "I am sorry, Sir. Forgive me. I will go now."

Richard knew she was not toying with him. Dove was not that sophisticated and worldly.

He told himself what had happened had been innocent. She was just a young girl who was smitten with the man who had rescued her from the cad and preserved her virtue.

But still, for a slave to conduct herself in such a way, uninvited, toward her Master could result in the slave being sold, or whipped at the very least. Such things were not to be tolerated, a slave touching her master in that way, a violation of the order of things.

But Richard did nothing to correct Dove. Instead that evening as Bess served the dinner he surprised her by asking how things had settled after the departure of the Timsleys. It had been weeks. Bess thought a moment and then assured him everything was fine, nothing had happened that had not already been taken care of by the Master and they had all settled down now. The Master need not worry about it any more.

He gave her pause when he asked further if Dove was all right and said he did not want her to be upset by what had happened and wanted her to understand she had done nothing wrong.

"No sir," Bess replied.

"Will you tell her that for me, please?" Richard asked. "Please tell her for me this very evening that she has done nothing wrong. I want her to know that."

Bess was puzzled by it but agreed she would. Her suspicions began when she saw complete relief flood over Dove's face as she delivered the Master's words that night, followed by a look of something else she could not quite determine. Later that night in bed, she realized the look had been one of pleasure – or of being pleased, or even delighted.

It was not Dove's place to be pleased by her Master. Bess began to worry.

She should have thought more about it when Dove said she should start sleeping in her own cabin, the sewing cabin, at least once in a while. Bess objected at first, but Dove countered that the others in the quarters were noticing that she always slept in the kitchen house and if they started grumbling to the Master about it he might reassign the cabin to someone else. So that night, Bess helped Dove carry a set of bed clothes and make up the long-neglected bed in the sewing house. She shared an extra candle with Dove, and with Dove assuring her she would be fine she went back to her own cabin next door and spent a restless night in the big empty bed. It was the first night in her life she slept completely alone.

A few nights later she woke when she heard a voice outside her cabin. When she peeked out her door she saw the back of a man standing at Dove's door. Bess started to barrel out to shoo him away but then she saw Dove's pale face in the moonlight turned up to the man, looking tenderly at him. Then she recognized the man's voice. It was Master Richard. She closed her door all but a crack, watching until Mr. Richard brought his hand to the brim of his hat and gave a small bow, then turned to walk away. Dove watched him walk away too, and then closed her own door. In a moment, Bess saw the cabin's window go dark as Dove put out her candle.

Bess began listening carefully after that. She barely slept, keeping her ears open for any sound from Dove's cabin. Not long after she blew out her candle and made sure her breathing sounded like she was sleeping, she would hear Dove's door softly open and hear Dove's bare feet going up the path toward the house. She tried to stay awake for her return, but often she fell asleep before she would hear the footsteps return and Dove's door close again softly. Over the weeks, Dove's return became later and later. Sometimes she would not return until the last hour before the sun rose. One morning, as the sky was lightening in the east, Bess was sitting on the step of the kitchen house, waiting.

"You be up at the house all night, again?" Bess said soft and low as Dove crept by, carrying a pillow from the house. Dove jumped and gave a little cry. "Why were you spying on me?" she hissed. "I only went to the privy."

"Not all night long, you didn't. You been up there keeping the Massah's bed warm for him."

Dove turned away, toward her own cabin. "You will never understand, Mother. I won't discuss this with you."

She knew Bess hated it when Dove called her Mother. "I your Mama," she would scold. "You keep talking like that and somebody gonna knock a black girl back down where she belong." It was not lost on Bess now. The implication that she knew nothing and Dove, at fourteen and with all her reading and writing and manners just like Miss Charity, was above her own Mama.

Bess followed Dove inside her cabin and shut the door firmly. "What I understand now is you not only his slave, you his whore too."

"Like you were the whore to The Captain and his crew?" Dove shot back sarcastically.

Bess slapped Dove across the face. So hard Dove's head turned to one side with the force and she staggered back a step. "That keep me 'live!" Bess cried out, leaning in with rage.

Dove put her hand to her stinging cheek, willing the tears away. She narrowed her eyes and said through clenched teeth, "Well, just look around you, Mother. Plenty of others made it here without opening their legs to every white man along the way. At least I know who the father of my baby is."

Bess brought her hand back to strike Dove again, but stopped. Dove said "is" not "will be." Dove was already carrying the Massah's child. It was as if all the air went out of her. Her legs went soft underneath her and she caught herself on the side of the table before she fell to the ground. She managed to sit on the chair.

"Then you already carry his child," she said, more as a statement than a question.

"I am going to have Richard's baby. That is true," Dove said quietly.

"Richard? Richard! What you think, calling him that?" Bess said, feeling the rage coming back. "What you think?" she hissed at her daughter. "You think you gone become Mistress of this plantation? You think he gone put you in a silk dress and set you at his table to show off to company? He still yo' Massah. He still own you. You his slave and always gone be – and 'dis chil' too. You think you not just another black slave gal to him?"

"Half-black. And our child will only be a quarter."

"But you still gone be as black to him as I is. If not to him, at least to ever'one else for sure. Ever'one who ever come to this plantation and ever'one in Charles Town too. You think they care you got a white papa? You think they care you baby papa white? You still just a black slave gal and yo' baby a black slave baby too, no matter how white you think it gone look."

With those words, Dove lost her determination. She knew the fantasy she had created for herself and Richard and the baby would never be real. Her child, even with Richard as its father, would still be a slave just like herself. And even if he came out with skin as white as rice and eyes as blue as the sky – or as blue as his father's, it would still just be a black slave baby. On that she deflated, and began to cry softly, her hand still on her cheek even though the sting was mostly gone.

Bess softened. Dove was so young. When Bess was this young and pregnant with her first son, she had a proud husband. She also had the support of her mother and her sisters and aunts all around her. They brought her special food to make the baby strong, and helped her with her work. When she started labor and pushed the baby out, there were loving hands with her to help her and to care for the baby.

Dove had no one like that here. The others in the quarters were too busy with their own children to give much help. The help Dove needed would have to come from Bess. She rose and went to her daughter and tenderly put her arms around her. "It gone be all right, now," she said softly, patting Dove's back while she wept on her Mama's shoulder. "It gone be all right."

That night, Richard stopped Dove's visits to the house. When she went to the side door on that final night, Old James was waiting and swung the door open wide just as she reached for the knob. It startled her, even more so when she looked up and saw Old James' stern, black face glaring at her. Even in daylight, the old man frightened her.

"You get on back home now, Dove," he said firmly.

"I've come to see Richard, Master Richard," Dove said just as firmly, drawing herself up. She had to show Old James that he did not frighten her and was not going to command her.

"The Master has informed me that if he wants to see you, he will send for you," he said with a tinge of satisfaction. Old James had heard all the talk of the situation and knew for the sake of his master and the entire plantation that this had to stop. It had taken some persuasive and frank talk from Old James almost all of the afternoon to get the Master to agree to that. In the end Richard relented and left it up to Old James to turn Dove away tonight.

"That is for the Master to tell me and not you," Dove said with disdain as she tried to brush past him, but Old James put out an arm and blocked her path. She would have to duck under his arm to pass, and likely if she did that he would grab her and throw her from the house. She did not doubt his strength.

"Not if you sully yourself, he doesn't," Old James said low and mean. "You think you can threaten the Master? You think you can make him do anything, gal?"

Dove stepped back, in disbelief. Sully. She knew what that meant.

She had heard the word during one of Miss Charity's afternoon teas, last summer. The ladies sat in Miss Charity's drawing room for an afternoon with their needlework that would conclude with tea being served. While Patience prepared the tea, Dove sat quietly in her alcove of the drawing room with her own stitching, ready if she should be summoned. After a while, the ladies tended to forget she was there and the conversation flowed freely.

"I'm afraid my Dianthus has sullied herself," Mistress Brownfield announced with disgust, "and just when I finally had her making a decent cup of tea."

Dove's needle stopped for a moment in midair. Although she was not sure what Mistress Brownfield meant, she certainly knew the light-skinned and haughty Dianthus. She always looked at Dove like she was dirt and never uttered a word that was not absolutely necessary. Even then it was spat out with contempt as if Dove was lower than a dog in the street.

"I told Nathan that he simply must sell her." In response there was the sympathetic clicking titter of surprised tongues and support around the sewing circle. "And that I want her out of the house by the time I return this day."

The ladies were completely in support of Mrs. Brownfield and in disdain for the fallen Dianthus; from "Oh my dear, what else could you do?" to "What will you do now, starting over with a new girl?" and finally, "What on earth gets into these girls these days, anyway?"

"Well, we obviously know what got into Dianthus," one of them said in a loud whisper, setting off a general titter of giggles until Miss Charity broke in saying, "Ladies, please!"

Even though Miss Charity struggled not to smile at the joke, as hostess it was her responsibility to remind them of their decorum and also of Dove's presence. She accomplished it with those two words and casting her eyes in Dove's direction.

After the ladies were gone and Dove carried the tray of empty cups and plates to Patience in the kitchen, she asked Patience what Mistress Brownfield had meant by saying Dianthus had sullied herself. Patience pressed her lips together and let out a loud "humpf," as though what Dove asked made her angry and disgusted.

"It mean she gone have a baby, that what it mean," Patience replied. "A baby Mistress Brownfield not please about."

"But I didn't know Dianthus was married," Dove replied, then remembering she was in Charles Town where a woman could have a baby without having a husband, added, "or that she has a man either."

"Oh, I know she don'," Patience replied in a whisper, then looking at the door she motioned for Dove to come closer and whispered, "Master Brownfield papa of that baby. That what sully mean. It mean a gal got a baby by the master, a baby that have no papa."

Dove was too shocked for words. It was the first she had heard of such things. She knew that she had no father herself, other than that her mama said he was a captain on a ship and that he was white, but on Master Wainwright's plantation, she had never heard of such a thing. It made her feel half sick.

"Don' you think Dianthus have any say in it either," Patience continued. "You think any slave gal can ever say 'no' to her master when he come 'round like that. Sometime a mistress even put her husband up to it if she too tire, or don' want another baby, or just can't stand her husband on top of her any more. But then, at least, the mistress mostly look the other way when the gal's baby come, so I 'spect Miss Brownfield not know nothin' 'bout this 'til she see Dianthus got a baby and then she figger it all out. Now she mad and jealous and Dianthus be sold. Dianthus too beautiful a woman to be in that house and she almost white, too. This be Miss Brownfield way to punish them both, Dianthus and the Master. Now he have to sell his favorite gal." Patience shook her head in sorrow and disgust.

Now, facing Old James in the darkened doorway, Dove felt the feeling of sickness she felt with Patience that afternoon come rushing back. Old James had implied that was what Dove had done.

"I would never do that. And I would never threaten him, James."

"That right," he said with sarcasm as he leaned in close. "Because I see to it that you don't. Now get on back home, gal, afore I have to call someone to take you. Your mama deserve better than that, don't she?"

When Bess later had to tell Master Richard that Dove was pregnant, he assured she had everything she needed during the pregnancy, and that her work was light, but all contact was severed. He got all the news he needed through Bess.

When Charity sent a letter asking when Dove would be sent to her that summer, Richard sent a reply that she was needed at the plantation and he could not release her. Charity was not pleased, but Dove also sent a note, reaffirming Richard's decision. There was much to be done here on the plantation. Like she was a favored niece being invited for a visit, Dove thanked her for the invitation and promised that she would see Miss Charity next year. She sent the note along with a gift she had sewn, easing the situation.

Richard and Charity, along with everyone else in Charles Town, were already distracted that summer. In England, James Edward Oglethorpe was campaigning for the establishment of a new colony, between the existing South Carolina Colony and Spanish Florida. Land west of the Savannah River would become part of the new colony, lessening the status of South Carolina.

Talk ran wild that summer; that Oglethorpe himself was coming to South Carolina as a precursor to receiving a royal charter, that he would be bringing along a settlement party, that he planned to negotiate with the Yamacraw for land, that the new colony would be populated by the dregs of English debtor prisons and the "worthy poor," that Oglethorpe would be seeking a complete ban on slavery in the new colony, that land ownership would be limited to fifty acres and handed over to indentured servants at the completion of their term. There was even talk that Catholicism would be completely banned in the new colony. Gentler speculations were that the new colony would be named for King George, perhaps "King George Colony" or even "Georgia."

As her belly grew larger, Dove seemed to shrink into herself. She sat listlessly most of the day in her cabin, ignoring her tasks. After the Master's dinner, Bess always went next door to help Dove with her sewing and mending. She fussed at Dove to eat the dinner she brought for her while she straightened up and swept out Dove's cabin. The people began asking about her, concerned they had not seen her. Finally Bess told them her daughter was having a baby, which sent them all into speculation of who the father was. Miss Dove had been too high up for any of the men from the quarters. Maybe it had been that young Jonathan Timsley after all. They had seen him coming around that last night and the timing would be about right, poor gal. Bess let the talk take that route, making sure not one of them suspected Master Richard was the father. If the baby came out whiter than Dove, it would be best if everyone thought someone other than the Old Massah was the father.

It was a clear morning, still early in November. The sun had just risen, orange and indigo in the eastern sky, when Bess went next door to check on her daughter. Dove was getting close now. It could happen any day. When she came through the door she could see that Dove had started. Bess ran down to the quarters to get the woman who served as midwife, then ran up to the house to tell the house maid that Dove was starting her baby. She would have the Master's breakfast ready as soon as things settled down enough.

The baby was not slow in coming, but it was not fast either. It took just about the right amount of time and Dove did fine. The baby was a girl, and Bess could see immediately that she was very light. It always took a while for black babies' color to come up after they were born but this was different. This child was white and going to stay white. Her eyes were blue; a cold, clear blue that would stay blue. There was a down of straight black hair on her head. Furthermore, she had a nose, jaw and brow just like her father.

The Master came down to the sewing house with his book as soon as the mother and baby were cleaned up and ready for him to see. While Bess stood to the side, he came quietly to the side of the bed, never looking directly at Dove and only momentarily looking at his daughter. The baby looked around the room with unfocused eyes, pursed up her lips and began to cry. She needed to be fed, but Dove let her cry. She was not going to bare her breast in front of the Master. Not ever again.

Richard sat in the offered chair, opened his book and dipped the pen in the ink well he brought along with him. "Do you have a name for her?"

Dove held her daughter and looked at Richard. It was the first time since Old James sent her away that she had seen him in the same room. He had not looked at her once since he came into the room. He was ashamed. It made her feel dirty and shameful. But what he had shared with Dove was nothing to be ashamed of. Nor was his daughter. Yes, she had picked out a name, a beautiful name she read once in one of Miss Charity's books, a name of distinction. It would be the finest thing she would ever give her daughter. But then something hardened in her. With ice in her voice she said, "Sukey. I am naming her Sukey."

Richard looked up at her in surprise. "But that is a slave name, Dove. Surely we can come up with something better than that."

"No. I said I am naming her Sukey. Even if you write something else in your book, that is what I will call her. Sukey. It will remind her who she is. All her life, she and everyone else will hear her name and always know who and what she is."

Richard opened his mouth to say something else, then looked away and slightly shook his head. He read aloud as he wrote: "Sukey, daughter to Dove. Born November seven, seventeen hundred thirty two." Without saying it aloud he added; 'father unknown' and closed his book. He stood and without another word, strode from the room. Dove, crying now, pressed her face against her wailing daughter's head.

Bess started to scold Dove, "You gone out your mind? You can't talk to the Massah like that." But then, seeing Dove's grief, she stopped herself. "Let me take this chil' for a while…Let me see if I can settle her down…Sukey."

Holding the swaddled child in her arms, Bess brought her own face close to the creamy face of her granddaughter, lightly rocking the child and saying the same words over and over, almost like a lullaby, "I'se yo' old grandmamma, Miss Sukey. I'se yo' old grandmamma, Bess. Ain't' nobody gone love you mo' than yo' old grandmamma Bess loves you. You gone see that fo' sure Miss Sukey."

Sukey grew and was the delight of Bess's life. While Dove did her work, Bess kept the child in the kitchen house with her. The people in the quarters could never get over that Sukey was a white child. The baby's father had definitely been white, and judging from how Dove was acting now, it had broken her heart. Dove barely talked to anyone and when her work was done she would just sit on her step, staring off into the woods like she wasn't seeing them. Bess mostly took care of the baby. When she brought the child to its mother, a look of pure pleasure and happiness would cross over Dove's face for a moment, but then the crease between her eyebrows came right back and she would start crying softly as she held the child. It was clear to everyone except Bess that Dove had lost her mind. Whatever had happened to her had just been too much.

When the baby was almost two, Dove came up missing one morning. For a while now, Dove had seemed much better and had started keeping little Sukey with her in the sewing house at night. Those nights, Bess would tiptoe over and check on them. If the baby needed changing or tending to, Bess would take care of it while Dove slept, but Bess took it as a good sign that Dove wanted the baby with her. Sometimes Bess would sit holding the baby for the rest of the night while Dove slept. Before long, when she needed something Sukey started reaching out for Bess first. That, all by itself, looked like it broke what was left of Dove's heart.

The morning when Dove came up missing, Bess had slept soundly through the night. When she went to Dove's cabin to check on things, Sukey was alone. Little Sukey sat up in the bed as Bess opened the door. She lifted her arms and said, "Mama," to which Bess would never be sure if Sukey meant Bess or if she meant Dove.

* * * * *

It was still early when Dove reached the rice field. She wore only her white shift. Her cap was gone and her unbraided hair hung down nearly to her waist. It was the hair that Richard had loved so much, that he would bring to his face as they lay naked together. She walked barefoot along the path by the canal that brought waters from the river to the fields. And she carried the pillow, hugging it.

It was the pillow that Richard lay against as the light came up outside the windows on the last night he allowed her in his bed chamber. As he lay there naked in the early morning light and reached out to her with the love in his eyes that she knew he still carried in his heart, and as she came to him after she was dressed to give him the kiss that she could not know would be their last, she noticed the stitching on the pillow ticking was coming undone. And with him teasing her, she had him lean forward while she exchanged it with the pillow she used when she slept with him.

"Better a small mend now than an impossible rend later," she said to him with a teasing tone. She promised she would have it mended and bring it back that evening.

How many times had she wondered if those words had set the process in motion that led him to ban her from his bedchamber and remove her completely from his life? Had her words made him reason that it would be easier on Dove if he turned his cheek to her then, instead of later on? That it would be easier on them both if he ended their impossible union and broke with her earlier instead of later?

But even so, it had been too late. She could not go on.

As she walked along the path, she hugged the pillow and everything it contained to her chest and bent her head down to bury her face in it one more time. Even now, it still carried the scent of him. For two years she had buried her face in his pillow at night, where the stain of him was still on the ticking. She could still smell the essence of him. For two years she had talked to him that way when she was alone at night, holding his pillow to her. She held him close like that while she slept. In that way, she kept the memory of what they had shared alive, even though it was not alive and never would be.

She thought now of what she had sewn inside the pillow. The things she had carried in her pocket. The things that were hers and hers to keep.

There was the ring she had braided of Richard's hair, stolen away the morning he asked her to cut his hair for him. Even though he rarely wore the formal wigs of his class, like every other man he wore his own hair pulled back smoothly and tied at the nape of his neck. And when he asked Dove to cut his hair she cut a longer piece where he would never see or notice and concealed it in the towel she carried away. She wove that hair, along with her own, into a circle. The circle, alternating with the silver and gold of Richard's hair and the dark black of hers, had no beginning and no end. Then after Sukey was born and had enough hair to be trimmed, she undid the circle and wove her daughter's clippings into the circle too. Now the circle showed all three colors; Richard's white, Dove's black and Sukey's fair brown.

Inside the pillow was also the golden button Miss Charity had given her the last time she left Charles Town, and the charm Mama had given her that Patience had made for Bess so long ago when she left Charles Town for this plantation. All were tucked safely inside the pillow and Dove had sewn the pillow closed.

The people would be coming to the fields soon to begin their day of work. Dove walked along the river canal until she found the spot she had selected. She waded out into the canal. Her linen shift billowed up around her momentarily. She waited until it absorbed the water and went back down.

She waded out until she found the spot she had found before, the perfect spot. Then she turned to face the rising sun. With the water almost up to her waist, she held the pillow close to her chest, just under her chin. Then she sat down in the water, the water coming up to her chin. She took one final look around her, at the river and the rice fields. She heard the morning sounds of the birds; a dove calling another, and the gentle breeze stirring the moss on the trees. Then she lay down.

The weight of the pillow held her down. It was all as she had planned. Because sewn inside the pillow were eight bricks. They were sewn in securely so their weight could not shift and release her if she struggled against them at the last moment. There was one brick for each week she had spent with Richard.

But Dove did not struggle. She was calm. As she lay there looking up through the water, she could see the sun lighting the morning sky. The radiant clouds showed red and orange and gold. And as she looked up and let out her last breath, knowing the next would bring the water into her lungs and end her life, and that breath formed one word. The word was not "Richard" or "Sukey" or even "Mama."

The last word Dove breathed was "Mercy."

* * * * *

They searched all day and everywhere for Dove. Bess said she would never have run away without her child and she could not have wandered far at night. They searched most of the day until Old James found her. He waded out into the canal as soon as he saw her there, in her white shift with her long hair floating around her.

Old James, with his face blacker than night and his hair and eyebrows like cotton. Old James whose permanent scowl and piercing eyes scared the children of the plantation and gave them nightmares. Old James who had been part of the plantation since Master Richard's father brought him here, long before Master Richard was born. Old James carried the body of Dove, still clutching the pillow, to the door of the kitchen house. Then he laid her down tenderly at her mother's feet. And Old James wept.

The Old Massah made a special place for them to bury Dove. She was not to be buried in the slave cemetery down by the river. Instead he said she would be buried just outside the family cemetery on the other side of the house. Bess prepared the body for burial, and after she picked up the sodden pillow and opened it to see what it held, she washed the ticking and stuffed it again so Dove's head would rest on it. Dove was dressed in her best with the treasures she had sewn inside the pillow placed in her folded hands.

Miss Charity was there for the burial. With the horses galloping at a full run, her carriage came rattling up the river road from Charles Town as soon as she got the word. Richard, knowing his sister would never forgive him if she was not notified, sent a rider with the news and instructions for him to ride without stopping and as fast as he could until the envelope was delivered.

Miss Charity wept openly over the coffin, set out in the central hall of the house instead of down in the quarters. Even Bess in her grief did not carry on as much as Miss Charity who was all but prostrate, saying over and over that Dove had been like a daughter to her. As the people from the quarters, all of them dressed in their best for their one and only time being inside the house, filed past the coffin, Richard finally had to quieten his sister with the warning she would upset herself so much she would have to go to bed.

Bess wisely kept Sukey away that day. Her granddaughter was too young to understand the meaning of seeing her mother laid out for burial. Bess asked a woman from the quarters to come to the kitchen house, to keep the fire going and to watch Sukey while Bess was up at the house. Bess knew the woman would be frightened in Dove's cabin, with Dove's spirit wandering around until the body was buried, so Bess set them up in the kitchen house. It was bad enough for her in the kitchen house, where Dove had been born and spent most of her time. The woman sang songs loudly and did not look around behind herself too quickly, lest she see Dove's spirit standing there watching over them.

It was the morning after the burial when Miss Charity sent word down from the house that she would like to see Dove's child. Bess had been expecting the invitation and Sukey's best dress and cap were freshly washed and ironed. As soon as she made herself ready and changed Sukey, she walked slowly up to the house, holding Sukey's little hand as the girl walked beside her. Sukey had not yet asked for her mother, but Bess was sure that would be coming soon.

As they approached the house, Bess picked up Sukey and carried the child on her arm. Sukey rested her head comfortably on Bess' shoulder. Sukey faced away from the house as Bess carried her toward it. As Bess stepped up on the veranda, Miss Charity spoke from the recesses of the porch where she was seated.

"You've brought Dove's child," she said warmly to Bess, but then with a catch in her voice she added, "I so wanted to see her before I left for Charles Town."

"Yes, Mam'selle," Bess reverted to her old title for Miss Charity. "This little Sukey." Then after a moment she added, "She very light-skinned, Miss Charity."

Charity reached out for the child, whose face was still turned away. Bess crossed the porch to Miss Charity, who remained seated but held her hands out to take the child. As Bess leaned over, little Sukey turned to face her aunt, and smiled down at the woman who was reaching out for her.

Charity almost gasped. Little Sukey had eyes as blue as...as blue as her own. Charity had seen Frenchmen in Charles Town with skin darker than this child. "She Dove's daughter, Mam'selle," Bess said firmly as she passed the child to Miss Charity.

Charity was silent, examining the child in wonder. How was this possible? Dove was half black, she knew that. Charity had expected her child to be the same light color Dove had been. But the child she held was white. Bess must be playing some sort of prank on her.

Bess was ready to take the child away from Miss Charity if she handed Sukey back, or worse yet if she threw the baby away in a panic of recognition. But Miss Charity's shock soon melted into recognition. She looked up at Bess, "She is my brother's child too, isn't she?"

Bess could not answer, but she quickly looked around to see if anyone else was hearing them. They were the only ones on the porch and the house was quiet behind them. "Please, Miss Charity. Please! Don't say that here," she said urgently in a low voice.

Charity understood and fell silent. She examined Sukey, who after studying her aunt with intense seriousness, leaned her head against Charity's breast and smiled up at her. Sukey lifted her hand, silently pointing to Charity, and then she softly placed her little palm against her aunt's cheek. It was in that moment that Charity fell completely in love with her niece.

"Oh, poor Dove," Charity said at one point, understanding what had happened.

"No, Mam'selle," Bess said softly, grasping the meaning of Miss Charity's words. "He not take Dove. She go willing to him."

Charity sat holding Sukey for a long while. While Bess stood by, she took the child's hand in her own and gently rocked her side to side as she sat on the straight-backed porch chair. Then she stopped and reached out and took Bess' hand in her own and after a long moment asked, in a choked whisper, "Oh Bess, what are we to do?"

After dinner that night, there was a tremendous argument in the library between Miss Charity and her brother. The door was already closed but the servants discretely withdrew from the upper floors of the house where they were clearing up in the dining room and went down to the ground level with its brick floors and doors that opened out under the veranda.

The sheltered place under the veranda was a pleasant place to sit during warm weather or when it rained, and while they could not hear the words they could still hear the heated exchange upstairs between their Master and his sister. As the servants stood there, Old James wondered out loud that he could not remember those two fighting like this since they had been young children. They generally were so patient and kind with each other. After all, they were all each other had. There was no other family left to them except each other.

For almost an hour the voices rose and fell. Bess came up from the kitchen house to see where the rest of the dinner dishes were. Then against Old James stern warning, she went up the inside stairs and gently knocked on the library door. Then she went inside. Bess was in the library with Master Richard and Miss Charity for quite a while longer. When the story was told later down in the quarters, they said with wonder that Bess had calmed them down. Before long, Bess came out with Miss Charity and took her upstairs to help her prepare for bed. And after asking Old James for another decanter, Master Richard stayed in the library that night, slowly sipping his whiskey with only one candle burning on the table beside him.

It had been another strange day.

* * * * *

"I will call her Mercy. Her name will be Mercy Wainwright. She is, and will be, my niece. My orphaned niece."

With Richard and Bess standing before her in the library again, after dinner and two days after her terrible argument with her brother, Charity recalled that the name was from a passage she had often read aloud with Dove. It was a name Charity loved. She had once told Dove that it was a name she would have given to her own daughter, if she had ever had one.

Charity came back to the kitchen house with Bess after the meeting. Mintie had finished the dinner dishes and was waiting for Bess so she could go home. It was late. Little Sukey was sleeping. Mintie, nervous with the Old Massah's sister in the kitchen, left as soon as Bess dismissed her.

Bess picked up and held Sukey. She felt the silky curls against the side of her face. She had lost three sons when the hood was thrown over her head in her garden that long ago day in Africa. They were grown men by now and would have forgotten her. She had lost Dove too, her only daughter. Poor Dove, barely laid in her grave. But none of that had hurt her as much as this was hurting her now.

Sukey; the sweet child. Sukey; all that was left for her. She walked around the kitchen house a while, cradling the sweet, sleeping child in her arms. Then she turned to Miss Charity and simply nodded her head.

So that night the three of them carried out Charity's plan. An hour after she left the kitchen house, Charity sent word down to the stable that she had to go back to Charles Town immediately. Her closed carriage was brought around to the front door as soon as the horses could be hitched to it. Richard came out on the porch with Charity, where she gave him the goodbye kiss on his cheek and bustled herself into the carriage. Richard shut the carriage door for her, bidding a safe journey to Charles Town loudly enough that all could hear. Then he stood at the top of the front steps, as was his custom when company was departing. Old James stood behind him at the front door as the carriage drove down the long lane to the road with its wheels crunching on the drive. They waited until the carriage went out the gate and turned toward Charles Town before they went back into the house and closed the door.

In the moonlit night they had not gone a hundred yards beyond the gate when Charity rapped on the ceiling of the compartment, signaling Benjamin to stop the carriage.

"Eyes forward Benjamin," she commanded him as let herself out. "Don't look anywhere else except down that road." Sometimes Charity had to make a comfort stop on the journey, but Benjamin was surprised she had to stop so soon. As instructed, he kept his eyes forward while Miss Charity hurried back down the road a bit before disappearing into the trees at the side of the road.

Bess stepped from the shadows, closely holding the little bundle that was the sleeping Sukey. She had given Sukey the drops, exactly as Charity had instructed, and the child was sleeping deeply. She would remember nothing of this. Miss Charity stood waiting.

"This your Aunt Charity," Bess said softly against Sukey's sweet head. "You gone go with her now. Your Aunt Charity is gone take good care of you. Old Bess can't give you that. You gone be a proper young lady now."

Bess held herself back so she did not break down in front of Miss Charity. Once again, she turned away from Charity a moment. She could not let go. She could not hand this child over.

She gently rocked the sleeping child in her arms, whispering urgently against her face. "Now you gone forget all about Old Bess," she told Sukey. "Old Bess your grandmamma. Always be your grandmamma. Old Bess your mama's mama. Old Bess love you. But this all Old Bess can do for you. Old Bess gone give you away because Old Bess love you more than she love anything in this world. You is gone be a proper lady now, Miss Mercy. You gone be white."

Bess stepped forward, holding out Sukey, now Mercy, for Mam'selle to take.

"Thank you," Charity said quietly with tears brimming. She knew this must be unbearable for Bess, giving up the child. "Thank you."

"No, Mam'selle," snuffing back her tears, "Old Bess say thank you. Thank you for loving this child, too. Old Bess say thank you for taking her for your own." She paused a moment, before she could continue. "But you make sure one thing. You must promise Old Bess one thing. You promise me that this child never know anything at all about Old Bess."

And Bess' English was suddenly perfect. "You must promise that she will never know anything about her grandmother."

Bess handed Charity the bundle, for a moment wondering again if she would release her hold on it. Charity understood and placed a sympathetic hand on Bess's arm and whispered. "I promise I will love her, Bess. So much more than you will ever imagine."

Bess let Sukey go with a silent sob and then stood watching while Charity hurried back to the carriage and got herself into it with the silent bundle in her arms. Bess heard Charity call out for Benjamin to continue. He clucked his tongue at the horses and they took off again at a quick pace.

The exchange had barely taken a minute. When it was quiet, Bess wiped her eyes with her palms and went ahead with Charity's plan. It was the plan that would assure Sukey's new life.

Resolutely, she went back to the kitchen house and took down her big garden basket. It was the strongest one with the big looping handle that she could carry over one arm. In the basket she placed a bundle of old cloths and her big butcher knife. She had freshly sharpened it with the stone while she waited to hear Charity's command come down from the house that she must return to Charles Town immediately.

Bess walked quietly but with purpose through the quarters to the barn. It was not Saturday and the people would be rising at dawn for a full day of work. No one was outside at this hour. Bess went on through the quarters to the barn, then out behind the barn where the hog pen was. The pigs were quietly slumbering in the pen.

One of them saw her and thinking Bess would be bringing something good to eat came over to the fence. Bess saw that the pig was the right size and came quietly up beside it, patting it to make it be quiet as she held it under the chin with her left hand. Then she plunged the knife into its windpipe between the lungs and the place where the squeal came from. Bess had cut up enough pigs to know the exact place. With a quick, hard slice from left to right, she cut completely through the windpipe and the artery next to it. While she held its mouth shut the silenced pig blew one gurgling gasp of air out the hole, struggled only a moment

48

as its lungs collapsed and then lay dead. Bess wrapped the pig in the cloths she brought to sop up the blood, placed the bundle in her basket and carefully made her way back to the kitchen house.

With only one candle burning she unwrapped the pig. She took Dove's needle and thread and closed the hole in the pig's throat. Then she washed the pig clean. She burned the rags in the fireplace, using the light from the fire to put Sukey's dress on the pig and wrap the pig's head in a triangle of cloth in the same way she wrapped up Sukey's head at night. She held the pig against her breast to see what it looked like and only the pig's pink cheek showed. Charity's plan would work.

When all was ready in the cabin, Bess undressed to her shift and waited. Charity said to wait long past midnight before she did the next thing and when Bess thought she had waited long enough she picked up the dead pig dressed in Sukey's clothing, wrapped Sukey's blanket around it and held the dead pig to her breast. Then she let out a long, wailing scream. The scream, for her lost Sukey, was genuine. Her screech set the dogs up at the house to barking.

As she banged out her door, she let out another long wail, "Suuuukeeeey! Oh Lawd, No. Not my Sukey!" Lights were coming on in the quarter and a few brave ones were beginning to poke their heads out their doors as Old Bess stood on the stoop of the kitchen house, screaming and holding the bundle tight against her breast. "Oh Lawd. Oh Lawd, no. Not my Sukey. Oh please, someone go get the Massah. My Sukey dead. Oh, Sweet Jesus, no."

She let her legs collapse under her a moment and sat heavily down on the stoop as she wailed. It was a real cry from deep inside her. She screamed up at heaven, where the Lord should be, watching down on her lie. After a while, one of the women came forward from the crowd that was collecting, just barely lit by the light coming from Bess's open door.

"Now Miss Bess, you just gimme that chil', honey," the woman said gently, reaching to take the limp bundle. "Gimme that chil'."

"No!" Bess screamed, rising and looking around at them wildly and holding her hand out for the woman to stop. "You ain' gone take my chil'," she cried out hoarsely, "No one gone take my Sukey. I got nothin' now. Got no Dove, Got no Sukey. You not gone take her. Not now. Not ever."

With that she turned and escaped back into the kitchen house and slammed the door behind her, wailing inside as she sat with her back against the door.

Old Massah was not long in coming, and was still dressed in what he had worn for dinner, but the house workers who followed him down from the house, carrying lights for him, knew that was not unusual. Old Massah often locked himself in his library at night when he could not sleep and sat drinking. And although he was not drunk, not even a tipsy, they could all smell the whiskey on him as he brushed past them.

Even though he splashed whisky on himself while he waited, he still made a mistake. Later they would begin to realize the Massah already knew Sukey was dead and that he came down to the quarters before anyone went up to the house. No one had to tell him. But maybe he had heard Bess from the big house. She certainly had been loud enough.

"Y'all get on back to your quarters now," he commanded clearly. They all turned toward their cabins and took a step or two, but lingered to see what would happen next. Old Massah tried to open the kitchen house door but could not budge it with Bess sitting against it inside, quieter now but still sobbing audibly. He pounded on Bess's door. "Bess you open this door, now. You hear me? Open this door and let me in."

Bess moved slightly away from the door and the Old Massah put his shoulder against it, partially pushing the wailing Bess aside as he shoved the door open. He should have asked a couple of the men to do it for him, but he shoved it open all by himself. Then he went inside and quickly shut the door behind himself, letting no one else in.

They could hear him speaking to Bess and Bess wailing. It went on a while before Bess was finally quiet. Then the Old Massah came out carrying the bundle that was the little dead Sukey. In the light that streamed out from inside Bess's cabin and in the fading moonlight they could all see Sukey's little pink cheek inside the bundle. He held her closely. Sukey had been his favorite, for sure.

"I am afraid little Sukey has died," he announced, as if no one knew. One of the women came forward with her hands open to take the bundle and prepare the body but the Old Massah held up his hand to stop her. "Stay there. It may be the fever. I don't want anyone else to handle her. Now if a couple of you will make up a box, we need to get her buried at first light."

Two of the men nodded. They would start on the coffin right away. The other folks crept back to their cabins. No one wanted the fever. That was sure.

And everything was going to Charity's plan. Everyone believed that little Sukey lay dead in the Old Massah's arms when he took the bundle back to Bess inside the kitchen house. He came back out, wiping his hands as though he had washed them and went back to the house.

Word came down from the house the next morning that the Old Massah was drinking. As soon as the sun was up he came to the door of the library and ordered Old James to bring him another bottle of whiskey. By ten o'clock he was sound asleep in his chair.

50

The box was placed on the stoop of the kitchen house and it sat there for a long while. Old Bess opened the door only long enough to drag the box inside and then slammed the door shut. No smoke came from the kitchen house chimney.

By noon, the woman who had reached out to take Sukey the night before banged on the door. "Miss Bess, Massah say we got to bury that chil' this mornin'. You come on out now. We take care of everything."

"Get away from this door," Bess hollered back at them. "Get away from this house."

"Massah want that chil' bury this morning, Miss Bess."

"Then you tell Old Massah he have to come down here and bury her his self," Bess yelled back.

As was planned, that settled it for a while. No one from the quarters was going to go up to the house to tell the Old Massah anything. If he asked, they would tell him what was going on, but they were not going up there on their own. All Richard and Bess had to do was to wait a while longer.

So nothing happened at all that day. No food was prepared in the kitchen and they said up at the house that the Massah was too drunk to eat it anyway. Old James said to let it rest until the next morning. If Old Massah was still drunk, he would come down and take charge of getting the child buried himself.

The next morning the Old Massah roused himself, unwashed and stinking of whiskey. He came down to the kitchen house and pounded on the door.

"Bess, goddammit! You open this door right now before I break it down. I swear to God I will break it down, now. You hear me, Bess? I said open this door!"

As the people stood around, the door opened slowly. A few gasped. Bess had smeared her face with ash as her ancient sign of deep mourning. For a moment she looked like a spirit coming out of the kitchen house door. She still held that bundle tenderly in her arms. Old Massah quickly put his handkerchief over his nose and mouth and pushed Bess back inside and followed her through the door.

Normally, it was the custom on the plantation for the dead to be washed and dressed and laid out in their coffin for all the people to come in and see before the burial, especially when the deceased was a child. But with Massah pulling out his handkerchief like that, it must mean that the body was beginning to stink already. It was too soon and it hadn't been that hot, but maybe it was a combination of the baby dying of fever and Old Bess holding little Sukey close and keeping her warm for almost two days now. After a long while, Old Massah came back out the door, carrying the little coffin with its lid on. He told the men who made the coffin to go get the hammer and nails. When they came back he set the box on the ground and told them to nail it shut.

One of the men began driving in the nails, but gagged at the stench and had to turn away. The other had to finish. No one asked to see the child.

They formed a ragged procession to take the coffin to the slaves' burying grounds and began singing the burial song, but when the Massah picked up the box to carry it, Bess came out of the house, sobbing, and fell to her knees in the dirt crying to the Massah to not take her Sukey away. He motioned to one of the women to go to her and in the end it took two of the strongest women to hold Bess back, so crazy she was that they were not going to bury her Sukey. Instead of leading them to the slaves' burying grounds where the men had already dug the grave, Richard led them to Dove's grave, barely a week in the ground herself. The Master would not let them reopen Dove's coffin to put little Sukey in her dead mother's arms, so they set the baby's coffin right on top of her dead mother's coffin and refilled the grave. On the way back to the quarters, they all said it had been a sad, sad time.

Some of the women who stayed behind from the funeral went inside the kitchen house and set things to rights, propping the door and window open for air, sweeping it out and scrubbing things down. Then after she was settled down they cleaned up Old Bess. Old James came down from the house and before they put her to bed he made Bess drink a full glass of whiskey the Old Massah sent down for her. The women said they would take turns so someone would be with Bess all through the night. When Bess stirred in her sleep and began sobbing they comforted her.

The next morning, Bess got herself out of bed, stirred up the fire and began cooking breakfast. It was as though nothing had happened. If Sukey was ever mentioned after that, even by accident, Bess would only say, "That sweet chil' in a better place now and wit' a white angel watching over her."

The other women in the quarters assumed Old Bess was referring to the nearly-white Dove whose body had been found in the river in her white shift and was buried in a white dress. It was the dress Dove had sewn thinking it would be her wedding dress one day. They would all cluck and hum in agreement. Yes, a white angel watched over Sukey, and they admired Old Bess for her strength and her faith.

And Bess, when she thought about it, would smile. She could have laughed right out loud at all of them, but she only smiled.

Because it had worked.

CHAPTER TWO

Charles Town
South Carolina Colony
1734 - 1746

Of course, Charity's role in this deception was more complex. For her brother, and even for Bess, when the death and burial of young Sukey was complete, it was finished. For Charity, the ongoing explanation of Mercy Wainwright was not.

During the drive back to Charles Town, Charity realized that her plan to introduce Mercy as her orphaned niece was not going to work. "Orphaned from whom?" would be the first question. Richard was known there, and short of his death notice appearing in the Charles Town paper, no one would believe that Mercy was his orphan. Along that line the next question would be, "Who was the girl's mother?" Certainly not the Widow Timsley. The marriage had never taken place and local gossip would have already known if the union had produced a child.

Charity and Richard's father had been among the early Carolina settlers. While he had not been fortunate enough to receive one of the original land grants King Charles II awarded to his loyal supporters following the restoration of his throne when Oliver Cromwell's Protectorate ended in 1663, their father had been a close friend of one of those eight men and shortly after the settlement expedition of 1670, for virtually nothing John Wainwright purchased a large tract of land that became the Wainwright plantation.

The town house that Charity now occupied had been one of the first real houses built within the city walls after Charles Town was moved from its initial location on the west bank of the Ashley River. On their father's death, Richard received the plantation, as well as the plantation house and its contents. Ownership of the town house passed to Charity. Although they respected each other's privacy, they knew they were always welcome in the other's home, and in fact they had known both homes all their lives.

When John first arrived in Carolina, the most pressing task at hand was to clear the forest so that crops could be grown. Although he ran cattle on the cleared land as a sideline, John Wainwright's first cash crop was the cleared timber. He worked alongside his slaves in felling oak and pine that grew as much as forty feet tall, trimming the limbs from the trunk, and loading the logs for transport down the river to the mill. He took a part of his share in milled lumber and a modest frame house was built on the land. That first house was entirely built of wood. The frame, exterior and interior walls, floors, and even the roof were made of rough cut pine boards that came from the property. Glass had to be imported so the windows were only covered with shutters.

But from the start, John had plans to build a substantial home on his plantation. When a layer of clay was discovered under the sand of the river, he began manufacturing bricks. Basically his slaves harvested the clay at low tide, packed the clay into molds, turned out the formed bricks to dry in the sun and then the bricks were fired in a kiln. When fired, the bricks turned to a deep red color. John decided the plantation house would be built from the brick he made right there on the plantation.

John's plans were quickly moved forward when he happened to meet the young Elizabeth in Charles Town, newly arrived from Barbados with her brother who held a Lords Proprietor grant for land nearby. Barely a year later, her brother died and she was left with the choice of returning to Barbados or staying and taking over the farm. She had already been working alongside her brother in every aspect of the farm so her decision was to stay.

Although it would appear to be a strategic union, Charity and Richard knew their parents had been deeply in love from the beginning. The first promise their father made to his bride was to build a proper house in Charles Town for her to live in while he ran their two combined properties. After that, as soon as he was able, he would build an even grander home on the slight rise of ground that bordered the two plantations and overlooked the river. Plans were drawn for the plantation house in the low country style. John and Elizabeth liked the plans so well that they decided to duplicate the house in town. However the size of a lot available to them along Tradd street, where John insisted they must build their house, precluded a home of that size, so the architect converted the plans to a 5/8 scale.

The Charles Town house, built of brick and tabby, was turned sideways in relation to the street, so the narrow end faced the street with the long first and second floor galleries, or porches, running down the side that faced the narrow formal garden. The back of the house was set against the side property line. The plantation house, when it was built, would also be brick and tabby, but would have wide verandas on all four sides with the long front of the house facing the river and the back of the house facing down a long carriage drive to the road that ran along the river back to Charles Town. All the furnishings, and even the window glass for the townhouse were ordered from as far away as England and Philadelphia, with the assurance they could be duplicated at the same or larger scale when the plantation house was built.

The result was that layout of both houses was the same and the rooms were almost identically furnished. Charity's father reasoned it would be easier for his wife and family to go between the two homes if they were as alike as possible. That had proved the case in the early years when the family often vacated the plantation for the safety of the city walls. Charity could remember more than one occasion of going to sleep in her bed in the plantation house only to waken the next morning in her room in the house in town. These days, the plantation house was small in comparison to the newer ones that were being built along the Ashley and Cooper rivers. But Richard had no interest in enlarging it, especially after the death of his wife and young son. The plantation house remained almost exactly as it had been when their parents resided there.

There had been another brother, David, who was the second son and the youngest child. David had gone to sea as a young man. According to English common law, the entire estate, including the plantation, would pass to the eldest brother. Second and third sons often established careers in the clergy or in the navy. After a full naval career, with only minimal decoration, they believed the brother had settled in England.

Charity supposed it would have been much easier on David if their father had left his entire estate to Richard. He certainly could have easily provided for Charity by putting funds in trust to provide her with a life income and a life tenancy in the town house with the ownership remaining with Richard. But the will had given the town house to her outright, along with a substantial amount of the family wealth. Perhaps, even then, her father somehow knew the potential for Richard's mismanagement and wanted to assure Charity some degree of security from that. But instead of seeing that, David had been bitter about having no inheritance and there had only been one or two letters from him over the years. Charity was not even sure if he was still living, or if he was that he was still in England.

But one thing was in her favor. He was younger than Richard, and if Richard had fathered Sukey - or Mercy as she had to begin thinking of the child now - then certainly David could have produced a daughter at his age too. On that night ride back to Charles Town, David became Mercy's father. Charity also decided that the dead mother would be French. That would explain Mercy's light, olive-toned complexion, her dark hair and thick eyelashes. That look was so prevalent among the French who settled in Charles Town, no one would question it.

Her trump card was that Mercy looked so much like Richard – his face was echoed in hers and most certainly in the arresting pale blue of her eyes. And so in turn, the child also favored Charity. She would have no problem introducing Mercy as her niece. While Mercy slept in her arms, she practiced saying it, how she would introduce and explain the child. "My dear brother David's orphaned daughter," and "My orphaned niece, Mercy Wainwright."

But she could not say that convincingly enough even for herself. It was a lie to say that the child was orphaned, so instead she had the inspired idea of saying it was only the child's mother who was dead, which in fact Dove was. She would say the child's father had abandoned her to Charity's care, which was also true. Mercy's father had indeed abandoned her. It was a lie she would tell so often over the years to come that in time she would almost believe herself. In reality, when all was said and done, there was very little about her lie that was not in fact true, and Charity was wise enough to realize that was the best kind of lie.

But even with that decided there was still the problem of how to bring Mercy into her own household. At a minimum, Patience would have to be told and Benjamin too. Charity knew instinctively that the more people she involved in her deception, the less likely it was to be a success. No, the fewer people who knew the truth, even among her most loyal servants, the less likely it would be that someone would slip up in the future. No one, other than Charity, could know.

The sky was beginning to lighten in the east when Charity had a sudden inspiration. If her brother David had in fact given Mercy over to her care, Mercy would have arrived in Charles Town by ship, not from the plantation. Charity rapped on the carriage roof again, Benjamin slowed the carriage and she leaned out the window to call up to him. "Do not drive to the house, Benjamin. We must go to the dock, posthaste. I am meeting a ship there. A passenger ship I fear has already arrived."

Benjamin whipped the horses back up to a run. It was fully daylight by the time they entered the city gate and then drove the full length of Broad Street through Charles Town to the docks, turning on Bay Street along the east wall that protected the city from the river. Indeed, a ship had arrived at Smith's Quay that morning. With the crowd around that dock, Benjamin had to stop the carriage to wait. From where they stopped, Charity could see that passengers were still disembarking. "Wait here, Benjamin," she commanded. "I will go ahead."

Although the sky was clear and it was actually quite warm, Charity hastily put on the hooded cloak she kept in the carriage. As she held Mercy in her left arm, she covered the child under the voluminous folds of fabric. Charity bustled herself out of her carriage, keeping her back to Benjamin while she closed the door herself. She walked away from Benjamin careful to keep her back facing the carriage until she was lost in the crowd.

To appear less suspicious, Charity uncovered Mercy as she pushed her way through the press of the crowd around the newly arrived ship. She took careful note of the name on its bow. This would become the ship that brought her niece to Charles Town. When she was sure she was out of sight of her own carriage she gradually brought Mercy completely out from under the cloak. With the drowsy child still in her arms she walked to the end of the gangway where the press of arriving passengers was beginning to slow and worked her way into the crowd. Then she simply walked back toward the place where Benjamin was sitting with the carriage.

"We were in time, Benjamin. Look! My niece Mercy Wainwright has arrived from England."

Benjamin looked down in surprise at the child his Mistress was holding up to him to see. Little Mercy looked familiar. He thought he had seen her somewhere before, but it was not possible. "Doesn't she favor my brother David?" she asked.

"David is her father. I'm afraid her mother has passed and he has given this child over to my care."

Although Miss Charity had made a mistake, Master David went to sea several years before Miss Charity bought Benjamin so he had no way of knowing her brother, he saw that the child did indeed look like the Wainwrights. Benjamin looked down, tipped his hat and smiled at the sleepy child, "Good morning. Nice to meet you, Miss Mercy."

Now there was only Patience to convince and Charity could begin introducing her new ward to the folks of Charles Town.

Patience thought Miss Charity's story seemed somewhat fantastic and that Miss Charity was nervous in telling it – the infant child of a long-lost brother who was all but forgotten suddenly arriving alone on a ship that had docked that morning. It was also odd that Miss Charity had only received word the night before, but maybe the letter was sent directly to Miss Charity at the plantation house and been overlooked during the uproar of events there. Patience could not deny that the child looked like the Wainwrights; Master Richard and Miss Charity and what she could remember of the young master David.

But it was not her place to question Miss Charity so she accepted the story. She set about making the arrangements for the unexpected arrival. The child arrived with nothing, and poorly dressed, too, Patience noted, so a complete set of basic clothing had to be secured right away. By nightfall Patience had procured a linen dress that fastened in back and an apron to cover the dress. Stockings would need to be bought and shoes would have to be made. Miss Charity accomplished a hasty conversion of the sitting room off her bed chamber into a nursery.

Charity presented her niece to her friends at that week's afternoon tea. She sent word ahead to the hostess, saying she had a rare surprise so excitement was already high and there was an air of expectation when Charity's carriage arrived, but nothing had prepared the women for the child Charity bore in her arms. Charity's friends, who were either childless spinsters like Charity, or married women with grown children, were enchanted. And from that week forward, little Mercy spent her afternoon teas going from one lap to another, with the ladies carefully keeping track of whose turn it was to hold the child next.

She was a calm and happy child and the ladies doted on her. They exclaimed how much she looked like her aunt and some even teased that if they did not know better they would think that Charity was actually trying to pass off her own daughter as her niece. Charity blushed at the implication, but was pleased by the teasing. It assured her that her friends had accepted the story, and it even made her feel a bit more connected to the girl, as though Mercy was the daughter she never had.

As the child grew, Charity's friends privately wondered how it was possible that she could be such a beauty and still look so much like her plain, spinster aunt. They decided it was Mercy's thick eyelashes and dark eyebrows, fuller lips, and her nicely rounded face that must come from her French background. Charity's face was so long and narrow, and with thin lips that barely seemed to be there. In fact, other than her blue eyes, Charity's pale face had always seemed completely devoid of color. But the color and the expression of their eyes were identical, and both had the same natural grace and deportment and displayed such impeccable manners so easily – something you were just born with, they agreed, a true sign of noble blood. No one could dispute that the two were what Charity said they were.

* * * * *

When Mercy was three years old, all of Charity's careful planning was almost undone, and by Mercy herself. That fateful morning Charity brought Mercy with her into the library while she worked on her correspondence. Like her brother at the plantation, Charity used this room as her office. Her writing table held a supply of her stationery, quill pens, and ink well. As she completed a letter she placed it in an envelope of fine paper and sealed it with sealing wax into which she pressed her sealing ring with the family crest bearing her initials. It was a pleasant morning and she enjoyed the task of correspondence. She had just finished a letter to Richard, giving him general news and an indirect update on the status of his "niece," when she urgently felt the call of nature and had to leave the room.

While Charity worked, Mercy played quietly in the library with a cloth doll with a complete set of clothes. The doll was a recent gift from one of Charity's friends and Mercy carried it everywhere, although she insisted on always removing the doll's silk gown, leaving the doll wearing only her shift, petticoat, and stays. And although Charity and Patience always redressed the doll each night, Mercy always removed the gown, as well as the doll's shoes and stockings, the first thing each morning.

When Patience came into the room with the ash bin and broom to tend the fireplace, Mercy was leaning across her aunt's writing table as she stood on her aunt's chair. Mercy was so intent as she daintily dipped her index finger in the ink well and then dabbed the ink on the doll's cloth face that she was not aware Patience had come into the room.

"Oh, Miss Mercy!" Patience exclaimed in a hushed voice. "Why you gone rune your bes' doll now?"

Mercy looked up in surprise and happily parroted Patience's words, "Bes' doll."

Patience crossed the room with her cloth to grab Miss Mercy's little hand and gently wipe the ink away from her fingers before any more damage was done.

Fortunately there were no stains on Mercy's clothes but the doll's face was almost entirely black.

"Why you rune your doll, Miss Mercy? You make her face all black."

"Bes' doll, Payshen. Bes' doll." Mercy was more insistent.

"That right. This your good doll, honey. Your Aunt Charity not gone like this."

"No, Bes' doll, Payshen," Mercy insisted. "This Mama Bess."

Patience stopped wiping the inked finger and looked at the child before her. "What did you say?"

"This doll Mama Bess, Payshen. Mama Bess."

It did not make sense. The child had not left Charles Town since she arrived by ship the year before. She had never been to the Wainwright plantation and Bess had not been to Charles Town in all that time either.

"How you know Mama Bess, honey?"

Charity heard the last of the exchange as she entered the room. She came to the desk, looked at the doll with its blackened face, then at Mercy, and at last her eyes went to Patience. For a moment the two women stood looking at each other, one horrified, the other still not understanding or believing.

Charity swallowed, took a deep breath and said, "I am afraid my deception and misrepresentation have been revealed." Patience still did not understand her. Charity sat down hard in her writing table chair. It was like the wind went out of her, "Oh, Patience. I have lied to everyone. I have lied to you and everyone in my house and everyone in Charles Town."

"You mean she is…" Patience began, not knowing how to continue.

"Yes, although this child is indeed my niece, she is also the daughter of Dove, and granddaughter of Bess."

Mercy looked up happily at the mention of her grandmother's name and repeated, "Bess. Mama Bess."

"But this chil' white, Miss Charity," Patience said, confused.

"Dove was half white and the father, my brother, is white, of course, so Mercy is quadroon, even if she looks white. Sometimes it just happens like this when they are only a quarter. They look white."

She told the entire story to Patience. Patience stood silently, listening but incredulous. She first learned how the child, Sukey, came to be: that Dove had loved Master Richard, that he did not take her against her will, as Bess's captors had taken her. She learned about Master Richard's rejection, and how Dove's suicide brought Charity to the plantation. That was the first time she had seen Dove's child, and that she knew for sure that the child existed for that matter.

"When I saw her there, I knew I just could not leave her like that, Patience," Charity wept into her handkerchief. "I just could not abandon her to that life."

After a moment, Patience placed a gentle hand on her Mistress's shoulder. "What you done, was a right and good thing, Miss Charity. You love this chil'. You don' need to worry. I loves this chil' too. But Miss Charity, I think I already know this Dove's chil' before. I thought I see Dove's stitch in the little dress she wore the day you brought her here, but I forget that 'cause I don't doubt you. I don't tell nobody. I happy to keep this secret. I keep it 'til I bury in my grave."

Charity took Patience's hand in her own, feeling a sense of relief. "It is good to have an ally. I am indebted to you, Patience. I am so indebted to you."

Patience knew what 'indebted' meant, but was not sure what an 'ally' was. It was something good the way Miss Charity said it. She was happy to be that for her Mistress, but she protested, "Now Miss Charity, don' you talk foolish. You don' owe me nothing. I happy to help you with this chil'. I not only do it for you. Dove always so sweet to Old Payshen. I do it for her and for Old Bess, too. Old Bess like a sister to me."

Charity found her life of deception was so much easier after taking Patience in her confidence. Having Patience as a reinforcement strengthened her story. Patience was even more devoted to the child than before, and after Mercy was put down for her nap later that day, Charity had Patience find her paint brush and together they painted the doll's face, hands, arms, legs and feet black with ink from the ink well. Patience held the doll close to the kitchen fire to dry the ink. When the ink had dried, Charity embroidered a red mouth and white eyes on the dolls face. They set the doll on Mercy's counterpane for her to see when she awoke, and Mercy was delighted with the change. "Bess," she exclaimed happily and hugged the doll closely. Bess was always her favorite doll after that and Patience stopped putting the doll's silk gown, stockings and shoes back on at night. Bess stayed barefoot and only wore her shift, stays and petticoat, just like the real Bess in Mercy's memory of her grandmother.

Charity began simple lessons with her niece and by age five, Mercy was reading almost everything. She also taught her niece the basics of arithmetic and read the most current books of knowledge aloud with her. Lest Mercy be lonely, Charity arranged for her to have friends to play with in the afternoons. She was happy to have the children come to her home to play with her niece, and also to have Mercy learning to go into others' homes when one of the other girls was hostess. It would help her form friendships and aid in Mercy's social development.

On one of those play afternoons when Mercy was seven years old, the girls were playing a complicated game in the front garden; complex because they gleefully kept changing the rules as they went along. While the girls played, Charity kept a watchful eye from her desk in the library, rising regularly to go to the window to watch.

Near the end of the play hour, a few moments before the girls should come inside for their afternoon tea before returning to their homes, Charity heard a change in the volume and timbre of the children's voices. She rose and quickly went to the front window just in time to see Mercy's playmates run away, likely back to their own homes, while a group of ragged children surrounded Mercy taunting her as she hid her face with her hands and burst into tears.

Charity went flying out her front door. Patience was coming around the corner of the house from the backyard, and not far behind her mistress. Patience chased the children from the garden, brandishing the broom she had been sweeping with as she ran after the children. "Don' you dare torment Miss Mercy, you white trash chil'ren," Patience yelled as she chased them. The children quickly outran the aging Patience. Patience came huffing back and let herself in through the front gate. Mercy's friends were gone too. Charity said that as soon as Patience caught her breath they would have to go to the girls' houses to make sure they were safely home.

In the moments after she came out the door and before they saw her coming, Charity recognized the rhyme they were chanting. It was a vulgar verse she sometimes heard among the rougher children playing in the streets, but it still shocked her now and especially that it had been directed toward Mercy;
.

> *"Yer pappy was a nigger and yer mammy was a whore,*
> *And you wouldn't even be here…"*

As she took Mercy's hand to bring her back inside the house, her niece hung her head, humiliated and embarrassed. Patience walked heavily three paces behind her mistresses, as was proper. She stopped as soon as Miss Charity stopped at the base of the steps.

"Your father was my brother, Mercy. Look at me, child," Charity said. Then she bent down to place her hand gently under Mercy's chin and raised her face to her. "Look at me. Do I look like a Negro to you? No. And neither was your father. And your mother was not at all what they said she was. As I have told you before and I want you to always remember, the lesson in this today is that just because someone says something about you does not mean it is true. Do you understand me?"

Mercy nodded, but as soon as Charity released her chin she lowered her face again. They trudged on up the stairs like that, hand in hand, with Patience not far behind.

* * * * *

In the spring of 1746, the year that Mercy would turn fourteen, Charity took her along on a visit to the family lawyer, Jean Faure. Although Charity had hired a tutor the past four years, he recently admitted he had taught Mercy all that he could. Charity was concerned with the continuance of Mercy's education and wanted Monsieur Favre to investigate potential schools.

"I don't want to send her to an academy where she will only be educated in what you might call 'subjects for girls'," Charity explained. "I do acknowledge it is important for her to be accomplished in music, dancing, drawing, embroidery, and French, but Mercy has an excellent mind and I want her to also study Latin, geometry, science, and perhaps even law, until she is at least sixteen. This is 1746, after all. I believe it is critical that my niece attend a school that will afford her a full education and that teaches boys and girls equally. I am prepared to send her to England, if I must, to accomplish that objective."

"It will be my pleasure to make your inquiries, Miss Wainwright," Jean responded.

"I trust you will let me know your selection at your earliest convenience," Charity directed as she stood and extended her gloved hand to him.

"Of course, Miss Wainwright," he said as he bowed over Charity's hand, then turned and added, "Miss Mercy." Mercy cast her eyes downward and gave the shallow curtsy as her aunt had taught, but she could not keep herself from looking directly at Monsieur Favre and smiling warmly at him as she rose. Fortunately her aunt did not see her boldness.

In the weeks that followed their meeting, it seemed to Charity that things took a turn for the worse while they waited to hear from Monsieur Faure.

First, news came by letter from Richard that Old Bess was dead. He seemed to only mention it as an afterthought. The letter was dated weeks earlier and apparently had not been posted for some time. She died peacefully in her bed in the kitchen house. She had not been ill or even complained of any discomfort, but simply died in her sleep. She was buried next to Dove in the space outside the family plot. Charity was distressed and debated whether to tell Mercy, but decided against it, other than just including it in a general announcement along with the other family news when they had their tea that afternoon. Before that she went alone to tell Patience. She took the news quietly and then asked if Miss Charity was going to tell Mercy.

Mercy had put away her dolls from childhood and scarcely remembered Bess now, even as a doll. She was appropriately sympathetic with the news, since she knew Bess had been a friend to Patience, and expressed her sympathies to Patience when she came to clear away the tea service.

Charity did not tell her niece that the letter also included hints of Richard's increasing financial distress. The yield of the plantation had been declining in recent years. Reading between the lines of his letters, Charity suspected that if Richard was more involved in the operation on a consistent basis it would not be so. She suspected he was shutting himself away in his library more than ever, leaving the day-to-day operation of the house and fields almost entirely to Old James. His letter hinted that he was considering selling off the far fields that had lain fallow for most of the past decade, saying they were too far from the house and quarters to be effectively farmed. His slave population was getting older, and at his age he was disinclined to procure any more to replenish his stock. The productivity of the older ones was declining and the initiative of the younger ones did not seem to be the same, even though they had the same task-oriented arrangement with Richard that began with his father. They produced less for themselves during their free time and looked more to Richard to provide their basic sustenance, depleting his diminished funds even further.

Against her better judgment, Charity decided she must go to Richard. She had purposefully stayed away from the plantation since the night she escaped with Mercy. He stayed away from her house in Charles Town too, lodging in a public house on the rare occasions he came to town. They stayed in touch through their letters, but now it was time to see what she could do to help Richard. She decided a surprise visit was what was needed. If she gave too much notice, Richard and Old James and the rest of them would likely pull themselves together and put on a show that everything was all right - as if it had always been.

She decided to take Mercy and Patience with her. With Bess gone and Richard likely just picking at meals from a tray while he drank away his days in his library, Patience would be needed in the kitchen if they were to have adequate meals for their visit. In the years since Charity spirited her away, Mercy had never returned to the plantation. She frequently asked to visit, curious about the childhood home of her father, as well as her aunt and uncle. Charity decided it might help Richard to see his daughter, remind him of what had once been. It was also long past time for Mercy to have the chance to meet her "uncle."

After the trip was decided, one day ahead of their departure she sent a note to her brother that they were coming and they set off in the carriage before Richard had a chance to refuse them.

Patience rode inside the carriage with them instead of up front with Benjamin. Mercy was excited by the trip and could scarcely take herself away from the windows of the carriage, even when Patience teased her about it. When they turned off the river road and down the long lane to the plantation house, she turned to her aunt to say, "It seems like I already know it, Aunt Charity. I have been here before, haven't I?"

Charity laughed. "Just look closely at the house, my dear. My father – your grandfather – built it exactly the same as the town house in Charles Town only larger. That's why it looks familiar to you. It's like it is the same house, only it is turned sideways."

But it wasn't the same. Where the town house was neatly maintained, its verandas and brick walks swept, and the garden carefully tended, Charity could see the plantation house was decaying and the gardens and grounds were overgrown.

As the carriage pulled up at the front door, Old James came forward, limping heavily and his livery frayed at the cuffs and showing wear. On closer inspection, Charity noticed that although Old James stood proudly to greet them, the left side of his face seemed partially paralyzed, as well as his left arm. Old James, if he had been about the same age as her father, would be close to eighty. With a start, she realized that meant Richard was fifty years old now, no – he was fifty-one this year. Charity herself was forty-eight.

Richard, appearing in the doorway behind Old James, was sallow and gaunt. His eyes seemed shrunken in their sockets and his shirt did not look fresh. He was poorly shaven and his hair was dirty. He had aged another lifetime in the last twelve years.

"Charity, welcome, welcome," he said as he came down the stairs. "It's been a long time."

"Absolutely too long, brother," Charity extending her hands for her brother to help her down from the carriage, then bringing her cheek up for him to kiss. Mercy came out of the carriage behind her aunt, unassisted. She seemed to be the only thing young and fresh in this dead and decaying place. "Richard, it is high time you meet your niece, Mercy Wainwright, David's daughter."

Richard's face went ashen. Although he knew Mercy was coming along, he was somehow half expecting to see little Sukey before him, not this well dressed, young beauty. She had the same mischievous grin as her mother, and for a moment it was as if Dove was standing there instead.

"Uncle Richard," Mercy said brightly, extending her gloved hand. "I do hope I am not an inconvenience for you, but I have absolutely begged Aunt Charity to show me the family home and plantation. I am afraid I made it quite impossible for her to refuse me any longer."

When Old James moved to take her traveling case, Charity thanked him graciously but told him to rest. Patience was here to help and would be attending to the ladies during their visit. If no one had any objections, Patience could also prepare their meals, unless Richard had already replaced Bess in the kitchen.

"James and I have been managing by ourselves, sister," Richard said sheepishly, confirming Charity's earlier suspicions about dinner on a tray in the library. Then he continued, almost flirtatiously, "but we would certainly be pleased to enjoy some of Patience's tasty delights while you all are here, wouldn't we James?"

Patience blushed even darker, flustered a bit, and then covered her discomfort by picking up Charity and Mercy's baggage to carry upstairs.

Throughout that afternoon, while Mercy walked with her Uncle Richard in the garden, or what was left of it, Charity conducted an assessment of the house and kitchen with Patience. Nothing had been done to the house for years and wear showed everywhere. Curtains were in tatters and all of the upholstered furniture was worn through. The dining room and drawing room wallpapers, special-ordered for the house by their father, showed water stains around every window. A few strips were missing entirely, presumably they had peeled away from the damp walls and were not pasted back. In the dining room, pieces of china her mother had once displayed so proudly were missing, presumably broken and not replaced, and all the silver was black with tarnish.

The library, where Richard spent almost all of his days and nights, sleeping upright in his chair, was a little better. It had been cleaned more recently, although several weeks worth of dust had accumulated on surfaces that were not used regularly. There was a musty smell from the books and when she removed one fine leather-bound volume from the bookcase the leather binding was cracked and the front and back panels were warped, a sure sign it had not been in the book press for quite some time. The book press itself, off in one corner, lay broken and covered with rust. Likely all of the books in the library were ruined from the damp. After examining the press, she brushed her hands with a sigh. The library her father had accumulated and tended so proudly and carefully was ruined through Richard's neglect.

"This whole house need a good cleaning, Miss Charity," Patience commented, pushing back the sleeves of her shift to show she was ready to get started.

"Yes, but I'm afraid it's long past that, Patience. Things have been let go too long. Mostly everything is ruined, I am afraid."

Old James came limping into the library, his eyes apologetic. "I 'pologize, Miss

Charity. Master Richard don't let no one but Bess and me in the house for a long time now and after she die I just can't keep up with things."

"You mean Bess was keeping this entire house by herself – and doing the cooking too?"

Patience looked sharply at her mistress, annoyed, but kept her silence. Patience did everything by herself too, with only one housemaid, and Miss Charity's house was most certainly not in this kind of mess. But then, Miss Charity did help out with polishing silver, arranging flowers and keeping things set out nicely. If a piece of her china was broken, which was almost never, she would not just leave a big gap on the sideboard where it used to be. Also Patience had to admit that the town house was smaller, and she wasn't partly paralyzed like Old James seemed to be. Even now he held his twisted hand oddly against his jacket, as though he could not move it.

"Not much cooking anymore, Mistress. Just Master Wainwright here and he usually don't want nothing 'cept in the evening, and then he don't eat most of that. I been cookin' for him bes' I can since Bess…"

"Of course, James. I'm sure you have managed. This is such a large house for only one person to be keeping. Why, when my mother was living, we must have had half a dozen house maids in here at least."

"Yes'm, Miss Charity." Of course Old James remembered. He had been the butler, or the black southern equivalent of the English butler, in those days. He would never have been asked to prepare so much as a cup of tea back then. Poor Old James, Charity thought.

The condition of the house and plantation grieved Old James. He had been the first slave Old Master John Wainwright procured when he arrived here from England. As a newly arrived African, the unseasoned young James was badly beaten by his previous owner. James was auctioned as a slave who needed a firm hand, and was only good for field work, but Master John had seen something else in him. First thing James did was help Master John clear this land and herd his cattle. As more slaves were bought James helped direct their work when he could, making the work lighter for his Master. With his own hands he helped Master John build the first house from the wood milled from the trees they cut down, and at night he slept just inside the door of that house, keeping watch while the master slept. Then, as now, he would have laid down his life to protect the man who had rescued him.

It was during that time James came to love his master. His sole source of pride and accomplishment came through his master and the plantation. He felt deep satisfaction when the first new crop of rice proved to be profitable and the master said they were on their way. When the master brought home the young Mistress,

James had been proud and thought he might cry with happiness. When the children, Richard, Charity and David, were born right here in this house, he loved them as though they were his own, but from a proper distance. James could always be relied on to keep things proper.

When the town house was built in Charles Town and the new, grand mansion was built on the hill by the river on the plantation, his heart swelled with pride. His place at both homes was always just inside the front door and never far from his master's side. He was proud to open the front door to greet and welcome their visitors. He directed the smooth running of the house and he indirectly managed the plantation as an intercessor or buffer between the workers and the Master. He made sure things went right, and it usually only took a "look" from him to set things right when they were not. He was fiercely protective, and that became even stronger with young Master Richard, who was not as strong and wise as his father had been.

That protection had proved disastrous with Dove. Sometimes he thought that had been the downfall of everything. What would it have mattered if he had let Master Richard continue with Dove? Maybe he could have set up Dove and the child in a house somewhere nearby and they would have all been happy. Other men did that. It had broken Richard's heart when Dove died. Old James would always carry the knowledge that he had done that to Master Richard – and to Dove too.

By then he had his Deed of Emancipation, signed by Master John on his deathbed, giving James his freedom. But he had never exercised it. This was his family, his home, where he belonged. He had no intention of ever leaving them. He considered leaving after Dove died, but there was nowhere else he could go, even free, so he stayed. Watching the decay of this house and the decline of the plantation for the last twelve years had been his punishment and his penance. A punishment he hoped would soon come to an end. Death would be his release and he would welcome it when it came.

"Well, Patience is here to help and Mercy and I can help, too, while we are here," Charity told him. There is no need to do up things for us, either."

"Yes'm, Miss Charity," Old James shuffled, relieved.

"Is there anyone we can bring up from the quarters to help us? A girl or two I mean? I think we can get this place cleaned and put back to rights in a day or two if we have someone to help us."

Over the next week, while Richard retreated to his library, Charity undertook a housecleaning project. When word got down around down in the quarters that Miss Charity was cleaning house, most of the women came up to help. They had long worried over the house falling into ruin with the Old Massah keeping everyone out of it.

For a long time it seemed like the more they did the worse things became. In the drawing room, Charity opened the long-closed curtains, only to bring several of them down in a choking cloud of dust when the entire portiere pulled out of the rotted window facing. The dining room carpet was so moth-eaten that it crumbled into shreds as it was being rolled up to take outside. The family portraits from England that her parents so proudly displayed were darkened with soot and either cracked or separating from their frames. Just the slightest fluffing of a cushion raised a choking cloud of dust.

But floors were swept and scrubbed. The surviving rugs were carried outside and beaten and brushed. Bed linens, including the feather bed covers and pillow ticks were removed and washed in a boiling pot set up in the kitchen yard. Bed curtains and coverlets were taken outside and hung in the sunshine to air. Forgotten corners were swept free of cobwebs. The remaining wallpaper was gently brushed with powdered lime and then carefully sponged with warm water, windows were washed inside and out, and even the mahogany rail of the central staircase was polished with the same tea leaf paste Patience stirred up at Miss Charity's. By the end of the week the old house showed hints of its former glory, especially when the sun did not shine directly through the windows.

After taking stock in the kitchen, and realizing the rice was mildewed and the flour was so full of weevils that it could not be saved, Charity told Patience to throw everything out. All the bins were scrubbed and aired and Charity ordered new provisions. The wood pile was restacked by the kitchen house door and the wood box beside the kitchen fireplace was filled. Patience even took the porch broom and thoroughly swept the kitchen yard so that it was only packed dirt once again. The cleaning spread down to the quarters and Charity noticed that things were being set to rights there also. It was amazing how just a little inspiration from the house carried over down there, too.

Still, she was troubled about Richard. He remained in the library most of the day and while he made an attempt to sleep in his own bed during their visit, she would often hear him creeping back downstairs as soon as he thought everyone was asleep. If she tiptoed down the stairs in the middle of the night, she could see the light of his candle showing under the library door. This could not go on. If nothing else, she needed to see Monsieur Faure about hiring a manager to run the plantation when they returned to Charles Town. Perhaps a man and a wife could do the job. The wife could serve as a housekeeper to assure the kitchen and the house were run properly. It would help to have someone keeping an eye on her brother too.

After a week, the house was running more as a normal household should. Patience was making some headway with the neglected kitchen garden and several boys were brought up from the quarters to help tame the worst of the formal gardens. Charity presided over meals served in the dining room, the table set with what was left of her mother's plantation china, (the best was always kept in the Charles Town house) and Richard was reminded to prepare himself for dinner with enough time that he was in his chair at the head of the table when Patience began serving.

They came to a point where Charity realized they had done all they could do. A girl was brought up to the kitchen permanently to help Patience, but none of the plantation women was qualified to be his cook. If things had been running properly, someone would have been training with Bess all along, but it was the same all over the plantation. There just weren't enough people to keep anything running properly. The only thing left to do was see Monsieur Faure about hiring a manager for the plantation. With a proper manager and housekeeper in place, perhaps they could take care of securing a cook. With only that item remaining, Charity told Richard over dinner that evening that they would be leaving in two days time.

The next afternoon as Patience built up the kitchen fire to begin preparation of the evening meal, she was relaxed and looking forward to being back in her own kitchen in Charles Town. She hummed a little as she built up the fire and started preparations for the meal. Returning to the fire, she stirred at it a bit with the poker before she added the last piece of wood. The fire was going good and she was thinking about going home. Then she made the fatal mistake of reaching into the wood box without looking first.

A snake lay in wait there. By then snakes were rare in the walled city of Charles Town, but she knew better here on the plantation. As soon as she felt the sting she knew what she had done wrong. Before she could yank back the snake buried its fangs into the pad her hand, just below the thumb, injecting its venom deeply. The kitchen girl stood screaming while Patience pried the snaked from her hand, its jaw locked and unable to release itself, still pumping its venom. Wrapping her hotly throbbing hand in her apron and holding it against her chest, she watched as the frightened girl ran off to the house for Miss Charity before Patience could tell her to bind her apron strings tightly around her wrist. Too late, she lay herself down on the bed, struggling to wrap the apron strings around the wrist by herself.

By the time Charity arrived, the hand was so swollen it looked like it could burst and the swelling was swiftly traveling up the arm, already past the elbow. Charity screamed out the door for Benjamin, then catching sight of Mercy running down from the house she commanded her niece to find Benjamin and have him ride a horse for the doctor. Then she helped position Patience on the bed so that the bitten right hand was on the floor, below her heart. Charity quickly tied off the arm at the shoulder, above the swelling, hoping to stop the spread of the venom. But by the time she heard Benjamin galloping away on the horse, the swelling had spread past the tourniquet. She knew nothing could be done.

"Bring me a bowl of cool water and a sponge," she commanded Mercy as soon as she returned. Charity plunged the sponge into the water, squeezed it out and bathed Patience's face and forehead. Patience stirred. Her breathing was becoming labored and her throat was swelling shut. She was clearly in pain, but remained calm.

She opened her eyes and looked around wildly for a moment, then focused on her mistress. The right side of her neck and jaw was beginning to swell. "I never tol' no one Miss Charity," she said. "I never tol' no one 'bout little Sukey."

"Yes, Patience, I know. Now please, don't try to talk."

Then Charity turned to Mercy. "We need ice. Run quick up to the house and ask Old James if he has any."

"But would it not be here in the kitchen house? If there is any ice it would be here, Aunt Charity." Mercy was wildly looking about the kitchen and beginning to panic.

"Just go ask him like I said!" Charity cried out sharply. Too sharply, but she wanted Mercy out of the kitchen house. She wanted to spare Mercy from what was to come, but more than that, she wanted Mercy to not hear anything else Patience might say.

"Promise me, Miss Charity," Patience looked up at her with urgency. "Promise you bury old Payshen in her white dress. Promise."

"Yes, I promise Patience. But please, do try to rest now. The doctor will be here directly."

"Promise you bury me in my white dress so when Lord Jesus look up and see Old Payshen coming maybe he think she an angel already and he swing the gates wide open." It was a sweet and simple vision that brought the tears to Charity's eyes.

"Yes, yes I promise, Patience."

"Keep talking to me, Miss Charity, please keep talking."

Charity knew nothing else to say. The right eye was nearly swollen shut and Patience's breathing was rasping and shallow.

"Let not your heart be troubled…" Charity croaked out with a dry mouth as she held Patience's hand. She swallowed and continued, "Let not your heart be troubled. In my father's house are many mansions…"

She saw that Patience's lips were moving silently in unison with her own as she said the words. How many times had Patience stood in the room as Charity read the evening devotional? This was a favorite for Patience. If ever asked, she wanted to hear about the mansions.

"There are many mansions," Charity repeated. "If it were not so, I would have told you. I go and prepare a place for you. And if I go and prepare a place for you, I will come again and receive you unto myself."

Patience' lips no longer moved. Charity bit her lips together and when Richard and Mercy came into the room they could see she was gone. Charity laid her head on her old cook's breast and wept for a long moment. Mercy came and put her hands on Charity's sobbing shoulders, comforting her.

"She loved you Aunt Charity."

"She loved everyone, Mercy. She loved everyone."

* * * * *

In the drawing room that evening, Mercy was angry. Mercy could not accept Richard's weak explanation and the argument rapidly escalated and grew more heated until Mercy was angry and defiant, and bordering on disrespect of her uncle. Charity pleaded for her to stop.

"But why can't Patience be buried there, Uncle Richard? I can not understand that."

"Because it is the family cemetery, Mercy. It is for the family."

"And Patience is not family?"

"No, she is not."

"But Bess and Dove and little Sukey are buried there."

"No, they are buried outside the family cemetery, not inside it."

"Then why can you not bury Patience outside the family cemetery with them. I don't see what difference that makes. Why can't Patience be buried beside them? She told me that Bess was like a sister to her. She had no one else like Bess and she knew absolutely no one else down among the quarters. I do not understand why you think Patience has to be buried down with the other slaves instead of there with Bess and Dove. She did not know any of the other slaves here."

"But Patience was not family. We cannot bury her by the family," Richard said simply, remotely, as if he were reciting a rule in school.

"But neither was this Dove, and neither was her mother, and yet they are not buried down in the slave cemetery. Why are they buried by the family burial ground when they are not family either?"

"It was different with them. That is all I can say about it. And I will not be questioned by you any further on this."

"But how was it different, Uncle Richard? They were slaves too. You owned them the same as Aunt Charity owned Patience. How is that any different?"

"It is not the same."

"How is it not the same? How can you even say that, Uncle Richard?" Then, it occurred to her, she would never have said it except that she was so exasperated and felt like she was losing the argument, an argument that had to be won for Patience's sake. "Unless Dove was your daughter," she said defiantly and with an expression that bordered on ridicule. "Is that it? Was Dove your daughter by Bess? Is that why you think they are family and they are buried there instead of down with the other slaves?"

Richard drew his hand back to slap Mercy for her impertinence, but Charity cut in, both with her words and her physical body. She stepped between Mercy and Richard, facing away from her brother to sternly scold Mercy, "Dove was not your Uncle Richard's daughter, Mercy. Do not say that now. Don't say that ever."

Richard stepped back and sat down weakly in his chair. He leaned forward and put his elbows on his knees and his face in his hands. He sat in silence like that for a long moment, then straightened up and looked up at them both.

"It's time she knows the truth, Charity," he said.

"No, Richard!" Charity was not prepared for the truth to be revealed to Mercy. She was planning to tell her someday, but not now and not here, and certainly not in this way. This was completely out of control.

But he leaned back and through his tears and a grimace that twisted his face into an unsmiling grin, he began and would not be stopped. Eventually Charity took his hand as he wept and she placed her other hand on his shoulder, standing beside him as he told Mercy his story. She braced herself for what was to be revealed. The truth that would reveal her own lies and the truth that would mean she would lose Mercy forever.

"It's time she knew that I once loved Dove. To my eternal damnation, and hers, I loved her. The forbidden fruit was too tempting and beautiful and precious. I knew from the start it was against the laws of God and against the laws of nature, but still, I loved her. I was too weak to resist. I loved her, Mercy. Even as black as she was, I could not help but love her. For a time, she was all I could think of. I woke with her in the mornings and could not wait until she came to me again at night."

Mercy knew she should be embarrassed by this intimate revelation, but she could not move. It was as if she was paralyzed and her feet were nailed to the spot she stood. She could only stare at Uncle Richard. Her Uncle Richard who had loved his black slave girl, Dove. She could not even look away to her Aunt Charity who was silently crying as this long-hidden truth was revealed.

"And then, after our last morning together, Old James made me realize that I had to let her go, that to save us both I had to send her away. And because I was weak that is what I did. I did not know that day that she was carrying our child. If I had known I would have run away with her. I would have taken her away from here and ridden as far west as we could go. Or I could have sailed away with her to Jamaica or even to New Orleans where we could have started a new life. Such things are not unheard of there. But I did not. I was too weak and too lazy to accomplish that.

"And since I kept her here, I condemned her and our child to a life of slavery on this damned plantation. And in doing that I also condemned myself to a life of slavery just as vile as hers.

"Then, when our child, Sukey, was born I still could have done something. I knew Dove hated and despised me by then for what I had done. But I still could have set her free and sent them both away; or even set her up in a house in a town someplace where I could care for them properly, maybe somewhere up north. But again I did nothing. I did nothing. Every time I had the opportunity, I did absolutely nothing."

Sobbing, he stopped until he could go on.

"And that was too much for Dove. She ended up taking her own life. That is why she is buried outside the family burial ground. When Sukey died a few days later, (Charity almost visibly breathed a sigh of relief at that, the truth had become so muddled in Richard's mind that is what he believed now) we buried her with Dove. And then when Old Bess died I could not do anything other than bury her next to her daughter. They were my other family. I loved them. Though it shames me before God and before my family, and even though I have lost my very soul because of it, I loved them."

Other than Richard's continued sobs, they remained in silence. Then Mercy came forward to her uncle, fell to her knees, folded her hands on her knees and put her face down on her hands, "Oh, Uncle Richard. I am so, so sorry. I did not know.

Please forgive me."

Richard placed his hand on the back of Mercy's head, but could say nothing.

Mercy raised her tear-streaked face and looked up at him. "And Uncle Richard, love is never wrong. I am sure Dove knew that, even with everything that happened. I am sure she loved you and forgave you and that Sukey would have forgiven you too, as I do. I forgive you too, Uncle Richard."

Richard leaned forward, bringing his lips to the top of Mercy's head, kissing her cap.

"You are a sweet girl and still so young my child. If only I ever had a daughter like you. If only my wife had given me another child to have after our son died, a daughter like you..." his voice trailed off, remembering his wife and son.

Then he raised himself and sat weakly back in his chair, clearly exhausted. He looked around at the room and then at his sister, and then down at his niece as though he did not know her, as though he questioned who she was and why she was there. "Have Bess make us something to eat," he commanded as though nothing had happened. "Charity, ask Bess to make some of her spoon bread and buttermilk that I love so dearly."

Mercy raised her head and sat back on her heels with her face a study of worry and disbelief as her Uncle Richard settled himself into a shallow sleep. And at that moment, Charity realized that her brother had lost his mind.

Charity and Mercy returned to Charles Town the day after Patience was buried next to Bess. As soon as they came through the city gates, she told Benjamin to take them directly to the offices of Monsieur Faure. Still in their traveling clothes, Charity and Mercy waited only moments in his antechamber before they were shown through to his private office.

Charles Town
South Carolina Colony
1746 - 1748

Jean Faure was more than happy to adjust his schedule at a moment's notice for the Wainwright ladies. Had they asked, he would have cancelled all his appointments and given them the rest of his day. Miss Wainwright and her brother were his first real clients. They were the first to take him seriously instead of treating him as a clerk who could handle routine items but then wanted Jean's father to step in for serious matters.

Jean's father had served Charity's father for years. He brought Jean into the firm as soon as he finished reading law. Back then, barely twenty one years old, Jean proved himself to the Wainwright family with his adept handling of the Widow Timsley. That affair earned him the gratitude of the family and respect within his father's firm and eventually a full partnership. As a result, Jean would always be grateful to the Wainwright family and would defer to the Wainwright ladies as often as possible.

But this was still a surprise. An office visit by them was rare. Generally, Miss Charity would send a message a week in advance inviting Jean to her house for an afternoon. It was always a pleasant visit in her drawing room, followed by tea and cakes; a rare treat in the life of a bachelor who lived in rented rooms. The afternoon was even more enjoyable when Miss Mercy joined them. Her aunt wanted Mercy to gain an awareness of family matters by sitting in on those meetings. Mercy was already showing a keen mind in those affairs, sometimes asking thought-provoking questions or seeking clarification when she did not understand the reasoning behind a law or rule. She would be annoyed, amused or sometimes even delighted the times when Jean was forced to admit that, in fact, there was no logic or reason.

When his clerk told him the ladies had arrived unexpectedly, he assumed the meeting to be a pleasurable one to discuss Mercy's education. He had sent the inquiry letters as soon as Miss Charity asked him to, but not enough time had passed to receive any reply. Rather than wait, and to speed things along, he had inquired about the schools after the letters were sent. He had a shortened list of possibilities ready. Two of the six academies were in the colonies. The best was in England, a school in Cambridgeshire. That school may be of more interest to Miss Charity, especially when he delivered the other news he had for her.

As Charity bustled into his office, hastily removing her carriage cloak as she came through, and followed by the beautiful Miss Mercy, he was glad he had not kept them waiting. Miss Charity was always calm and collected, calculating even, in her dealings with her attorney. From her hastened deportment and her rush through the customary greetings, the matter she brought with her appeared urgent. Even Miss Mercy, who smiled warmly at him from under the hood of her cloak, seemed preoccupied.

Mercy was such a rare beauty. Jean had been twenty-four the first time Charity brought her niece to his office to see about formalizing documents for her ward. The child had been beautiful even then, with her big blue eyes, dark curling hair, and thick eye lashes. All during that first meeting she was calm and seemed to be intent on their conversation, instead of fussing or sleeping as most toddlers would. Over the years, as he handled Charity's legal affairs, he had watched Mercy grow. She was educated and poised beyond her years, and now, almost fourteen and beginning to blossom into a young woman, it was nearly impossible for Jean to not stare at her beauty. With a pang of sadness, he realized it would not be many more years before Charity would be asking him to prepare the property contracts and trust arrangements for her marriage. He pledged silently that he would faithfully and aggressively represent her interests.

After he ordered tea for them and while they settled into the comfortable chairs around the table he used for his meetings, instead of talking to his clients across the clutter of his desk, Jean sought to put the ladies at ease by giving them a brief report on the school letters he had sent. "I have not yet received replies to my letters of inquiry, but I am happy to tell you that I have narrowed the list down to six academies. Actually there are some new academies that have been started here in the colonies. West Nottingham Academy in Maryland already has a favorable reputation and Linden Hall in Pennsylvania is very well received, even though it is a boarding school exclusively for girls. I presume that is due to their aggressive emphasis on complete education – curriculum, character, culture, and conditioning."

"I like the sound of that. I have complete confidence you will finalize your selections, posthaste, to review with us, Monsieur Faure. I want Mercy to begin with the commencement of the next term in the fall."

"Yes of course, Miss Wainwright," Jean replied amicably.

It amused him that Charity was one of the few people in Charles Town who pronounced his surname correctly. In nearly perfect French, she would say FAH-ray, with only the slightest emphasis on the first syllable. Most people here, especially those of English backgrounds called him Mister fa-REE, some even shortened it to the single syllable name "Free." His friends and colleagues sometimes teased him by calling him "Frenchman" or even "Frenchie", and over the years the combinations had evolved into the name "Freedom," and even "Johnny Freeman" when they were in their cups. Jean did not mind, he had been born here and felt no connection whatsoever to France, or even to England for that matter. But it would have pleased his father to hear Miss Wainwright pronounce their family name correctly.

His grandparents had been murdered in France during the purge of the Huguenots and his orphaned father had survived only by his wits on the streets of London until King William sent ships of French refugees to Virginia in 1690. Soon after arrival there, Jean's father made his way down the coast to Charles Town and set himself up as a lawyer. He was never formally educated in law, but he was a voracious reader and the law books he prominently displayed in the window as soon as he hung his shingle above the door were enough to launch this law firm.

Now there was a lull in the conversation. Jean had learned the best thing to do was to give the clients a moment to collect themselves. Then if that did not work he would gently ask, "Now what can I assist you with today?" After a moment, he asked that of Miss Wainwright.

"My brother is losing his mind," Charity gasped out, then brought up her handkerchief to hide her tears. Mercy reached across and gently took her hand. "Aunt Charity," she said in a gentle and comforting tone. Richard had to bite his upper lip to keep the grin from his face. It was a declaration he heard often from women of the Wainwright's class; women who felt no other recourse than to come to him when the man of their concern disagreed with them or behaved badly.

"Perhaps you can share with me why you think that," he suggested gently with his hands folded on the table. He had laid down the pen he was holding, showing that she had his full attention and also that he would write nothing of what she revealed.

"Well, it's everything," Charity said, dabbing her eyes before she continued with her litany of concerns: Richard's drinking, complete neglect of the plantation, the rice fields choked with weeds, the house in ruins. "My mother's china and silver...the wallpaper and rugs...and even my father's library are all ruined by his neglect. He won't even let anyone into the house to clean it, only Old James and Bess...did you know Bess had died Monsieur Faure?"

Jean had not heard. "I am sorry to hear that, Miss Wainwright. I know how your brother depended on her, as well as James."

"And I think Old James must have had a stroke... he is paralyzed on one side with his face sagging down and carrying a stick to get himself around...he can't do anything really, but James is the only one Richard will let in the house. I had to clean the house myself when I was there, with Patience and Mercy and some of the women from the quarters helping of course, and then..." She paused a moment to collect herself and take a deep ragged breath.

"Then my Patience was bitten by a snake the last afternoon we were there and Richard refused to let us bury her..." Charity gasped and sobbed a moment before she could continue. Jean wisely decided to let his client talk herself out before he tried to make any sense of what she was telling him.

"Poor Patience," Charity continued. "There was nothing that could be done to save her and then there was a big argument in the library and Richard refused to let us bury Patience beside Bess and Dove by the family cemetery where she would want to be – not in the slave burial grounds down by the river. There was a terrible argument and I thought he was going to strike Mercy and I had to step in between them." Charity sobbed, unable to continue. Mercy turned to face her aunt as she held her hand, rubbed her arm and patted her shoulder. Charity calmed herself enough to continue.

"And then, he finally agreed, but then he turned right around and told me to have Bess make him something to eat. Bess! She had been dead and buried for at least a month by then. You see, Jean, he has lost his mind and the plantation is completely falling apart.

"At first I thought we just needed to hire a manager – a husband and wife to take over things until Richard can pull himself together, but now I don't think he can even stay by himself there. I don't know what to do. What are we going to do?"

Jean was silent and thoughtful for a moment. "I am going to have to betray your brother's trust in what I am going to tell you." He paused. Charity nodded her understanding.

"Mister Wainwright asked me to come to him earlier this spring. It was a month or two ago. Bess was still alive when I visited. He wanted to review his will. When I was there I saw the house was not being kept up quite as well as it should be. And although he took more of the fields out of cultivation again this year, the remaining ones were being planted when I was there. "

"That hardly seems like anything confidential," Charity observed. But Jean lifted his hand, indicating he was not finished.

"I am afraid, that during that visit, your brother revealed to me that he is gravely ill. That was the reason he wanted to review his will. He has consulted multiple doctors, both there at the plantation and here in Charles Town,"

"But, I had no idea he had been here in town," Charity exclaimed.

"He did not want you to know. The doctors all agreed that he has a tumor in his liver. About six weeks before my visit they had prescribed tincture of opium, or laudanum, to help him manage the pain." Charity, and even Mercy, gasped at that news. "What prompted him wanting to review his will and set things in order was that the doctor found additional tumors of the lymphatic system. The cancer is spreading and your brother knew that it was only a matter of time."

"Oh, poor Richard," Charity said softly. "Why did he not tell me? I should be there with him – or bring him here to care for him."

"During that visit, his express wish to me was that he wanted to live out his days at home. The doctor showed James how to prepare and give the doses of the drug, and even with James' impairment, they still thought he was able to do that and care for Mister Wainwright, with the help of Bess, of course. To provide the quiet Mr. Wainwright needs for his rest, most of the house was to be closed up. I understand the drug eliminates his appetite so Bess had a challenge of preparing anything that he would actually want to eat, and then that he could keep down. I noticed during the visit he ate very little, even when he was making an effort for my sake."

"Oh, poor Richard. I was doing everything wrong," Charity observed.

"Well, he should have told you, but I am guessing it was his pride that kept him from doing so. Without that, how would you have known to do anything other than what you did?"

They were quiet while Charity and Mercy processed the news Jean had shared.

"What are we to do?" Charity asked.

"I think the best thing all of us can do is follow his wishes and let him live out the time he has quietly in his own home. James knows to send word to me immediately if he needs to. If you like, I can dream up a pretext of something about his wills and make another visit to check on things. I can see if he thinks any changes are needed."

"Yes, yes. Whatever you think. I am so, so sorry. I feel like such a meddling old woman."

"No, you were only acting out of love and concern for your brother. That is nothing to apologize for. If he had told you what was going on I am sure you would have understood." There was a pause and then Jean continued, "There is another matter I need to discuss with you Miss Wainwright."

"Yes, of course."

Jean paused another moment and Mercy wisely realized he needed to speak to Charity privately. "Please, excuse me," she said quickly, "I will wait in the anteroom."

"I have no secrets from my niece on my legal matters, Monsieur Faure. Mercy may stay."

"No, it is fine Aunt Charity," Mercy said.

After Mercy left the room, Jean continued. "I apologize, but I could not continue with Mercy here. I am not sure you would want her to know this." Charity felt the blood drain from her face. It was something about Richard's will, something Mercy should not hear. "While I was visiting your brother, he completely rewrote his last will and testament. I can attest that he was of sound mind then, even if he may not be at this time. I have long been an advisor on his financial matters and I advised him against his most recent estate decisions, but I am sure you understand that in the end, I can only represent what a client wants, even if it goes against my advice."

"Yes, of course."

"At a very minimum, I need to inform you that your brother's estate is insolvent. His funds are depleted and his creditors are pressing for payment. For that reason, I must advise you to maintain the complete separation of your funds and property from his and to not acknowledge any of his creditors' demands."

"Yes, of course," Charity repeated. She was embarrassed by this revelation.

"His creditors know to only send their demands to this office, and to not even bother your brother any longer. However, if any of them should try to contact you, you must forward their requests to me to handle. Do not in any way acknowledge them. If they should call on you in person, refuse to see them and ask Patience - oh, I am so sorry and do apologize - ask your maid or whoever answers your door, to direct them to this office."

"Yes, I will. But do you think they would actually do that?"

"I have seen as much in these cases."

He paused, allowing Charity to absorb what he had said. The plantation was lost. She needed to be careful to preserve her own home and funds. It was more than she should have to deal with on top of everything else he had revealed.

"There is more, I am afraid," Jean continued.

"Oh dear," Charity said. "I was afraid of that."

"Your brother asked me to prepare his will so that you and your brother David receive minimal bequests. That, of itself, will acknowledge your relationship to him, but also remove the possibility of his creditors pursuing collection from you through those funds. At most you would have to surrender the amount of the bequest to them."

"I do appreciate your guidance to him."

"The next thing is that he wanted the plantation, the house, all of the contents of such to be sold and used to satisfy the creditors."

"Yes, of course."

"But prior to that, your brother's wish is that at the time of his death, all his slaves are to be given their freedom."

Charity blanched. She knew Richard did not approve of slavery, but that he understood and accepted that it was a necessity for any plantation to operate. He had been a fair and honorable master. This was understandable of him, but to grant more than one hundred slaves their freedom wiped out most of the remaining value of her brother's estate. She swallowed. So much to absorb in so short a time. "It is Richard's wish. I think we must respect it," she finally said.

"Beyond that, he directed first that each slave over the age of twelve years be given an amount of cash from the sale of the property. With the present state of his affairs, I doubt the sales proceeds will cover that bequest, provided a buyer will even be forthcoming."

"What are we to do then? How can we respect Richard's wishes?"

"We can not. And you must not. The sale proceeds will be divided ratably to the servants after the creditor claims are satisfied. I will eventually have to declare the estate bankrupt. I think Richard's people will understand and will be grateful for their newfound freedom, even without the cash he intended to bequeath to them."

Charity was silent for a long while, and then began gathering her things to take her leave. It had been a most distressing meeting. She could see it had been distressing for Monsieur Favre as well. She graciously concluded, "I suppose it is the best that can be done. I am proud of him for his persistence in granting their freedom."

Jean smiled at her. "I appreciate your understanding and your support. I am determined that we must protect your interests, and those of Miss Mercy as well.

"There is yet another matter I need to discuss with you. Some potential good news after all. I was going to wait and tell you when we discussed schools for Miss Mercy."

"Yes?"

"I have received a preliminary notification from your brother David's solicitors in

England, inquiring of the status of you and your brother. It appears your brother passed away in Cambridgeshire earlier this year and you are both named in his will."

"Oh dear," Charity said thoughtfully. "I cannot pretend to feign emotion over this. We have not seen or heard from David in twenty years or more. He was most disagreeable with Richard over our father's will." Charity could have bitten her tongue. She had just revealed she had no contact with David since long before Mercy arrived in Charles Town.

Jean looked at Charity, waiting. "There was no mention of Mercy in the solicitor's letter."

"No," Charity barely breathed. "I guess there wouldn't be."

"Did he know of her?"

"No."

"There is one more matter, Miss Wainwright and it is the primary reason I needed to speak to you without Miss Mercy. Your brother, Richard, gave over to me for safekeeping his inventory of the slaves he owns so I can prepare their deeds of emancipation. He was meticulous with his records, although of course, Bess is still shown as living and owned by him in that record." Charity could only nod. "That record also shows that her granddaughter, Sukey, is still living."

"Yes, so she is," Charity said in non-committal agreement.

Jean looked at Charity, waiting.

Charity recalled that if there had been only one thing their father had stressed to his children, it was that complete honesty was required at all times with their lawyers. A lawyer could not represent you if you lied to him. Charity took a deep breath and held it a moment, then let it out as if it deflated her. She could no longer keep this from Monsieur Faure. He knew too much.

"Sukey and Mercy are one in the same," Charity confessed. "Sukey was Richard's daughter - his daughter with his slave, Dove. She was his daughter and she was also his slave. I knew Dove and after she died and I saw how white Sukey was I could not just leave her there to that life. So I concocted a scheme with my brother and Bess. Sukey was my niece. That was no lie. The lie was that she was David's daughter instead of Richard's. I created another mother for her and brought her home and raised her as my own. My life since then has been one of lies and deceptions. Of that I am guilty."

"I think you are only guilty of loving your niece, Miss Wainwright," Jean said gently. "Of that, and providing her a loving home."

"Others would not be so kind."

"There is no need for them to know. When the time comes I can quietly process her deed of emancipation and record the name change so she can legally be your heir. She will not have to know about it unless you decide to tell her. And I have one additional item, a request, actually."

"Yes?"

"With your permission, I would like to be Miss Mercy's sponsor for this year's governor's ball. I hear Governor Glen himself will actually be in attendance."

For as long as anyone could remember, the governor's ball was held every year in June. It was late enough in the season that the daylight extended long into the evening. It was early enough that the summer heat had not really set in yet. It was late enough in the spring that flowers were in full bloom. Yet it was not so late that people had vacated the city for the cooler air of the plantations or even the northern colonies.

During the five years Governor Glen had been absent after his appointment by the Crown in 1738, the finest of Charles Town still attended. He had attended in 1744, but had already vacated for the summer when the ball was held the next year. Now, to appease the people of Charles Town, he was committed to attending this year. Young ladies of age and the correct social standing would be accompanied by their fathers, announced, and given their first presentation to society. When a girl's father was no longer living, an uncle or other suitable sponsor could present her. As the family solicitor and longtime friend, and as a respectable citizen, Monsieur Faure was a perfect sponsor for Mercy.

"But she is not yet fourteen," Charity responded in surprise. Mercy would not be fourteen until November, five months away. "But yes, I would be most grateful and indebted to you."

"May I ask Mercy, then?"

"Yes, certainly."

Mercy was brought back into the room. She was pleasantly surprised by the offer, just as Charity had been, and accepted Jean's invitation immediately. Then she teased, "All this time to discuss only that? My Aunt Charity must have put you through quite an interview, Monsieur Faure."

"Yes, she did. As she should, Miss Mercy, and please call me John, Or Uncle John if you prefer."

"Yes, Uncle John," Mercy said with an amused and almost-teasing look, but still pronouncing his name with the softened French "zh" sound. "I suppose I had better practice my dancing so I won't embarrass you, especially if the governor himself asks me to dance." Then she thought a moment and continued with an amused tone, "Although I hear he is a terrible bore, intent only on discussing politics. Perhaps I should also brush up on that too, so I do not embarrass either of you, or end up being sent out of South Carolina all together."

* * * * *

With Jean's invitation there was much to do and Charity sprang into furious action. On the way home they stopped at the dressmaker. The woman and her staff were fully booked with orders for the ball, but Charity agreed to take fabric that was already in stock and offered to pay double the fee to assure the dress was completed on time. Charity would attend the ball as chaperone to her niece, of course, but she could wear one of her existing gowns. She would only be a matron in the background, for the evening anyway.

Charity found out that two other young ladies who had been friends with Mercy since childhood would also be presented that evening and that a dance tutor and musicians were hired for the girls. The tutor had finished giving them dancing lessons the previous year when the girls all reached twelve years of age, but a refresher would ensure the girls were ready and confident the night of the ball.

Although it was unlikely to be performed at the Governor's Ball, the tutor taught them the new and hugely popular Virginia Reel. Rumor was that Governor Glen did not care for these modern dances, especially those that took inspiration from lowly Scottish dances as did the Reel. In reality, their tutor knew the girls would only need to know the minuet for the ball. It was the Governor's favorite, and likely would only be danced at a slow pace.

The girls were drilled on the basics of the minuet: keep a perfectly straight back with eyes facing forward, arms extended gracefully with the elbows at waist level and relaxed, fan primarily in the left hand, but always in the hand away from your partner.

The minuet began with a deep curtsy to the musicians, then a curtsy to your partner, after that it was simply a repeat of three almost bouncing steps on the ball of the foot followed by a slight dip on the fourth count while mirroring the lead and elaborate poses of the male partner. The tutor was adamant they should never, ever take steps so vigorous that their upper bodies showed more than a hint of movement. After three afternoons the girls could do the minuet blindfolded, and hoped the ball would include at least one subdued trot of the jig, if not a full session of the Virginia Reel.

To ensure she would be rested and refreshed that evening, Charity insisted that Mercy stay in bed the entire morning on the day of the ball. Then, since she would eat only lightly after her stays were laced, she had a large breakfast, followed by a bath. The day before, Mercy's long hair had been washed, and although her hair did not need curling, it had been tied up in curling rags since then to tame her curls. A hairdresser had been hired to come to the house later that afternoon to arrange Mercy's hair. For the hairdresser, Mercy would be dressed in the entire ensemble except for the gown itself. She would wear a covering wrap while the hairdresser and her assistant prepared Mercy's hair.

Charity still wore her mob caps and could not get used to women leaving their hair uncovered, even for a formal occasion such as the ball. At most these days, it seemed women wore only a small circle of lace on top their head that barely covered their hair. Charity was not sure she approved, but that was the fashion and Mercy's thick and lustrous hair would be put up for the ball. The dressmaker also stitched a hooded cloak of almost weightless silk for Charity to wear for the drive to the governor's house, protecting her hair and clothing from any dust that may arise from the road. The entire day had been scheduled to the quarter hour to assure Mercy and Charity would be ready when Jean arrived that evening.

Jean Faure closed his office early to go home to make his own preparations. Closing early did not matter anyway; it was as if the entire town was shut down that afternoon in anticipation of the ball. As he walked to his house, only the bars were open that afternoon. After he passed Harris's Tavern on Bay Street, four men came tumbling out the door and staggered along behind him. One of them shouted, "Johnny Freeman, you old bastard!"

Jean was not one to acknowledge such conduct by drunken men in public, especially in the afternoon, but since his name was used he stopped on the empty street and turned to face them.

"Finished for the day already, Johnny boy?" the ringleader, a florid man named Simon Bricks, shouted at him.

"Yes. If you gentlemen will forgive me," Jean said firmly, with a slight bow, then turned away and continued.

"I heard that you are hobnobbing with the gov'nor tonight Johnny boy!" Simon called out after him again, more aggressively this time.

Author's note: the term 'hobnobbing', which originated around 1605, originally carried the implication of drinking together in a raucous manner. Over the years the term changed to mean casual social interaction. In 1746, either meaning would have carried an implied accusation of Jean's inappropriate behavior with the governor.

Jean turned, "It is true that I will most likely see the governor at the ball this evening, if that is what you ask."

Jean calmly stood his ground as Simon came forward; swinging his walking stick and apparently intent on something he had to say. "And I hear you mock the governor, Sir, by taking your colored wench with you," Simon said with a muffled belch. The other three sneered, showing missing and blackened teeth.

Jean was shocked at the insult. "I will escort a young lady whose mother was French, so she is - as you say - only if you are now including the French in your ignorant definition of 'colored,' Mr. Bricks." He paused a moment to let that sink into Simon's rum-sodden brain. "But then that definition would also include me, I might say. This is none of your concern. She is from a good family. One of Charles Town's finest, in fact," Jean added, turning to go.

"The finest of Charles Town, indeed," Simon mocked. "To look at her, anyone can see that her mother must have been a ni…"

He never got the word out. Jean's crunching fist to his mouth saw to that. Simon went down like a load of bricks. Jean cupped the stinging knuckles of his right hand in the palm of his left, thinking he might have broken something. There had been an audible "pop" when his fist connected with Simon's jaw. He was unsure if it was the bone breaking in his hand or the teeth that were now missing from Simon's bloodied and gaping mouth.

"Anyone else?" he asked the other three men standing there, rubbing his hand.

They stood there stupidly for a moment. They were surprised Jean had not demanded satisfaction by lightly slapping Simon with his glove, or throwing his glove down before him, in challenge to a duel, the expected response to defend a young lady. They had followed along for that sport. They expected Simon would challenge the upstart young Frenchman, it would be Simon taking the risk, but the punch and their companion now lying unconscious at their feet was not what they expected. They knew Jean was an expert. Reputation was that Jean had been challenged only twice in his entire lifetime: the first challenge was only to first blood by small sword but the second, with pistols, was to the death.

Jean gallantly gave both challengers the chance to withdraw when he met them on the dueling field, but then dispatched them both, the first with a harmless slice to his opponent's wrist that drew the required blood, the second with a single shot through the heart. None of Mr. Bricks' companions cared to be the third on the list, so they scattered in the opposite direction, leaving Simon lying where he had fallen.

Where only moments before Jean had been whistling a tune in his anticipation of the coming evening, he now walked the rest of the way home in a dark mood.

The drunken Simon's challenge of Mercy's parentage was likely only wild conjecture. Although most people would discount the rant of a drunken lout, it was too sensational a story about one of Charles Town's leading families to be ignored. If the rumor started it would spread like wildfire. Jean knew Simon would be spreading his story again as soon as he came around, especially after Jean had embarrassed him in front of his companions.

He wished he had remained calm, that he had even sneered at the accusation as invalid. It was unlike him to lash out like that, but he just could not let that word, "negro" – or even the more coarse version of it, be spoken about Mercy on the streets of Charles Town, however deserted those streets were. It was his only way to silence the drunk at that moment.

Now, if he was asked about it, the only thing he could do was to discredit Simon as a drunkard and his accusation as ungrounded, wild speculation. He would have to carry on with the plans for the evening. To cancel their plans or to do anything else would only give credence to the rumors that were likely spreading already. After her presentation this evening, it was less likely Charles Town society would do anything but embrace Mercy as one of their own. At a minimum, he would need to inform Charity privately of what had happened so she would be ready to respond. It would be next to impossible, but he would need to tell her before they arrived at the ball.

Jean arrived promptly at six o'clock. Charity was ready and watching for him in the library, seated in one of the window seats that overlooked the street. She had intentionally delayed Mercy's preparation so she could have a few moments privately with Monsieur Faure before Mercy came down. To do so, she kept the hairdresser waiting after her arrival, then lingering in the library while she reviewed yet again the plans for her niece's hair, and all the while seeing that the woman was increasingly impatient to begin. Finally she released her, estimating she had a good ten minutes to share the devastating news she had received that afternoon.

Jean was shown to the library and the door was closed. With little formality, Charity blurted out the news that her new cook, Sepia, told her that afternoon. Sepia, the half-French, freed slave Charity had just hired, and whose cooking and housekeeping were already surpassing the late Patience, timidly explained to Charity that it was being discussed across the back fences and in the kitchens of Charles Town. It was exactly the same news Jean had to share with Charity. They were both surprised, and even more alarmed, that the other had already heard. It meant the rumor had spread more than they realized.

"What are we to do?" Charity cried out in anguish.

"We will ignore this and go ahead as if nothing has happened," Jean insisted. "If anything is said tonight, we will ignore it. If we are pressed, we will deny it categorically. Have you thought what you will say if you are asked?"

"Oh it would only be my closest friends who would even say anything to me about it so I would say I have already heard and how preposterous it is. If they should persist, I will say something like – 'after all these years we have been friends, do you really think I would keep such a thing from you?' I will insist truthfully that Mercy is my niece, my brother's daughter. Beyond that, I will simply remain silent and give them my worst glare if I have to."

Jean smiled at her in approval. "I was thinking of something similar myself. Deny and discredit will be our strategy. Denounce it as a rumor started by a drunken and jealous fool."

"I have said nothing to Mercy. Do you think we should?"

"Absolutely not. It is possible nothing will be said and telling her would only ruin the evening for her. I also think it is better if she is genuinely surprised and shocked if anything is said. She is the innocent and should remain and appear as such. If she looks at all like she knows and is in collusion with us on this, it will destroy her credibility as well as her social chances."

"Hopefully, I am making too much of this," Charity said wearily. "I hope it will just blow over. If only this wasn't the night of the Governor's Ball, that might be easier. People are always ripe for rumors, however untrue, when they are dressed up and pressed together in an overheated space as they will be tonight."

Just then they heard Mercy's footsteps overhead. They quickly went out into the hall, arriving at the foot of the stairs just as the hem of Mercy's gown appeared on the upper landing. She descended the staircase slowly and regally, as Charity had taught, but with a look of eager anticipation and a shy smile toward Jean. As she reached the final step, she stopped and extended her left hand as she had been taught. Jean stepped forward and took her hand at the fingertips to bow over it, lightly kissing the back of her hand.

Mercy was absolutely breathtaking. Even Charity, who had already seen the gown many times, held her breath for a moment. The gown was pale ivory silk, the rustling petticoats underneath were of stiffer silk in the palest pink, the sleeves of the gown came just below Mercy's elbows with a generous blossoming of lace showing from sleeves, the lace only slightly lighter than Mercy's pale wrists and hands. Her rich and luxuriant hair was braided and coiled high on her head with a crown of small white roses worked into the front. A few curling tendrils purposefully escaped, giving an air of innocence, and Mercy's lightly powdered face, neck and décolletage were as flawless as alabaster. Her blue eyes blazed from under her thick dark lashes and her full lips were moist and red in anticipation of the evening to come.

"Do I look all right?" Mercy asked, suddenly worried at the complete silence.

Jean took a deep breath, "Stunning…breathtaking…"

"You are absolutely beautiful," Charity said, suddenly choked with emotion. Could this be her niece? Was this really the little girl who only days ago played in the front garden with her friends, who blackened the face of her doll, whom she had rescued from a life of slavery on her brother's plantation? Was this stunning beauty in front of her really Mercy?

Mercy gave a silent, but delighted giggle at their reaction and then quickly came down the remaining step. "I feel all grown up. But I feel like I am only pretending to be a lady like when I used to get dressed up in Aunt Charity's things when I was a little girl."

"You are grown up," Charity insisted.

"You are not a little girl any longer, Miss Mercy, you are a beautiful young lady now," Jean agreed.

"Shall we go?" Mercy asked.

The governor's house was large by Charles Town standards and was similar in both size and layout to Uncle Richard's house on the plantation. As soon as Mercy arrived, she was ushered upstairs to join the other young ladies who would be presented. Charity went along with her, to help with any last minute preparations that were unnecessary in Mercy's case, but the other girls' mothers and maids fluttered around like butterflies until the butler knocked on the door and everyone except the girls went downstairs to the main hall.

The girls' fathers and Uncle Jean stood in line to join the girls at the top of the stairs. As the first girl began her descent down the staircase, the butler announced her name, her father's and mother's names and that they were from Charles Town. The second girl was from a plantation up the Ashley River and the butler said the name of that plantation instead. At the foot of the stairs each young lady was escorted to a reception line, and introduced to each person, the final introduction being the governor himself. As the introductions were completed, each girl, now a young lady, and her father went to join her mother in a second line, then all eyes turned up the stairs again to watch as the next girl was announced and presented.

Mercy was third in line. At the top of the stairs, Uncle Jean offered his right arm, so that Mercy took it with her left hand. As she descended the staircase the butler announced, "Miss Mercy Wainwright, niece of Miss Charity Wainwright of Charles Town and of Mr. Richard Wainwright of Wainwright Plantation. Miss Wainwright is escorted by Monsieur Jean Faure, Esquire."

As Mercy descended the stairs, Charity was alert and ready for any change in the tone of the muffled comments by the assemblage, but the people either had not heard the rumors or were too well-bred to comment in this setting. Or maybe they were nervous about what they would say to the governor when they went through the line themselves after all the young ladies were presented and had danced with the governor. Twelve young ladies came down the staircase and were introduced and, as expected, the musicians began a minuet. Custom was that the governor would dance with each young lady in the order presented, but apparently he was unaware of this custom or decided to ignore it when he came directly to Mercy and extended his hand in invitation. Mercy, although surprised at this faux pas, recovered quickly enough to curtsy to the governor, take his extended hand and allow him to lead her to the middle of the hall.

As her tutor predicted, the minuet was danced at a slow pace. Even so, the governor was perspiring profusely. The hall was already stifling with the crowd of guests and abundance of candles. Mercy privately wondered when he would accept the South Carolina climate and begin leaving off his high collars and the enormous, powdered wig.

"I suspect you young ladies would prefer something more modern like the Virginia Reel for dancing, would you not?" he asked Mercy as they took three lightly bouncing steps past each other, then dipped. Mercy brought down her chin as she smiled up at him over her fan while she dipped, afraid she would burst out laughing as she visualized the governor leading the reel. "I am afraid I am bound by tradition," he explained as they passed again.

It seemed the minuet was going on forever. Rather than have him think her mute, Mercy asked him a question off the topic of dance. "Are you finding South Carolina to your liking, Sir?"

"Oh, I am fraught with nothing but problems from morning until night with the responsibilities of governorship, Miss Wainwright."

"I should think the good people of Charles Town would require little governance," Mercy said with amusement.

"But its citizens are not all as delightful as you, my dear."

Mercy cast her eyes down a moment, as the compliment demanded, but then looked up with a smile indicating her acceptance. "I should like to hear of your work in more detail, my Lord," she replied as they came to face each other while dancing four more counts.

The governor laughed, "No, I am not a Lord, Miss Wainwright, only a politician I am afraid, so "Sir" will be quite enough, thank you."

Finally the dance ended and the governor went to the girl at the first of the line. He dutifully danced with all of them, assuring their passage into Charles Town society. Those watching noticed he did not seem as delighted with the rest of the young ladies as he had with Miss Mercy Wainwright. After he finished the dances, his receiving line was reformed and the general dancing could begin. Uncle Jean escorted Mercy to the floor for the next dance. After that they joined Aunt Charity at the edge of the hall until a young gentleman asked Mercy to dance. Then Jean paired off with a protesting Charity who agreed, but only for one dance.

Later in the evening the governor sought Mercy out for another dance. The evening was growing more relaxed with people drifting out onto the galleries for the breeze from the bay and venturing into the gardens, so the hall was less crowded. "I did not expect to find such a rare beauty in the colonies," he said.

"I am sure you have many surprises here. Are we really so different from England?"

"The climate is ungodly, but I am adapting and determined to make a success of it. The crown requires it, you know."

"You mean you have actually met King George?" Mercy asked with genuine interest.

"Ahh, a Royalist? Yes, I was introduced to the King when I received my commission here. Stuffy old gentleman, I'm afraid. And rather dense, I might add. I still wonder why on earth he bought back this colony. It would do him good to get out of the palace once in a while, I am sure."

Mercy glanced around them quickly to see if anyone was hearing such treason. "I am only teasing you my dear," Governor Glen laughed. "Only to see your reaction. But yes, I did meet the king once, and he has placed many demands on me to assure a successful governorship this time."

They danced several dances together while he willingly explained the situation of South Carolina as a royal colony. After years of dissatisfaction among the population and petitions to the Crown, the Lords Proprietor sold the colony back to the crown in 1729. The King had high expectations for his new investment and was fraught with economic distress from the transition. Mercy asked enough questions and showed enough interest in the political situation that Governor Glen found himself talking openly and freely with her.

"And there is, of course, the problem of the constantly growing number of free Negroes," he added.

"How exactly is that a problem?" Mercy asked him. "They have worked for their freedom, bought it themselves and make their living offering their skills in the market. I should think that is what you would want in a growing colony, increasing the revenues and thereby increasing taxes paid to the colony and to the Crown."

"But their population keeps increasing, more and more of them offering the same skills. It can only lead to poverty and them wanting even more funds from the Crown for their survival," he replied, almost whining.

"But the same happens with everyone else coming here, wanting to work. They either make a living or they move somewhere else where their skills are required. Or they take some land further west and clear it for farming. I can't see how that is different just because someone's skin is brown."

"But free colored people can not go into Georgia, if that is what you are talking about. They can be seized and taken as the property of the trustees, to be sold or exported as the common council might direct," he said, quoting from memory the January 9, 1734, prohibition on slavery passed by the governors of Georgia.

"Then that is not fair. If they have earned their freedom, why should they not have the full advantage of it?"

"They are different, savages at heart I am told."

"Then you are told wrongly, Sir," Mercy bristled. "The freed colored people I know of are all eager to do good work, even the seamstress who sewed this dress for me for instance. They provide for themselves and their families, and are not at all, as you say, savages."

"Still, she takes work away from a white seamstress," he argued. "It would be better for them, and for us, if they would return to their own land when they are freed."

"How can you say that? They are no longer African. Many are mixed, the progeny of slaves and their English masters. Some are quadroon or octoroon. They are still considered colored, of course, but are sometimes even as white as I. And would you also force the return of indentured servants to Ireland or wherever they came from when their contract is complete? Would you also send the French back to their country now that the Catholic Church no longer murders them?"

"Ah, the French. A problem where ever they go," the governor observed in French.

"My mother was French," Mercy replied defiantly before she could stop herself, speaking also in French and surprising the governor. Then suspecting his French may not be as good as he was pretending, reverted to English. "And the father of Monsieur Faure, our family's representative who is my sponsor this evening, was also French. Do you think he should be forced to return to France? We only consider ourselves to be Carolinians here, not half French, half English or half anything else. I think the sooner the Crown recognizes that the better it will be not only for England but also for the colonies too."

"My dear, I did not seek to insult you," the governor apologized. "You have a wonderful mind and intriguing opinions. I guess I have some things to learn, don't I?"

Mercy was instantly apologetic and slightly embarrassed for voicing at her opinions so strongly. She smiled up at him as they finished their dance and replied, "There is no need for apology, Sir. As my aunt will tell you I was reared to value an honest and energetic discussion. I will stand ready to assist you, Sir, in that course and in any way that I am able."

The governor took her offered hand, bowed to kiss it, then released her saying quietly that he must dance with the other young ladies too, lest a scandal be concocted by the good women of Charles Town who were watching them like hawks from the perimeter of the room.

They were indeed being watched, but not for the reason the governor suspected. As the evening progressed, Charity sensed a growing unease with her friends. Conversations abruptly ceased when she approached or were obviously steered to another topic, eyes met hers and quickly darted away. There were whispers behind fluttering fans, and mostly Charity noticed the increasing scrutiny of Charles Town society of her niece as she danced with the governor. It was almost as if she could watch the story making its way around the room.

Jean asked Mercy to dance immediately after she danced with the governor. He kept her dancing through two more tunes. As the third number ended and the floor emptied of dancers, he said quietly, "I implore you to remember that everything your aunt has done, and will ever do for you, was in love for you." Then he escorted her back to where her Aunt waited.

"I am afraid I have a terrible headache, Jean," Charity said, dropping formalities. "Would you please take me home?"

"I will come too," Mercy declared. She was unaware of what was happening around them. Jean thought such an early departure was unwise; in effect admitting the rumor was true. It was still early; the first candles had not even burned half way down. But he could not deny Charity her request. The three went forward together, making their excuses audibly to the governor as they thanked him for the evening. Mercy and Charity sat quietly on the settee in the receiving hall while Jean summoned their coach. No one else came to bid them a good night. Mercy became worried that their early departure was the result of her outspoken comments to the governor, or that she had danced too much with him, and felt her cheeks burning with shame. Charity took her hand and held it until Jean said the carriage was ready.

The next morning, Charity rose early. She had scarcely slept. Mercy also rose early and came to find her aunt in the library long before the breakfast dishes were laid in the dining room.

"I am so sorry, Aunt Charity," Mercy began.

"Why – whatever are you talking about, my dear?"

"I spoke too freely with the governor last night, and I danced too many dances with him too," Mercy's chin trembled. She had never felt more shame.

"Oh my dear, that is not it. Not it at all. I think the governor was quite enchanted with you, as he should be. He spoke favorably of you to Jean. There are just things going on right now that you would not know, and are not to worry about. I have decided you will go to school in England this fall, near the house your father has willed to me. I am closing up this house and we can go there together and stay while you are in school. I have always wanted to see England and we will see it together. Would you like that?"

"Why, yes, Aunt Charity. That would be wonderful. I so dreaded leaving you to go to school."

It was enough to distract Mercy until an uninvited guest called later that morning. Prudence Brownfield rang at the front door shortly after ten o'clock and was shown into the library where Charity was working on her correspondence. Mercy had been with her most of the morning but had momentarily gone upstairs to fetch a book they were discussing when Mrs. Brownfield arrived.

"Charity, you must forgive my intrusion, but I simply had to come and tell you there is something unbelievable being told around town about you and your niece."

"On the contrary, Prudence," Charity retorted. "I am quite sure you could not wait to run over here and tell me the rumor that I have already heard. I am surprised you were not here at first light."

"Really!" Mrs. Brownfield was indignant. "I only thought, as one of your dearest and oldest friends, that you must know what is being said. I have only your welfare in mind."

"Oh, do sit down, Prudence," Charity said weakly. "I am already aware of what you have come to tell me. Can I offer you some tea?"

Mrs. Brownfield's disdainful face said she would not now, nor ever, drink tea or anything else Charity Wainwright had to offer. Charity could see Prudence believed what had been said.

"They are all saying that Mercy is colored. That she is the daughter of your brother and his slave, not some made-up brother and a fictitious French woman. Is that true Charity? Have you lied to me and the rest of us all this time?"

"Prudence, I assure you my brother, David, was most definitely not made up. You know that is true, Prudence. You met him before he left home all those years ago. As I recall you were even smitten with him for a while."

"That is absolutely and completely not true," Prudence puffed up in indignation.

"No, I suppose not. You would never have allowed yourself to be interested in the second son would you? There was no fortune in that."

"I did not come here to be insulted by you, Charity Wainwright! We have been friends for too long for this. I only came here to warn you, to let you know what was being said."

"You came here to revel in it, that's what you did."

"Well!"

"Well, what? Do you really believe what is being said, Prudence? Do you think I lied to you and everyone else when I said Mercy was my niece? When I brought her into this house? You were as enchanted with her as anyone else. Does she look like a colored slave girl to you, Prudence?"

Prudence faltered. "You are forgetting that I was also in this house when you used to bring that slave girl - that...that Dove - down here from the plantation. She used to sew for you, did she not? And she would sit right here in this very room listening to our every word, too, didn't she?"

"She could have heard every word you said if she had been sitting out in the kitchen house, Prudence."

"I did not come here to be insulted, Charity," Prudence said again and then raised a single eyebrow of satisfaction and paused before she continued. "When I think about it I realize your niece looks just like that girl, Dove. Take away her blue eyes and straight hair and she looks just like her mother. I only thought it was my duty as your life-long friend to warn you about what is being said. I only thought you should know that people are talking about it, and they are not at all happy that you brought her to the governor's ball and even let the governor himself dance with a colored girl, even if you want to pass her off as your niece."

"She is my niece," Charity shouted, rising from her chair so abruptly that it fell backwards to the floor. "And you have done your duty, Prudence, although I suspect you have taken great pleasure in finally putting Charity Wainwright in her place, haven't you?"

"You are mean. You are spiteful. And you are hateful," Prudence said with a voice like ice.

"Not even half as much as you, but I guess I have let you rub off on me haven't I? I should have told you a long time ago what I thought of you when you made your husband sell your maid, Dianthus. You couldn't stand that he preferred her over you, could you?"

"And you, Charity Wainwright, you have always been jealous of me because I had a husband and you didn't, you...you...old maid!"

"I could have had plenty of husbands if I had wanted to. I just did not feel like I had to marry the first one who asked me because I wasn't going to get any more offers."

Prudence's mouth fell open, then she shut it, eye's blazing indignantly. "I'm leaving," she declared.

"Good – get out of my house."

Prudence crossed to the library door, flung it open, and turned back to Charity. "And one more thing. I stuck up for you on all of this last night. I told everyone who would listen to me that it was not possible. I said I knew you. But no more. You are on your own now, Charity Wainwright. You can come up with your own reasons why you disgraced the governor by letting him dance like a monkey for half the night with your high-yellow, colored gal."

Mercy came halfway down the stairs, but froze on the spot when she heard the argument begin. She had never liked Mrs. Brownfield and could not understand why Charity would count her as a friend, except for the Brownfields' position and that Charity had known them forever. In a way, she was amused to hear her aunt speaking to Mrs. Brownfield as she was. That was, until she realized what the argument was about. The two had argued in the past, then after a few days or weeks they would eventually soften, one would apologize to the other and their friendship would resume. Yes, they had argued before, but never like this.

As Mrs. Brownfield slammed out the front door, Aunt Charity also came through the library door, apparently on her way to the front door to open it and shout something else after the departing visitor, but as she came through the door she looked up and saw her niece standing on the stairs, tears brimming and her face frozen in shock and disbelief.

"Oh Mercy," Charity said softly as the anger went out of her.

Charity let Mercy run back up the stairs and slam the door to her room. She let Mercy have the space to cry by herself for a while. She had lied to her niece as well as everyone else. Her niece deserved the truth, more than anyone else. She had to find a way to explain it to Mercy and to ask for forgiveness.

Finally, she went up the stairs and knocked softly on Mercy's door. There was no sound from inside, and for an awful moment she thought Mercy might have gone out her window and run away. It was what Charity deserved, but not Mercy. Then she heard a small sniffle from inside and she gently opened the door.

"Mercy," she said softly. "I am so, so sorry."

Silence.

She pushed the door open wider. Mercy lay face down on her counterpane, all skirts and petticoats on the feather bed. Even like that, Mercy was beautiful. She felt her heart go out to her niece, but it could never be the same again. She crossed the room and sat tentatively on the edge of the bed. Then she put her hand on Mercy's shoulder, the shoulder closest to her. Mercy came up all at once to bury her face as Charity's arms went around her. For a while, all they both did was cry.

Finally it was Mercy who broke the silence. "Last night, as we finished our last dance and just before we left the ball, Uncle Jean asked me to remember that everything you have done, you have done in love for me, Aunt Charity. I did not understand what he meant, but now I think I do."

Charity sobbed a moment, realizing that Mercy had still called her "Aunt Charity." The bond was still there. "I have always loved you, Mercy, like you were my own daughter. You are my niece, but I have loved you more, I think, than I could have loved any daughter. You have been the joy of my life."

They embraced, and finally cried out, Mercy said, "Tell me about her, Aunt Charity. Tell me about my mother."

So over the rest of the morning and most of the afternoon, the two sat together, their backs against the headboard of Mercy's bed while Charity told Mercy the story. There were moments they laughed together - how Charity had fooled Benjamin into stopping the carriage right after they left the gates of the plantation – "he must have wondered what I had been drinking or what was wrong with me," to how Patience and Mercy had painted the doll's face, arms, hands and legs black that long ago afternoon.

"I think I have always known," Mercy said thoughtfully. "I had memories of Mama Bess and the plantation that I could not convince myself I had only imagined, or even dreamed."

"She was a special woman - and your mother too. I am so proud that you have their blood running through your veins, and you should be too."

"I guess I am, no matter what people say. I guess that also means I really am colored, and a slave." She thought a moment and shuddered. "Does this mean that I belong to Uncle Richard, then?"

"Only for a while," Charity replied. "He has drawn up papers for all his people to be freed when he dies. Jean told me that the day we went to see him. That was what we were talking about for so long in his office."

"Then Uncle Jean knows about me too?" Mercy asked.

"Yes. But don't believe for a second that it changes how he feels about you – about us."

Mercy stopped a moment and then laughed out loud. She laughed so hard she couldn't stop and the tears ran. Charity did not understand, especially when Mercy could only manage to say, "the governor, the governor..."

When she finally collected herself enough, she repeated the conversation she had the night before with the governor, "there I was lecturing him about the rights of free colored people to stay here. I really was impertinent to him, rude almost, but I told him we were all Carolinians here instead of half-English, half-French, and half-anything. Just wait until he finds out what half of me he was dancing with - a half black girl," and Mercy dissolved into near-hysterical laughter again."

"No, you are only a quarter, my dear. But you are entirely and one hundred percent Wainwright. Always remember that."

They were quiet a while, then Mercy asked, "What are we going to do Aunt Charity? No one will speak to me – or to you because of me."

"Oh, this will blow over eventually. They can't prove anything without Jean and I am sure he is doing everything he can to discredit the rumor as the ramblings of that drunken simpleton, Simon Bricks. Eventually they will either decide they believe it or they don't. Either way, we won't be here. We are going to go to England. We can live in your Uncle David's house. A couple of years away from here will do us both good. After that, you will be old enough to decide on your own what you want to do. I may even decide to stay in England permanently myself, as your old dowager aunt. Nothing could be more respectable there, I assure you."

"But what about Uncle Richard, mmm, Master Richard and the plantation."

"He doesn't want us there, Mercy. I love him dearly and he loves me, but he has to do this on his own. I have come to accept that. If we are already gone when the time comes, Jean can take care of everything. There won't be anything left anyway and it is better for us if we are away. People can't say anything worse about me for abandoning my brother in his hour of need than they are already saying. I don't need to stay here just to try to please them."

* * * * *

Richard Wainwright died in his sleep barely two weeks after the governor's ball. It was as much a relief for him as it was for those around him. Jean accompanied Charity and Mercy to the plantation for the burial. The next day, as they stood on the veranda with Old James, Jean read aloud the letter Richard had prepared for his people, announcing their freedom. Some fell to their knees in thanksgiving, others shouted in jubilation, while others looked completely bewildered at their new status. Charity wisely knew some would make a success of it, some would not, but all were better off. They would not be sold along with the land and house to a new, unknown master, if a buyer ever came forward.

After that announcement, Charity stepped forward and told the story of her deception with little Sukey. Some of the older ones, who remembered that time, laughed and clapped their hands in delight at the story. Old James was confounded, but relieved. When Charity was finished he came to Mercy, with tears in his eyes, and told her how he had wronged her mother. He told how he had separated the Old Massah from her mother, and that even at the end, Master Wainwright still asked for her. "I see now that nothing better could have happened to you than what came to be," he said.

As soon as they returned to Charles Town, Jean sent a letter to the school for young ladies in Cambridgeshire, England, announcing that Miss Charity Wainwright wished to enroll her niece, Mercy, in their school, and the elder Miss Wainwright would be taking up residence nearby in her late brother's home in Cambridge. Charity began closing up the house, but in the process realized it would be better if Jean would take up residence there during their absence, giving up his own rented rooms. In exchange for keeping watch over the house in their absence, Charity insisted he should live there rent free. She also suggested he bring Old James to the house as his butler and to hire a woman from the plantation to do his cooking. Old James was too old to make the transition to freedom and Jean would need a cook since Sepia would be going to England with them.

It was early August when the *Endurance* docked in Charles Town. At noontime, two days later Charity and Mercy stood at the rail on the deck of the tall-sailed passenger ship, watching cargo being loaded. Sepia was down in their cabin below, unpacking the trunks they had kept with them for the voyage. The larger trunks were already stored in the hold of the ship. Charity told Sepia to join them on deck as soon as she was satisfied things were set to right.

It was a festive atmosphere, punctuated by the occasional arrival of a coach at the end of the pier, bringing fellow passengers for the voyage. Charity knew it was a time of new beginnings. She was happy to be leaving and for a moment she mentally ran through a number of rude and childish gestures she could make as the ship sailed away, knowing of course, she would do nothing more than wave goodbye to the good people of Charles Town.

To amuse them, Mercy made up a little game of guessing by the amount of luggage being unloaded if the arriving passengers were bound only for Virginia, New York or Boston, or if they would be joining them for the entire voyage to England. Although there was no way to tell immediately, they both made mental notes so the outcome would be determined as they became acquainted with their fellow passengers.

As they watched, a new carriage with a team of perfectly matched white horses pulled up. Two footmen began unloading the voluminous luggage as a well-dressed couple alighted, followed by two excited young boys who had to be their sons. When the man stood, straightened and faced the ship, Charity nearly gasped. It was Thomas Squyres.

When land first became available in the Carolina colonies, Thomas' father, William, procured land adjoining the Wainwright plantation. Lord William Squyres was a titled nobleman in England. William, with his wife Lady Elizabeth at his side, developed the plantation in South Carolina. Thomas was born on the plantation in 1700, but was properly christened in the Anglican Church in Elm of Cambridgeshire the next time his parents returned home. It was their second son Thomas, who inherited the plantation in the South Carolina colony. The manor and title back in England went to Thomas' brother, the first born. Even without his father's title, Thomas still had the regal bearing and presence of a gentleman. Even now, deference was automatically given to him and his wife on their arrival at the port.

Years ago, their fathers had conspired that Thomas and Charity would marry, merging the two plantations into one. She had many suitors, but Thomas was the only man Charity would have married. Although the match was arranged by their fathers, she loved Thomas deeply. In fact, she had loved him too much to hold him to their contract when she realized he did not love her in the same way. They remained amicable friends. Thomas remained unmarried for years, making

Charity wonder if she had made the right decision until, in 1730, he married Mary Sanders, who was almost ten years younger than Charity. Now, as Mary also came forward on the dock, Charity smiled and waved down at them. Mary, surprised to see Charity, waved back enthusiastically and called up something that was lost in the din of the dock activity.

Charity turned urgently to Mercy, "That couple is Thomas and Mary Squyres. His father was an English duke or an earl or something and his father had the plantation next to my father. As a young girl I was once betrothed to Thomas, but I released him. We are all good friends now. I suspect they are traveling to England and will be on the ship with us for the entire voyage. Please, let me introduce you but say nothing else – of the plantation and our family. I will explain everything to you as soon as I can. Please, Mercy, I implore you – say nothing."

Mercy was more shocked by what her Aunt had revealed in the past few seconds than anything else she could remember. Her Aunt had been engaged to this man? The son of a titled Englishman? She had never mentioned any of this? "Of course, Aunt Charity."

"Here they are now!" Charity exclaimed cheerfully, more for Mercy's information than in greeting to the couple approaching them.

Thomas came forward and bowed over Charity's extended hand and lightly kissed it as she curtsied deeply before him. Mary Squyres also took Charity's hand and greeted her warmly as the two women gave a brief curtsy to each other.

"Thomas and Mary, I don't believe you have met my niece. Please allow me to introduce Mercy Wainwright."

Mercy silently repeated Charity's performance, extending her hand to Mr. Squyres as she curtsied deeply to him. She joined hands at the fingertips with Mrs. Squyres as they exchanged a shallow curtsy.

"My, my," Mary exclaimed with a southerner's drawl, more noticeable in contrast to Thomas' refined speech. "We heard you had adopted your niece, Charity, but I had no idea she was such a fair beauty!"

"Yes, my dear, departed brother," Charity continued with a forced smile and gaiety. "Mercy's mother was a French beauty, as I am sure you can see. We Wainwrights have always been as plain and colorless as rice, I'm afraid."

"Oh now, Charity!" Mary protested. "You mustn't say such things. I have always envied your blue eyes and pale complexion, even in the hottest of weather. Can you believe this heat?" Mary was already flushed and blotched red in the noonday sun. Thankfully the conversation was steered away from Mercy.

In the next several minutes, Charity confirmed they were sailing all the way to England and then would travel on by coach to the small town in Cambridgeshire where Mercy was to enroll in the academy for young ladies.

"But our niece – my elder brother's daughter, is enrolled at that self-same academy!" Thomas exclaimed. "If you will allow me, Charity, it would be my pleasure to arrange an introduction of the two young ladies before the term begins. We are staying at the family home in Cambridgeshire during our visit. Perhaps you will come and see us there?"

Charity swallowed hard, but then agreed, "How very kind of you Thomas. It would be our pleasure to call on you and your family. Thank you."

By the time they returned to their cabin to prepare for the noonday meal, Mercy was bursting with questions. But Charity, thinking instead she should quickly repack and get off the ship before it was underway, retired to her bunk with a cool cloth on her forehead. "This is a complete disaster," she moaned, pulling the cloth over her eyes. "Or it might well become one."

As it was, Charity had revealed to Mercy almost all the situation in those first few moments. It was a novelty for Mercy to think of her aunt having a romantic attachment to anyone, especially the dashing Mister Squyres. It gave an additional dimension to her aunt that she had never considered before. Instead of seeing her aunt as a middle-aged matron, she saw Charity as a young woman, desired, heart-breaking (since she had apparently rejected Mr. Squyres all those years ago) and a contemporary of the gay and charming Mary Squyres.

During the voyage, Charity seemed younger than her years, blossoming in the company of her friends. And if they had heard any of the rumors of Mercy's parentage before their departure from their plantation, they were too mannerly and well-bred to mention them. They treated Mercy as though she was completely what Charity represented her to be, a beloved niece. They questioned nothing.

The long voyage passed too quickly and they soon found themselves settled in David's cottage in Cambridge. It was small, but exceptionally comfortable, as Charity suspected David's home would be. Sepia could easily keep house with Charity's assistance. No sooner were they settled, than the Squyres sent their carriage and footmen to bring all three ladies to the manor house for a visit before Mercy and their niece, Hope, were settled at school. Mercy and Hope became good friends, and were teased about the coincidence of their names. "Mercy and Hope – it sounds like the title of a country parson's sermon," Uncle Thomas would say to the girls over the dinner table.

After the girls were enrolled in school and Charity settled into her brother's cottage she began taking long walks with her sketch book in hand. She had not sketched for years but she enjoyed drawing the landscapes and making studies of the local flora that she colored with her brush and paint box. When the girls had their holiday from school at Christmas, Charity and Mercy were again invited to the Squyres home. Thomas and Mary announced they would be sailing back to South Carolina on the first ship that spring, to arrive in time for the spring planting. They invited Charity to sail with them, but she declined, saying she was content in the cottage and would likely stay until Mercy finished her schooling. "I might even just stay here permanently," she teased.

They could see that England agreed with Charity. Her cheeks now showed a rosy glow from her walks and she woke each morning eager for what the day would bring.

But two days after Christmas, Charity was soaked to the skin by a cold rain as she took her afternoon walk. When she returned home she could not seem to get warm, even though Sepia built up the fire in the sitting room and made her mistress stay beside it. By that evening, Charity had a dry cough and struggled to breathe as she lay feverish in bed.

As Charity's condition deteriorated, the best doctors in all of Cambridgeshire were called to attend her. Varying treatments were ordered. To increase her fever and drive out the pneumonia, the fire in Charity's bed chamber was built up and she was covered under multiple layers of heavy quilts. As the patient became delirious and struggled to sit up, gasping for breath, she was forced to lie down and was restrained to assure complete rest. On the second day, one physician insisted she be bled and three bleedings, letting a pint of blood into the basin each time, were performed at twelve hour intervals. As Charity grew weaker, a scalding hot poultice was applied to the soft skin on the underside of each forearm where it would draw the poison from her lungs. In spite of her doctors' valiant efforts, and with Mercy lying prone beside her on the bed weeping, Charity died after only three days of treatment.

It was six months to the day from when she stood up and turned her chair over during the argument with Prudence Brownfield. Sepia whispered that it proved an old superstition among the slaves was true, that if someone's chair turns over backward when they stand up, that person will die within six months. Although she was not superstitious in the least, if Charity had remembered it, she might have been more careful until that six months was over. At a very minimum, she would not have been walking in the rain two days after Christmas.

Mercy was grief-stricken at Charity's death, but was determined to finish the schooling her aunt so wanted her to have. She wrote to Jean and said she would return to South Carolina after she had completed the two years. Then the two years became three as Mercy continued reading law and science. She enjoyed a social life in Cambridgeshire, both at school and Squyres Manor where she was invited by Hope every time they had a school holiday. In England, no one suspected she was quadroon, and such things were not even defined or important any way.

Ultimately, with Jean pressing for her return to settle Charity's estate, she promised she would return to South Carolina in the spring of 1749. Thomas and Mary Squyres would be returning to South Carolina and she could sail with them. She did not tell Jean that she had decided to sell Aunt Charity's house and then return to England. She would leave South Carolina and the people of Charles Town forever and live out her days as a scholar in her Uncle David's comfortable cottage in Cambridge, England.

PART TWO

MARY

CHAPTER FOUR

Cambridgeshire, England
and South Carolina Colony
1749-1750

Squyres House in Cambridgeshire became a second home to Mercy. She was welcomed during breaks from school, and the girls became such close friends that Hope declared they were sisters.

Hope's father, who was Thomas Squyres' elder brother, inherited his title, along with the manor house and the surrounding park. When she was at Squyres House, Mercy addressed Hope's parents by their formal titles of "Lord Squyres" and "Lady Squyres" only on her first arrival and at formal occasions. Other than that, they were very relaxed about such protocol in their home.

Uncle Thomas and Aunt Mary came from South Carolina every two years. Their sons, Andrew and Timothy, were born in South Carolina, but like their father, were christened at Elm in Cambridgeshire. Andrew was not christened until he was almost two years old. Thomas and Mary always arrived in the fall and stayed through the winter, returning with the first sailing of spring. It would have been better for them to come in the spring and stay until the fall and escape the low country summer, but Uncle Thomas needed to be in residence at his plantation during the planting, growing, and harvest. Rice cultivation was very demanding and winter was the only time he could take his leave from that responsibility.

Mercy and Hope were at Squyres House all of the summer before the third year of their studies. They visited the cottage in Cambridge several times, where Sepia was paid a salary to keep the house. It seemed like an extravagant waste of money to Mercy, but Jean insisted in his letters that it was a small expense and he would retain Sepia's services until Mercy returned to South Carolina.

Hope's bond with Mercy deepened when she learned her uncle was once betrothed to Charity. It was a romantic story for the girls and to Hope especially, who longed to go to South Carolina to see her uncle's plantation. Now with this revelation, she also wanted to see the Wainwright plantation and Aunt Charity's house in Charles Town too. Mercy tried to discourage her, vaguely saying that tenants now lived in Aunt Charity's house and the plantation was sold after Uncle Richard died, but Hope would not be dissuaded.

"But there is no reason why we could not stay with Aunt Mary and Uncle Thomas," she insisted. "The Squyres Hall property joins the old Wainwright plantation, does it not? Surely the new owners would allow us to have a look, if only on the pretense of visiting your family's cemetery. And I would so love to see your Aunt Charity's house, even if only on the outside. I imagine Aunt Mary would accompany us there. I shall beg them, if I must, to allow me to sail back to

South Carolina with them next spring."

Mercy struggled to find excuses, the most persuasive being that she did not know if she would return to South Carolina at all. But even that was weak. Hope already knew that Mercy had to return, even if only temporarily, for the settlement of her Aunt's estate.

When the girls returned to Squyres House for the Christmas holidays, Mercy knew as soon as she saw Thomas and Mary Squyres that they knew the truth about her. She could not keep it from Hope any longer. Hope must learn it from her instead of someone else. Such a secret revealed, even accidentally, by the South Carolina Squyres would be devastating to the trust of their friendship.

Hope's mother, Lady Margaret, usually walked with the girls in the gardens, but with the entire house preparing for Christmas, they found themselves walking alone one afternoon. Mercy knew she had to take advantage of the rare opportunity to tell Hope the true story of her background.

Even in winter, the landscape at Squyres House was beautiful. They walked far into the park, until it became wild and untamed, before they turned back. It was still daylight and quite pleasant when they reached the edge of the formal gardens. They were cozy and warm in their hooded school cloaks so they lingered, taking one path after another.

"I know you have sensed that I am less than eager to return to Charles Town, and even South Carolina for that matter," Mercy finally began.

Hope linked her arm through Mercy's as they walked, "Please forgive me, Mercy. I fear in my eagerness to see South Carolina, I forget that it will be grievous for you to return there, with both your Aunt Charity and your Uncle Richard now absent. I am ignorant of knowing what it is to have no family, and I fear that makes me inconsiderate in remembering that for others."

Mercy leaned closer to Hope, thinking what a good person she was. "You are so kind, Hope. But that is not entirely the reason I do not wish to return."

They walked on a while longer. Hope was not sure what else to say.

"It is true I have no family. I fear I also have no friends there either - or none that will receive me, at least. You see, Hope, in Charles Town and in South Carolina, I am a person of color. I am colored."

Hope stopped as she turned to stare in wonder at her friend, not understanding. Then she laughed aloud and gently shoved Mercy away. "You are playing a joke on me, Mercy."

Mercy stood looking at Hope soberly. "I wish that were true."

Hope was confused, started to reply several times but could not. Then she simply said, "I do not understand."

"I am what is called quadroon. I am one-quarter black, or African. My mother's mother came from Africa, as a slave."

"But I thought Charity Wainwright was your aunt. How can that be?"

"Yes, she was, but only because she chose to acknowledge and claim me as her niece. I am her brother's daughter. But I was his daughter by his slave. A slave named Dove."

"So…your mother was a slave too?"

"Yes. My real father, whom I always called Uncle Richard, owned her. When I was born – and until he died – he owned me too. I belonged to him and was his slave – his property, even though he gave me to his sister."

Hope again turned to face Mercy. She studied Mercy's face intently for a long while. Then she drew down her chin, laughed, and declared, "I could just kill you for teasing me so, Mercy. Who put you up to this? Was it Uncle Richard? Or was it Andy and Timmy? Those boys – this sounds just like them. I will be the laughing stock at dinner this evening when you tell this, won't I? 'If only you could have seen her face,' I am sure you shall say. I could just kill you for teasing me, Mercy!"

But Mercy remained sober, staring at Hope. They moved to sit on a bench under an arbor by the side of the garden walk.

Finally Hope insisted, "It can't be true, Mercy. You are as white as me. Paler, actually." she said holding her forearm next to Mercy's, "Just look. Here it is the middle of winter and I still seem to tan and freckle no matter how much I stay out of the sun, while your skin is always as pale as cream. Your eyes are blue and mine are brown. How can anyone possibly say you are not white?"

"It doesn't matter there. People in Charles Town know my mother was a slave."

"Are you still a slave there? Is that why you do not wish to return?" Hope asked, worried and confused.

"No, Uncle Richard – my father – freed all of his slaves when he died. We were all given a Deed of Emancipation, which really doesn't mean much except that I am a freed slave in South Carolina. If I so much as cross the Savannah River into the Georgia colony I could be seized and sold as a slave again."

"I have never heard of anything so ridiculous," Hope protested.

"The intent of that law was to discourage settlers from taking their slaves into Georgia, since they know they can lose them. But the result is that free people of color can't go there either."

"But you are safe in South Carolina?"

"Technically, yes. Aunt Charity took me after my mother died and raised me all those years as her niece – her white niece. When Uncle Richard died and I was freed, our lawyer, Monsieur Faure, filed papers to legally change my name to the name Aunt Charity gave me and that I was always known by. I could not legally use the Wainwright surname otherwise, even though it belonged to my father. Since my mother was a slave I had no right to his name or his family.

"At the same time, Aunt Charity confirmed me as her heir. But even though she named me in her will before that, it wasn't legal for me to inherit from her until my name was legally changed, and then, after that was done, she reconfirmed me as her heir in a codicil to her will. Until then, I was only Sukey, the slave girl. I think that might be where I got such an interest in law, just trying to understand how all of that could be."

"Then you were actually raised as the person your aunt said you were."

"Yes, I had white friends. I shared a childhood tutor with other white girls. I was given dance lessons and I was presented into society with other young ladies at the Governor's Ball. I even danced with Governor Glen himself. No one yet knew."

"Did you know?"

"I only learned the truth the next morning. The rumors somehow began the day of the ball. Jean - Monsieur Faure - still does not know how it started. We left shortly after that for England. It was already planned for me to come to school here, but Aunt Charity decided to close up the house and come along too. She inherited Uncle David's cottage in Cambridge earlier that summer, so it gave her a very good reason to come along with me and stay here."

"Was she in trouble then – for what she did?"

"Only socially. But I doubt any of her friends would have received her, or even spoken to her after that. They thought she betrayed them and all of her class. I am sure there was even talk that she embarrassed the governor by letting him dance with me, a colored girl. It would have been a very lonely time for her if she stayed behind when I left for school."

"I just can't understand it," Hope said after a while. "It all sounds so strange."

"It's really not so different here, Hope. Think of what would happen if your aunt chose to bring up the illegitimate daughter of a scullery maid as her niece and then presented her to the king when she was invited to court. The differences are not so readily visible here as they are in the colonies, but the distinction between the classes is quite the same."

Hope nodded, understanding a little better.

"I just wanted you to know this. You are the first person, other than Monsieur Faure, who knows. You are the first person I have ever told."

Hope took Mercy's hand in hers and leaned so there shoulders touched. "I am so happy you told me, Mercy. It is so interesting. My life is so boring."

Mercy leaned back and laughed comfortably. "The daughter of a lord and lady who lives in a castle is boring?"

"It's not a castle, and you know what I mean. I will never have any romantic secrets. When I marry it will be someone selected for me by my father. Your parents must have been passionately in love. Oh - do you want me to keep it a secret?"

"It doesn't matter so much here. I think Thomas and Mary must know already. I don't see how they could not. I don't wish you to go about telling everyone, but no, you don't have to keep it a secret."

They sat a while longer, and then Hope looked at Mercy like she had just realized something.

"What?" Mercy asked. "What is it? Tell me!"

"I think...I think you must be in love with this Monsieur Faure - Jean? He sounds so romantic."

"Ha! He is as old as Aunt Charity," Mercy protested. "Besides, I will never fall in love. I am going to stay here and become a scholar and live in Cambridge forever. I will be a very old lady someday, surrounded by books, and you will come to tea and we will scratch our whiskers and talk about the old days when we were girls together at school."

Hope laughed. "We have to come up with pet names for ourselves before we finish school, you know. Black and White? Pepper and Salt? Coffee and Cream?"

"Just as long as mine isn't Sukey," Mercy agreed. "I can't for the life of me understand what my mother was thinking. Supposedly she was educated, especially for a slave."

"And mine can't be Piggy. Not under any circumstances."

So the girls were laughing and gay as they walked back to the house, and Mercy felt the burden of her secret lifted. At least it was with her best friend, Hope.

* * * * *

On Christmas day, with her parents' permission, Thomas Squyres announced over their dinner in the grand hall of Squyres Manor that Lady Hope would accompany them back to South Carolina after she was finished with school in the spring. Hope was ecstatic. "Won't it be such a grand time, Mercy, all of us in South Carolina together?"

There was just enough hesitation from Thomas Squyres for Mercy to realize she was not welcome on the voyage, nor would she be welcome at their home in South Carolina.

Furthermore, their complete refusal to address her by anything except her Christian name since their return, even on the occasions when Hope was addressed as "Lady Hope", showed their lack of acceptance of Mercy as a social equal. At a minimum she should be called "Miss Mercy," if not "Miss Wainwright" at those times. They might as well call her "Sukey." Even the household servants took notice of it and wondered. It was all right for their niece to associate with the quadroon Mercy Wainwright in faraway England, but never in South Carolina.

She was angry, but instead of throwing down her napkin and saying exactly what she thought before she stormed away from the table she calmly said, "Oh, but Hope, did I not tell you? Monsieur Faure has already booked my passage."

"No, you absolutely did not!" Hope protested. "On what ship?"

"On what ship are you sailing?" Mercy asked of the Squyres without looking at them.

"The *Endurance,* of course," Thomas replied, uncomfortably.

"No, that is not my ship," Mercy said cheerfully and sipped from her wine glass. "I am so sorry, Hope, but we will not be sailing together."

She lied. Jean had already booked her passage on the same ship. And it was too

late to write to him to change her return to Charles Town to another ship. She
would have to change the booking herself. At that moment she would rather
swim back to South Carolina than to set foot on the same ship with the Squyres.

Hope was disappointed. "Do you suppose he could change it? Oh well, you will
come and see us when we are all back in South Carolina. Won't it be such fun?
Aunt Mary, you simply must take us into Charles Town. Mercy has told me so
much about it."

Mercy gave a long, unwavering glare down the dinner table at Thomas Squyres
and then at Mary, revealing she knew exactly what had happened, and that they
would never be forgiven. Before breakfast the next day she took her leave of
Squyres House, never to return. She only told Hope she wanted to spend the rest
of the holiday at her cottage in Cambridge. She needed to prepare things there for
the final term of school and give instructions to Sepia for preparing the house for
their return to South Carolina in the spring.

Although she could not help it, Mercy was distant with Hope during their final
term. Hope sensed the estrangement, but assumed it was because their time at
school was ending. She tried to steer Mercy's thoughts toward the time they
would share in South Carolina, but Mercy knew that was not going to happen.
She had booked passage for herself and Sepia on the *Temperance*, sailing four
weeks after the *Endurance*. The Squyres would be fully at home on the
plantation by the time she arrived in Charles Town. With any luck, she could
complete her business there and return that fall on an earlier ship than Hope
would be taking home.

While they waited for the *Temperance*, Mercy went to London to refresh her
wardrobe before the trip. Her expenses at school had been small and there was
still a sizeable balance of the money Aunt Charity brought to England. If she was
going to be shunned in Charles Town, she intended to be stunning. With the
proper clothing of a young lady she would show them all. She ordered four
complete changes of day dress, plus two gowns for evening wear, although she
presumed she would have no occasion to wear them in Charles Town. There
were also numerous hats, gloves, shoes, reticules and even an outrageously
fashionable French parasol. Sepia was also completely outfitted and her new
clothes were finer than anything she had ever worn. Mercy gave the dressmaker a
fair bonus for having the order ready in time for the sailing.

The voyage passed without incident and they even arrived in Charles Town a few
days earlier than expected. Mercy went directly from the ship to Jean's office,
only to find he was no longer associated with the firm. She found him in the
library at Charity's house, not yet expecting them, but he said he would move that
day to the rooms he had already rented so Mercy could move into her house
immediately.

"Why are you no longer with the firm?" Mercy asked as soon as they settled in the library.

"We had a difference of opinions that led to the eventual parting of ways," he explained vaguely.

"Because of your support for my Aunt Charity and me?" Mercy asked him outright.

Jean was silent. Mercy was pleased that he simply chose not to respond to her question instead of glossing things over with platitudes or, worse yet, lying about the cause.

"I am so sorry, Jean," Mercy said. "You do not deserve such treatment."

"Nor do you, my dear."

"What will you do?"

"I have been considering a move to Augusta. They are sorely in need of lawyers. I have also thought about giving up law entirely. I have grown as weary of it as I have of Charles Town. I think I should like to try my hand at farming."

Mercy said nothing. It was the most Jean had ever revealed of himself to her.

"I suppose we have business to conduct first," she said, hoping to cover the uncomfortable silence that was settling over them after his revelation.

"There is no hurry, Mercy."

"I plan to return to England as soon as I can, Jean," she said. He looked shocked.

"Oh, Jean. There is nothing for me here. I could spend the rest of my days sitting here in Aunt Charity's library waiting for someone to call. And we both know that will never happen. I won't live out my life as a prisoner here."

"I will come to see you."

"Of course, that it not what I meant."

"Are you intent on returning then?"

Mercy looked at him, and this time she was the one who could say nothing.

"We need to discuss your Aunt's trust. Your grandfather established it to provide for your Aunt throughout her life. She used it freely and it was not intended to last in perpetuity – or forever, that is."

"I know what perpetuity means," Mercy bristled at the implication she did not. "Are you saying there is no money? Why did you allow me to keep Uncle David's cottage open if that is so?"

"No. No, there is still a good balance in the trust, but I do not think it can last for your lifetime," he explained. "You must look for another income. I suggest leasing out the cottage in Cambridge. I have checked and it will provide you with a fair income, much better over the long run than selling it outright."

"Or I could sell this house when I go back to England."

"I am afraid there is currently no market for selling it, Mercy," he said.

"Then I will rent it," Mercy argued. When Jean hesitated she demanded, "Is there no market for that either? Am I so tainted then?"

"I had hoped you would stay here, or in South Carolina at least. I thought you might settle down here, marry, and have a family."

"Who would ever want to marry me, Jean? You forget that I am a woman of color. No white man could ever marry me." Then she added with an edge of sarcasm, "Or are you suggesting that I marry a footman or a blacksmith or some other tradesman of color?"

"Things are changing Mercy. In Virginia, families are claiming themselves as white if they are one-sixteenth black or less."

Mercy was instantly angry at that. "So, if I breed myself with a white man and then my daughter does too, I can hope that my grandchildren might be allowed to say they are no longer colored?"

Jean was silent.

"I am sorry Jean, forgive me. That was crude."

"But true, I'm afraid," he said. "I had always hoped that one day I would be making the arrangements for your dowry and your marriage trusts."

"Why do you think I would ever want to sell myself to another man?" she replied.

"What do you mean by that?"

Mercy turned away from him and walked toward the library windows, looking out at the street.

"A husband, a master, what is the difference? A husband is his wife's master as much as he is master to his slave, the only difference is that a husband cannot sell his wife to another and cannot kill her with impunity as he can with his slave. Remember that I have been a slave once, Jean, and I am not voluntarily giving myself over as a slave again, in marriage or anything else."

"But it would not be like that, Mercy. You mustn't be so cynical."

"But even if I was completely white my husband could use force to make me obey him. He could cancel any contract I make, take my money and squander it and leave me in complete poverty with no recourse to me whatsoever."

"Not if the trust is set up correctly."

"A husband can break his wife's trust, Jean. I know that much."

"Not if it is set up with multiple beneficiaries, he cannot. At least none that I have set up have been successfully challenged in that way."

Mercy turned back from the window in surprise to look at Jean. His comment gave her pause for thought. She was amazed at his strategy. "Really? That possibility is intriguing. Exciting, actually."

Jean grinned at her in approval and almost chuckled. "Your lecturer at the Inns of Court wrote to me that your true strength was in legal reasoning. He said the worse thing that could happen was for you to take a legal apprenticeship and be forever saddled with the endless copying of legal documents and clerical duties. He encouraged me to take you into my firm, even as a woman, in reading law and preparing legal arguments for our cases."

"Oh, I loved it, Jean," she said, temporarily distracted from their previous argument. "You know that I was only allowed to be there because of Lord Squyres' influence, and then I was only to be an observer and keep silent, but I soon found I could not help myself, especially when the men in his lectures were so blatantly obtuse." Jean had to laugh.

"I loved reading the laws, understanding them - or not understanding them, as the case may be," she added. "I loved arguing why laws could or could not be applied to a case. But I realize now I will have to satisfy myself only with the pleasure of study. Even in England, I can never be a barrister or even a solicitor."

"Not unless you find your way in and are willing to fight for it. I think you would be marvelous."

"Do you know they are planning to start a course of study in common law at the

University of Oxford?" she asked.

"Yes, but I understand it will be several years yet before it is really underway."

"But still, just think of it! I heard William Blackstone speak at Cambridge. His argument is that the study of law should be university-based, where the concentration of foundational principles can be learned instead of just haphazardly learning law through apprenticeships and the Inns of Court. Can you imagine how much better that will be? Students will all learn from the same books and their education will be standardized. I wish I was starting now instead of when I did. How much better that would be!"

Jean laughed in delight at her enthusiasm, took her hand, and led her to Aunt Charity's settee where tea was waiting. Old James came tottering in to check on them, surprising Mercy that he was still functioning, and even alive for that matter. He greeted Mercy warmly, welcoming her back to Charles Town. Then he made a few minor adjustments to the tea tray and gingerly made his way back out of the room.

"At least some things don't change, do they?" Mercy said, looking up with a smile after Old James was out of the room.

Jean leaned forward and kissed Mercy, surprising her. "No. They don't."

* * * * *

The summer passed too quickly, even though Mercy was quite alone. She sent notes to her childhood friends, telling them she was back in Charles Town and inviting them to call at their convenience. Those invitations all went unacknowledged, confirming Mercy's outcast status.

Lady Hope came to Charles Town to see Mercy at midsummer, unannounced and alone, that is if being accompanied by a maid and driver could be considered traveling alone. On her arrival, she announced that she would be staying a week. Every day she made Mercy get dressed in one of the new dresses from England and they went out in Thomas and Mary Squyres open carriage with its fine pair of matched white horses. Everyone in town knew the carriage and strained their necks to see who it carried.

When they entered a shop, Hope audibly announced herself when greeted by the proprietor or his help. "I am Lady Hope Squyres of Cambridgeshire," she would say extending her gloved hand to be bowed over by a gentleman, or she would give a deep curtsy to a lady who had no choice but to curtsy in return, and to Mercy as well. If Hope saw someone else in the shop she thought Mercy might remotely know, she would link her arm through Mercy's arm and add, "I am here visiting my dearest friend, Mercy Wainwright. We were together at academy.

We are more like sisters, actually."

It cost Hope nothing and she even thought it was a lark. In the evening, they would dissolve into fits of laughter, especially when Hope would mimic the response of a particularly reticent Charlestonian.

When the week was over, a grandly dressed Hope made Mercy come out with her to the waiting carriage to see her off. Standing at Aunt Charity's gate and with every eye in the neighboring houses along Tradd Street upon them, she kissed Mercy's cheek and gave her a long, bone-crushing hug.

"I am so sorry that Uncle Thomas and Aunt Mary have been such prigs," she said loudly for their audience. "Just remember that you are always welcome in my home, Mercy. My door in Cambridgeshire is always open to you. I love you more than I could ever love a sister, my dear, dear Mercy."

Mercy hugged her friend again, feeling her heart would break at the separation. She returned the sentiment to Hope, saying that wherever she lived, Hope would always be welcomed there too.

"I know you are never coming back to England to live," she said more quietly so only Mercy could hear. Mercy began to protest but Hope added, "And I know you will marry your Jean Faure. And if you don't, I think I will sneak back over here and marry him myself!"

Mercy burst out laughing through her tears and pressed her handkerchief quickly to her nose. Both girls were smiling and waving as the Squyres carriage drove away.

In late August, word came that the old plantation house had burned after being struck by lightning during a storm that blew in off the ocean. One Sunday afternoon, Jean took her to see it. The new owners had been restoring the house before the fire and the gardens had been resurrected to something of the original plan. But now the gardens' centerpiece was only the blackened brick shell. Some of the ancient live oaks along the edge of the river had been toppled by the storm, giving a raw and injured look to the landscape. The new owners were temporarily living in the old wooden frame house that John Wainwright built when the land was first cleared. They were amazed it had survived the storm. After visiting the family cemetery where her father, mother, Old Bess and Patience were buried, Mercy quietly asked Jean to take her home.

* * * * *

As the weeks passed, Mercy was amazed to realize the depths of affection she had for Jean. After Hope's comment, Mercy recognized the feelings that had always been there, and as far back as she remembered, but they were deeper now and different. Regardless, it was impossible and could never be.

At the beginning of September Jean asked her to marry him. Against his advice and his wishes, Mercy persisted in her plans to return to England. Charity's house was sold at a fair price, considering the circumstances, and her passage was booked. The night before her ship was scheduled to sail, they sat together on the veranda in the cooling breeze of the evening. Everything Mercy would take was packed. The new owners bought most of the furnishings along with the house. Mercy kept a few things: the Wainwright silver and china, Aunt Charity's writing desk and books, and all of the paintings of the Wainwright ancestors. Those things were now in crates and would be shipped to her cottage in Cambridge.

It was a beautiful and leisurely evening, and they lingered on the porch until it was long past time for her to prepare for bed. It would be the last time she would sleep in Aunt Charity's house. "I am buying a farm in Georgia," Jean said unexpectedly. "The land has been cleared and a peach orchard has been planted. It is on a creek in St. Paul Parish, west of Augusta. There is a small house on the property, but in time I can build something better."

"Then you really do intend to leave Charles Town, too," she said.

"Yes, I need a new start, same as you, away from here and away from everything."

Mercy looked up at him as they sat side by side. "If that is what you want, then I am happy for you Jean. Truly I am."

Jean looked at her intensely. He said quietly, "What I want is you, Mercy. I have always loved you."

"Jean, don't," Mercy said, turning away and preparing to stand. "I leave for England in the morning."

"I am asking you to marry me, Mercy."

Mercy rose and went to the porch railing with her back to him. She pressed her hands to her temples, shaking her head slightly side to side. She was incredulous. "Do you honestly believe that you can marry me, Jean?"

Jean was silent.

"Are you truly forgetting I am a person of color and you are not? Do you think there is a minister or a judge anywhere who would marry us, a black woman and a white man?"

"You don't look anything other than white, Mercy. They would never know."

"You want me to lie about it?" she cried out, growing more agitated. "I have had enough lies."

"No. You would not have to lie, Mercy. We won't be married here in Charles Town. We can go to Savannah to be married, or even Augusta. They won't know us. They won't even ask, I'm sure. In truth, I look more colored than you, don't I? With my brown eyes and this curly black hair they will ask me if they ask anyone. If they ask you, we will go somewhere else. We can keep going until we will find someone who will marry us. I will not stop. I want to be your husband, Mercy."

"That does not make any sense, Jean," she said sadly. "Even if we can find someone to marry us, it still would not be legal. We would always have to lie about it and worry about being found out. We cannot lie about it forever."

* * * * *

Mercy was standing with Sepia on the deck of the ship the next morning, waiting for it to sail. Jean stood sadly on the dock. She had promised to write. That would have to be enough. He would go to his farm in Georgia. She would go back to Cambridgeshire. She knew she would never see him again. After so many years of him looking out for her, he would never lay eyes on her again.

She watched him standing there on the dock. With the flurry of everything around them as the ship prepared to sail, his eyes never left hers. People jostled him on the dock and pushed past her on the deck of the ship but the look between them was never broken. "Oh, what am I doing?" she finally asked of no one in particular.

Then she turned to Sepia. "I am not going. Run and tell the captain we are getting off the ship and not to sail until we do. Also tell him we need our things from the hold." Sepia looked at Mercy like she'd lost her mind. "Well, don't just stand there. Get our things. I'm going to stay here, Sepia. I'm going to marry my Monsieur Faure."

Sepia had been listening at the window last night. She gave a cry of delight and clapped her hands, then went running off. Jean had been pushed to one side in the press of the crowd on the dock, waiting for the ship to sail. Mercy waved and called out over the din to Jean until she caught his attention. "Yes, Jean," she called out. Jean shook his head and cupped his hand to his ear, signifying he could not hear. "Yes. I said yes!" She was waving wildly and shouting, again and again. Jean still could not hear her.

The sails were being raised. The ship would be sailing at any minute. A portly gentleman standing next to Mercy at the rail cupped his hands to his mouth and bellowed, "The young lady said she says 'Yes.' She...Said...Yes!"

Jean heard that. Other passengers heard it too and were laughing, clapping their hands and cheering as he came running to the gangway. The purser stopped him there – visitors had gone ashore already, but Mercy went running and came down the gangway to meet him. He swept her up and swung her around in a circle. Sepia came running back on the deck, carrying two hastily packed bags, and all the ship's porters following her carrying the rest of their luggage.

"Are you certain?" he asked when he finally set her down.

"No," she swallowed and replied honestly. "Do I have to be?"

He laughed and said, "I can be sure enough for both of us." Then he kissed her soundly.

* * * * *

Their first problem was a place to stay. The new owners of Aunt Charity's house were given the keys as Mercy left that morning. Jean was keeping his rented rooms until the purchase of his farm was complete. After that, he would sail to Savannah and then travel by boat up the Savannah River to the falls at Augusta. From Augusta, he would travel over land some fifty miles west into the Georgia colony to take possession of the farm. After Mercy and Sepia disembarked the ship and it sailed away, they simply sat on Mercy's trunks that were piled on the cobblestones of East Bay Street. Mercy and Sepia sat on the small trunks that were packed with their clothing for the voyage, surrounded by the larger trunks and the crates containing the portraits, silverware and china that the crew had hastily unloaded while their captain waited impatiently to sail. They could do nothing else. If they left, all of her abandoned belongings would be carried away.

Mercy knew she would not be allowed in any of Charles Town's hotels or even the public houses. Even in her fine clothing and with a maid accompanying her, her status as a woman of color was too well known here. They sat for a long time while Jean made inquiries, representing her as his client. The hotel managers were less than friendly with Monsieur Faure, and even more so when they found that he was trying to rent rooms for the woman who had been the vehicle of his mockery and disgrace. Jean was ordered to leave more than one establishment.

As they waited, Aunt Charity's dressmaker, Mary Botts, and another woman paused as they walked by. Many of Mary's clients required her to come to their homes for her work, preferring not to be seen patronizing the shop of a woman of color. Both Mary and the woman she was with were elegantly dressed and both were very light, but not as light as Mercy.

"Why, Miss Wainwright," Mary exclaimed. "I 'most didn't recognize you."

"Good morning, Mary - I mean, Mrs. Botts." Mercy realized Mary was the first person other than Jean who had spoken to her since she arrived Charles Town nearly three months before. Even today as she sat by the dock with Sepia, obviously stranded, people she recognized crossed to the other side of the street to avoid her. Mary introduced the other woman as her new assistant, Doretta, who curtsied politely to Mercy, while trying not to stare.

Of course Doretta knew who Mercy Wainwright was, she had heard the talk, but she just could not believe how white Mercy actually was. How could anyone ever have suspected she was anything else?

"We got no place to stay," Sepia blurted out. "Miss Mercy done sold Miss Charity's house and then she decide to get off the ship this morning and marry Mister Jean instead. So now we got no place to stay."

"Sepia!" Mercy was aghast.

True, Sepia had every right to speak around Mercy to the women. Mercy was only her employer and they were all on the same social standing now. But still, Mercy was shocked to have their status laid out like that to women she barely knew, and on the street, too.

"Well, Mister Jean ain't had no luck finding a hotel for Miss Mercy and night comin' on soon, so I 'spect we gone be sittin' here on these trunks all night. We got no place else to go." Sepia looked like she could burst into tears at any moment.

Mary smiled and put a calming hand on Sepia's arm. "Yes, you do. You all are staying with me."

Later on that evening, after the trunks and crates were settled in the shed behind Mary's little house in the colored section of town, and Sepia and Mercy were dressed for bed, Mary asked them to share a cup of cocoa in her sitting room, an expensive treat to welcome them into her home. Her house was small, but beautiful, as Mercy might have expected it to be. Mercy kept reminding herself that she was the same as Mary now. She asked Mary to call her Mercy, without the Miss, and Mary insisted Mercy do the same with her.

After Jean was sure they were settled, and had thanked Mary profusely for her hospitality, he left for his rented rooms. The women sat talking long into the night. Sepia was sent on to bed, but Mercy was not sleepy and Mary was genuinely eager to talk, keeping Mercy actively engaged in conversation.

They talked about England and her friendship with Hope – Mary had seen them riding in the Squyres carriage and could barely contain herself to keep from cheering for Mercy. Their talk drifted to Aunt Charity, with Mary declaring, "Your Aunt Charity was always so kind to me."

"I just can't get used to thinking of myself this way," Mercy confessed. "I am sorry; I don't mean any insult by that."

"Why would you be used to it?" Mary replied gently. "Your aunt raised you as a white girl from the time she brought you here as a little baby until you come out at the Gov'nor's ball. It just about as easy for you to think of yourself as colored as if I suddenly find out I was white." Mary's language became less formal as they relaxed and talked more openly. "I am only sorry it have to come to an end. I was so proud when you went to dance with the Governor. I sew happy stitches into that dress, every last one of 'em."

"Then you knew already?"

"Honey, I knew the first time your Aunt Charity bring you to me."

"But...how?"

Mary put the tips of her index and middle fingers to the base of her nose, at the nostrils.

"You got no shelf here. Colored folks never do, no matter how white they look. You look at white folks, they got this unusual little shelf right below they noses. I think the Lord make it so they snot don't run down they thin little lips and straight in they mouths."

Mercy snorted in laughter, falling back into her chair. She felt the base of her own nostrils. There was nothing there, no ridge, no shelf.

"And then, they was also the first time I fitted you. You didn't need no stays, girl! You already got a tiny waist and a nice big butt and bosoms too. Why you think it is those white ladies all wear they stays so tight and put on a bustle? English ladies all got a body like a tree trunk, straight up and down, and flat butts with no titties. They all want to look like us. They know that what they mens like. And they know what they mens want."

Mercy was laughing so hard now she could not catch a breath. "Stop," she protested, putting her hand on her side to stop the pain.

But she did not protest too strongly. She realized Mary would never say these things to a white woman. She was treating Mercy as an equal. And while that itself was new and a bit shocking for Mercy, it was also comforting. There were other people in the world, and even in Charles Town, who were exactly like her.

Finally, it was time for bed. Mary brought a candle to the room Mercy would share with Sepia. Sepia was sound asleep. "Thank you for your kindness, for taking us in," Mercy said as she kissed Mary's cheek goodnight.

"Ain't nothing," Mary replied, lightly patting Mercy on the back as she hugged her. "You gone be all right now, Mercy. You gone be all right."

* * * * *

While they waited in Charles Town for the purchase of Jean's farm to be finalized, they sought a minister who would marry them. First they went to Jean's church and were flatly refused. Aunt Charity's pastor, who had christened Mercy, rudely showed them to the door, saying the mixing of the races was an abomination and against the laws of God. Before he slammed the door in their faces, Mercy shouted back that she must have missed reading that part of the Bible.

They tried other churches in town, where they were not so well known, but the ministers were alert to the structure of Mercy's face and skull and discretely asked if she had any African blood. Since she responded honestly, they were told they could not be married.

As they sat visiting with Mary late one evening, discouraged, but with Mercy more determined than ever, Mary suggested her own church and pastor. They could come to the preaching the next Sunday morning and Mary would introduce them after the service.

Mercy and Jean slipped into the crowded pew beside Mary, feeling all eyes on them, but welcoming. Mary had affirmed that everyone was welcome in their church, regardless of shade. Mercy stole some glances around them as the hymn singing began and was amazed at the variations of color, from as black as she remembered Old Bess and Patience being to as light as herself. When the people caught her eye, they nodded warmly to her, recognizing her as their sister. Mercy was completely swept up in the singing of the first song, an ancient African form of chanting with the leader calling out the verse and the rest answering with the next line. It stirred something deep within her - an old and faint memory of Old Bess, possibly singing the same song. She began to cry softly, but not before Mary's arm went around her waist, supporting her. Jean held her hand and sang strongly beside her.

After the long sermon, with the congregation participating by shouting out their agreement with the preacher's declarations and proclamations, and a final hymn, the congregation rose to make their way out the back of the little church. Mary introduced Mercy and Jean to everyone she knew, which was essentially everyone in the church. People took Mercy's hand enthusiastically, welcoming her and saying they were praying for her, which also touched her deeply. By the time they made their way to the preacher, with Mary beaming at him and eager to introduce her friends, Mercy felt like she had come home.

They visited briefly with the preacher - others were still waiting too. For a moment Mercy was afraid Jean was going to tell the preacher they wanted to get married. Mercy tightened her grasp on his arm, just above the elbow and slightly shook her head when he looked at her. She did not want to cause problems for Mary. The request would wait.

"Maybe he can pass," Mary declared, looking thoughtfully at Jean as they walked back to her house for Sunday dinner.

.

"No, Mary," Mercy said, wondering how her new friend could suddenly be so confused. "Jean is white. I am the one who needs to pass."

"I know that," Mary said indignantly. "What I mean is maybe he can pass - for colored."

CHAPTER FIVE

St. Paul Parish, Georgia
1750 -1757

With Mary's comment the idea was born. Jean easily forged his own Deed of
Emancipation, dated the same day Mercy was granted her freedom and also
signed by Richard Wainwright's attorney, Jean Faure. In doing so he showed his
name as Johnny, a more believable name for a freed slave. He also filed a name
change, as he had done for Mercy, changing his legal name to Johnny Freeman.
Slaves often took the surname of Freeman when they were not sired by their
master or had multiple owners before they were freed. If anyone asked, he could
truthfully say he had worked for Master Wainwright in the big house on his
plantation. He would just not explain that his work had been as Master
Wainwright's attorney.

They were too well known in Charles Town, but when they arrived in Savannah
they would seek out a colored church, show their papers, and ask to be married.
If that did not work, they would try at every colored church from there to
Augusta.

They set out by ship for Savannah. Mary and others from the church came to the
dock to see them off. Sepia decided to stay in Charles Town. She would start
work the next week as a seamstress for Mary. Old James also stayed behind, too
old to make the trip and start yet another new life on the farm in Georgia. Mary
promised she would look after him. She employed him in her house with only the
lightest of duties. It would give him a place to live out his days in the dignity he
deserved.

In Savannah, they sent their crates ahead while they waited for a boat to take them
up the river. Savannah was founded only in 1733 and it was still a newly-raw
town. It was at the mouth of the Savannah River and it was building up rapidly,
following the formal design of James Oglethorpe. They strolled the streets,
enjoyed the parks, and fell in love with the city. They even considered staying
there instead of going on to Augusta. But Savannah was too close to Charles
Town and someone might recognize them.

They searched for a church in Savannah with no luck. "Johnny" said it should be
expected since the ban on slavery was only ended earlier that year. There were
not yet enough free persons of color to support a church. Mercy and John were
still not married when they boarded their boat for Augusta.

There were a fair number of passengers on their boat. They made good progress,
nearly twenty miles a day. Sometimes their stops at night were little more than
camps along the river, sometimes on the Georgia side of the river, other times on

the South Carolina side. John always asked for a minister each time they stopped. Finally a minister was located in one of the South Carolina stops. Although there was not yet a church building in the new little town, he held services and performed weddings from his home. He said he would marry a free couple.

The next morning, Mercy and John knocked at the minister's back door and showed their papers, explaining they were going further west into Georgia to start their new life on their farm there and wanted to be married as Christians. They were congratulated and married by the minister with his wife serving as witness. The minister recorded their names in the Bible John had brought from Charles Town for the occasion. Mercy became Mercy Freeman. She was almost eighteen. John was thirty-nine.

* * * * *

John paid a premium price for a new wagon and a strong team of horses when they arrived in Augusta. Their luggage and some of the crates were loaded in the wagon. The rest, including the Wainwright portraits, Aunt Charity's china and silver, and her writing desk, were put into storage at the dock until they could return for them. They would know what furniture they needed after they saw the house on the farm. Basic furniture could be bought in Augusta. Finer furnishings could be ordered from Savannah.

The farm was not as developed as John had been led to believe. Most of the pine forest was still not cleared. The peach orchard was planted with as many trees as the seller promised, but at least a third was dead or dying. The house was really just two small cabins made from whole logs cut on the property, joined by one long roof over an open space between called a dogtrot. One of the cabins had a dirty and uneven plank floor of rough pine. The floor of the other was simply dirt. The furniture the sellers left behind was unusable.

"I suppose I should have kept more of Aunt Charity's furniture," Mercy observed after John carried her across the threshold.

"Not for this, you shouldn't have," he declared, kicking an overturned bucket that lay by the door. "I am sorry, Mercy. I had no idea it would be this bad. I will take you back to Augusta and rent a place there until I can get the new house built."

Mercy gave him a light kiss. "This is our first home together, John. I love it and it will be beautiful in time, I'm sure."

For all its faults and shortcomings, Mercy and John fell in love with the farm. It was on the edge of the piedmont, or high land. From there it was downhill all the way to the sea. Some people said that thousands of years ago the ocean came all the way up to St. Paul Parish and Augusta, and that the land south of there had all been under water. That made some sense. The high land of the piedmont was mainly clay. Down below was made up of sand hills and then sandy loam beyond that to the ocean. It was strange to Mercy to think that all of the low country had once been under the sea.

The high ground where they were now was quite different from the low country they were used to. Even the air of the farm was different. There was no dank smell of swamps and no salt air from the sea. Instead there was the fresh smell of the pine forests that surrounded them.

They observed their first Christmas together, alone in their cabin. Mercy thought how different it was from the year before, when she had glared down the dining table at Thomas and Mary Squyres in the main hall of the elegant Squyres Manor in Cambridgeshire. Now she was in her own home, however humble, with a husband who loved her - worshipped her even. The present was definitely better.

Mercy was pregnant. It was not a surprise to her. John was a passionate and tender lover and she never refused him. Their joy in each other's bodies knew no bounds. On Christmas day she told John their baby would arrive that summer. Their child would be the first to have the new family name of Freeman.

Spring brought the heavy fragrance of wild honeysuckle from the woods. The surviving peach trees, when they bloomed that first spring, only added to that heady fragrance. As she grew bigger with the baby, Mercy left the shutters of the cabin open and sat outside under the sheltered dogtrot whenever she could. She even moved the table and chairs to the porch and they ate every meal there. She said it was like living in paradise. John bought a load of smooth-planed lumber and hired a man to put a floor in the second room. When that was finished he replaced the rough floor of the main room. He said he wanted his son to have a smooth floor with no splinters when he started crawling.

John was busy tending the orchard, pruning the trees to increase their yield and replacing the ones that had died. Mercy helped him carry water from the stream to water the young seedlings. It would be a poor harvest that year with nothing to sell. But they did not need to worry just yet. There was still money from the sale of Aunt Charity's house and Uncle David's cottage, and also what remained of Aunt Charity's trust and John's savings. They bought basic furniture in Augusta and started plans for a larger house on the property. Mercy loved their little "dogtrot," as John called their cabin, and said she was in no hurry to move. The main room was comfortable and homey with cozy chairs by the fireplace, a cooking table nearby, simple rugs on the floor, and Aunt Charity's elegant writing desk by the window.

That spring a neighbor traded some young hens for supplies and by summer they had pullet eggs. Mercy was frying some of those eggs for breakfast on the first day of August of 1750 when her labor began. She went to the door and called out to John, who was picking okra and tomatoes in the kitchen garden by the house. That evening, John delivered their child, a girl. Mercy wanted to name her Mary Hope; for Mary Botts who had helped them find their way and for Lady Hope, who would always be her friend. John agreed it was a beautiful name, even without considering the two women for whom the child was a namesake.

* * * * *

There was a dramatic change in Georgia in 1750. The first years of the colony proved to be a failed experiment of relocating the population of English debtor prisons and of social programs of helping "the worthy poor," by giving them fifty acre plots for farming. With little preparation for this new vocation, few of them were successful. Most just barely survived. By 1750, many of the immigrants were selling their partially improved property, if they could find a buyer, or simply abandoning their land and making their way elsewhere. Within months of arriving in St. Paul Parish, John tracked down the owners of the three adjoining farms and made generous offers. He now owned two hundred partially-cleared acres. The only occupied farm adjoining theirs belonged to a young couple from Virginia, Lancaster and Alice Lovett. The Lovetts were also newly married and expecting their first child.

It may have been because they were all so young and full of hope, and so different from the worn-out immigrants around them, that Mercy and John became close friends with Lancaster and Alice. Their son, Richard, was born two weeks after Mary Hope. The path between the two cabins was well-worn. Alice and Mercy often shared their chores, the cooking, washing and mending, and tended their babies together.

At their first meeting, when Alice came to introduce herself, she quietly observed Mercy's struggles with housekeeping. Mercy confessed to Alice that she had always had at least a cook and maid until she left Charles Town and that she knew nothing about keeping a house. Alice showed Mercy how to build a cooking fire, some simple cooking and cleaning methods, and even how to do her laundry. She had endless patience with Mercy; in fact she showed sympathy that Mercy had never been taught these things. In time, with Alice's gentle encouragement, Mercy began to believe that even if she would never be an excellent cook or housekeeper, she was at least a competent one. And in the quiet times when the chores were finished and their babies were sleeping side-by-side, safely barricaded on the bed with pillows, Mercy taught Alice to read.

Although Alice came from Princess Anne County in Virginia, where education was readily accessible, her father believed education was wasted on girls. Alice was ashamed of her ignorance and hid it expertly. Mercy only realized her new friend could not read when she shared a letter from Lady Hope. The effusive letter congratulated Mercy and John on the child and expressed her deep appreciation of the baby's name and her wish to see her namesake the next time she visited the Squyres in South Carolina. Then she related a funny story that Mercy had trouble reading aloud since she was laughing so much. She finally handed the letter to Alice saying, "Here, you can read it yourself." From the look on Alice's face she realized she could not, and their reading lessons began.

With the ban on slavery lifted in Georgia colony, large scale farming became feasible. Rice and indigo planters poured into the low country, bringing their slaves with them. Most of these planters were given huge land grants and they added even more land to their holdings by buying up the old subsistence farms. The land was quickly cleared of timber for the new plantations and put under cultivation.

In the next twenty-five years, the slave population of the settled land of the colony, which extended into the wilderness about sixty miles west of the Savannah River, would increase from fewer than five hundred slaves to over eighteen thousand. This huge increase in the demand for slaves could only be met with shiploads brought directly from Africa.

As more slaves arrived there was a more visible and clear distinction between the black and white races. In that division, Mercy came down easily on the side of the whites. With her fair skin and blue eyes, no one would look at her and think she did not belong with the newly arriving planters and the English and Scottish immigrants. Without doing anything, John and Mercy simply became white again. They bought another large farm that adjoined their property. The owner was moving to the low country with hopes of starting a rice plantation as soon as he could buy enough slaves. John and Mercy now owned more than six hundred acres, but they had no intention of ever buying slaves.

Mary Hope was a sweet-natured baby, but she could also be strong-willed. Long before she could talk, she had her own idea of how things should be done. While John only laughed and gave in to her, Mercy resisted. Mary Hope often glared at her mother and Mercy would glare right back at her. But if Mary Hope began to cry, Mercy would pick up her daughter and nuzzle her, as Old Bess had done for her so long ago, crooning, "I'm your mama, Miss Mary, ain't nobody ever gonna love you as much as your mama loves you."

Mary Hope had her father's olive complexion and dark brown eyes. She even had his curly black hair. People sometimes looked at the baby oddly. Mercy knew they were questioning Mary Hope's heritage. But then they looked at John and saw how much the baby looked like her father. They all knew John was a Frenchman, and that had to be where his daughter's coloring and curly hair came from.

When word got around the area that John was a lawyer, people just started coming to see him. What they needed was generally routine and simple; a bill of sale for a team of horses, a statement demanding payment, a letter of agreement, or even just a letter written to relatives back east. John would see his clients at the table in the dogtrot. Mercy would leave the door open as she went back and forth, bringing tea and cakes to their visitors while they met with John. Then, when a document was needed, John would explain that Mercy's handwriting was so much better than his, and if the client thought it was all right, he would have her prepare the paper. Mercy, sitting inside the cabin at Charity's writing desk, would have the document almost finished by then, waiting only for the amount of the contract, and the names of the parties to be filled in.

The one document John always had to prepare himself, since Mercy flatly refused to participate in any way, was the bill of sale for a Negro. There were slaves in St. Paul Parish, not as many as the low country where the huge plantations were blossoming, but still enough to require the supporting commerce. When a client was buying a slave for the first time, John would give counsel about the investment they were making and the ongoing expense it required. He made the comparison that they would not be wise managers if they neglected or mistreated a horse or cattle, and neither should they endanger their investment in a slave. He correctly suspected some who came to him were only seeking to meet the required minimum of twenty slaves to attain the status of calling their property a plantation.

During these meetings, Mercy would shut the cabin door to the dogtrot, or even leave the house. John would explain that his wife strongly objected to slavery and that for his small operation, only the peach orchard, it was more profitable to hire the hands he needed during harvest instead of bearing the expense of maintaining a workforce of slaves all year round. John hoped to plant some sound economic reasoning in the minds of his fellow farmers.

Money was in short supply in the parish, especially so far from Augusta, so John often took goods in trade from his clients. He might be paid in household goods, garden produce, hens and eggs, or sometimes even the promise of a share of a farmer's crop. As the demand for his services increased, Mercy began storing the surplus in the second cabin and in time that extra room was entirely given over for that purpose. People began coming to see Mercy when they needed something, like a new cooking pot, some extra eggs or even a setting hen. Without quite realizing what was happening, Mercy became the owner and operator of a general store. Mercy's storehouse was the first place the neighbors would come when they needed something. Eventually John hung a shingle over the door saying "Freeman's Store." Below that he put up a second shingle reading,

John Freeman, Esq.
Law Office
Letters Written

When John's service to a client required him to travel to Augusta, Mercy began organizing a wagonload of goods to take and went along with him, leaving Alice in charge of the store in her absence. It was a two day drive to Augusta, meaning they were gone five days including a day for trade.

The road just outside their cabin had once been a trading path to Augusta.

It reached far west into the Creek Indian settlements, branching out to smaller trails and thinning out as it went. Some even said the trail went as far as the Mississippi River, but Mercy could not imagine one road going that far. Coming east into St. Paul Parish, all those smaller individual trails merged into one that ended in Augusta. But with the Indians moving farther and farther west, the road in front of their store was now relatively quiet.

> *Author's note: The Upper Trading Path, originally used for trade with the Native American tribes, ran west into St. Paul Parish (Warren County) from Augusta. Through Georgia, the main stem of the road led past present day Warrenton, Indian Springs, Griffin and Greenville.*

While John conducted his legal business in Augusta, Mercy would drive the wagon around town, selling the wares she brought with her and refilling the wagon with goods she could sell in her store; coffee, tea, sugar, lengths of fabric and lace, needles and thread. The store's stock was growing steadily with each trip. She also would take special requests for things she did not keep in stock, such as shoes, tools, guns and powder, filling them to order. She gave a guarantee that if customers did not like what she brought back from Augusta, they did not have to take it. But the guarantee was rarely used. People came to trust and appreciate Mercy's knowledge and happily took what she brought back for them.

Soon the trip was being made every second week, whether John had legal business to conduct or not. Every two weeks Mercy had a packet of letters from the surrounding farms to post in Augusta and brought back the mail for their part of the parish. She provided the service free of charge as a courtesy to her customers. People only had to come to her store to pick up their mail instead of going to Augusta.

She came to look forward to those times together with John. Once, when they were leaving Augusta, the wagon fully loaded with stock for the store, he turned to her and said, "I am afraid people will say we are no longer carriage people, Mrs. Freeman."

Mercy laughed out loud. "A carriage, on this road? Remember how Aunt Charity's carriage was always rattling and shaking to bits and that was only on the River Road. No, thank you, Mr. Freeman, I would rather ride in this sturdy wagon than be sitting by the side of the road with a broken axel or ruined wheel, regardless what people may say about me."

When harvest time approached, she offered to buy a farmer's small indigo harvest for cash money outright. The farmer happily took her offer. It was too small of a harvest for him to take to market himself, even with the generous subsidy paid by the Crown for indigo, almost all his profit would be consumed by hiring the team and wagon he did not own himself. Mercy owned the horse team and wagon and made the trip already. She took the indigo to a buyer in Augusta and made a small profit on the transaction. Word got around that Mercy Freeman would pay cash money for a crop and by the next spring, other small indigo farmers were lining up to sell their harvests.

Mercy only paid the farmer when a crop was loaded in the wagon at her store. She received payment a few days later when she delivered the crop to her buyers, so there was little risk. Certainly none of the risk and the grueling physical labor the farmers bore in bringing their crop to harvest. But the prices she paid were fair and she soon had a reputation for honesty with the area farmers. She started buying peach harvests and other crops that came to harvest later than indigo, and making one trip right after another with a fully loaded wagon during the extended harvest season.

After finishing the harvests of the second year, Mercy was weary of the trips and wanted to be home more with Mary Hope. She asked around and hired a young man from a nearby farm to help. At eighteen, Andrew was the eldest son of a large family newly arrived from Maryland, part of the great migration south by those seeking refuge from the French and Indian Wars. The family had fourteen children and had left almost everything behind. Now they were struggling to get their long-neglected property on a productive basis. They needed the income to survive until the next harvest. Andrew would take the wagon to Augusta each week. He would deliver goods to Mercy's buyers, and make the rounds to her suppliers, filling the wagon with items from her list. She had understandings with her regular buyers and suppliers and they promised to give Andrew the same prices they would give Mercy herself.

She kept careful records of any discrepancies with those businesses in Augusta. She rode along with Andrew every three months, rectifying her list and assuring favorable ongoing relationships for business. By the third year she was earning more from her enterprise than John was earning in his legal business. Similarly, Alice Lovett was earning more from her work with Mercy than Lancaster was earning from farming.

It was then that John and Mercy began plans for the new house. They agreed on the building site, near enough to the dogtrot cabin that they could still use it to conduct John's legal business and for Mercy's store. John laughed and teased her when Mercy insisted the new house had to have a dogtrot too, but the architect he hired in Savannah adapted that request into a long central hall on the first floor with wide double doors at both ends, effectively creating the same air flow and the feeling of being outdoors but still sheltered, that Mercy so loved about the cabin.

The architect's plans were impressive, and Mercy loved the symmetry of the design. The house would be two full stories tall, crowned with a hipped roof. It would be as wide as it was long, so that all four sides of the house were the same. The ground floor would have four rooms; a drawing room and library on the left side of the hall and a dining room and sitting room on the right. The same basic layout was repeated on the second floor providing four large bedrooms.

Two identical fireplace structures would be situated on the shared wall between the drawing room and the library, and also the wall between the sitting room and the dining room. Two fireplaces would share one firebox, opening on both sides, so that one fire heated two rooms. The setup would be repeated on the second floor so each bedroom would have a fireplace. The two symmetrical fireplace chimneys would run through the attic and show above the roof. A total of eight matching dormers would light the attic, with two dormers set into each side of the tall, hipped roof, bringing light and ventilation to the attic.

A wide veranda would wrap around the entire first floor with columns supporting the roof that sheltered the space below. A shallower gallery on the second floor would allow glass-paned doors to open into all the bedrooms. The house would be situated on the site to face the prevailing southerly breezes.

Since lumber was plentiful, the house would be almost entirely built of wood felled and milled on the property. The only materials they would have to buy were bricks for the fireplace chimneys, and the windows and doors. Window glass had to be shipped from England and their house would have four windows in each room, a major expense. Mercy particularly loved the architect's design for the first floor windows that went all the way to the floor. When raised, those windows were actually more like doors and would give each room direct access to the veranda. The whole house would be light, open and airy.

The first step of building the house was to build a mill to saw the wood. A spot was found where the creek could be dammed deeply enough to provide a flow of falling water would be strong enough to turn a mill wheel. The mill parts would be ordered from the Netherlands, the best producers of circular saw blades and mill parts. While the dam was being built, their Savannah architect heard about a bankrupt sawmill in the north that used the same machinery the Freemans would order, but at a substantial savings. John made a fair offer and the machinery was disassembled and shipped to Savannah, then brought up the river on longboats. From Augusta it was brought overland in special wagons. Then it was reassembled and connected to the new waterwheel. Boards from the first trial runs of the new machinery were used to build a shed to shelter the machinery. With that complete, the gears to the water wheel were engaged and the first sawmill in St. Paul Parish was in operation.

At first, John and Mercy hired some of the poorer farmers from along the creek to work the mill, thinking steady work would help them. But the men soon complained that the mill was filthy and they would be absent for days after they were paid, drinking until their earnings were gone. After a few months, Mercy wrote to her old friend, Mary Botts, in Charles Town, explaining the situation and saying that if any of the men in Mary's church were interested in the work, to let her know. She explained they would have to live in the open to start, but would be given the first lumber from the mills to build their own cabins. Land was set aside next to the mill for a settlement and John was even providing hardware, doors and simple glass windows for a standard three room cabin. She promised they would pay those men the same that they were currently paying the poor white farmers, who did not seem to want the work.

The same day Mary received the letter, six men and their families set out across South Carolina on foot. Their color ranged from rich brown to darkest black. Although freed men, their darker tones excluded them from the employment offered to lighter-skinned former slaves. In Charles Town they barely survived on day jobs in the roughest and least desirable work. The mill in Georgia colony paid well and would give them the chance for a new life. Eight more families followed within a week, and then two more. Mercy sent a letter with the next post thanking Mary and telling her to send no more. In all, sixteen families migrated from Charles Town to work at the Freeman mill.

With the crew of freed men, the mill quickly settled into a smoothly run operation. After the worker cabins were built, a steady supply of lumber was provided for the new house. It had been wise to use the first practice cuts of lumber to build the cabins. By then, the lumber produced was the best in the area and there was a new little community beside the millpond above the dam, laid out in two orderly rows with eight cabins facing a common lane running down between the two rows. Each cabin had a garden plot and one or two outbuildings.

The workers were grateful and asked John if they might also build a church at the end of the lane by the millpond. John donated the lumber, nails and other hardware for the church and enough lime for two coats of whitewash. John and Mercy were invited for the first service in the new church with its proud little steeple that would hold a church bell one day. The first service would be followed by a shared celebratory lunch on the grounds.

Mercy and John, with little Mary Hope walking along between them, walked down the neat lane of tidy cabins built of newly-milled pine. As they approached the church they could see that tables were set up under the trees. All the workers and their families were quietly lined up outside and dressed in their best to greet the Freemans. None of them had been to services since they left Charles Town. Although Mercy would have preferred to sit further back, the best seats on the front row were reserved for the Freemans. Jean and Mercy stood until every one had entered the church before they sat on the church pew that smelled of newly milled pine.

The hymn singing went on at least two hours before the preaching began and Mercy once again found herself emotionally swept up in the music. One of the workers, who had been elected by the others to serve as the preacher because he could read, delivered a simple but moving sermon. A final hymn was sung and the first service was complete. Everyone filed out. Dinner would be next.

Mercy was somewhat surprised that the congregation left the church so quickly and did not wait for Jean and her to leave first, but as soon as she came out the doors she saw why. All the families were lined up again outside, facing the door and beaming as they waited for the Freemans. The preacher and another man were proudly holding something between them that was covered with a cloth. She was moved to tears when the cloth was removed to show a hand-lettered sign that would be nailed above the door;

Mercyville Church
1756

As soon as the cabins and the little chapel were finished, work began on the new house. The first step was milling the pine logs to the specifications laid out by the architect. John soon saw that he had underestimated the amount of timber needed and spent a week hastily riding the property marking additional trees to cut. As the lumber piles grew in the mill yard, the brick order for the foundations and fireplace structures began arriving. Brick was expensive, especially transported this far from the river, so John and Mercy kept careful count of each delivery. The brick was stacked in neat rows next to where the foundation was staked out. Following the brick, wagon loads of sand for the mortar were added to a growing pile.

When the lumber order was nearing completion, the architect arrived from Savannah, bringing the first crew of selected craftsmen to assure a premium quality of work. Finish carpenters, glaziers and painters would follow in later months when the house was ready for their work. Local men were hired to assist the craftsmen, working under their direct supervision with all of the work coordinated by the architect. A tent city, of sorts, sprang up at the construction site to house those men. Their presence provided an unexpected and brisk business for Mercy's store.

Every evening Mercy and John took Mary Hope to look at the progress. After the foundation was finished, an immensely tall scaffolding was built where one fireplace would be. Then the fireplace structure began rising layer by layer to the sky. Mercy was amazed at the height, but realized two stories with ten foot ceilings plus the space between the ground and the first floor, added to the height of the hipped roof above the second story and then the added extension above the roof to assure the chimneys would draw properly meant the chimney structures would be almost fifty feet tall.

After the chimneys, the frame of the first floor was built, finally giving an outline of the house to come. The subfloor was laid on the joists and the interior walls were partitioned, giving an idea of the dimension of the rooms. The rooms seemed large, especially after living in the dogtrot, but as she walked through the skeleton walls of the first floor, Mercy realized the house was larger than Aunt Charity's had been in Charles Town. It approached the dimensions of her father's house on the plantation. She was not sure she wanted such a large house.

On the day the craftsmen started putting up the smoothly-planed pine boards for the interior walls, work came to a complete standstill. The plan had been to nail the boards horizontally, but the architect stopped the work almost immediately. John and Mercy were called to the house and for the next hour the architect argued that it did not look right and that the boards for the interior walls, at least for the ground floor, should run vertically.

He also wanted them to be in alternating widths of twelve and sixteen inches, providing a pattern around the rooms in lieu of wallpaper. Mercy was inclined to agree, but John was adamant it would not happen. The amount of lumber required to provide that many boards ten feet long and in those specified widths, instead of the random widths and lengths already available, would be nearly doubled. In addition, a horizontal framework would be needed on top of the existing frame of the walls to provide an anchor for the vertical panels. The project would be delayed until the wood could be cut and milled.

As the discussion grew more heated, Mercy took John's hand and asked if they might take a walk while they thought about it. They walked a good long while, all the way around the mill pond, before John was open to discussing the change.

"It may delay us a few weeks for now, John," Mercy observed calmly, "but we will be looking at those walls every day for the rest of our lives. I don't mind living in the dogtrot a little while longer."

When they came back to the new house, walking hand-in-hand, John surprised her by telling the architect the walls should not only have the vertical board placement on the first floor but also on the second. The attic could be walled in the horizontal pattern.

Even though the lumber had already been planed in the mill, after the walls were up, they were scraped and then sanded smooth, removing any trace of the remaining saw marks. When those boards were painted, the walls would look as good as plaster and were much more practical in the humid climate. The interior and exterior doors and the windows were installed as soon as they were shipped from the mill in Philadelphia. The planks of heart pine flooring would be installed last, followed only by the trim work.

The bedrooms and central halls were painted in varying shades of white paint, less expensive and easier for the painter the architect brought in from Savannah. The dining room was done in a pale green and the painter and his crew did such an excellent job of mixing paint that there was very little variation in the color between batches. The drawing room was painted a light shade of gray. Aunt Charity's portrait, when it was finally hung over the mantle, was beautiful against the color. Jean said the old painting seemed so much more colorful in their new home than it had in Charles Town.

With the total cost running much more than they originally anticipated, Mercy and John promised each other to move in only with the bare minimum of furnishings. All the bedrooms did not need to be furnished and they could complete the drawing room and dining room over a period of time. They did not want to have to use any of Mercy's money from Aunt Charity and Uncle David, nor dip into John's savings more than they had originally planned.

But then, John came back from conducting some legal business in Savannah, insisting Charity accompany him back there the following week. A wealthy lady, newly widowed, was leaving Savannah to return to Philadelphia where she had her primary residence. Eager to leave, she wanted to sell the entirety of her furnishings for one lump sum. Her attorney contacted John, who gave her a deposit of earnest money until he could return with Mercy. As busy as they were, Mercy went along on the long trip to Savannah, thinking they should not spend the additional money. It was a staggering amount, even for an entire household of furniture.

But as the childless widow took them through the house Mercy realized they could not pass up the opportunity. The husband died soon after the house was completed. The furniture, all crafted in Philadelphia of the finest woods and fabrics, was so lightly used it all looked new. The widow's drawing room was elegantly furnished and even included a pianoforte that was part of the deal. The finely polished mahogany dining room table seated twelve, and was matched with a massive sideboard that Mercy knew would fit perfectly between the two front windows of their new dining room. As an added incentive, the widow told them she would also include all the carpets, bedding and linens, curtains and even the fine dining room and drawing room portieres, four for each room, and exactly the number John and Mercy needed. The woman had beautiful taste. Mercy agreed and John gave the happy widow a draft on the bank in Charles Town that held his savings in full payment. A mover was hired to pack up the contents of the house and ship them to Augusta. From there wagons would bring the crates overland to Mercyville.

After they returned from Savannah, one thing Mercy steadfastly refused was the exterior color the architect had chosen for the exterior walls. It was a color scheme Mercy said she liked early on. In one of their first meetings with the architect, she mentioned that although Charity's house back in South Carolina had been brick, there were also many frame houses in Charles Town. She had always admired a smaller frame house close to Charity's on Tradd Street. With black shutters, white trim and yellow walls, she always thought it looked so cheerful and welcoming. The architect took note of that and incorporated the color scheme into his plans.

But when Mercy found out the additional cost of yellow paint, dramatically higher because it required enormous amounts of precious yellow ochre, exacerbated by the amount of paint that would be required to cover the outside of the house, she flatly refused, saying it was a ridiculous waste and the outside should all be painted white. They had spent too much money already. She firmly dug in her heels, or at least that was how John described her stubborn refusal, and neither the architect nor her husband could dissuade her.

By the time she left for her next quarterly trip with Andrew to Augusta, Mercy was frustrated with the lack of progress on finishing the outside paint. The painters were taking too much time so carefully painting the white trim and columns. She kept telling John they could just paint it all at one time, since they were using only one color. He agreed with her but nothing changed. She left for Augusta in a huff, snapping at the architect in front of John that she wanted the painting to be finished when she returned. There was simply no excuse that he was letting it drag on this long. The wagons had already started bringing their new furniture from Augusta, for heaven's sake.

It was good for her to be away for a while. She had successful meetings with her buyers and suppliers and found some new items for the store she was excited to bring home. She was in good humor when they left Augusta and could barely wait to be home. She would apologize to John for her impatience and to the architect too. She had almost yelled at them the day she left. She brought along a supply of John's favorite tobacco and a bag of the same for the architect as a peace offering.

The sun was setting as they came up the road to the cabin at the end of the second day of their drive home. From that vantage point the new house towered over the little dogtrot cabin. Happy to be coming home, she was filled with a rush of pride at the new house that stood glowing in the setting sun. John and she had built it together. It was almost like a symbol of the life they had together, so new and bright and shining.

As they drew closer she could see the painting was finished. The painters were busy gathering up the last of their things and putting them in their wagon. Obviously John and the architect had been rushing them to complete the job for her homecoming.

"Drive on up to the house, please," she told Andrew.

As the wagon, still loaded with her market purchases, pulled up the new lane and stopped at the foot of the stairs up to the veranda, John came out the front door to greet her. Mercy smiled warmly at him, a little shy with the realization she would soon be apologizing to him. She looked up again and saw that the golden color from the light of the setting sun was permanent.

John looked sheepishly through his eyebrows at her, with his hands palms up at his sides. Mercy stood up in the wagon and put her hands on her hips. "John Freeman! What have you done?" Then she laughed and clapped her hands together like a child on Christmas morning. "Oh, I love it! I absolutely love it!"

John helped her down from the wagon. She could barely take her eyes away from him or the house. It was perfect, just as she had imagined. The new house was finished. She threw her arms around John.

"You are spoiling me, Mr. Freeman," she mock-scolded him as she hugged him. "Are you always going to give me everything I ask for?"

"I can't help myself," John replied, kissing her with passion he usually reserved for the privacy of their bedroom. "I really can't."

The house was painted a bright and sunny yellow. With the pale brown of the new wood shingles on the roof, the dark reddish brown of the chimney bricks showing above, the crisp white of the columns supporting the veranda roof, and the facings around each window and door, it looked so cheerful and welcoming. Mercy would always smile when she looked at their house and remembered how John surprised her that afternoon.

* * * * *

After the new furniture arrived and their personal possessions were moved from the dogtrot, Mercy and John decided to give an afternoon party to celebrate. The Lovetts were invited, along with other neighbors nearby and even the customers who frequented the store or were clients to John. They even invited the poor white farmers along the creek. John was not sure, but Mercy insisted they could not exclude them.

The next afternoon, they invited the residents of Mercyville. Mercy had not wanted to hold two separate parties, especially dividing the events between their black and white friends, but the guests at both events were given the same tour of the new house and were equally invited to make themselves at home as identical lunches were served on the veranda. John finally convinced her that two parties would be the best thing, and the way it was separated provided roughly the same number of people invited both days.

Two women from Mercyville, who had sometimes worked in kitchens in Charles Town, helped Alice and Mercy prepare the food. Those two women helped serve the white guests the first day and a slightly uncomfortable Alice helped Mercy serve the second day. They could never have managed a combined party without bringing in help from Augusta. Mary Hope said she liked the second party much better; especially the singing and dancing that went on long into the night.

With the living quarters of the dogtrot vacated, Mercy wanted to set it up as a school. John argued that he was already using it for his law office, but Mercy insisted that did not preclude it being also used for a schoolroom. In fact, the presence of his law books might encourage her students. She opened her little school with Mary Hope and Richard Lovett as her first pupils. She taught them every morning until lunch time. Alice watched the store during that time and Mercy was nearby if Alice needed help. During school hours John saw his clients on the porch. If John needed the privacy of his office, Mercy gave the children a recess or moved their lessons out to the porch.

Mercy also knew there were children of the workers in Mercyville who should also be educated. Many of their parents were barely literate themselves and lack of education would mean those children would have fewer opportunities to improve themselves. With John accompanying her, she asked to speak to the congregation after church, offering her services as teacher. She intended to bring the Mercyville children into her classroom with Mary Hope and Richard, but the preacher immediately offered to set up school in the chapel so an evening school could be established. Mercy taught the four children who were old enough to begin lessons. Since school was in the evening and would finish after dark, the parents were allowed to accompany their children. The first night, she asked the parents to sit in the pews behind the students. Mercy could see they were closely observing everything and were learning right along with their children. She made sure she saw the recognition of understanding among the adults before she proceeded to the next lesson. Before long, every adult in the village crowded into the pews, eager to learn the reading, writing, and arithmetic that Miss Mercy was teaching.

Another change that year was that John decided they should cut no more trees from their own property. The cleared areas were planted in peaches and orchard grass was allowed to grow between the rows, but there was still a problem with erosion of the cleared areas. For a while the crew only cut single trees in the forest that John had marked for harvest. Even though the pine forest soon replenished itself, John decided anything else would be too much. He had seen soil erosion ruin other farms. Rather than continue cutting, word was sent out from the store that the mill would begin buying felled trees from surrounding farms.

An oily and unshaved farmer named Seth Pryce took it upon himself to organize the farmers along the creek in selling their lumber to the mill. Before long, he demanded higher prices for the raw timber than the resulting lumber could be sold for. John balked and there was a stand-off with Pryce. As the supply of logs waiting to be cut at the mill dwindled, Pryce came to the store almost daily, bringing his pitiful wife with him. He asked to see random merchandise, handled it with his grubby hands and asked endless questions and then left without buying anything. It was intended to harass Mercy. Pryce terrified her, but she was determined to never show him her fear. She faced him boldly and spoke directly to him. Even more than she detested Pryce, Mercy felt sorry for his woman, who jumped when he spoke, flinched if he moved too suddenly, and seemed more like a beaten dog than a human being.

Pryce eventually accepted John's offered price, but only if he alone would be the one to drive the farmer's logs to market in his own wagon. He would also receive the full payment for the delivery. John suspected Pryce had intimidated the other farmers into using his service, for which he was likely taking a handsome cut of the proceeds. But without the timber they would either have to shut down the mill or harvest too much from their own land, so the undesirable arrangement was established. After unloading the logs at the mill, Pryce always came to the store, swaggering and spitting tobacco juice where he pleased, and waving his chit to be paid as it if were a victory banner. Mercy did not want to be alone with Pryce. She made sure John was in his office on the days Pryce was scheduled to make a delivery. To be on the safe side she started keeping John's loaded pistol under the service counter.

* * * * *

A year later Mercy was teaching arithmetic when she heard a carriage come up the road and stop outside. Carriages were lighter than the wagons most people in the parish drove and sounded different. She was so intent on the lesson that she barely noticed the sound of fine ladies' shoes tap-tapping across the porch and going in the store.

Likely it was a woman from the low country, lost and asking directions. Many of the low country people came to the piedmont hills during the summer months to escape the heat and sickness. They mainly stayed in Augusta, but sometimes they came out into the country as a lark when they were bored. The road to Augusta was more defined than it used to be, but this woman had still lost her way, probably too stupid to tell east from west by the sun. She would track mud everywhere and leave after getting directions without so much as a thank you, as if she were vastly superior over country folks. Mercy decided Alice could deal with the inconvenience and continued the lesson.

It was quiet for a while, and then she heard urgent footsteps coming across the porch. Alice opened the door and motioned for Mercy.

"There's a lady here to see you," Alice whispered. "She asked for Mrs. Faure, but

I think she wants to see you."

"Me? Who is it?"

"She looks like a lady, but she's different. I think she's mulatto," Alice lowered her voice to a barely audible whisper on the last word, making Mercy want to laugh.

Mercy looked around Alice at the woman who was standing across the porch in the doorway of the store.

"I think it's high time I came out here to see my friend and my little namesake, don't you?" Mary Botts called out.

"Mary!" Mercy exclaimed, crossing the porch to greet her old friend. Alice's eyebrows went up almost to her scalp when Mercy kissed Mary on the cheek and hugged her closely. The two laughed merrily and swayed back and forth as they hugged. Mary was so fashionably and grandly dressed, even as she traveled, that Mercy felt dowdy and worn out next to her. When Mary pushed her away to arms length for a look, Mercy smoothed down the skirt of the wrinkled day dress she wore for teaching school and working in her store. "You look absolutely wonderful," Mary said genuinely, putting her gloved hand to Mercy's cheek, "so happy and healthy. It is wonderful to see you, Mercy."

It had been six years at least. Finally they broke away enough that Mercy could turn to Alice. Alice stood with her hands folded, but unable to mask the questioning look on her surprised face. Who was this unusual woman?

"Alice, please let me introduce my dear friend, Mary Botts. Mary simply rescued Sepia and me when I was left without a place to stay in Charles Town. She was my Aunt Charity's dressmaker long before that and," she turned to Mary, "I think you sewed my first real dress for me didn't you? And Mary, this is my friend, Alice Lovett."

Mary smiled graciously at Alice and curtsied deeply. Alice, to her credit, returned the curtsy and then in the frontier fashion bravely stuck out her hand for Mary to shake. Mary took Alice's hand warmly, holding it in both her own hands as she smiled and said, "Mercy has written so many good things about you, Mrs. Lovett. It is truly a pleasure to meet you."

"Alice. Please call me Alice," Alice said, feeling awkward. This colored woman really should use a "Miss" used before her first name, but Mary Botts had already addressed Mercy without the "Miss" so Alice did not want to be a prig about it, and especially in front of Mercy. And it seemed like Mary Botts was someone important, anyways. Maybe she wasn't really colored after all. She had heard that some French women could look like that sometimes.

"Thank you Alice, and please, you can call me Mary if you like. Everyone does."

Mary was taken into the school room to see it and to meet her namesake, Mary Hope. Mary Hope was enchanted and was impertinent enough to ask, "How long will you be staying?"

"Mary Hope!" Mercy scolded. As much as she tried to instill good manners, Mary Hope was growing up wild out here on the frontier.

"No, Mother. I only meant to say that I hope Aunt Mary can stay with us a long time," she explained sweetly, then turning to Mary, "Can you?"

Mary laughed musically and replied, "Well, when I left Sepia in charge of the store I promised her I would be back in time for the fall orders, so I guess I could stay until then, that is, if your mother and father will have me for that long."

That afternoon, after Mary was settled in one of the extra bedrooms, she sat with Mercy and Mary Hope in the cool shade on the veranda. Mary Hope could scarcely leave Mary's side; she was so enchanted by their visitor. Mercy had to gently scold her daughter as she lightly fingered the lace at Mary's elbows, traced the embroidered sleeve and bodice of her dress, and admired Mary's hair and the hat she still wore. Mary only giggled and hugged the child to her, with Mercy protesting that she was only encouraging Mary Hope's bad behavior.

Athenia, the woman Mercy had hired from the village to do her cooking and housekeeping, was almost bursting with pride when she came out on the porch with Aunt Charity's best tea service. It was too fine and precious for use on the porch, but Mercy let it go, understanding Athenia's need to celebrate this occasion. Athenia knew Mary from the Charles Town church and was completely grateful to Mary for sending them here to this new life. There, she had been too dark to be hired in a house and her husband only worked the filthiest day jobs whenever he was lucky enough to get them. Mercy could see Athenia wanted nothing more than to take Miss Mary's hand and show her around her new cabin, the mill, and all of Mercyville.

"Athenia, I just had an idea," Mercy said. "Do you think we could give Mary a tour of the village after church on Sunday, and then maybe after that we could all have our lunch up here at the house? Do you think everyone would want to do that?"

"Oh, yes'm, Miss Mercy. They all be so happy to see Miss Mary again and I know everyone want to have church meeting with her."

Alice and Lancaster arrived at the house early on Sunday morning. Since the Freeman house was on their way to church, the Freemans and Lovetts always walked to church as a group. It was a pleasant walk, with Richard and Mary Hope running ahead and Alice and Mercy walking arm-in-arm. This morning, with Mary joining them, it was almost like a party. They walked past the store and then on down the path to the mill and finally to the village. Mercy looked ahead to the end of the lane and saw that the entire population was lined up outside the church door, waiting for them - or actually waiting for Mary.

Mary graciously walked toward them with her hands outstretched, greeting the first in line with a kiss. She slowly made her way down the line, taking the men by the hand, kissing the women on both cheeks and calling each one by name. She knelt down to talk to the children and held the new babies born after the people had arrived here from Charles Town. Everyone beamed at her, a few with tears running. It was a wonderful reunion. At the end of the line Mary announced that she felt like she had come home.

After a powerful hymn singing, the preacher shortened his sermon. As he brought the sermon to a hasty conclusion, Mary leaned into Mercy's shoulder to whisper behind her fan, "Seem like someone can smell all dat fry chicken." Mercy choked into her handkerchief and her shoulders shook with suppressed laughter. Mary Botts had not changed at all.

Mary took her time with the tour of the village, entering each cabin and exclaiming over it as the family beamed with pride. She walked slowly up the lane, arm-in-arm with one person after another. They all went as a group to inspect the mill. Although it was idle on Sunday, the men proudly showed her the workings of the machinery. Mary said she loved the smell of the fresh sawdust and praised how open and airy the shed was.

Then the group made its way to the Freeman house. Most of the women had gone ahead to help. Athenia was bossing and calling out orders, making sure everything was right. Long tables filled with food were set up in the shade of the side veranda with some of the older children assigned to fanning away the flies. After the blessing, Mary was told to go through the line first and she politely took a little bit from every serving platter and dish. Looking at the abundance of food, Mercy wondered if every garden had been picked bare and if there was a chicken left to scratch in the village. As soon as their plates were filled, everyone settled around the porches and lawn to eat.

"Your Aunt Charity would be so proud of you," Mary said quietly to Mercy as they sat on the veranda after lunch. Some of the men organized a game on the grass. It was an ancient one that was most likely brought from Africa. John, Lancaster and Richard joined in, ignoring the teasing and laughter as they struggled to understand the rules. Sleeping babies were laid on blankets under the shade trees and Mary Hope sat on the edge of the porch with two girls close to her age, carefully keeping their Sunday dresses clean while happily swinging their bare feet in simple rhythm.

After a while the girls were called away by their mothers and Mary motioned for Mary Hope to come sit on her lap. Mary Hope reclined across Mary's lap with her head against Mary's shoulder, relaxed and secure.

"You are so pretty, Aunt Mary," Mary Hope said, fingering Mary's curled hair.

"So are you," Mary said, hugging Mary Hope to her and kissing her cheek.

"I wish I had blue eyes like Mama, though."

"Don't you like my brown eyes?" Mary teased. Mary Hope giggled. Mary continued, "I got my brown eyes and all this curly hair from my great grandmamma."

Mercy caught Mary's eye and gave a slight shake of her head.

"Then I bet she was pretty too," Mary Hope said.

"She came from Africa," Mary said, ignoring Mercy.

"Maybe my great-grandmother came from Af'ica too, and that's where I got my brown eyes and curly hair," Mary Hope concluded as she dozed off.

With the dishes washed and the leftover food on the tables combined and covered with a cloth, the women scattered on the lawn, drifting into quiet conversation or lightly napping. The game finished and Lancaster and John challenged the other men to a fishing contest. Richard came running up to ask his mother if he could go too, and then ran to catch up, with Alice and the other ladies with her on the porch smiling at the sight. Alice, Mercy, and Mary talked in hushed tones while Mary Hope napped on Mary's lap. Mercy was so relaxed leaning back in her rocking chair that she did not realize she had drifted off until there was a sudden and frantic commotion at the edge of the lawn. She came fully upright just in time to see children scrambling back to their mothers as Seth Pryce staggered into view, clutching his bullwhip in his hand.

He was one of those poor white crackers who loved making a big show of cracking his whip. It made a big, snapping pop and he cracked that whip often, just to show that he could. It was coiled now and Mercy was determined it would stay so. He did not need to be frightening the women and children with it on this Sunday afternoon.

Mary Hope was now awake and left Mary's lap to stand beside her mother's chair. Before he spotted Mercy on the porch, Mercy turned to her daughter and said, "Sweet Pea, I need you to be a good girl for me. I want you to go through the house and out the back door and then run down to the mill pond and tell your father that Mr. Pryce is here to see him. I need you to run as fast as you can, do you hear me?"

Mary looked at Mercy with concern, "Shall I go with her Mercy?"

"No. He is less likely to notice Mary Hope going by herself. Now, Mary Hope, walk across the porch and don't start running until you are through the back door and across the yard. Tell him it's Mr. Pryce. You hear?"

"Yes, Mama."

"Now go."

Mercy waited a moment until she was sure Mary Hope had enough time.

"Mary," she said as quietly and calmly as if she was discussing the weather. "My pistol is in Aunt Charity's desk in the top right drawer. The drawer is locked and the key is in the top left drawer under my ledger book. Would you please go and bring it to me, and keep it hidden so he won't see it. Go around the veranda and through the back door so he won't see you. It is already loaded, so be careful with it."

Mary nodded then rose, holding her teacup as calmly as if she was going to fill it. She circled around the veranda to the back door.

Only then, Mercy rose and stepped into the sunshine at the edge of the porch. Alice came to stand beside her. In the yard, Pryce pulled a flat bottle of cheap whiskey from his pocket and took a long drink from it. The women in the yard were silently gathering their children and slowly inching away from the intruder and well out of the range of his whip. When they were at a safe distance they stood, with babies in arms and quieting hands on the older children. All of them were waiting for what would happen next.

"My husband will be here momentarily, Mister Pryce," Mercy called out confidently across the yard. Although her knees were weak and almost shaking she willed her voice to be strong and authoritative.

Pryce looked up at her in mock surprise, squinting one eye as if the light hurt his eyes, "Y'all having some kind of nigger picnic here, Miz Freeman?"

Mercy remained silent as Pryce came unsteadily toward the porch.

"Stop right there," Mercy commanded when he reached the base of the stairs below her. "My husband will be here momentarily."

"Y'all do love your niggers up here don't you," he said and cackled drunkenly.

"Sorriest bunch a nigger lovers in the parish, and all right here in Niggersville."

"I said John will be here in a moment, Mr. Pryce. But for now, I can see you are drunk and you need to shut your stupid mouth until you can speak to him."

Pryce glared at her with pure hatred. He was standing so close she could smell the stench of cheap whiskey and soured sweat on him. She could see the individual whiskers on his unshaved chin. She could even see the broken blood vessels in the whites of his eyes. She wanted nothing more than to turn and run away. For a split second, Mercy thought he might decide to use the whip on her. But she put the thought away and glared back at him, standing her ground.

"No, ma'am. I 'spect you will do just fine. I got a message for you and your husband from the boys. A real important message."

"You can give your message to me. I will tell Mr. Freeman. Then you can leave."

"The other farmers, the <u>white</u> farmers, and me has been talking."

More likely, you have been stirring things up, Mercy thought, but said nothing. She raised one eyebrow and waited.

"We don't like it one bit that y'all is paying all these heathen niggers to work in your mill instead of hiring good Christian men. It ain't right. Not one bit right."

"These are Christian men too, Mr. Pryce. They were in church just this morning."

The insult was not lost on Pryce. There was no white church in this part of the parish yet. Likely it had been months since any of the farmers he referenced had been in any sort of worship, unless they considered the shabby old log cabin way down the creek that sold home brewed whiskey to be such a place.

"Only 'cuz y'all give 'em a nigger church is why. Why, we heard you was even using your little church to teach all your niggers to read and write and you know that's again' the law now."

The new Georgia law he referred to, passed in 1755, only prohibited teaching slaves to write. Teaching slaves to read was allowed since it was necessary for them to be able to read the Bible. Mercy was careful, even though the people she taught were not slaves and technically exempt from the law. But she doubted Pryce was intelligent enough to realize the distinction between reading and writing. He definitely did not understand the distinction between these people and slaves. To him, every person of color was a slave.

.

"Forced ignorance by law, if it comes, will be a tragedy, Mr. Pryce. But as long as it is legal, I will teach anyone who wants to learn - including you. I may even continue teaching, even if such a law is implemented, as my civil protest."

Her words were beyond him; even if he had been sober he would have struggled to understand what she was saying, but the defiant words gave her confidence to continue facing him.

"Don't need none of your learnin'," Pryce shouted at her.

With that he spit a long and reckless stream of tobacco juice. Mercy forced herself to maintain his gaze and not look where the errant blast of spittle landed on the top step, just inches from the hem of her skirt. Mary took her arm at the elbow, letting Mercy know she had returned. "I got it," she said softly to Mercy without moving her lips.

"I come to warn you, Miz Freeman, both you and your nigger-lovin' husband. The boys don't think it right that you hire all them niggers instead of white men to work your mill. You is takin' money away from the good Christian men who deserve it."

"They had their chance," Mercy shot back at him. "If they had ever bothered to come to work more than three days a week when we first started the mill they would still have their jobs today. You can't run a mill only half the time and a mill does not run itself without workers."

"Y'all can't run a mill without the wood either, now, can ya?" he sneered with an evil grin.

"What do you mean?"

"What I mean, Miz Freeman, is that if you don't clear out all these here niggers and hire the men back, we ain't gonna sell timber to you no more. We all decided we don't do business with niggers."

Mercy took a deep breath. This was getting out of hand. Where was John? Without fully realizing what she was saying she spat out, "You and your boys haven't been so particular about doing business with me, though, have you?"

"No, and when you get rid of your niggers, we will be happy to keep bringing our timber to you, same as afore."

"I don't think you quite understand what I am saying, Mr. Pryce."

Pryce stared at her as if she was talking gibberish.

"I am quadroon, Mr. Pryce." Mercy was vaguely aware of Alice's gasp behind her. "So even if I fired every free Negro in Mercyville, you would still have to deal with me, wouldn't you?"

"I don't rightly understand ma'am." Pryce did not know what she meant by quadroon.

"It means that I am one-fourth Negro. My grandmother was a slave. She was raped by a white man as soon as she left Africa, so my mother was half-white. I am the child of my mother's white master. My mother was his slave, so I am one quarter. I am as much a 'nigger' as you call us, as anyone else standing in this yard."

Pryce glared at her and wobbled unsteadily. He was not sure if he believed what she was saying. It was not possible. She was making fun of him.

Mercy felt Mary's grip on her arm, reassuring her. "So am I," Mary said levelly to him and with pride. "I am octoroon, or one-eighth Negro."

"Is she yo'r mammy then?" Pryce asked.

Several of the women in the yard snorted in laughter in spite of themselves.

"No, Mr. Pryce. If she was my mother, I would be one-sixteenth black. Half of one-eighth is one-sixteenth, not one-fourth. And if I was only one-sixteenth, I would be legally white in every colony on this continent."

"Y'all are all God-damned abominations, ever last one of you," Pryce raged, starting up the steps. At the same time, John and Lancaster came through the door from inside the house. Mary Hope had told them to circle around and come through the house, and as they came through the central hall, they were hearing the last words Pryce shouted at Mercy.

"Stop right there, Pryce," John commanded. Pryce came up another step before he thought better of it and stopped. Then he turned and started down the steps and toward the path. John went down the steps toward him.

"This is an abomination, the deggidation of the races, the work of the devil, and evil in the eyes of God!" he railed drunkenly, brandishing his whip. "Y'all will all burn in the fires of hell."

"Tell your men..." John began. He said it three times before he had enough of Pryce's attention to stop the tirade. "Tell your men that we will no longer buy any of the wood that Seth Pryce brings to us. Tell them our business arrangement is hereby cancelled, Pryce."

Pryce looked up at John stupidly. "You can't do that. What you going to do without wood? You can't run a mill without wood."

"No, Pryce, you misunderstand me. I only said we would not be buying wood from you. Go back with that message. I will send that message around too. Tell them I will even come and get their wood at no charge. You are finished here. If you so much as set foot on my property again, or threaten my wife, I will shoot you as a trespasser and a scoundrel. Now, get off my property."

Pryce pointed the whip up at them, ready to shout out something else, but realized it was futile. He was completely cut out of the deal. His plan had backfired. The farmers would sell directly to the mill now. He turned, took a sloppy swig from the whiskey bottle, and staggered away down the path.

Mercy was weak with relief. John came back up the steps, but before he could reach her she turned to Alice, taking both her hands, "I am so, so sorry, Alice. I never should have lied to you."

"You never lied to me, Mercy. I never asked you about it, so how could you have lied? To tell you the truth, I always wondered about John, but never about you. It does not matter. Not to me. You are my sister. How could a little thing like this change that? I still love you."

"I'm colored too, Alice," Mary said lightly, handing the pistol to John. "Just so you know."

Alice laughed, "Yes, I know that now. But honestly? I thought you must be French."

"People think that a lot. I guess it's because of my stylish dresses. But John is French, did you know that? His name used to be Jean Faure in Charles Town. I forgot and that's why I said that when I first came here. It's still hard to think of him being Johnny Freeman."

"And here I was all along thinking that John might be colored," Alice said, shaking her head.

"People think that a lot. But I don't think it's my stylish dresses." John echoed Mary's words, making them all laugh.

Mary Hope observed, "Mama if you are a quadroon, and one quarter, does that make me one eighth, then? What is that, what was that word?"

"The word is not important, Mary Hope," Mary said, cutting in. "What is important is that you are you. But the word is octoroon, and you are the same as me. It means we both have a great-grandmother who came from Africa."

And with that, Mary Hope was happy. She was just like her beloved Aunt Mary.

Everyone was nervous after Pryce's visit, but on Monday the gears were engaged with the turning mill wheel and the buzzing of the saw resumed. Alice opened the store and Mercy resumed lessons with Richard and Mary Hope. For a few days they were all jumpy and, under John's strict instructions, no one walked alone on the paths between the Lovett and Freeman houses, near the store, the sawmill, and the village. After a week they breathed easier, especially when the first white farmer showed up with his own lumber, insisting John did not need to send a wagon and driver. "We is all happy to be rid of that skunk, Mr. Freeman," he said. "Sorry if he made you think otherwise."

* * * * *

The summer was hot that year. It was good growing weather, but that was about all it was good for. Mercy dismissed both schools until fall when the weather would be cooler. It was too hot for the students to concentrate and she needed a break anyway.

She confided to Alice and Mary one afternoon when they were sitting in the shelter of the dogtrot, fanning themselves between breezes, that she just did not feel right. She wondered aloud if she could be pregnant again, but Mary said it was likely just the heat. She was feeling the same and she was long past the age of having another baby.

Mercy had expected they would have more children, especially when Mary Hope had been conceived so quickly after their wedding, but that was not to be. Alice was the same. It looked like Richard would be her only child, too. Long ago, Alice and Mercy promised each other that they would watch over the other's child if one was ever left motherless. Beyond that, they were raising Richard and Mary Hope like they were brother and sister.

A few weeks after Seth Pryce's visit, Mercy woke as the morning sun began shining into the bedroom. She lay completely uncovered, but still wet with sweat. Her shift was nearly soaked through. John was sleeping deeply beside her and snoring softly. Since they moved into the new house, John had approached their marriage bed with increased vigor. She supposed it was nature telling him to fill this big house with children. He had been amorous again when he came to bed that night and Mercy had willingly accepted him in spite of the heat, amazed at the passion he displayed in spite of his advancing age. He was forty-seven years old. She was twenty five.

Feeling exhausted and like she had barely slept, Mercy got out of bed quietly. She would wash at the basin and change into a fresh shift before John woke. But before she started her toilette, she stepped out onto the second floor gallery, peeking out first to see if anyone else was there. Even though the sun was rising, the sky was still very dark. Maybe there were thunderclouds overhead, blotting out the sky. Rain would only cool things down for a little while, and then make it hotter when the sun was fully up. She went to the railing, fanning herself. It was only marginally cooler on the gallery. The sun was showing brighter now, lighting the porch. She would have to go inside soon; she could not stand outside like this, half-dressed, even this early in the morning.

The dawn was strangely quiet. Then she realized it was too quiet. There was no morning sound from the birds in the woods, calling out as they woke with the dawn. The sky overhead was still black. Mercy looked up to see the clouds, but instead saw stars shining. It was night time. It was still the middle of the night. She looked again at the sun, rising through the trees. It was not the sun at all. It was the mill. The mill was on fire.

"John!" she screamed, running back inside. "John. Wake up. Fire! The mill is on fire."

John sat up in bed, looking at her like it was a dream. "What?"

"Fire! The mill is on fire! Or something down there is. Get up! We have to get down there.

John ran out onto the balcony and came back almost immediately. "That is two fires, at least," he said, pulling on his breeches and thrusting his feet into his shoes without putting on stockings first. Mercy was similarly rushing through getting dressed.
.
Mary was knocking on their door, carrying a candle with Mary Hope following close behind her. "What can I do?" she asked.

"Stay here with Mary Hope." Mary said.

"You are staying here too, Mercy," John was adamant.

"I am going, John. People may be hurt. I am coming with you."

John knew better than to argue at this point. Lancaster was already downstairs, after banging on the door he had opened it and was calling out to John and coming up the stairs, Alice was right behind him screaming out for Mercy. They had seen the fire from their house too.

John went to the wardrobe, pulled out his rifle, and went to Mary. "Can you use this?"

Mary looked it over in less than two seconds. "Yes."

"Keep Mary Hope and Richard here with you. Do not leave this house. Bolt the doors after we leave and don't let anyone in. If anyone breaks through, shoot him. If the house catches fire, take the children out the back and into the woods. Do what you have to do to protect yourself and the children."

Mary nodded. Then he added something that made her blood run cold. "If we don't come back, take Mary Hope and Richard with you back to Charles Town."

With Mary Hope restrained by Mary, terrified and screaming out after them, they went running down the path. Mercy and Alice gathered up all the quilts they could carry before they ran out of the house. Soaked in water at the mill pond they could help beat out small fires. Mercy stumbled once in the dark as they ran, but the quilts helped cushion her fall. Her knees were skinned and she could feel the blood running as she ran.

When they arrived, the scene was an inferno. Flames were shooting high from the mill shed's roof and the church at the end of the lane was completely in flames. Wisely, the people had realized the church could be rebuilt. All their efforts were focused on dismantling the sawmill's machinery and removing it from the burning building. The men were ripping the machinery from its mountings, mostly by sheer muscle. The women and older children had formed a line, passing buckets filled from the mill pond down the line to where they were thrown on the hottest parts of the fire.

With Mercy screaming after him, John ran directly into the burning shed to help the men. "John, stop! Get out of there. Get everyone out of there, now. Oh, Sweet Jesus, let it go. Let it go, John."

Looking up, Mercy could see that the flames were breaking through the underside of the shed's room. Individual shingles were glowing bright red and orange; and glowing embers were beginning to fall like rain on the men below. Still, they continued wrenching the machinery loose. The main saw blade assembly was freed, and several of them began dragging it from the building, with Lancaster helping and shouting out instructions. The bucket line was going faster than ever, but the fire was even bigger. One bucket was used to douse a man whose nightshirt was set aflame from the falling embers.

"John!" Mercy screamed and screamed, feeling like something had torn loose in her throat. "Get out! Get out!"

John looked around at Mercy. Then he looked up at the burning roof above them, just as the last bracket of the saw feeder assembly came loose. There was a shout from the men and they picked up the long tray-like table and started carrying it out of the shed. John was helping them. Whole, burning shingles were raining down on them now. "John!" Mercy screamed and screamed again. Alice was fighting her and holding her back, afraid she would run in to get him. Mercy struggled and fought against Alice, trying to free herself. Buckets of water were thrown on the men as they half-ran with the feeder assembly, soaking them to keep the fire off their clothing.

Then, to Mercy it seemed as if everything had suddenly slowed down, like something had broken inside her head and like time wasn't passing. The men were closer to the doors and closer to being out from under the burning roof, but they were barely moving. She looked up and saw the flames licking high up into the night sky, and the roof completely glowing bright orange and yellow with flames now. The buckets of water were being thrown on the men coming toward the door. The long arches of water did almost nothing to protect them from the inferno above. Mercy looked up and saw the burning roof beginning to sag under its own weight. It hung there for a long moment. Then it let go.

She looked to John, at the far end of the table with another man. He was looking at her and running toward her. She tried to scream again, but nothing would come out. She was looking into John's eyes and he into hers when the fire, falling like a curtain from above, struck him and the man running beside him, knocking them to the ground. Then John was gone.

* * * * *

Mercy was only vaguely aware of things in the days that followed.

First she was aware of the sweet scent of Alice's dress when Alice spun her around from the horrific scene and pressed Mercy's face into her breast. She thought that Alice must have used lavender soap the last time she bathed.

Then she was aware of standing on the veranda with Alice and Mary while a lumber wagon drove by on the lawn. Seth Pryce lay on the back of the lumber wagon and the white farmers walked slowly behind the wagon, holding their hats over their hearts as they looked up to where Mercy stood. She was aware of the rope marks burned deeply into Seth Pryce's neck.

She was aware of Mary Hope's small hand slipped into hers as they stood by the open grave that would receive John's body. The men were using ropes to carefully lower the coffin into the hole. All the people of Mercyville surrounded her, some of them crying. She could not cry. She could barely take a breath. There was another fresh grave nearby, someone else she knew but could not remember now. They were standing near the ashes where the church had been. Alice and Mary were there beside her too, holding her up, holding onto her, comforting her, but Mercy knew if it wasn't for Mary Hope's small hand in hers, she would have jumped down into that hole for her body to be buried with John. Her heart was there with him anyway.

Warren County, Georgia
1781-1795

Mary Hope Freeman Lovett was thirty-one years old. She had one child, now three years old, and was married to a man who did not love her. He had even refused to live with her. Her life was over.

She had also come to the sad conclusion that nothing would ever change in Warren County, Georgia. They were all part of a new country now and had been for five years. Georgia was a state, instead of a colony, and as the old colonial system was thrown out old St. Paul Parish had been divided up and redrawn into new counties with new names. The place Mary Hope lived, and had always lived, was now in Warren County. She had a new address without ever having the benefit of moving.

Mary Hope wanted to travel. She wanted to see Savannah and even go on to Charleston, as Charles Town was now called. Her mother, Mercy, and Aunt Mary, as everyone called Mary Botts these days, still called it Charles Town. Since Mary Hope's father died, they had never changed anything else so why would they change that? Mercy had been presented there at the royal governor's ball in 1746 and had even danced with Governor Glen. The two old ladies had told that story so many times that Mary Hope almost felt like she had been there too, dancing, of all things, the minuet. How quaint.

Mary Hope had been to Charleston only once. Surely it was not unreasonable for her to go there again, but Mercy was impossible. Aunt Mary, who had to be at least a hundred now, and Mercy were as firmly ensconced in this old yellow house as the church bell was in the tower above the old church down in Mercyville. Except that bell had a lot more activity than those old women ever did. Her mother-in-law was the same. Miss Alice came down the path and opened the store every day. You could practically set a clock by her. After she closed the store she would come and sit on the porch for a while with Mercy and Aunt Mary where they would tell the same stories and remember the same old times and hum and cluck their tongues until Mary Hope thought she would scream.

Richard, her husband if she could even call him that anymore, had been away from Mercyville. When they called for men to join the fight against England, Richard Lovett left his mother and joined them. Miss Alice begged him not to go, practically threw herself on the ground and clutched at his ankles to keep him from going, but he went anyway. After that, Mercy said for Mary Hope to be nice to Miss Alice. After all, Miss Alice had nobody else. Her husband, Lancaster, went up north to Virginia to look after things after his father died and had died there himself. Miss Alice almost never got over that – him dying and her not being there with him.

Mary Hope's one and only trip had been to Charleston. When Richard joined the colonial army, Charles Town was as far as he got. He was there when the South Carolina militia routed the British from Sullivan's Island on June 28, 1776. News of that victory, the first defeat of the British, encouraged the Continental Congress gathered in Philadelphia enough that they went ahead and signed the treasonous Declaration of Independence from King George on July 4, assuring their own executions as traitors if the colonists were not successful in the war that followed. Richard hoped to join the militia as they moved north to defend the capital, but he was part of a garrison left behind to defend Charleston should the British decide to return and attack the Charleston harbor again.

He was gravely disappointed, bored to distraction, and sent long letters home to Miss Alice, clearly homesick. Even though Mary Hope and Richard had had an understanding since they were twelve years old, he only wrote to her occasionally. By Christmas of 1777, Mary Hope was driven to vexation that he had found another girl in Charleston. There was snow that winter and after it melted and it looked like spring, Mercy finally agreed to let her go to see him. Travel by sea was too dangerous with British warships patrolling the coast, so it would be a long, overland trip all the way across South Carolina. Aunt Mary went as her chaperone and they stayed with Sepia who now lived in Aunt Mary's old house in Charleston. Aunt Mary knew the city and Mercy was assured she would keep a close eye on Mary Hope and prevent any mischief.

Richard was happy to see them, but only too late Mary Hope realized he would have been equally ecstatic to see anyone from home. By then she was pregnant. When that was revealed, Aunt Mary all but forced Richard into the marriage. It was not an ideal situation, but when Mary Anna was born back in Mercyville, and only seven months after the wedding, she had the last name of Lovett and both grandmothers, Mercy and Alice to look after her. With two women named Mary in the house already, they called her Anna.

Baby Anna took to her Grandma Mercy, even more than she took to her mother it seemed. While Mary Hope lay in her bed for days after giving birth, barely able to move, Mercy would carry little Anna around the room, singing softly and talking to her new granddaughter. Once, when Mary Hope knew her mother thought she must be sleeping, she clearly overheard Mercy softly crooning, "I'se your old grandmamma, Miss Anna. I'se your old grandmamma Mercy. Ain't nobody ever gone love you more than your old grandmamma Mercy loves you, Miss Anna."

"Good Heavens, Mother!" Mary Hope exclaimed rising up on her elbow in bed. "I am her mother, am I not? And why are you talking like one of the people down in the village?"

Mercy turned to face Mary Hope as she nuzzled the baby's cheek against her own, gently rocking as she continued defiantly in the same softly crooning voice, "Your grandmamma a quadroon, Miss Anna, and your mama is octoroon. But you is white, Miss Anna, you is white."

"Yes she is, Mother. And I simply won't have any of that talk. She doesn't need to know anything about all that nonsense. As you said, Anna is white." One sixteenth was enough, even in Georgia. Her baby was white.

Without responding, Mercy laid the baby in her crib. "She asleep now," she whispered. "Good night, Mary Hope."

No one else called her Mary Hope since she was a little girl, but Mercy called her that when she wanted to remind her daughter who she was and her place in the household. Mercy put a finger to her lips, shushing Mary Hope who was sitting fully upright and staring daggers as her mother tiptoed out the room.

Although Charles Town fell to the British in the siege of 1780 and some five thousand troops, including Richard, were captured, the ultimate defeat of Cornwallis at Yorktown in 1781 ended the war. Richard came home, but refused to share the bed in the rooms Mercy had given over to Mary Hope and Anna. He slept on a sofa in the library for two nights. On the third night, Mary Hope made sure Anna was sleeping in her cradle, took a candle and went down to him. She had made herself as pretty as she could and wore only a light wrap over her shift. Her hair was down and freshly brushed, inviting.

Richard stirred on the sofa as she sat gingerly beside him. She placed a palm on his chest, feeling his strength beneath the night shirt. It had been three years. She leaned forward and kissed him, only to have him come fully awake and push her away roughly.

"It's only me, Richard. It's Mary, your wife," she said warmly, leaning into him again.

He grabbed her face in one hand and shoved her away roughly. "Go back upstairs, Mary."

"But I am your wife," she replied.

"I said go back upstairs."

Stung by his rejection and willing herself to be silent, and even more strongly not to cry, she picked up the candle and crossed as calmly as she could to the library door.

"I leave in the morning," he said. In her surprise, Mary Hope turned to face him. "I am going west." She stood silent in shock. "You and old Mary tricked me into this marriage. We are married in name only."

It was final. Mary Hope knew her life was over.

A year went by and then two with no word from him. Then came the day when Miss Alice came running up from the store as soon as the post wagon came. Mary Hope, Mercy and Aunt Mary were sitting on the porch for a few moments after lunch before they resumed their afternoon work. Miss Alice had a letter from Richard. He wrote that he bought a farm in Hancock County, only one county over.

"Well now, that is really going west!" Mary Hope said sarcastically, making Aunt Mary snort in laughter. All the women knew the complete story by now. There were no secrets in Mercyville.

"You should go to him, Mary. He asked about Anna in his letter," Miss Alice said hopefully. "I think he may have softened his resolve against you."

"I am not dragging my daughter across open country to God only knows where just so her father can have a look at her like she is a monkey in a circus! If he wants so all-fired much to see her he can just come back here." Aunt Mary nodded in agreement

"You could leave Anna here with us and go by yourself," Mercy suggested.

"I said I am not going!" Mary Hope almost shouted.

But after a week, with the three women working on her, Mary Hope agreed to make the trip. Strategically, all agreed Richard would be more agreeable if his mother, Miss Alice, accompanied Mary Hope. They were packed and set off in the delivery wagon early the next morning.

They reached the Lovett plantation by nightfall. Their driver stopped several times to ask or confirm directions and, as they drew closer, the reference to the Lovett farm became "plantation" instead, meaning Richard owned the required acreage and more than twenty slaves. He had established himself as part of the growing planter class. Mary Hope wondered where his money had come from, and decided it must be from the settlement of the Lovett estate back in Virginia and kept secret, even from his own mother.

Richard was more annoyed than welcoming with their surprise arrival. Even with his mother he was less than cordial. A servant showed them to rooms upstairs and said dinner would be served within the hour. Barely changed, Miss Alice and Mary Hope went to the dining room and were seated. Richard was nowhere to be seen. The first course was served and eaten. After it was cleared, Richard burst through the doors from the central hall. It was obvious he had been drinking. He sat insolently at the head of the table, took up his napkin, and signaled impatiently for the servants to serve the next course.

After the seemingly endless dinner was finished, with Richard tapping his whisky glass to be refilled so many times Mary Hope lost count, they moved to the parlor. It was elegantly but haphazardly furnished, lacking a woman's touch as Miss Alice quietly observed. After they settled, Mary Hope was startled by movement in a darkened corner. A handsome black woman, in a silk dress of the darkest russet, rose languidly from the chair to take Richard's empty glass and refill it from a decanter on the bureau. Richard slouched in his chair facing them. Mary Hope felt dowdy and countrified next to the elegantly dressed woman.

"Now ladies, to what do I owe this unexpected pleasure?" he said with obvious sarcasm.

"Richard!" Miss Alice exclaimed. "I am your mother."

Richard raised his glass to her and nodded impudently in his acknowledgement. "Muthah," he drawled.

He still had not looked directly at Mary Hope. He spoke in the lazy drawl of the emerging planter class he strove to emulate. His words came from the back of the mouth, slurred together, almost as though it was too much effort to bring them forward and someone else needed to do it for him, as apparently everything else was. Mary Hope, Mercy, Aunt Mary, and even Miss Alice, still spoke as upper-class Charleston residents, their speech more closely aligned with their counterparts in England. With the new separation from the Crown, English ways were falling out of favor and the planter's drawl was becoming popular. But rather than being fashionable, Richard's speech made him seem more like a spoiled and petulant child.

Mary Hope began. "When your letter came last week, your mother wanted to come to see you, of course."

"And she has. And she has." Richard agreed as patronizing as if he spoke to a child.

"You must have realized when you wrote she would want to see you."

"I do not recall including an invitation in that letter," he observed, pausing as if he was trying to remember, "to anyone."

They were all silent for a moment. Miss Alice looked horrified, ill almost. Mary Hope wanted nothing more than to run from the room and drive away in the farm wagon, even without her luggage.

Instead she swallowed. "I am your wife, Richard. I cannot understand why that is so disagreeable to you. We were always friends; as far back as I can remember. This is no way to treat us now."

Richard threw his hands out to his sides, palms up, as though he could not object, and sloshing his drink in the process. "Guilty. Guilty as charged, Mrs. Lovett," he mocked her sarcastically. The woman standing behind his chair barely concealed her smile as she reached to refill his glass. She was purely evil, Mary Hope decided.

"Richard, I have always loved you," she continued, ignoring the woman. "We have a child. I want to have more children. I cannot understand why I have become so distasteful to you, but I still want to have a family. If you do not want me here, we do not have to live together, Richard, I can remain in Mercyville."

For a split second, Richard looked at her with remorse, but then the bravado returned.

"And can you not understand, my dear wife, I do not wish to have any more pickaninnies with you? Our child was a mistake, and a freak of nature."

Miss Alice came bold upright and was aghast, but firm. "Richard! You will cease such disgraceful talk! Mary is your wife and Anna is your child. As such, you will show them the proper respect they deserve! What on earth has happened to you?"

Author's note: The term pickaninny is thought to originate in the 17th century, an Anglicized form from the Portuguese "penque ninas" or 'little children.' The term was initially used for small children of any race, but by the end of the 19th century was used exclusively for black children. The context of the term as a racial slur did not occur until the early decades of the 20th century. Miss Alice's strong objection to her son Richard's statement about her grandchild Anna would be in reaction to the second sentence.

"You forget, my dear mother, that my wife is a nigger."

With that, Alice bolted up, crossed to her son and slapped him soundly. It left an immediate and dark red hand print on the left side of his face. "You are no son of mine. I could not have produced such a cruel and odious creature as you, sir. You are not my son."

"No, I am not, mother," Richard said sadly, ignoring the slap. "The son you knew died in Charleston. I am all that is left."

He leaned back in his chair and put his hand to his shoulder. The hand was immediately taken by the women behind him. Then Richard looked at Mary Hope, the first time since their arrival. "I was ill in Charleston. After you came to me and we were married, I was ill. The scourge of the streets, they called it. I am no longer able to father a child, Mary, not for you, and not for my Delilah here. Not for any one."

As the full meaning of his words sank in, Mary Hope felt her cheeks burn with the shame of it, but also realized with relief that she was safe. If he was being truthful, the illness he carried had been contracted after she conceived Anna in Charleston. He could not have passed it to her.

After another pause, she rose to her feet to leave. Miss Alice stood also. "You are sorely wrong, Richard," Mary Hope said, glaring down at him. "Our daughter is white. With only one-sixteenth blood, she is legally white in every state of this country. She legally carries your name. You can not and you will not disown her. I will drag you through every court of this land if you try. But if you will not let me love you, I will let you go. You need not trouble yourself with us, any longer. We will go at first light."

"Forget me, Mary. Forget all about me," he said sadly as Mary Hope and Miss Alice reached the door.

"I can not," Mary Hope replied, not turning to look at him. "I will not."

But after Miss Alice was through the door and starting toward the stairs, Mary Hope did turn back as she closed the door. She saw Delilah, so appropriately named, kneeling in front of Richard, holding both his hands in her own and looking up at him tenderly as he wept. For a moment, before her hatred of Delilah began, Mary Hope was glad of that.

When they were back in Mercyville, Miss Alice withdrew into herself for a long while, barely stirring from her house as she grieved for her son. Mary Hope, on the other hand, was energized. She took over opening the store for Miss Alice, giving over the daytime care of Anna to her mother and Aunt Mary. Augusta was growing rapidly and with the lands relinquished by the Cherokee to the west being opened for settlement, their road from Augusta was busier than ever. People on their way west stopped for provisions and to water their horses. Mercy let travelers camp at no charge in a meadow down by the creek. The increased business at the store came in handy, as demand for the lumber produced by the mill was leveling off. They still sent lumber east to Augusta every week, but newer mills to the west were supplying the demand in that direction.

Mercy stayed up at the house while Anna napped in the afternoons, but Aunt Mary always came down to the store, 'just to keep Mary Hope company,' she would claim. She actually enjoyed helping with customers and sitting in the shade of the dogtrot with Mary Hope when they were not busy. Her eyesight was beginning to fail, but she could still see well enough in the bright light of the porch to sew and she made dress after little dress for Anna. Miss Alice eventually recovered enough to come down to the store in the afternoons, helping out inside or sitting and visiting with Aunt Mary.

Their only unpleasantness was during the summer months when the low country planters came north. They were often coarse and enterprising. Their rice plantations were enormously profitable and solely by virtue of that wealth they believed themselves to be royalty in the new order of things and above everyone else. The men would order the three women about in the shop, never satisfied with the service and disparaging of the goods offered. Their women were even worse, looking around with their noses wrinkled up as if something smelled bad and generally lacking in basic social graces. If they asked if there were satisfactory accommodations anywhere nearby, Aunt Mary would reply, "most of your people find the campgrounds down by the mill pond most agreeable,' so sweetly that Mary Hope could barely keep from laughing out loud. Aunt Mary would be cackling with laughter as they drove away.

* * * * *

Although she never knew her father, Anna grew up with four women who adored her. She had to mind and was expected to be diligent with her studies. She was a pleasant-natured and easy-going child and was never a problem. And she carried with her the confidence that she was loved.

Even though her mother would sigh and go in the house when they started up, Anna loved to hear the stories that Grandma Mercy and Aunt Mary told her. After dinner they would usually sit on the porch of the house and Grandma or Aunt Mary would start with 'do you remember…" and they would be off and running.

From them, Anna learned that Grandma Mercy had a grandmother named Bess who came on a ship from far away Africa. She had another family there before she was captured. Bess had a daughter who was named Dove and Dove had been Grandma Mercy's mother. But Dove died and Mercy had been raised by her father's sister, Great Aunt Charity, who was the lady in the painting in the library and had also been a good friend to Aunt Mary. Great Aunt Charity had a slave named Patience who helped keep Mercy a secret. Grandpa John had been Grandma Mercy's husband and he was also from Charleston, but his father and mother were from France. He had saved Great Aunt Charity's brother from marrying a woman who would have stolen all his money and had a bad son who was mean to Bess and Dove. Grandpa John died in a bad fire down at the mill a long time ago, and it still made Grandma Mercy cry a little when she told it.

She loved all those stories and heard them so many times she almost felt like she had been there too.

Miss Alice was her other grandmother. Miss Alice was always sad except when she saw Anna. When Georgia claimed lands between the thirty-first and thirty-fifth parallels all the way to the Mississippi River, a nephew from Virginia passed through on his way there and invited Alice to come with him. It was rough, unsettled country, but in her letters she wrote that it reminded her of those first happy days when they were all settling in St. Paul Parish. As boundaries were redrawn over the next two decades, the nephew's land was part of at least three different territories, but ultimately it would become Shelby County, Alabama. Miss Alice was happy and said she would live the rest of her life there. Her house in Georgia was closed up. Someday, if Anna wanted it, the house would be hers.

If she asked about her father, she was told he was Miss Alice's son and lived far, far away. But she had never known him so she really did not ask about him much.

Anna always helped in the store, but when she was sixteen and finished with her studies Mary Hope decided it was time for Anna to go to Augusta and learn the business they did there. Until Mary Hope was satisfied Anna understood the business and could conduct it herself, Anna would ride along to market in the delivery wagon. Mary Hope even promised that after their transactions were finished she would take Anna around town and show her things. They would eat in a restaurant and even stay in a hotel.

Aunt Mary sent off for patterns and fabric to make both Mary Hope and Anna new dresses to wear in Augusta. Augusta had been the state capital continuously now since 1786 and it was an important city. Aunt Mary knew the importance of a woman's wardrobe in such a place and was determined to have Mary Hope and Anna properly presented when they went to town.

The trip was timed so they only stayed on the road one night each way. They arrived in Augusta late Tuesday and were up early on Wednesday, making their deliveries and refilling the wagon with their purchases. Anna was introduced to the merchants who had done business with her mother and her grandmother before her. Seen as the successor in the family enterprise, Anna was treated with the respect due her. She asked intelligent questions and Mary Hope was proud of her conduct.

As they climbed back up in the wagon at their final stop, and Anna's eyes were shining with the excitement of the day, she looked across the wagon bed to the next wagon where a young man stood, holding the reins of his horses. He was tall and fair and had ginger hair, a color Anna had never seen. He looked openly at her and lifted his hat, smiling a broad smile that gleamed white. Mary Hope immediately stepped between them, firmly taking Anna's arm as she sat down on the wagon bench so Anna had no choice but to sit. Anna could not help looking back over her shoulder as they drove away. He was still looking and she smiled back at him in spite of herself as they drove away.

The next time they were in town and the wagon stopped outside the same merchant, he was suddenly there, graciously offering her a hand as she stepped down, using the spokes of the wheel as a ladder. Then he offered a hand to Mary Hope. When she was down, he removed his hat and formally bowed toward them, "Samuel Newman the Third, of Newberry, South Carolina, at your service, Madam."

"Thank you, Mr. Newman, but we do not require further assistance," Mary Hope said politely, but firmly.

"Thank you, Mr. Newman," Anna said more graciously, offering her gloved hand. He took her hand and bowed over it, "Samuel, please. Miss?"

"Anna. Anna Lovett, sir."

"Miss Lovett," he said with a smile. "A pleasure to make your acquaintance, Miss Lovett."

Mary Hope turned back, "If you will excuse us, Mr. Newman, we have an appointment."

"Certainly," he agreed, and bowed again, "Mrs. Lovett. Miss Lovett."

Mary Hope took Anna firmly by the elbow and led her to the shop. A good thing since Anna was looking back over her shoulder at him and almost stumbling the entire way.

As they were finishing dinner at their hotel restaurant he came to their table, graciously bowing again as he greeted them. "Are we staying in the same hotel?"

"There is no way I could know that, sir, since I know not where you are staying," Mary Hope replied, pointing out the obvious.

"We are staying here, Samuel," Anna said in a more friendly tone, ignoring Mary Hope's warning look and smiling up at him. "We always stay here when we are in town conducting our business. Mother says it is the best and most respectable in Augusta."

"My mother says the same. She always wants to stay here when she is in Augusta too," he said.

"Would you care to join us?" Anna asked impertinently. The invitation should come from her mother, but she was afraid it would not. "We have only just ordered our dessert and will also enjoy coffee after that."

Samuel could not pull out his chair and sit quickly enough. Mary Hope recovered to ask, "Is your mother at the hotel with you?"

"No, ma'am. Not this time. My parents send me here every second week to conduct business for them. I have seen you at the same suppliers and wholesalers we use. I suspect we are on much the same schedule."

"So it seems," Mary Hope agreed.

In spite of Mary Hope's reticence, they had a pleasant conversation over dessert and lingered over a second cup of coffee. Mary Hope then insisted she retire for the night, indicating Anna should too; they had an early start in the morning.

"It was a pleasure to see you again, Samuel," Anna said warmly as they took their leave. She offered her hand, ungloved this time, and his lips brushed her knuckles as he kissed it, sending a thrill of recognition through her. Mary Hope also offered her hand and he bowed graciously over it and bade them a good night. When Mary Hope asked for the bill at the desk, the maitre d'hôtel said it had already been paid by the young gentleman they had dined with.

Three days later they were back at home and Anna was helping Mary Hope in the store. In between customers they were unpacking their new purchases and putting them on the correct shelves. She wore her hair up under a cap and a long apron to protect against the dust. It was almost time to close up when the door opened. One more customer, the last one for the day. Mary Hope was still kneeling behind the service counter, but Anna turned around to greet the late customer.

"Oh!" she exclaimed. "Samuel. What are you doing here? I mean, what a surprise!" She was trying to tuck any errant hair back up under the cap and smoothing down the soiled apron. Mary Hope came up on her creaking knees, staring at their visitor before she found her tongue. "Are you lost, young man? Newberry, South Carolina, is the other direction from Augusta."

"I came to see you," he laughed. "I apologize for barging in like this, but I did not want to take time to write asking if I could come and then wait for a reply. I know it is terribly rude and I can go if this is an inconvenient time. I just…I…"

Anna was smiling up at him. His blustering was so endearing and she had noticed a slight furrow of worry between his eyes, endearing him even more.

"Mr. Newman," Mary Hope huffed and rolled her eyes. "That is absolutely the worse speech I have ever heard. Come on, we are having supper soon. Grandma Mercy and Aunt Mary are making fried chicken and okra tonight. There is always plenty for one more. Help us close up and then come on up to the house with us."

"Thank you ma'am. Thank you most kindly."

They went up to the house. Introductions were made to Grandma Mercy and Aunt Mary, who looked like they were about to burst with questions at the sudden appearance of this dashing young man all the way from Newberry. But, thankfully, they held their tongues.

The two elder women kept him entertained in the library while Mary Hope took Anna upstairs and helped her with her toilette. There was not enough time for a full bath, but she helped Anna wash from the basin and change into one of her better day dresses, undo her hair, brush it and put it back up. She even dabbed a bit of her perfume behind Anna's ears before they went back down.

"I should have told you more about having a beau before now," Mary Hope said. "Just try to remember to not stare at him and try to look at someone else in the room once in a while, although I know that won't be easy. My, he is a fine-looking young man, isn't he? And so well-mannered too."

Anna nodded.

"And also, you can't, under any circumstance, be alone with him yet. I will tell you when that is all right, but it won't be this evening, or even tomorrow. If you are going to have young men calling now, we will have to talk more about this, starting first thing in the morning."

The fried chicken and okra turned out to be chicken and rice gumbo since tomatoes and okra were in abundance in the garden. It was likely the same thing most of the families were eating down in the village that evening too. While Grandma Mercy went down to the village to notify Beattie, the woman they sometimes used to serve in the dining room, Aunt Mary scurried around and stirred up a batch of her light biscuits to serve with butter and peach preserves. While they were baking, she poached six peaches, then halved them and removed the pits. Just before serving, the middles would be filled with sweetened cream for their dessert. Even though the women usually ate around the table in the kitchen house, or pulled it outside the kitchen door when the weather was nice, the dining room table was set with Great Aunt Charity's silver and china and Mercy brought out a bottle of wine she reserved for special occasions. They would eat the simple gumbo with spoons from soup plates, but at least it was elegantly presented.

When Anna and Mary Hope finally came downstairs, Grandma Mercy and Aunt Mary were entertaining Mr. Newman in the library. Aunt Mary was obviously relieved. They had run out of topics they could discuss with this unannounced gentleman caller. While they were waiting, Grandma Mercy was trying to keep the conversation going by commenting on the surprising new growth in Augusta, even though she had not been there for years. Mary Hope and Anna entered the room, with Mr. Newman standing as they entered, and then settled on the settee. Mr. Newman was seated facing the portrait of Great Aunt Charity. He asked about it.

Anna inwardly groaned. Now her Grandma Mercy and Aunt Mary would be sure to launch into a long and detailed narrative of the Wainwright family history. Anna looked up at the portrait, remembering how the long and colorless face staring down from the painting frightened her as a child. It had been painted by an English artist who visited Charleston. The painting was large, showing Charity in full length. She wore a huge white ruffled cap under an elaborate hat, layers of petticoats under an overskirt that ended high above her ankles. The dress was elaborately laced over stiff-looking stays that pushed up a minimal bosom. She was standing in the family parlor of the house in Charleston, with a view of the bay incorrectly shown beyond the windows.

As a child, the pale blue eyes seemed to follow Anna around the library, but now she saw the kind generosity behind those eyes and the ready smile behind the lips. Perhaps that was because what she now knew of Great Aunt Charity. Thankfully, Grandma Mercy delivered an abbreviated history of the woman in the portrait.

But then she directed Mr. Newman's attention to the smaller portraits of her grandparents on the opposite wall of the library, and finally a simple depiction of the Wainwright plantation in South Carolina, painted by a traveling artist, that was actually more like a diagram of the plantation than an actual painting, although it did have a good likeness of the old house and the surrounding gardens. She explained the house was gone now, destroyed in the great storm of 1749. The new owners built a new house on another part of the plantation.

There was also the flat-looking portrait of her family by a traveling artist who came to the plantation. It showed Charity, Richard, and their brother David as an infant with their parents. She explained that most of the background on that type of portrait was painted in advance by the traveling artist with the members of the family filled in after he was hired. It was not an accurate depiction, but Grandma Mercy kept it because it was the only likeness of her father, Richard Wainwright, even if he was only a young boy.

Anna was holding her breath, hoping Grandma Mercy would stop. But beside her, Aunt Mary was looking like she was just getting geared up to jump in as soon as Grandma Mercy ran down. This was a disaster!

Samuel was holding his breath, too, as he listened to Anna's grandmother, but for an entirely different reason. He was beginning to realize Anna was too far above his station. His family only had a small farm near Newberry and his father operated a small store, not as large as the one he had seen here. Last week, he had spent all the money his mother had allowed for his room and board in Augusta by making the grand gesture of paying their bill for dinner. He had to spend the night in the wagon behind the livery where his horse was quartered. He had been dishonest in leading them to think he was staying at their hotel. He could never have afforded that. Now, it appeared Anna was from a grand old South Carolina family with its roots going all the way back to a grand house in England. His mother's and father's families had fled by Conestoga wagon to South Carolina in 1758 during the French and Indian wars, leaving almost everything they owned behind. Edgefield County was already crowded by other refugees and they had to spend all their savings and take on mortgages just to buy their small farms. His own father had exceeded and improved his station by starting his small store and becoming a merchant, but his background could never measure up to the Wainwrights.

"Of course, no portrait exists of my mother," Grandma Mercy continued. Anna, with a small smile frozen on her face, inwardly groaned. "She was the mulatto daughter of Richard Wainwright's cook Bess."

Thankfully, Mary Hope interrupted, "Mama, dinner is waiting and I don't believe the young people are interested in hearing all this right now. Maybe we can all go on into the dining room?"

Knowing where Grandma Charity was heading, Aunt Mary was closely watching young Samuel's face when Mercy revealed the parentage of her granddaughter to this potential suitor. She was alert for any tightening of the jaw or the muscles around the eyes that might reveal his hidden distaste, if he felt any. Instead there was a slight relaxing of those muscles. She took it as a good sign.

They settled at the dining room table, Grandma Mercy sitting at the foot of the table with the head, as always, set for John, but the chair vacant. It was a custom that widows were often afforded and Mercy still observed when they ate in the dining room. It also indicated her status as a widow to Mr. Newman. Grandma Mercy motioned for Samuel to sit on her left and Anna on her right. Mary Hope sat beside Samuel and Aunt Mary sat across from her, on Anna's right. Aunt Mary had told Mercy that she wanted to sit where she could see Mr. Newman's face. She would see what his words did not reveal.

He was curious about other things but was too polite to ask: the status and lack of presence of Anna's father, the relation of Aunt Mary, who appeared to be French and might possibly be the sister of Mercy's dead husband, and most of all - the gigantic detail about herself and the family that Anna's grandmother had just shared as glibly as if she was discussing the price of cotton.

Beattie served steaming plates of gumbo from the sideboard and then left the room. She would wait outside the dining room until Charity rang the bell for her to clear the course and serve dessert.

"Are you shocked that Mercy is quadroon, Mr. Newman?" Aunt Mary asked.

"Aunt Mary!" Anna protested, wishing she could dissolve through the floor.

Samuel set down his wine glass and swallowed, then touched the napkin to his mouth before he spoke. Someone raised this boy right, Aunt Mary observed.

"Quite honestly, yes, ma'am, I am. But not for the reasons you are thinking. My parents are strongly in opposition to slavery and my father sees it as a failed institution…"

"So did my husband," Mercy interrupted him appreciatively. "But please, do continue."

"In fact, they have taken great encouragement from recent actions in their home state of Pennsylvania to overturn laws forbidding marriages and progress to restore full rights to free persons of color, although they must keep silent on those topics in these parts, I fear. They taught us not think of other races as inferior to the English, just under different circumstances. No, Mrs. Botts, to me it is just that Mrs. Freeman does not appear to be in the least bit colored, in spite of her high ratio. My surprise, I believe, is that most people in her situation would never reveal it, especially here in the southern states, and would most definitely claim themselves only to be white."

Aunt Mary raised her glass to him approvingly and took a sip, but did not toast.

"How can your parents be opposed to slavery and live in South Carolina, Mr. Newman?" Grandma Mercy asked, taking up her gumbo spoon. "The two situations are mutually exclusive are they not?"

"My parents both came to South Carolina with their own families before they were married. My father was from Erie, Pennsylvania, and my mother's family was from Bucks County. The French and Indian Wars made it impossible for them to stay there so they came south as refugees. Every place they tried to stop along the way was too full already and, with no land available, they had to keep going. They finally were forced to stop in Newberry. They could go no further since Georgia was not yet open to settlers. They were able to buy farms there and my father began a store, similar to the one you ladies operate here. Even though the two farms are combined as one these days, it is still a small farm, and not large enough for a profit to be made from holding slaves. He was wise enough to realize that."

Mercy nodded in understanding – and approval. Slavery was failing in all but the largest plantations of the low country. Holding slaves was not profitable for the small farmer. Some were slow to realize that, and many were selling or even freeing their slaves to avoid the ongoing cost of maintaining a work force between harvests. John had been one of the early ones to realize that and counseled his clients along that line. Of course, she realized most of those who could afford it would still have slaves as servants in their houses, but it was still an improvement.

"So instead of slaves they had ten children," Samuel joked.

The four ladies burst into surprised laughter. "Ten children!" Mary Hope exclaimed. Then she looked into her wine glass and added, "What a wonderful family that must be."

"Well, we didn't always think so when we were all still at home, ma'am, but mostly I have to agree."

"Oh, tell us about them," Anna said, genuinely interested. "How many brothers and sisters are there?"

"I have three older brothers, William, Walter, and John, all married now," he blushed at the word 'married' but plunged on. "Then my twin sister Mary is to be married soon." He blushed even deeper, charming Mercy and the older women thoroughly. "Then there are my sisters Zilpha and Beth, seventeen and fourteen, and two more brothers, Jonathan and Lemuel, they are twelve and nine, and lastly Margaret Eve – or Marnie we call her. She is only eight years old and thoroughly spoiled, I'm afraid."

"Oh, no, surely not," Mary Hope said warmly.

"Well, she is the only one of us who was allowed to keep a cat, and in the house, too. I think Mother just gave up by then. He sleeps on the foot of Marnie's bed."

They all laughed at that, and Aunt Mary looked approvingly looked at him, then around the table at Mercy, Mary Hope, and finally Anna. Mercy rang for the table to be cleared and dessert to be served.

After dinner they moved back to the library, so Beattie could clear again. After they were settled, Mercy abruptly asked, "Do you understand the sequence of Anna's heritage, Mr. Newman?"

"I think so ma'am."

"My mother, being one half Negro was mulatto and I am one quarter, which is quadroon. My daughter, Mary, who is also half French, is one eighth which is octoroon."

"The same as me," Aunt Mary piped, but was silence by a look from Mercy.

170

"But for one-sixteenth, there is no descriptive term. Do you know why that is, Mr. Newman?"

"I believe so, ma'am," he said quietly.

Anna wanted to hide her face behind her hands. If this was what "having a beau" was going to be, she would have to refuse the next invitation she received. Or at least until Grandma Mercy and Aunt Mary had passed.

Mercy waited. Samuel looked around at them and said quietly, "I believe one sixteenth is white, ma'am – or can be when the person does not appear to be colored."

"Exactly. Anna is white. Legally she can represent herself to be white. She can legally marry a white man. If you will forgive me, my late husband was a lawyer, Mr. Newman, which is why I am inclined to speak so bluntly – perhaps too bluntly."

She continued, "Now, I am sure you are aware there are people, especially people in the southern colonies – I mean states – who consider someone who has even one drop of African blood to still be colored, no matter how white they look. Do you believe that Mr. Newman?"

Samuel paused. "I honestly have not had any occasion to consider that until now, ma'am. But, logically speaking, I could not support that line of thought. I assure you, though, that it matters not to me, either way. I was not brought up like that."

Mercy relaxed back into her chair, "Then you have my permission to call on my granddaughter."

"I'm not sure he will still want to, Mother," Mary Hope said. "I do apologize, Mr. Newman, but Anna is my mother's only grandchild."

"No need to apologize, Mrs. Lovett." Samuel replied. "And yes, I would be honored to call on Miss Anna."

"You can sleep in my room tonight," Aunt Mary declared. "I will sleep on the trundle in Anna's room."

"I do not want to put you out of your own room, ma'am. I am quite happy to sleep here on the sofa, or even on the porch. Sometimes, I even sleep in the wagon," he added before he thought.

"I still be sleepin' in Anna's room anyway," Aunt Mary insisted. She fixed her gaze on him, letting him know she would be protecting Anna's virtue and reputation with a gentleman in the house.

* * * * *

Anna's interview with Samuel's parents was more relaxed. When the invitation came, Mary Hope accompanied her. They traveled by wagon to Augusta, where Samuel rode to meet them. He drove them the rest of the way, his own horse tethered behind.

The Newman home and farm were modest. The visitors were received in the parlor, an adequate room, but still cramped with the number of people. Samuel's younger sisters simply sat on the floor beside their mother, and his father stood behind Mrs. Newman's chair during the first meeting. After that, they were never all together in the same room. The older brothers and their wives went to their homes and Samuel and his younger brothers were busy on the farm and the sisters helped their father in the store. It was a different life than Mary Hope and Anna were used to, but the family seemed content and happy with one another's company. Mary Hope and Anna were simply folded in with them as though they had always been a part of the family.

The one exception was Samuel's sister, Beth, who was fourteen. Anna sensed Beth was jealous of her, but realized it would be the same with any girl Samuel chose. She made a special effort to engage Beth in conversation and even invited Beth to join her and Samuel for their evening walks, although Samuel usually insisted that his little sister stay home.

They fell into a pattern. They saw each other every second Wednesday when Anna and her mother went to Augusta. After meeting Anna and her family, Samuel's parents gave him permission to make the full trip to Mercyville the week between. Although he was old enough to do it without their permission, it gave him leave from his duties at the store and on the farm to be away. He rode on horseback instead of coming by wagon, considerably cutting the time required for the trip.

During his visits, the two began a custom of taking a long walk around the mill pond. A path was worn by the generations of the village. It was a picturesque spot. Generally Grandma Mercy or Aunt Mary followed them, far enough behind to give them privacy in their conversation. The most physical contact was Anna's hand on Samuel's offered arm as they strolled, and sometimes a stolen kiss when they rounded a corner and their chaperone would momentarily fall out of sight. Anna took advantage of one of their walks to talk about Beth. Samuel was clearly annoyed with his sister's conduct.

"She is never going to like me if you don't let me warm her up," Anna observed. "It would not offend me if she had accompanied us on our walks when I was visiting at your home."

"She doesn't need to come with us all the time," Samuel stated. "She has to realize that."

"She seems very close to you though. It has to be hard for her to see you with someone."

"Mother should make her understand what it means to court someone."

"Is that what you are doing then, Samuel?" Anna said, half teasing and raising her face up to him.

"I do hope so, Anna," he said, his lips seeking hers, "I do hope so."

In the times between visits, Anna began walking the path in the early evenings. It made him seem closer to her and eased the loneliness and longing she felt for him. She should not walk alone and Mary Hope came with her sometimes, but generally Grandma Mercy was the first to offer. She would walk with her arm through Anna's. Mercy took advantage of these times alone to retell all the stories, making sure Anna knew them. Mary Hope had grown impatient with hearing them, but in the calm setting Anna could more easily picture the familiar scenes. "Some day I reckon you will be telling these stories to your own granddaughter, Anna. Of course, there will be more to tell by then."

One evening they paused by the little church at the water's edge. Mercy remembered the first church, almost identical except it had no bell in the tower. She recalled the day it had been dedicated and her feeling of belonging. They paused by John's grave.

"I wanted him buried here, instead of up by the house. I was off somewhere in my mind those days after he died, but I remember that being one the thing I insisted on. I wanted him buried here by the church."

"Yes, Grandma," Anna said quietly. She knew this story.

"Did you know that the old slaves, the ones who came from Africa, wanted to be buried by the water because they believed the water would take their souls back to Africa? That was where they wanted to go when they died instead of the white man's heaven."

Anna paused. She did not know that. It did explain why the slave burial grounds on the plantations she had seen were almost always by the water.

"When I die, Anna, I want to be buried right here too. Right here beside John."

Anna caught her breath and her throat tightened. She began to cry. "Oh

Grandma, I don't want you to die. I don't."

Mercy pulled Anna to her and held her closely, Anna's head against her shoulder as she wept. "Hush, now child. I will still be here a while. I want you to know I have had a good long life. Thanks to my Aunt Charity and Jean Faure, my life has been so much better than it was supposed to be. Without them I would have been a slave all my life. I have been free and I have been happy. You and your mamma have been a special part of it, too."

Then she whispered, not sure if Anna could even hear. "I'se your old grandmamma, Miss Anna. I'se your old grandmamma Mercy. Ain't nobody ever gone love you more than your old grandmamma Mercy loves you, Miss Anna."

* * * * *

Samuel Newman and Mary Anna Lovett were married in Upson, Georgia, on October 27, 1795. When they and their parents met with the Baptist minister before the wedding, Anna honestly and legally represented herself to be white. Her mother and grandmother nodded in agreement. Aunt Mary, took a breath as if she was going to say something, but stayed silent. From this point forward the line that came down from Old Bess was, without question, white. It saddened Mercy a little, feeling something had been lost and that, in time, those who followed might even forget.

All of Samuel's family was there. Mercy Wainwright, Aunt Mary Botts, and Mary Hope Freeman Lovett were there for Anna. Alice Lovett, in failing health, was unable to make the trip, but sent her warm regards. There was no reply to the invitation sent to Anna's father, Richard Lovett.

CHAPTER SEVEN

Warren County, Georgia
1795-1818

On March 14, 1794, the United States Patent office granted a patent to Eli Whitney for an invention he titled "The Cotton Engine." It was a simple device, a wood box with a hand crank attached to a drum inside the box. The drum was covered with metal spikes, like the teeth of a comb. There was an opening at the bottom of the box and another opening on the side. The top of the wooden box had a funnel opening. While the crank was turned, raw cotton could be fed into the top of the engine, or "gin." The spikes on the drum pulled the cotton through the gin. Cotton seeds fell out the bottom, ready to be planted for more cotton, and combed cotton came out the second opening, ready to be pressed into bales. Mr. Whitney was slow to perfect his patent and the machine was easily copied and was widely available.

It was singly the harshest punishment ever to be inflicted on the black race in America.

Overnight the large-scale farming of cotton became immensely profitable. Previously only a sideline on most plantations, with enormous amounts of hand labor required to remove the stubborn seeds from each boll, the cotton gin meant that a bale of cotton could be seeded and carded in minutes rather than days. Ignoring the depletion of the land it was grown on, vast tracts previously cultivated in indigo and rice were converted to cotton at the next planting. In Hancock County, Richard Lovett converted all his land to cotton and cleared even more. Even the formal gardens were plowed under and planted in cotton, a crop that was being called "white gold." It was the same across the South. Cotton exports would increase from less than 500,000 pounds in 1793 to more than 93 million pounds in 1810.

Under the new system, slaves became expendable. The previous calculations of the profitability of a slave had divided the costs of buying and maintaining the slave over the number of years the slave could be expected to work in the fields. Now, even though prices in the slave markets were soaring, a wide rule of thumb became that three years of field work from a slave was enough. If a planter could get that before a slave was worked to death, it was profitable. The task system of slavery all but disappeared and slaves worked from sunup to sundown, under the constant watch and frequent lash of a hired manager called an overseer.

Slaves were extremely valuable and in short supply. In South Carolina it became illegal under any circumstance for an owner to grant freedom to a slave, including the death of the owner. Slaves could only be sold. The recognition of people of mixed race as white became even more restrictive with the denominator in the fraction increasing or being abandoned all together. The rights and freedom of previously free persons of color were restricted. They began leaving for the northern states.

Of course, not every slave had to be bought in the marketplace. Children born of slaves were also slaves and automatically belonged to their mother's master. Children would be put to the fields as early as age six, supposedly with reduced work, but at harvest every hand available was pressed into service plucking the cotton bolls from the sharp pods while dragging long sacks of the stuff behind them along the rows.

Not content to merely let nature and the human heart take its course, many owners became active breeders of their slave stock. When a male of particular strength, stature and endurance emerged he was mated with every women of child bearing age on the plantation, and sometimes hired out to others for the same purpose. If the woman objected, sometimes already "married" to another, she would be put under the lash until she submitted. Many saved themselves from torture by submitting without protest. Within generations, the stature of the slaves seen in the field, both male and female, changed. They were taller, more muscular and enduring. They were also darker. And the planters justified their actions by saying the blacks they owned were inferior and without morals. House servants, often half siblings to the children of the masters they served were treated only marginally better.

At home in Mercyville, Aunt Mary and Mercy often discussed the topic with Samuel. Anna hated the discussions and Mary Hope quietly excused herself, privately aggrieved at what must be transpiring at Richard's plantation in the next county. Their previous optimism that slavery was becoming an obsolete institution and would soon pass away was dashed. Slavery had changed from the system it had originally been and was rapidly growing. Like a cancer, it was reaching into every corner of their world.

During one conversation, Anna was chilled to the bone when Grandmamma Mercy seemed to speak as though from somewhere else, "The Devil and his demons have been unleashed on an ignorant and godless South. He will not be content until every man, woman, and child, white or black, is destroyed."

Then she quoted from the prophet Isaiah; "His fury is upon all their armies: He hath utterly destroyed them, He hath delivered them to the slaughter. Their slain shall be cast out, and their stink shall come up out of their carcasses, and the mountains shall be melted with their blood. They shall call the nobles thereof to the kingdom, but none shall be there, all her princes shall be nothing. And thorns shall come up in their palaces; nettles and brambles in the fortresses thereof."

Mercy turned to Anna and Samuel, "Only the scorched earth will remain. Before that comes, you young ones must take your families and get as far away from here as you can."

They would never forget her words, but the seeds for such devastation were now only being sown. At harvest, some sixty years later, Mercy's words were a gentler description of the devastation that was to come.

* * * * *

In spite of the human misery surrounding them, their part of the world was not without its challenges, but it was still peaceful, idyllic almost.

After a deep cleaning and new paint, Samuel and Anna moved into the house Lancaster and Alice Lovett built so long ago. Mercy, Mary Hope and Aunt Mary were close, but not too close.

A month after they moved in, word came from Samuel's eldest brother William that their parents had been killed instantly when their horses bolted on the road near their home, possibly frightened by a snake. Their wagon was overturned. Samuel's sister Mary had been gravely injured and died soon after. William wrote that he and his wife would move back to the farm to raise the younger children. As the oldest male heir, they all knew the farm was his now anyway. It was a sad time for all of them. He wrote that the younger children were adjusting and their sister Zilpha, although grieved, would soon marry the young man she had been courting. Their parents had given their consent and a wedding date had been set.

However, Beth, at fourteen, was grief stricken and was becoming withdrawn. She was insolent and angry during the day and they could hear her weeping every night. William and his wife were at a loss at what to do.

Back when they were courting, Anna told Samuel she wanted a large family. From Old Bess on down they had all been only children. She knew her mother wanted many children, but could never have another. Anna and Samuel had a large house. She had seen how close Beth was to Samuel. As they walked along the path around the mill pond several evenings later, she suggested to Samuel that they start their family by inviting Beth to become a part of it.

Samuel would have never suggested it, but he hugged Anna tightly to hide his tears. He could not love Anna more than he did at that moment. They met Beth in Augusta the following month. As soon as she came down from William's wagon she hung on Samuel, until she was all cried out. Then she only gave Anna a perfunctory peck on the cheek, barely acknowledging the sister-in-law who had made this possible. Anna hoped Beth would eventually come to love her too.

Mary Hope was especially delighted when her first grandson, Jonathan, was born the next year. He was soon followed by the twins, Samuel and Emily in 1797. Every day Mary Hope either went to the Newman's house or brought the babies home to stay with Mercy, Aunt Mary, and herself. The babies were well-tended.

In fact, Anna had to remind the old ladies to let baby Jonathan down to crawl or he would never learn to walk on his own. She would tease, "I think you ladies will still be carrying him when he leaves for the academy."

Aunt Mary was the first to pass, and it was quietly in her sleep just as the peaches were coming into bloom in the spring of 1798. No one really knew how old she was. Her birth was never recorded and she was taken from her mother as an infant and raised in the house, much the same as Mercy had been, but as a house slave. Her talents with a needle assured her survival after the old Mistress freed her in her will. The Christmas before she died, Aunt Mary guessed she was near to ninety years old. She recalled her days as a young slave girl in her owners' town house within the old walled city of Charleston. She recalled vividly the siege and starvation of the city during the Yamasee War. From guessing her age at that time she estimated herself to be approaching the age of ninety, if not there already.

They buried Mary Botts in the cemetery down by the little church on the banks of the mill pond. Before they closed the coffin, Mercy tucked into Mary's hands the ornamental scissors and pincushion that Aunt Charity had once worn suspended from her belt. Mercy had given them to Mary years before, and although wearing such things was out of fashion, Mary had treasured them.

Mercy's death was not as easy. A stroke that summer paralyzed her left side, much the same as Old James had been paralyzed so long ago. Mary Hope assisted her each morning, getting her mother dressed, brushing and arranging her hair for the day and feeding her breakfast. Mercy was not patient with her disability. Where she had always been articulate, her speech was now limited to monosyllabic words she struggled to form. She was frustrated and often used her good hand to throw things away from herself, swearing in her frustration. Her young great-grandsons were frightened by her twisted face and would only remain with her when Anna held them on her lap and sat beside Mercy. It broke Mercy's heart, but she was delighted to see the children, the first boys in the family she would always say before her words became even more difficult.

The final afternoon of Mercy's life, Anna and the children sat with her in the library. Anna turned to see tears streaming down the old woman's face.

"Grandma," Anna said taking Mercy's hand in hers. "Grandma what is it?"

Mercy turned slowly to look at her, exhausted. She took a painful breath and said in a voice barely above a whisper, "'member."

"Yes, Grandma, I remember."

Mercy struggled, slowly forming each word, "'Member. Bess. Dove. Char'y. Wain. Wright. 'member, Anna. 'member me."

Tears were brimming, Anna said, "Of course, Grandma, I will always remember you."

"Tell," her eyes were urgent.

"Yes, I will tell my boys and their children too, Grandma. Now please, stop. You are tiring yourself too much. I know. I remember, Grandma. I will always remember."

They sat for a while, then Mercy said, "I'se...You...Ol'...Gran'...Ma...Mercy..."

Anna set the baby on the floor, sat at Mercy's feet and laid her head on Mercy's lap and softly crooned the words herself, remembering for her Grandma, "Ain't nobody ever gone love you more than your old grandmamma loves you."

When she looked up again, Mercy was gone.

They buried Mercy beside John. There was no minister present, so after recounting the simple statistics of her mother's life, Mary Hope invited each person standing at the grave to share a memory of Mercy if they wanted to do so. There were the families from the village, families from the surrounding farms, and the poor whites from down along the river. Others came from as far away as Augusta. They all had something they wanted to say. Mercy had lived a good long life, sixty-six years in all, and her life had touched each of them in some special and uplifting way.

The burial became more of a celebration than a sad occasion as stories were shared. They even laughed a few times, remembering this woman and her undefeatable spirit. As the final hymn began, an ancient song with its roots in Africa that Mercy loved, hands were joined with no regard to color, as Mercy would have wanted. Leaving the little cemetery and walking back up to Mercy's house, where lunch would be served on the lawn, Anna commented to her mother that she felt strangely uplifted, instead of grieved. "What else would you expect from her?" was all Mary Hope had to say.

* * * * *

Anna hoped Beth would mature as she grew into a young woman, but even after her eighteenth birthday, she still wanted her brother's full attention. She continually schemed to dominate him. She was petulant and jealous of her nephews and niece to the point Anna did not want to leave them alone with their aunt. In the fall of 1798, against Samuel's wishes, Beth simply announced she would marry John Harrison. Mr. Harrison had not spoken to Samuel, so it was a complete surprise. Samuel immediately objected, adamantly in fact, and Anna thought she noticed a hint of satisfaction on Beth's face at her brother's objection.

It was not that Samuel held John's background against him, but all the Harrisons were barely one step above the poor white crackers. It seemed the term originated because the men who lacked the means for real weapons, carried bullwhips that they loved to swing around faster and faster until they snapped back the handle, making a loud "crack." The term stuck.

John sometimes worked as a blacksmith. Samuel had misgivings about Beth adapting to the life of a poor blacksmith's wife. She had adapted so quickly to the comforts of the Newman household and was even disdainful of what was freely given to her. What concerned Samuel most was that John was often out of work and was prone to drunkenness. Even more worrisome was that, when he drank, he was prone to fighting. He was not even kind to Beth, from what they could see. But, realizing her declaration to marry John earned her Samuel's full attention, Beth was insistent, if not insolent, and Samuel could not object. Even though he had been her legal guardian, she was old enough now to marry without his consent. Anna could not admit to Samuel how much she looked forward to Beth's wedding, and hoped they would see less of her after she was married.

Their family continued to grow; Lemuel arrived in 1799, Lovett in 1801, Amanda in 1805, and Levina in 1808. With six children and the old Lovett house bursting at the seams, Mary Hope invited them all to move in with her. The house Mercy and Johnny Freeman had built was somewhat larger and the airy attic could be easily partitioned for more bedrooms for the grandchildren. They were soon comfortably settled. Even though the Wainwright ancestors often looked down from frames that hung crookedly on the wall, some of the furniture was ruined, and the walls were always smudged, Mary Hope was happy to have the house full.

As soon as Beth learned of their move, she demanded that Samuel let her move into the old Lovett place. By then, John was drinking more than ever and was absent about as much as he was home. He only worked at a job until he was paid and then disappeared until his money was gone. Beth had three small children, all poorly tended. When John was absent, Anna insisted Samuel take basic provisions to his sister. It was not fair for the children to suffer because their father was a drunkard. Samuel had just delivered at least a month's worth of staples to his sister when she made her demand. Samuel refused adamantly, saying it was not his house to control. He explained as carefully as he could that the house belonged to his mother-in-law. It had been the home of Mary Hope's husband's parents.

Lacking even a horse and wagon, Beth walked the five miles to see Mary, dragging her children along with her, to demand that, as family, she should be allowed to live in the vacant house. It was just sitting there empty anyway. Samuel intervened and said she had no right to make such demands of Mary. She was not related to Mary at all. A fierce argument ensued between brother and sister, and Samuel all but threw Beth off the property with her screaming at Samuel from the road that his "bitch wife was behind all this," and that they would be sorry. Anna felt sorry for the children, having to see that. She continued sending provisions to the now sullen Beth and consistently absent John solely for the benefit of her nieces and nephew.

* * * * *

More people than ever were moving into Warren County and a new settlement sprang up west of Mercyville. It was being called Warrenton in hopes of becoming the county seat. Although the new town was just south of the old trading road, people began taking a shorter route from there to Augusta, bypassing Mercyville. By 1810, when Warrenton was incorporated, there was not much left of Mercyville anyway. To most, it was only a tiny settlement around an old log cabin trading post on the old road.

After almost sixty years of operation, the sawmill was closed. The machinery was worn out and would be too costly to replace for the small amount of lumber that was being milled. Samuel and the two remaining workers closed it down, dismantled the machinery and sold it for scrap.

Most of the families in the village were gone by then. The few remaining grandchildren of the original families said goodbye to the Newmans and made their way north. They knew a trade and could read and write and do sums. Better lives awaited them in the northern states.

After sixty years of use, Samuel declared the empty cabins were not safe, and they were pulled down. The wood was given to the white farmers along the river who used it for firewood. The Newmans preserved only the cemetery and the little church. It was still whitewashed and each year when winter was over, Anna and Samuel took the children down to the cemetery to tend the graves. They unlocked the door of the little church, swept it out and gave it a good airing while Grandmother Mary told the stories. The children happily helped with the cleaning and listened to all the stories, since each one would be rewarded with a turn at ringing the church bell when they were finished. Anyone who heard the bell knew the Newman children had tended the old graveyard and it was officially spring.

With their road rarely traveled, the little store became more of a nuisance to keep open than it was worth and it was closed too, although Mary still went down every day to sweep out the dogtrot and then sit for a while remembering. Samuel and Anna were now dependent on the peach harvest for their income. The trees were fully matured and bore wonderful fruit. Samuel kept busy between harvests tending the orchards. He pruned the trees and cut the lush grass between the rows of trees and sold the excess hay they did not need for their own livestock. The rest of the time he kept busy cutting out pine seedlings that sprang up in the orchards. He had to do the same with their road to keep it open and passable. They knew the pine forest could reclaim the orchards and all their land quickly. When that happened there would barely be a trace to show they had been there.

The loss of Mercyville would have been overwhelming for Mary if Warrenton was not booming close by. A new Baptist church was formed. Ground was secured south of town near Long Creek and a church was built. Although Samuel did not really care for the Baptist's position on slavery, their inclusion of free black congregations appealed to him, even though that position was continually diluted as the church sought to attract the elite planter class away from the Anglican Church.

The family started going to services every Sunday. Mary went with them. Since her support for the Mercyville church was no longer required, she gave generously to the new little church. The deacons appealed to her generosity frequently when money was needed for special funds and she regularly obliged them.

Beth joined the church as soon as she heard Samuel and Anna belonged there. Anna had to give Beth credit, she put forth an effort. The children were clean and behaved themselves for Sunday morning services. Beth would soundly thump them on the head with her knuckles if they did not.

John rarely came to church, but Beth made sure he was freshly bathed and shaved when he did. By this time, Beth was discontent and pushing John to make a better living. She could not be faulted on that, but Anna felt it was more for Beth's benefit than for her family. She wanted to improve her standing in the community and especially at Long Creek Baptist Church. John leased a livery with a forge and became a blacksmith in his own right. The commitment to paying the rent assured he worked almost every day, and Anna was happy to notice that Beth and her children sometimes wore new clothing and shoes - cheap quality to be sure, but still new. John was finally providing for his family. With no more income from the mill and store, Samuel decided they should stop sending provisions to his sister.

Forty miles to the west they were building a new capital city to replace Louisville. In 1803, the Georgia state legislature called for a centrally located town to be established with the name of Milledgeville, in honor of the man who was the first governor of the State of Georgia. The site selected was on a pretty stretch of land overlooking the Oconee River. The current was swift there and it became a gathering point to ship cotton bales south. A rough and ready town of simple wooden houses and cheap hotels sprang up. Decent residents kept away in the early years, discouraged by the gambling, dueling, overcrowded taverns, and bordellos. But with the construction of the new statehouse in 1807, fifteen wagons moved the state records and the treasury from Louisville. There were plans to build a grand governor's mansion on the hill north of town, with the suggestion that fashionable residences for more respectable and affluent citizens would soon follow in the neighborhood surrounding the mansion. The capital was two full days of driving from Warrenton, but Sparta was conveniently located midway with overnight lodgings available for travelers.

Although Samuel and Anna no longer had the mill income and the store profits, they still lived comfortably. Mary still had some money from Mercy, money that had originally come from Aunt Charity's trust. As Mary and Mercy had always done, Anna and Samuel adjusted their living expenses so they did not have to use it, but it was there as a comfort and a cushion against disaster. Samuel knew that Anna and his children would be well cared for if the Lord took him early.

In 1814, Anna assumed she was past the age of having children. She was thirty-six and her baby Levina was six years old. Her oldest son, Jonathan was eighteen and from the looks of it would be married soon. He was popular, and the young ladies at Long Creek Baptist flocked around him after church. Anna had miscarried a year after Levina and decided that meant the end of things. Although Samuel was concerned with her advancing age, she realized she was pregnant that spring and that fall a healthy baby daughter was born. They named her Oratio. And then, only a year later she had another son, Henry. Henry would be the last of her little flock. After Henry was born, she teased Samuel, reminding him that she had said she wanted nine children when he came courting.

Although Louisiana was opening for settlers, and creating a lot of excitement in Warren County, Samuel declared they should be content where they were. Mary was now sixty-five years old. It would be unwise to uproot her to move the family west and they simply could not imagine leaving her behind. It would be up to their children to go west, if they decided to.

Their only grief was their relationship with Beth and John. At first, Beth was annoyed when Samuel stopped sending provisions. Then John was almost surly when he saw Samuel at church and Beth completely stopped speaking to Anna – rudely looking through her and ignoring Anna's greetings. Beth's children taunted their younger cousins, but young Lovett would have none of it and had given and received more than one Sunday morning black eye with his cousins. It was a strained relationship and Anna tried to time their arrival at church to avoid confronting Beth and John.

In 1817, when Henry was two years old and Oratio was three, Beth suddenly warmed to Anna. On Sunday mornings she openly admired Anna's hat or dress and could not compliment the children enough. Anna knew she should appreciate the change of heart, but she felt there was something of a black widow's sting waiting behind Beth's false smile and her eyes that remained as cold as a serpent's.

The reason for the change in Beth was apparent soon enough. One Wednesday afternoon a deacon of the church rode out to the Newman place, as the settlement that had once been Mercyville was now called. Declining Anna's invitation to come in for some refreshment, he told Samuel the deacons had requested his presence at a meeting after church that Sunday.

The deacon was usually friendly, but now he would not look Samuel directly in the eye. Deacon meetings with members were serious, meaning some infraction of the church covenant had occurred – or, even worse, that one of the Lord's commandments had been broken. If the deacons were involved it was one of the more serious commandments. Perhaps there was an issue with John. He had been censured by the deacons once before for drunkenness and fighting. Had he persisted in that behavior?

"A deacon's meeting? What is all this about, Brother Castleberry?" Samuel asked. The deacon was a third or fourth cousin to Samuel, whose mother had also been a Castleberry. The deacon was of the same branch of the family that came south from Pennsylvania more than sixty years earlier. The deacon would only respond that it would be revealed soon enough that Sunday and rode away.

Samuel and Anna discussed what it could possibly be, but could come to no conclusion. As she dressed for church that morning she was filled with a sudden and dreadful realization. It was Samuel who was being accused of something, not John and Beth. Samuel - who diligently provided for his family and even those beyond it. Samuel - who had never said a cross word to his wife and only disciplined his children with loving guidance. Samuel - who had been a faithful husband to her all these years. Samuel - who maintained the little cemetery and church on their property even though he had no family connection to it. What on earth could anyone accuse Samuel of? Anna had to sit on the edge of the bed for a moment to collect herself. What could it be?

Church members could sit in the audience during a Deacon's meeting if they chose to. As the Newman family arrived that morning, Anna looked around at the other faces as they made their way to the doors. Most looked down or looked away as she approached. Those who met her gaze seemed to Anna that they did so with either a look of anguished sympathy or complete hatred. She sat in the pew feeling as though her stays had been laced too tightly that morning. The church was completely full. With no place left to sit on the crowded pews, most of the men were left standing. In the crowded room the air was hot and oppressive. Beside her, Mary sensed Anna's discomfort and took her hand, squeezing it strongly and indicating her own strength. Whatever it was, Mary would be there.

The service went on for an eternity. After the final hymn, as if no one knew about it, the preacher announced a deacon's meeting would be held and church members who desired to were invited to attend, but were to keep silent. No one moved.

Samuel's cousin, Brother Castleberry, took the pulpit as head deacon and after clearing his throat said, "It grieves me to convey to the deacons that an accusation has been made by one member of our church against another. It is a grave accusation of the most egregious nature: of lying to God and to the bride of Christ himself - the church. Should the deacons find this accusation to be true, it will mean the excommunication of the member from this congregation, and the eternal damnation of his soul to Hell."

There was a collective intake of air among the spectators. They had not expected something this exciting to transpire. Mostly these meetings were about fights between church members, both of physical and verbal natures, with punishment and retribution meted out by the deacons. Nothing like this had ever happened.

Anna swallowed and took in a deep breath of relief. It could not be Samuel. It had to be someone else. Her relief was only momentary as Brother Castleberry continued. "I will now ask the accuser to come forward and address the Board of Deacons with his accusation."

All eyes roamed the room, seeing who would rise. After a dramatic moment, John and Beth stood and went forward. "Women are to keep silent in the church, saith the Lord," Brother Castleberry reminded her. Beth nodded and took John's arm firmly, as though encouraging him.

John, wadding his hat in his hands, seemed to be mute. Beth gave him a little nudge and he started, almost as though he was reciting what he had been told to say. "My accusation is against my wife's brother, Sam Newman. He knowed his wife is a nigger, but he brung her to this church and to mix with these good Christian people anyhow. He lied to all of us, saying she was his wife, and he lied to God."

Beth nudged him again. "Oh, he lives in sin with that nigger, against the laws of God."

After an initial moment of shock, a general cry of surprise and disbelief went up, until Brother Castleberry shouted them into silence.

"Samuel Newman, come forward."

Samuel stood to rise and Anna stood with him. He turned to tell her to stay with Mary, but her look told him that she was coming. She took his arm and went with him to the front of the church. She could feel all eyes on her, looking at her as though they had never seen her before and judging if what John said could be true. Whispers were exchanged behind hands.

"Women are to keep silent in the church, saith the Lord," Brother Castleberry reminded her. Anna nodded in acknowledgement. But instead of casting down her eyes as she should, she stood, looking in defiance at John and Beth, the deacons and the congregation.

"What do you say Samuel Newman? Are the charges by John Harrison true?"

"No. They are not," Samuel replied.

"Then why would John Harrison make such an accusation against you, sir?"

"I suppose it is because I quit sending food to my sister to feed his sorry children."

There was a titter of laughter in the audience until Brother Castleberry raised his hand for silence. "Is there no truth to his accusation?"

"No, there is not."

There was a rustle through the congregation. John had just become guilty of the sin he had accused Samuel of – lying to the church and lying to God.

"But her grandma was a nigger!" Beth burst out, pointing her finger at Anna. "I saw her before she died and I know it's true. She was quadroon."

"Silence!" Brother Castleberry scolded Beth.

"And if my sister was able to do simple fractions, she would realize that even if my wife's grandmother was quadroon, or one-quarter Negro, my wife is then one-sixteenth. And that, sirs, is the law and my wife is legally white in every state of this union. My wife and I were legally married in South Carolina. Neither she nor I have lied about this, because she is white."

"She is still a nigger, Samuel," Beth yelled at him, her eyes bulging. "It only takes one drop of nigger blood to make her a nigger and she is a nigger! And she ain't your wife! You was never legally married to her!"

The audience erupted into loud discussion as the deacons went into a conference. There was much head nodding and shaking among the deacons, with emphatic whispered words accentuated by hands chopping the air. After a long discussion, Brother Castleberry came back to the pulpit where John and Beth were waiting on one side, Samuel and Anna on the other.

He addressed Samuel, "Samuel Newman, are you aware that a person still has the evil mark of Cain upon them even if they have only one drop of blood of the Negro race?"

186

Ignoring the question Samuel countered, "Does not verse two of the thirteenth chapter of Romans command us as Christians to obey the laws of the land when it says, "whosoever resists the powers ordained by God, resists the ordinance of God and shall receive to themselves his damnation?"

Castleberry was flustered. He did not anticipate the accused would be quoting scriptures. Generally they cowered, mutely awaiting the deacon's decision of their punishment. He held up his hand for Samuel to stop.

"But you knew the position of the church?" Castleberry was not to be dissuaded.

"No, I did not."

"You are lying, sir."

"No he is not." Anna could stay silent no longer. "Samuel never lies."

"In saying that Madam, you are lying yourself. No one is without sin."

"But you said he lies. I said he does not. Even though Samuel may sin, I have never once, in all these years we have been married, known him to lie. No one here can truthfully say they have."

"Silence!" Castleberry's mind was made up and he was losing the argument to this woman. "It is still the decision of this board that you have lied to this church, and thus, to your eternal damnation, you have also lied to God. It will be entered in the book that you are excommunicated from this church, as well as from the family of God. May God have mercy on your soul."

There was silence in the church. Samuel looked at John like he could kill him, then at his sister with something he had never felt in his life, pure hatred. Beth, only then realizing the grave error she had made, looked horrified and then looked away from her brother's glare.

They made their way back to the pew where the children were silently waiting. Jonathan was pale beyond belief. Mary was holding her little grandson Henry on her lap, with Oratio sitting beside her on the pew not understanding what had happened. They all silently gathered up their things and made their way out the back of the church. But just as they reached the door, Mary turned back to say. "No court in this land will ever say my daughter is colored. You are all hypocrites under the scriptures, and you are so full of hate, Jesus himself would not know you if he was here today. I will not be a part of this sad excuse for a church any more, either. See how you all can get along without my money now."

Author's note: In the records of the Long Creek Baptist Church of Warrenton, Georgia it was written that John Harrison, the husband of

Elizabeth Newman, had a quarrel with his sister-in-law, Anna Lovett Newman that he took before the church. Samuel Newman was charged with perjury by Brother Castleberry. Samuel Newman was excommunicated as a result of the church agreement. Later, in September 1828, it was also entered that John Harrison was excommunicated for immoral conduct and his wife Elizabeth Newman was excommunicated for "not hearing the church."

Beth and John came to the house that afternoon, dragging their children with them. Beth had worked herself into a full crying jag by then, and as soon as Samuel opened the door she hung on him, crying hysterically and begging him to forgive her.

Samuel only turned to his eldest sons and said, "Remove this woman from my person."

Then he turned in silence and went back into the house. John led an incoherent Beth away, saying he told her it was a bad idea to come to the Newman house. Anna stood silently in the doorway as John dragged Beth away. Beth turned around time and again to call out, "I am sorry Anna. I am so, so sorry." Eventually they were just specks way down the road and then they were gone.

* * * * *

What happened tore the family apart.

Unable to face the shame from people he thought were his friends, Jonathan left for Mississippi within the month. The girl he hoped to marry refused to receive him; or rather her father would not allow him to see her. Samuel gave his eldest son an amount of cash and a horse and they all hugged him goodbye, although Oratio could not be coaxed out from her hiding place under her bed. He was twenty-one. They could not force him to stay. Samuel and Lemuel soon followed. There was no future for them either in Warren County. Emily, now twenty, went north to Pennsylvania where they still had family in Bucks County.

Anna grew weary when she thought of moving and starting over. She was almost forty years old, too old to start new somewhere else. And there was her mother to consider. Mary was nearly seventy now and steadfastly refused to go anywhere. Even though she had not seen or heard from him for years, Richard was still living in the next county and she was still married to him. Regardless what the rest of them did, she was going to stay put. Who would tend the orchards and pick the peaches if they left? She said many times she was not afraid to live alone and would manage fine.

Possibly sympathetic to their plight, a neighboring farmer came to them in the early months of 1818 with a generous offer to buy their farm lock, stock and barrel. He wanted to add to his own orchards and the Newman land was adjacent to his.

At first they refused, but he came back with a second offer, this time carving out the two houses and the land around the mill pond that had once been Mercyville so ownership would remain with Mary Hope Freeman Lovett. After two weeks of discussion and consideration, Samuel and Anna accepted the offer. They were free to leave. Letters were sent back and forth to the sons in Mississippi. All were married now and Jonathan shared news that his wife was pregnant, with the baby due in the summer. Anna warmed to the idea of moving since it would bring her closer to her first grandchild.

They were packed by April. By then, Jonathan and Samuel had decided their opportunities would be better in the new state of Louisiana and their families were moving west again, this time to Ouachita Parish. They found some promising land for Samuel and Anna to look at there. It was six hundred miles from Warren County. Samuel and Anna hated leaving Mary alone in the old yellow house, but she assured them she would not really be alone. She had hired a couple to cook and help her take care of the place.

Anna thought her mother looked very small and old as she stood waving bravely from the porch of the dogtrot as their loaded wagon started down their road to the main road. Samuel wanted to make it to Ouachita in thirty days. It would be hard driving. Anna wondered if she would see her mother again this side of heaven.

CHAPTER EIGHT

Mercy Plantation
Hancock County, Georgia
1820 - 1837

Mary Freeman, as she thought of herself these days, was never lonely. True, the big old house was quiet, but there were the Wainwright portraits in the library, mother's and father's graves down by the old church, and a letter every week from Anna and Samuel with news of their new life in Louisiana with the children and grandchildren.

Mary was pleased, and read Anna's last letter aloud in the cemetery to Mercy and John. It was about Anna holding her new grandchild and whispering, "I'm your old grandma Anna. Ain't nobody gonna love you like your old grandma loves you." Anna was a good girl and would remember the stories. Mary knew that she would also become a part of those stories some day too.

Her days were quiet, but not silent. There was always a racket from the kitchen. Her new cook, Chloe, was clumsy and things could be dropped and banged around with a huge commotion just while making a simple pot of tea. Mary had one of those new cook stoves installed in the kitchen house. It had four lids on the top that could be opened to feed and tend the fire underneath and it seemed Chloe just loved to rattle those lids. Mary did not mind. It was a friendly commotion, not like someone banging things around in a sullen fury.

Chloe's husband Curley, (and they swore that was his real name) was always whistling or humming beneath the library windows as he went about his chores tending Mary's old azaleas and the new camellias she let him plant along the perimeter of the porch. Curley had a definite talent in bringing plants to bloom and keeping them healthy. The yard had never looked better. There was a planned cycle to his plantings that followed the seasons, divided further into cycles that followed the months, and then even seemed to follow the weeks so something was always blooming from early spring until late fall. There were subtle variations from one week to the next, depending on the season. Although she had few callers, especially after Beth turned the town against the family, it was never a lonely life.

Chloe made a cake for Mary's seventieth birthday and the three of them had a little party on the side veranda. It was a white cake and the middle had a surprise layer of a delicious sauce of preserved raspberries. Mary said she could not remember having such a delicious and light cake. There were letters from Samuel and Anna and their children and their wives, and even a birthday drawing from one of the grandchildren. Amanda was fifteen now and was allowed to have callers. Levina, at twelve, was jealous of Amanda. Oratio was six and little Henry was five. Mary realized it was not going to be long until she would have trouble keeping track of all of them. She already needed help from Chloe to remember all the names and ages of her great-grandchildren.

Other than being so old, she felt fine. Sometimes she would catch herself thinking she was only forty, or twenty-five, or even fifteen again and then look in the mirror and wonder who the old woman was looking back at her. Maybe that was old age, not recognizing your own face in the mirror. Chloe continually cautioned her to be careful, especially when she went up and down the front steps. Mary had been going up and down those same steps since this house was built and wasn't going to forget how to now, but to humor Chloe, she would hold onto her cook's hand and let her be the guide.

Her life was pretty much the same from day to day. Nothing much really happened until a letter from her husband's attorney came in the mail. It was mixed in with the other greetings and she almost missed it. The attorney, Robert Tucker, Esq, regretted to inform her that Mr. Richard Lovett had passed away on November 6, 1820. As his wife, she was the sole heir to his estate - so even in death Richard still ignored their daughter. The attorney should like to call on her at her home at her earliest convenience to discuss the transition. Mary sent a letter in reply and Mr. Tucker arrived almost immediately. It was the week before Christmas.

After the departure of the children, Mary kept only a simple Christmas. When Mr. Tucker arrived, the front door and hall were already decorated with the usual lush garlands of magnolia leaves and ribbon. Curley made up the garlands and Chloe hung them with Mary standing by, supervising. After decorating they always had a cup of Chloe's egg punch, sweetened with a bit of bourbon and sprinkled with nutmeg and cinnamon.

On Christmas day, Mary gave them their gifts and then Chloe would serve a special dinner for Mary in the dining room, with Chloe and Curley eating the same dinner out in the kitchen. After reading her letters and Christmas greetings again in the afternoon, Mary would have tea and after sitting by the fire a while she would go to bed. It was nothing at all like the bedlam Anna and Samuel would enjoy with their enormous family. She could only imagine.

A visitor was a rare treat and Chloe almost had herself in a state, bossing Curley through a complete cleaning of the house while cooking all of her specialties. Mary teased Chloe that they were only having one visitor, who may not even stay the night, but she was happy for the change and grateful to Mr. Tucker for providing it. It was good to have some anticipation in the house again.

He arrived with his carriage wheels crunching on the freshly-swept gravel of the drive. Mary, dressed in her best dress, which still had some good years of wear left in it, came out onto the veranda to greet him. After bowing over her hand, he followed her into the library where tea and cakes were waiting, with a beaming Chloe standing by and ready to serve.

"Madam, I must express my sincere condolences at your loss."

"Why, thank you Mr. Tucker," she replied graciously, "but it is actually no loss. I am sure you know that Mr. Lovett and I never lived together after our marriage. In fact, I think it has been at least thirty years since I last saw or heard from him."

Mr. Tucker cleared his throat. Even though he knew the circumstances, he had still expected a grieving, or perhaps even bitter, widow. But Mrs. Lovett met his eyes with a purely contented gaze. "Would you care for another piece of Chloe's Christmas plum cake, Mr. Tucker? She has been baking all week in preparation for your visit. The pecans are all the way from Bryan County, I am told."

Mr. Tucker glanced over to Mrs. Lovett's maid, who shyly ducked her head at the mention of her name. "Yes, that is mighty nice of you Mrs. Lovett."

"Please, Mr. Tucker, call me Mary. I have not thought of myself as Mrs. Lovett in almost forty years. May I call you Robert?"

"Yes, ma'am. Of course."

They paused a moment, savoring the cake.

"Well, enough of polite conversation," Mary said. "What did you need to see me about Robert?"

Robert swallowed. "It is pretty straightforward, Mrs. Love...um, Mary. With your late husband's death, everything passes to you. Lovett plantation and everything on it belongs to you."

"I do not want it, Robert. Can it be passed along to my daughter instead?"

"No, ma'am, it cannot. Under the terms of the will, and the law, if you refuse the property it is to be auctioned off to settle the estate. After fees, duties and commissions, the remaining funds will be distributed to you. Then you can do anything you want with the money, give it all to your daughter if you like, but that would not accomplish transferring the plantation in its entirety to her."

"Why not?"

"Well, everything would be sold; the furniture, the paintings, everything in the house, the machinery, the land, and the slaves. She would be hard-pressed to buy everything back, even if one buyer bought everything."

"Do the slaves have to be sold?" she asked.

192

"They are part of the estate. If you refuse, then everything, including the slaves has to be sold."

"You must understand that I find the notion of slavery abhorrent. Can I not give the slaves their certificates of emancipation and sell the rest?"

"If that is your intent, ma'am, you could accomplish that by taking possession, freeing them, and then selling off what is left. However, most of the value of the estate is in the stock of slaves."

"You speak of those people as though they are cattle, Mr. Tucker."

"I meant no offense, Ma'am. I was just stating what could be accomplished. But Ma'am…"

"Yes,"

"If I may be so bold, may I suggest that the slaves on Lovett plantation are not ready to be emancipated. It would be a disaster that would only result in their ruination. They are only trained in growing and harvesting cotton and can scarcely manage taking care of themselves, let alone their children. They are dependent on the master for everything. To free them would be to destroy them."

Mary was silent a long moment. "You are very passionate about this, aren't you Robert?"

"I do apologize, ma'am."

"No, no need to. I just need to think a moment," she paused. "Is there no manager on the plantation to watch over them?"

A look of contempt flickered across Robert's face, "Mr. Elias Garrett is the overseer. He can only be counted on for his continued abuse."

Mary fell silent, looking at the portrait of Aunt Charity staring down at them.

"Did my husband ever share my heritage with you, Robert?"

Robert's immediately downcast eyes revealed the truth. Richard had betrayed her to his attorney along with everyone else. "I questioned it ma'am, but now that I see you I understand that he was mistaken. Mistaken if that is what he believed to be true."

"Oh, he was not mistaken, Robert. You see, my great-grandmother was a slave on the Wainwright plantation in South Carolina. I am one-eighth, an octoroon, so technically I am still Negro by Georgia law. Does that invalidate my husband's will?"

Robert was thoughtful a moment, then simply said, "No. A free person of color can still own property in Georgia and can receive property left to them by any white person. In your case, since you were married to Richard and he recognizes and names you as his wife in his will, the property can, and absolutely will, pass to you."

"Did Richard free any of his slaves in his will?"

"No."

"I remember the one time I called there. We had not been married very long. I wanted him to let me come to him, or to still have a family with me. His mother even went with me..." Mary lost her train of thought remembering the meeting. What had she been talking about? Robert waited patiently.

"Oh, what I was going to say was that when we were there it seemed there was a woman with him in the house, possibly a companion of sorts to him. I always wondered about her, what happened to her."

"Delilah?"

"Yes, yes - that was her name. I met her just that one time and it was not the best of circumstances." She paused. "Is she still living there?"

"She is still living, but she is no longer on the plantation, ma'am."

"Did Richard free her then?"

"No, ma'am."

"What happened to her?"

"She was sold in the culling of slaves last fall."

"What?"

"After being there with him almost forty-five years, taking care of his every need, Richard had her beaten and sold with the culling last fall," Robert said, barely able to conceal his anger and contempt.

Mary would have dropped her teacup and saucer if Chloe had not been there to catch it.

She felt a buzzing in her head. "He must have been out of his mind," she realized.

"Yes, ma'am. Quite."

"What became of her?"

"I arranged for several third parties to be at the auction. One of them was able to successfully bid for her and then sold her to me. I signed her Declaration of Emancipation that same day, so she is a free woman. I gave her a sum of money and pay the rent on a house for her in Macon. She is heart-broken, but I do get a weekly letter from her."

"She can read and write then," Mary said, slightly encouraged. Then she looked up at Robert. "It was a brave and selfless thing you did for her. I want to pay you back from Richard's money. That is, assuming he had any."

Robert nodded with a small smile. "No need to do that, Mrs. Lovett. It was my choice and I am happy to do it. I thought she deserved better than he ever gave her, especially at the end. And, yes, there are substantial funds left to you."

"What is this culling you spoke of?"

"It is unusual, but not unheard of. Each fall, after the harvest, the slave stock – or population - is reviewed and a number are sold off rather than continuing the expense of keeping them through the winter."

He briefly described what he witnessed at the Lovett plantation each fall, his presence illogically required by his client as Richard and his overseer made their selections, literally pulling the selected ones from their families, their mothers and fathers, their children. New slaves, fresh stock, were bought each spring and just thrown in with the rest of them. He hoped to never witness it again. Even though he gave her a watered-down child's version, Mary was appalled.

"How utterly barbaric," she said.

There was a long pause. Robert, sensing Mary was deep in thought, making her decision, waited.

"So, I can't just free the slaves, I cannot pass the property to my family, who would likely not want to keep slaves either, and I could not in good conscience sell the property and its people to someone else who would only perpetuate the system. I am not left with any reasonable choice, am I?"

Robert slightly shook his head in agreement.

"Can I rely on your loyalty and your guidance, Robert?"

Alan E Bailey

"Absolutely."

"Then I suppose I have no choice but to remove myself from here, and take up the ownership and management of the Lovett Plantation."

* * * * *

Rather than subjecting Chloe and Curley to what she suspected the horror of the Lovett Plantation would be, she left them as caretakers of her house by the millpond, promising that she would return periodically. She was sure to need a rest from what lay before her. Her hastily-packed trunks were loaded into Mr. Tucker's carriage and she rode back with him the following day.

In spite of Richard's apparent wealth, she was surprised at the neglect of the house and gardens. It reminded her of the story of Aunt Charity and Mercy traveling out to the Wainwright plantation and finding it in a similar state.

An elderly black manservant, in a jacket and cravat that showed him to be the butler, waited at the bottom of the steps. A ragged young boy ran forward, taking the horses and Robert's driver jumped down from the driver's seat to open the carriage door for them.

"Master Robert!" the old man said happily, "Welcome back, sir."

Mary lightly touched Robert's hand as she came down from the carriage. She curtsied to the butler as Robert introduced her as, "Mrs. Lovett, your new mistress."

"Please, Robert," she softly scolded, then turned to the butler. "I would prefer to be called Miss Mary – or simply Mary, if you please."

"Miss Mary," the butler made the change effortlessly. "Mary" would be completely inappropriate, and Julius would still refer to her as Mrs. Lovett when not addressing her directly.

"And you are?"

"I am Julius, Miss Mary."

A deeply tanned man in a green cutaway coat and wide brimmed hat came running around the side of the house to meet them. He slowed to a walk the last few steps and stuck out his hand, showing his poor manners. Instead of taking his hand and accepting a handshake, Mary lightly extended her hand, palm down, as a lady should, even in these modern times. He remembered himself, took her offered hand at the fingertips, lightly bowing.

196

"I am Elias Garrett, Miz Lovett, at your service."

"Mr. Garrett." Mary acknowledged him, but did not add any further pleasantries. She already did not like him. He had the slimy air of a snake about him, someone who would stab you in the back with a smile on his face, she thought. Ignoring Garrett, she turned back to Robert and said, "Shall we have a look around?"

After a short pause for refreshments that Julius served from a tray on the front veranda, Robert gave her a perfunctory tour of the house. It was gloomy and had an air of death about it, but there was nothing a good cleaning and fresh air could not clear away. As a start she said, "I wonder if we might open all these drapes and let some sunshine into these rooms."

"Yes, Miss Mary," Julius agreed with enthusiasm. It seemed like it was something he had wanted to do for a long time.

The layout was much the same as her house back in Warren County and also the house Richard's parents had built: a long central hall, dining room and living room, sitting room and library downstairs, a long staircase to the second floor where four bedrooms were situated, then an attic above that. A detached kitchen was behind the house, situated in a kitchen garden. As the realm of the cook, the kitchen was neat and orderly. The cook herself, a woman of generous proportions named Dilsie, was a study of tidiness. Although cautious and avoiding the eye of her new mistress, Dilsie still greeted her warmly, the one bright and welcoming spot it seemed.

A number of outbuildings could be seen at the end of the yard. They walked toward those, inspecting a barn, sheds and the ever-present gin house and cotton warehouse; now empty of the harvest but with bits of the fiber still clinging to the rafters, doors, and rough wood siding. A lane ran beside the warehouse and disappeared around a corner.

"Where does that go?"

"It leads down to the quarters, Ma'am," Elias said, as if his words would assure her not wanting to continue.

"Let's have a look then," she said, taking Robert's arm and leaving Elias standing with his mouth hanging half open.

It was evening and the workers were returning from the fields. The crop was finished and they were plowing the stubble under. Elias proudly said the work would be finished by Christmas. Mary noticed he fingered the whip coiled at his side and his eyes darted around the area as he spoke.

Their entrance into the clearing that housed the quarters was unnoticed at first. Then it set off a flurry of activity near to panic as mothers grabbed up their young children and corralled the older ones. In just a few moments, everyone was assembled in front of the cabins they were assigned. Sometimes as many as twelve to fifteen people were standing in front of one impossibly small cabin, barely eight feet by twelve. All eyes were on her, but there was not a sound.

Mary stepped forward, forcing a pleasant smile to her face. Then she realized. These people thought it was another culling. "Did Richard ever come down here?" she softly asked Robert.

"Only for the culling," he replied quietly.

"Then they think this is what that is."

Beside her, Elias showed his whip, bringing it up and rubbing the coil of it with his free hand, making sure it was seen. "Put that down!" Mary said sharply to him before she could stop herself.

Elias looked at her, stupidly. "Are you having trouble hearing me, Mr. Garrett? I said to put that whip away. Now!"

Elias put the whip back down to his side, but could not stop his sullen look at this woman, talking to him that way.

She stepped forward. Robert stayed with her. "Hello," she said. "I am Mary Lovett, Mr. Lovett's widow, but I would like you to call me Miss Mary, if you please."

Still there was silence. "I am just having a look around and wanted to come down and say hello to you. We can get better acquainted later. I am sure I will come to know each one of you soon. But for now, don't let us interrupt. Continue what you were doing."

"What is this, a garden party?" Elias mumbled under his breath.

Mary turned to him with an eyebrow raised in surprise and then gave him a withering look. "Do you forget that I am now your employer, Mr. Garrett?" she demanded quietly but forcefully. He stopped.

Mary bowed lightly and gave a shallow curtsy to her people, then turned to go, but as she did her eye caught a movement beyond the crowd. A small boy, very light-skinned and clad only in a rough linen shirt against the chill evening came toddling from the other end of the lane toward her, crying. He could not be more than two years old. His nose ran, his legs were filthy and his feet were bare, but worse were the scabs on his scalp - apparently a bad lice infestation.

198

Mary turned back and stepped toward the boy, "Whose child is this?" willfully keeping the reproach from her voice. How could someone neglect a child so badly? Eyes around the quarter were downcast. Mary looked around but no one would meet her gaze, except one woman, holding two young children close as they stood with her. She glared back at Mary.

"Is this your child?" Mary asked of her.

"No, ma'am," she replied, with a voice bordering on hatred. "He not."

"Whose is he?"

"He mama sold in last culling. Dey say leave him be." She looked like she would spit on Elias Garrett if she could.

"Don't you dare sass Miz Lovett, Laura," Elias warned, pointing his whip at her. Laura glared back defiantly at him. Whip me all you want, her eyes said, it is still the truth.

"Laura was merely answering my question, Mr. Garrett. And put that whip down before I take it away from you. How could you sell this child's mother and leave him here alone? How could any human being do that to another, especially to a mother and her child?"

Elias was silenced. Mary went to the child and picked him up. He was filthy and she could see lice nits in his hair, or what was left of it. Still, she cradled the wailing child to her breast.

"Laura, can you give him something to eat?" she said.

There was a long pause. "Got nothing to give him, Mistress. My chil'ren hongry too."

Mary turned on Elias. "Why is this? Why do these people have no food?"

Mary was appalled to learn that from first planting to last harvest only seven pounds of rice and beans was issued on the first of the month for each man, woman and child. Then she was angered when Elias told her the rations were cut back to five pounds a month during winter.

"And obviously, it is not enough."

"Just following the master's orders, ma'am," Elias replied defiantly.

"If any of you has any food left, please raise your hand," she called out.

199

One woman timidly raised her hand before her husband pulled it down, giving her a look. Mary went to her. "How much do you have?"

"Got a little rice left, Mistress. Been careful, but not much left, but we stretch it out 'til next time."

Mary, still cradling the child, walked back to Elias. "I want you to give five pounds of rice and five pounds of beans to every man, woman and child on this plantation before dark, Mr. Garrett. Is that clear?"

"But they get their Christmas next week, Miss Lovett. They will all have plenty then."

"And go hungry until then? I do not follow your line of reason, Mr. Garrett. I would not expect a cow to give milk if I starved her and I would not expect a racehorse to run. Am I clear? Do you understand me? Is there enough in the storehouse to do as I have ordered?"

"Yes, ma'am."

"Then get started. And, Mr. Garrett."

"Yes."

"Starting now, the previous five pounds of bean and rice per person per month, is changed to that amount each and every week – distributed every Saturday. Is that understood?"

"Yes, ma'am. If that is what you want."

"Yes, it is what I want. I will not have these people starved."

She turned to the people, who still stared at her, amazed at the exchange. "Can someone help me by taking this child to be cleaned up and fed?" Laura stepped forward, holding out her arms and Mary handed him over. "Thank you," Mary said.

Mary stamped all the way back up to the house with Robert and Elias almost trotting behind her to keep up.

"This is inexcusable, shameful! How could my husband have allowed this?" she ranted. Robert was encouraged. Elias was increasingly agitated as he continued on to the building where the rations were stored.

But instead of continuing on to the house she went to the kitchen and burst through the door. "Dilsie?"

"Yes, ma'am," Dilsie answered cautiously, with her head down. Master Richard rarely came to the kitchen, but when he did, and especially when he burst through the door, it was not good.

"What have you prepared for dinner?"

Dilsie began naming off the dishes she prepared to welcome to new mistress to the plantation. When she was finished, Mary asked, "Is there a smokehouse?"

"Yes, ma'am," Dilsie answered even more cautiously, thinking the mistress was not pleased with the dinner menu she had planned. Master Richard had been like that, sometimes throwing what she had prepared on the floor and commanding her to make something else.

"Do we have any ham?"

"Yes, ma'am. Still four nice ones. Smoked real good now."

"Go down and bring up two of them. Mr. Tucker will help you, won't you Robert?" she ordered, while tying on an apron and looking around the kitchen. "We need to make biscuits, and a lot of them. Can you show me where the flour and soda is, and do you have any buttermilk? I will get them started."

"Yes, ma'am." Dilsie was almost apologetic. She made light bread rolls for the dinner. She should have made biscuits instead.

"Dilsie," Mary looked at her now, "I have just ordered Mr. Garrett to issue new rations to the quarters, but it's going to take time for the rice and beans to cook and they are all hungry. Do you think you can help me carry this supper down there and divide it up the best we can? I think if we make up a batch of ham biscuits to go with it - at least one apiece for everyone - it can get them something to eat in the mean time. Can you help me with that?"

"Oh yes, ma'am," Dilsie said enthusiastically. 'Praise Jesus!' she thought.

As often as she dared, Dilsie saved the scraps from the master's table and took them to the quarters instead of feeding them to the hogs like she was supposed to do. It was obscene to feed the hogs when the children were hungry. In doing so, she risked being beaten and even sold off the plantation. At a minimum, she could have been taken out of the kitchen and sent to the fields. But she could not help herself. Now the mistress had commanded her to do what she had wanted to do. She sprang into action, feeling a celebration in her heart.

Mary pushed things aside on the work table to stir up the biscuits and as soon as they were ready, they were filled with a slice of smoked ham. When the platters were piled high with the biscuits, Mary picked up the tray and Robert helped Dilsie carry the pots containing what would have been their dinner and they went back to the quarters.

The first of the rice and beans had been issued and was being cooked at a communal fire. It looked like they could scarcely wait for even the rice to cook. The beans would take longer. Mary walked among them, handing out the biscuits. "Eat this now," she said, "but don't eat too much at once. You don't want to get sick. Be sure everyone gets some."

The last part was unnecessary, she realized, as she watched older siblings making sure younger brothers and sister had food before they served themselves.

"Bless you, Miss Mary," Laura said quietly.

"And bless you too, Laura. It is a bit like the feeding of the five thousand isn't it?" Mary replied. "No one is going to go hungry on this plantation while I am here. I promise you."

So much had happened in the few hours since she arrived that Mary felt a little giddy. Robert took the tray and had her sit down. Then he handed her one of the biscuits. She had not realized how hungry she was herself. Robert took one and began munching it. "Delicious!" he said.

Eventually, after the dinner pots were emptied and Dilsie had cut up another ham to add to the simmering rice and bean pots, they walked back up to the house. Elias was subdued and pensive. Robert seemed amused. He had to try hard to keep himself from grinning outright. At the base of the steps to the house Mary turned to Elias, "You will come to my office first thing tomorrow morning," she commanded. Then to Robert – "Oh, I do have an office don't I?" Robert nodded. "We have much to discuss, Mr. Garrett. Good night."

As she went through the front door she was suddenly exhausted. "Oh, my," she declared, sitting weakly in the chair Robert quickly brought to her and feeling every one of her seventy years. After a few moments they moved to the dining room table where Dilsie had still managed a simple supper for them, beaming at the new mistress as she served plates prepared at the sideboard.

"There is so much to do here, Robert. I had no idea. Everywhere I look shows neglect. I don't know. I am not sure I can do it."

"You have already made an excellent start, Mary." Robert said, grinning at her with admiration. He raised his glass in toast. Mary found her glass and raised it as her eyes met his.

"To Lovett Plantation," he said with a nod. "And to a new beginning."

Mary paused. "I don't like that name, Robert. I want to start by renaming this place right here and now. From now on, this plantation will be called "Mercy" in honor of my dear, departed mother.

"To Mercy Plantation, then," he revised his toast, and this time Mary joined him.

Mary was refreshed and filled with new energy when she rose with the sun the next morning. She dressed herself and found her way to the plantation office where she would meet with Elias. It was a small, frame structure with a central desk backed with a tall shelf of pigeon holes holding a clutter of documents. There was a map of the plantation on one wall and a simple, straight-backed chair facing the desk. She took the chair behind the desk, slightly more luxurious but still Spartan. Elias came in just as she was seating herself and she realized it was his chair she was taking, but she sat down anyway.

"Oh, good. I'm glad you are early, Elias. I have much to cover with you."

Over the next months, she adopted the role of a beneficial matriarch with Elias, while realizing he chafed under her close management. Each day they would discuss the work of the previous day, what was planned for the present day, and what was coming up. She kept careful notes of their meetings. "I have to write things down or I don't recall them later," she explained, and he came to hate those lists. Nothing escaped her notice and he could let nothing slide. She postured her comments and questions so that he had no choice but to agree with her, or to look incompetent as manager. But she covered only one improvement per day, giving him time to think over and absorb the significance of what she said.

"Elias, I have been reviewing the crop yield per acre over the past ten years and it appears, that in spite of my late husband's increased punishments and disciplinary tactics, the yields have declined. It would appear his approach has not led to increased yields, don't you agree?"

"Elias, I understand the meeting house was given over a number of years ago for housing our people. I have checked and all the other plantations in the area have a meeting house. I believe we should build another meeting house, don't you agree?"

"Elias, I have been reviewing the record of punishments on the workers and there are a number of inconsistent punishments. I believe that for discipline to be respected that punishments must be consistent. Until further notice, I will give final approval on punishments prior to their administration. Don't you agree?"

"Elias, I believe the workers will be happier if they live as families with their families. I see we have ten to twelve workers living in each cabin and there are rarely families that large. I don't think it is Christian for men and women to be living together who are not married. I think we need to occupy the workers this winter with building new cabins until each family has a cabin. Don't you agree?"

"Elias, I am not sure rice and beans is an adequate diet, especially for children. I think we need to add an allotment of meat and corn meal to the rice and beans. Don't you agree?"

"Elias, I simply cannot condone adultery and fornication among anyone on this plantation. Don't you agree?"

"Elias, I believe for a man to lie with a woman, black or white, is still fornication or even adultery if he is married to another. Don't you agree?"

"Elias, I want to start a new program this next harvest, paying the workers a small amount for each bag of cotton they pick and bring to the gin house. I am thinking three cents a bag. It will give them a little money and begin teaching them the value of things. But I am not forgetting you, Elias; I will also pay you an amount for each bag they pick, on top of your salary. I think that will help raise our yield per acre, since they will know all year the more cotton there is to pick, the more they will earn at harvest time. Don't you agree?"

"Elias, I want to start an evening school in the meeting house to teach the children their letters and how to read the Bible. It is not against the law to teach them how to read, only how to write, and I will only be teaching them from the Bible. I believe it is the best path to their salvation, bringing them to our Lord and Savior, Jesus Christ. Don't you agree?"

And finally,

"Elias, I find myself sorely in need of white female companionship on this plantation. I think your wife might enjoy coming up to the house for tea – say tomorrow afternoon. Don't you agree?"

Lucy Garrett arrived promptly the next afternoon, overly dressed for tea in her Sunday-best dress, hat and gloves, and a fancy fringed shawl that did not quite go. Mary was ready and heard the timid knock on the front door and opened it before Julius could come to the door.

"Mrs. Garrett, I am Mary Lovett. Please do come in."

"I warn't sure if I should come to the front door like this, Miz Lovett, but Elias said I was to," Lucy said apologetically in a thin and small voice that sounded more like a half-grown girl than a young woman. "I never come up to the big house afore."

"Yes, perfectly correct and well done," Mary praised.

Lucy looked around meekly, trying not to gawk. She reminded Mary of a scared little rabbit, all dressed up like a child would do. She must have lain awake all night dreading the visit. Mary also noticed a fading bruise on her left cheek, almost hidden by the bonnet, and when she reached out to take Mary's offered hand, there was the ring of a fresher bruise around her forearm, above the wrist between the sleeve of the dress and her glove. Mary's heart went out to her.

They went to the library, where Dilsie was just finishing tea.

"Hey, Dilsie," Lucy said, before she caught herself. She warn't sure if white folks was supposed to talk to niggers in the big house.

"Good afternoon, Mrs. Garrett." Dilsie said respectfully, but still in a friendly way. It was apparent to Mary the two already knew each other and were friends, and Dilsie was guiding her friend through this meeting.

Mary sat and patted the chair beside her for Lucy to sit too. She poured tea, careful to make each motion slowly and carefully so the wide-eyed Lucy could do the same. It was only small talk, but she could see that Lucy relaxed some when Mary said, "I have sorely missed having female companionship here. I am so happy you could come."

"Oh, Miz Lovett. I ain't much good at company. I never been anywhere fancy like this afore. Never been nowhere really, 'cept afore me and Elias was married and come here I lived over in Warren County, just over the river. But my family was all just crackers there. Elias don't like me sayin' that, but it's true. He wants a big house like this someday too and told me it would be good for me to come and have a good look at it. I'm happy to come to visit and keep you company, but I just don't want to lie to you, ma'am. I don't think you will want to visit with me."

"Why, I am from Warren County too! See there? We have something to talk about already."

After a while, Mary was amused that young Lucy was trying to hide that she was looking at the room. Lucy turned back, "Sorry ma'am. I just cain't help lookin'. Everything is just so beautiful here. I never seen anything like it."

Mary rose, bringing the observant Lucy to her feet too. "Lucy, let's have a look around the house. I have been so busy since my arrival I've barely had time to look at it myself. We can explore it together."

For the next hour they went through all the rooms. Mary opened drawers she had not opened before, poking through the contents. She pulled books from the library shelves, reading the titles, and stopped to look at paintings. The house, with all the curtains open and most of the windows raised to bring in fresh air, was not quite as gloomy as it had been. It was clean, but otherwise the decorations were gaudy and tasteless. Mary would have to focus on her home sometime soon to see what could be done to make it more pleasing.

Still, Lucy was amazed. She reached out to touch things, then ducked her head and apologized. Mary only laughed and when she could, picked up objects and handed to Lucy for closer inspection.

When they settled back in the library, and after Mary poured them another cup of tea, she began describing her plans for the school she was starting in the new meeting house. A new shingle roof was being put on the big house; the roof had leaked like a sieve the last time it rained. After that work was finished in the evenings, Mary paid the older children a penny for every discarded shingle they picked up from the ground that was of a large enough size. Her plan for the first lesson would be to paint letters of the alphabet on those shingles, having the students practice in the dirt until they could make the letter, then using one of several brushes to paint the letter on the shingle. The shingles could be propped on a rail she had nailed up around the school room, about three feet off the floor. As the students learned their letters they could begin placing individual letters on the rail to form words.

"Do you think that sounds like a reasonable idea for teaching them how to read, Lucy?"

Lucy ducked her head, "I wouldn't know, ma'am. I never went to school."

"But you can read and write, can't you?"

"No, ma'am. My folks didn't know how so they couldn't learn me to. I used to want to read, something fierce and awful, but Elias says I'm too...well, that I cain't never be learned how."

"Oh, nonsense. There is nothing to it. I will show you sometime. Maybe we can start the next time you come to tea."

"Oh yes, ma'am," Lucy said and beamed a smile. It was the first time she smiled since she arrived and it was a lovely smile.

At the door, Mary took Lucy's hand. Please, Lucy, I want you to call me Mary when we are together like this. That is how friends do it."

"Yes, ma'am, I mean, yes, Mary."

"And I want to tell you, just between us, that I understand your husband. I want you to know you always have a place to come to here at my house, and that you will always have a safe place here at Mercy plantation, with or without your husband. This will always be your home for as long as you want it to be."

"Yes, ma'am," Lucy was embarrassed and covered the bruise on her arm, but was pleased.

Mary's method of teaching the alphabet and reading was successful. As they had with Mercy's school so many years ago, the parents stood in the back of the meeting house during the lesson, closely observing. At the end of each lesson, Mary would arrange enough letters on the rail to form a word. At first they were simple: she would arrange one or two student's names, letting them see what their name looked like in letters. Then she used other words that showed where they were; Mercy Plantation, Hancock County, and Georgia. There was so much to teach she had to be selective.

* * * * *

By April, 1821, Elias was increasingly frustrated at having to take every decision to Mary, but she did not relax her hold. Mercy Plantation had settled into a comfortable routine and its people were looking better fed, if not healthy. Her announcement of the program of paying three cents for each sack of cotton they picked that harvest sent a wave of excitement and optimism through the quarters. None understood numbers yet, so Mary switched her lessons to the story in Genesis about Noah building the ark, and any other biblical reference she could find pertaining to arithmetic. If ever there was a surprise visit by the sheriff she wanted to be able to prove she was only teaching her people the Bible.

She estimated the best pickers could earn as much as twenty dollars at harvest. Families pooling their money together could accumulate eight hundred dollars in five years, the price to buy one slave. She only had five years to make the first of them ready for freedom.

Disaster struck Mercy Plantation the week after Easter. Prior to the fall culling of the previous year, two slaves ran. One was caught and returned almost immediately. He did not survive the punishment Elias administered to him. The other, Jimmie, who ironically was one of the strongest field workers and best pickers, and thus would have been immune to the culling, was not captured. Before Mary arrived, Elias had administered several whippings to his wife, Peggie, and their fifteen year old son, trying to make them tell where Jimmie had gone but they apparently did not know because nothing could be beaten out of them. As time passed, Peggie grew more hopeful that Jimmie made it to Canada and that he would someday have enough saved to buy the freedom of his family.

Then Jimmie was brought back to Mercy Plantation in chains, running awkwardly between two horses as they came trotting up the drive. Mary went out and ordered the men to stop and release him.

"He is a dangerous one, Ma'am."

"He is my property and you will do as I say. Now!"

Jimmie collapsed to his knees, exhausted and defeated. Seeing him as she arrived with the others, running up from the quarters as the word spread, Peggie screamed and had to be held back. Elias had two men bind him with ropes and take him to the barn. Unlike the old days, he knew he would have to discuss Jimmie's punishment with her royal highness, Mrs. Lovett.

Mary stamped down to her office with Elias at a trot to keep up. When they were inside she slammed the door and spun to face him with the expression of an angry wildcat.

"What now? What now, Mr. Garrett?"

Elias sat in his chair, leaned back and put his foot on the desk, and casually pushed back his hat. Mary wanted to slap him. "Well, ma'am, he has to be punished, and as you say, punishments have to be consistent here at Mercy Plantation."

Mary walked around and pushed his foot off the desk, and then sat down. "And I suppose now you are going to have the joy of telling me exactly what that punishment is."

Elias's eyebrows went up and his eyes narrowed in his mockery. "Well, ma'am, there are two options. Only two things to choose from when a nigger runs away." He paused. Mary looked at him. "I am waiting, Mr. Garrett."

"The first is removing his toes so he can't run. What we do is, take a really sharp ax and..."

"Stop!" Mary interrupted holding up her hand, then placing her palms to her temples. "I am not going to destroy a man. Where is the sense in that? Crippling a worker so he is never any use?"

"Oh he can still work, chop cotton and pick it. He just ain't never gonna run again."

"I won't have it."

"Well, looks like you only got the second choice then ma'am." Elias said patronizingly with an evil grin.

"And that is."

"Forty lashes. Administered by me."

"But that will kill him, the state he is in."

Elias thrust his hands out, palms up. "Six one way and a half-dozen the other. Like you said ma'am, consistent punishment is the key to effective discipline."

Mary looked away, staring out the window, then she turned back. "I guess the only choice is the whip." Elias jumped up ready to start the beating. Mary held up her hand, stopping him. "But not today. Not until he's had a chance to recover enough that he will survive his punishment. I will decide that, and I will be present for the punishment. And Mr. Garrett,"

"Yes, Ma'am?"

"I will inspect the whip before you begin."

Two days later, rather than prolong the agony of waiting, Mary consented that Jimmie was ready. Completely horrified, she stood outside the barn while his hands were tied at the wrist and the rope looped over a rafter, then pulled up. He was stripped to the waist and stood, waiting.

Peggie stood in the circle surrounding the barnyard, supported on either side by two women. She had promised Jimmie she would be there, that she would watch and not look away. Even now her eyes looked to be frozen open. Elias uncoiled and recoiled his whip. Mary walked to Elias, her hand extended to take the whip. She inspected the full length of it for any embedded objects, but it was smooth. She handed it back to the overseer.

"Jimmie, you understand the punishment and why you are to receive it," she said, feeling like she was in a bad dream. "I have decided forty lashes instead of the other punishment. I am sorry this is necessary."

She stepped back and Elias's whip rang through the air, cutting deeply into the flesh of Jimmie's back. Mary could hear him take a breath in and hold it, determined for Peggie's sake to not make a sound.

Naively, and perhaps to calm herself, Mary had associated Jimmie's punishment with the three whippings Mercy had given her as a child. The first time was for lying. The second, for impudence, and the third and final, for giggling in church when she knew better. She was twelve years old. All three times, Mother had hugged her in her left arm, while three to four sharp slaps of the willow switch were administered to the backs of her bare legs, leaving welts that lasted for hours. Mother had cried more than Mary, especially the last time when Mary was more angry than hurt, insulted at being treated like a child when she was already a young lady. What was happening to Jimmie was not even remotely similar.

Elias drew the whip back, feeling its length, swung it around behind him again and administered the second of the forty lashes. A groan escaped Jimmie's mouth, he pressed the side of his face into his arm, pushing against the pain, shook his head as if to clear it and took a breath, bracing for the next.

Mary swallowed, and felt the tears on her cheeks. Elias administered the third lash, cutting more deeply than before. Jimmy wobbled on his knees, but then forced himself to straighten them and stand. Mary realized Elias was just getting started, there were soft, muffled sobs from behind her. As he wound up and brought the whip down for the fourth, Mary stepped in front of him,

"STOP!"

The whip whizzed by her ear, catching and cutting through the fabric of her skirt.

"I said stop, Mr. Garrett. Can you not hear me?"

"That's only three." Elias said, coiling the whip with a glistening sheen of sweat on his forehead. There was a glazed look about his eyes.

"Julius?"

"Yes, ma'am."

"See that Jimmie is cut down and that Peggie and he get back to their cabin. I will be there shortly. Mr. Garrett, I determine the punishment on this plantation and this is more than enough. I will meet with you tomorrow morning regarding this matter in my office. Do you understand me?"

Elias looked at her with pure hatred and for a moment she thought he might strike her, but he visibly collected himself and with a slight shake of his head, wiped his sweating forehead on his sleeve and focused his eyes on Mary as he seemed to come back to himself.

She turned and went to the house. She picked up the decanter of Richard's whiskey from the library and told Julius to gather up some clean cloths and follow her. She went down to the quarters, found Jimmie and Peggie's cabin and knocked on the door.

As mistress of the plantation she was entitled to just walk on in, but she could never bring herself to do that. A wizened old woman came to the door, and seeing Mary, fell to her knees, taking Mary's hand and bringing it against her cheek as she wept. "You saved my Jimmie, Mistress Mary. Jesus bless you, Mistress Mary. Jesus bless you. You saved my boy."

Mary wondered how this woman had escaped Richard's cullings. The family must have hidden her away somehow. She overlooked that the old woman had broken one of the cardinal rules of the plantation system - that a slave should never, ever touch the master. She only asked, "May I come in?"

Jimmie was already lying on the table, face down. Peggie was gently bathing his wounds with cool water, crying softly as he winced in pain. When she saw Mary she looked up and smiled through her tears. "I am so sorry," Mary said. "This is wrong."

"Jimmie would'a died if Mister Garrett finish him," Peggie said. "We thank you, Mistress for saving him."

Jimmie was angry. He could only look the other way. Away from where his mistress stood.

"I brought whiskey. Give him a cup of this to drink. It will help ease the pain for now. We also need to wash the wounds with it, to keep them from getting infected and to start healing."

Peggie took the whiskey and dabbed a bit to her cloth. She wasn't going to use enough of the precious whiskey to make a difference. "May I?" Mary asked. She took a ball of cotton from Julius, soaked it until the excess whiskey ran on the dirt floor, then liberally dabbed Jimmie's wounds after she warned him, "This will sting."

As she completed the bandaging of the wounds to keep out the flies, she talked softly to Jimmie. "The next time you leave here, Jimmie, you will walk out the front gates with your family, and all of you will have your Deeds of Emancipation in your hands. But before that, you need to be ready. You are smart, Jimmie. You know you can't just run up north and take the jobs they will offer. You will never make enough that way to live and save enough to buy even your old mother here. You have to have a good trade and be able to read and write and do your numbers. It will take a while, but you can do it if you want to. As soon as you are up and around, I want you to start coming to my reading lessons in the meeting house."

Jimmie was sullen and silent.

"I have to work out the rest of your punishment with Mr. Garrett. I have some extra work around the house, and my husband let the gardens go. Maybe you could do that on Sunday afternoons for a while, say one Sunday afternoon for each of the remaining lashes. You would be learning some basic carpentry skills, and painting and gardening. Those jobs pay well up north, I'm hearing."

Jimmie nodded. He still could not speak to his owner.

At the door, Peggie also took her hand. "Thank you, Miss Mary. You a kind woman."

"Oh no, my dear. But I try. I really do try."

* * * * *

The more she visited with Lucy, and from her interaction with Dilsie, Mary came to realize that Delilah had been a calming and positive influence in the house and on Richard. None would reveal the reason for her departure, except to say that Master Richard was just not in his right mind. She came to gain a respect for the woman she had despised so long ago, and eventually felt a deep need to meet her - just to see her face to face again.

She shared this with Robert Tucker, seeking his counsel on contacting Delilah. He was reluctant, saying Delilah had taken time to adjust to freedom and her new life. Eventually he said he would contact her. There was no response. When Robert sent a second letter, thinking perhaps the first had been lost, she sent a short reply saying she wanted only to be left alone.

After Jimmie's interrupted punishment, Elias was sullen and withdrawn. He was barely responsive in their morning meetings, nodding almost imperceptibly or not at all when Mary pinned him down with one of her "Don't you agree?" questions. She wanted to fire him but worried about Lucy if the Garretts left Mercy plantation. She also realized she would only be unleashing one of Satan's worse demons on another group of slaves at another plantation. It was best to keep Elias, however frustrating he was, where she could control him.

She also knew it was not over. She began to grasp that his retaliation would take on a larger form. Mary's school was only marginally legal and her treatment of her workers, while increasing the yields of Mercy plantation above the average yields of her neighbors, was increasingly resented by other planters in the county. Her softness could undermine what they could expect from their own workers.

She began to prepare for the inevitable visit from the sheriff. She was careful with the school, making sure nothing was present that could be considered to resemble pen and ink, or even slate and pencil. Letters on the rail were always arranged in a bible verse, one that would be considered admissible to teach slaves; "God is Love" was replaced with "Shalt Not Lie," "Shalt Not Steal," and even "Master and Slave He made Them."

It was on a Sunday afternoon; when she would least expect the sheriff to be conducting his business, that she saw him coming up the lane on his horse. She was sitting on a low stool in what once had been the rose garden. Richard had plowed the roses under for cotton, and it was now being put back into roses. Jimmie was working to lay out a path in a circular route through the rectangular garden. Mary sat with her parasol shielding her from the sun and talking to him about her plans for the garden. Jimmie still was nearly silent, but it was now a companionable, rather than a sullen, silence. He listened carefully and although he would never meet her eyes, she felt a bond growing between them.

Mary stood and waited for the sheriff to dismount his horse at the front steps before she called out, "Sheriff Tate, what a pleasure to see you." The sheriff was already thrown off his planned agenda – being greeted warmly instead of a show of guilt and fear. He walked over to where she waited.

"I am afraid the late Mr. Lovett completely destroyed these gardens, Sheriff. You will have to forgive me for breaking the Sabbath, but I find it more of a worship experience than toil, being out here in God's nature. Jimmie is helping me and he is doing a fine job, don't you agree?"

Although it looked to be nothing more than a long rectangle of manure and straw at the side of the house, now intersected by a crude path outlined in stones, he nodded in agreement to her question.

"To what do we owe this pleasure, Sheriff Tate?"

"Well, Miz Lovett, I have been hearing some complaints about your school. You know you can't be teaching the niggers, ma'am. It's against the law."

"Has there been a change in the law?" Mary asked with surprised concern.

"No, ma'am. It's always been against the law in Georgia to teach 'em to read and write."

"Oh, but sir, I only teach them to read. So they can read the Bible and their heathen souls can find the Lord's path to salvation. I think it is best for them to know the Lord's way, don't you agree?"

The sheriff was beginning to look confused.

"Come, Sheriff Tate, let's walk," she said, motioning with her eyes to Jimmie, who was surely hearing everything. She wanted the sheriff to think she didn't trust her workers either. "Will you help me up to the house? I want to get my reticule. I don't like leaving it in the house when I'm out. Don't you agree?" By now she had a grip on his arm, just above the elbow and squeezed the bicep almost painfully until he agreed. Yes, how could he not agree?

They walked down through the quarters, where the people were finished with their Sunday dinners after spending the morning worshipping in the meeting house. Some sat on stoops visiting. Children played at endless games or lay napping by their mothers. There were smiles when they saw their Mistress, or at least until they recognized the sheriff there with her. Sheriff Tate realized it was a far cry from the last time he was here.

Old Mister Lovett, half-crazed at his loss when the two slaves ran, wanted the sheriff to make the wife and son of one of the men tell him where they were. Tate, seeing how badly beaten the two already were, went back and told the old coot that he couldn't do anything more. If they had not told Garrett already, then they didn't know. An enraged Lovett had thrown a full glass of whiskey at him, barely missing his head before it shattered on the wall. He could have arrested Lovett right then and there, but the plantation masters were rarely arrested unless they killed or attacked one of their own kind. The face of the woman standing behind him all during that meeting, Delilah, showed recent signs of her master's wrath. It was a sad place.

As they walked past one of the fields planted in cotton Mary continued, "Sheriff Tate, one of the first things I did after coming here, after renaming the plantation for my dear mother of course, was to compare our yield per acre to previous years and to learn what I could about our neighboring farms. I think my late husband's approach of decreasing food rations to his people when their work was lacking was self-defeating of itself, don't you agree? I increased their food rations and the crops look like they are doing very well, don't you agree? You can't expect a starving cow to give you milk, can you?"

As they entered the meeting house, "My husband took away the meeting house, but I had this new one built. I think the Lord's guidance helps workers to understand their place and obey, don't you agree? This is where I teach them the Lord's word."

There was only a large open bible on the pulpit and a row of shingles standing on a rail with upper and lower case letters proclaiming "God is Love." He could see nothing indicating there was any kind of school here. They left the meeting house, Mary's grip on his arm guiding their path as she rambled on and on.

"I have told my foreman, Mr. Garrett, that I simply cannot abide fornication and adultery in a married man. Don't you agree? I told him that for a man to lie with a woman other than his wife, even a Negro, is against the Holy Scripture and a man is to treat his wife in the same loving kindness as Jesus Christ showed to his church. Don't you agree? I think the number of mixed and very light children I see in my own quarters shows that it is happening right here on Mercy Plantation and under the instructions of our Lord and Savior Jesus Christ, I have commanded it to stop. Don't you agree?"

"I know Mr. Garrett is frustrated with the changes I have made here at Mercy Plantation. I hope he did not seek to involve you, just because of a recent disagreement we had regarding the discipline of one of my people. In the absence of my late husband, I must be master of the plantation and, as Christ instructed, I only want to show Mr. Garrett the Lord's way and his loving kindness. Don't you agree?"

Mary could see the sheriff only wanted to be away from here. Mean crazy, like Mr. Lovett had been, was something he could understand, control, and correct. Bible crazy, like Miz Lovett was looking to be, was something he could not. Her wide-open, unwavering stare and that placid smile, showing just a hint of teeth, were unsettling. She looked almost ready to turn him into a burnt offering on some hidden altar down in the woods. Mary realized it would not be long until he was running to his horse.

Mary managed to keep him engaged in conversation until they were back at the steps where one of the boys had his horse ready and waiting. She stopped, opened the drawstrings of her reticule and pulled out a hand-full of gold coins, making the Sheriff's eyes bulge that she was carrying that kind of money around on her person. It should be hidden away in a lock box, or even in the bank, but it was just another signal that Miz Lovett was half out of her mind.

Mary counted out one hundred dollars in gold, put the rest back in her purse, took the sheriff's hand and poured the coins into it. "Just a small token of my appreciation, sir."

"Ma'am, I cannot accept this."

"Oh, it is only a gift sir. It is a gift to signify my appreciation for your continued protection - of me and of my home. I am a solitary widow here, unused to being on my own, and I do so appreciate knowing I can depend on you when I need your kind assistance and protection."

"But, ma'am, I cannot take this. It will look to be a bribe."

Mary looked right and left, as though she was alarmed that they might be observed. "Oh, but it is not a bribe, Sheriff. I would never break the law. This is merely a sincere expression of my gratitude. I'm sure you have things you need at your jail – more bibles perhaps? Or perhaps your wife needs something nice that is difficult to provide on your salary. They only pay you a pittance, I am afraid. So please, take it and know that it makes me happy to give it. Since there is no church here I am able to attend, it is merely a part of the offering I would make to my church and the servants of the Lord as they do his work – as I am sure you are doing too."

Sheriff Tate buttoned the coins into his vest pocket and mounted his horse. He tipped his hat as he turned the horse to ride away. Mary stood with her placid and unblinking smile, watching him with satisfaction. She could almost hear old Aunt Mary cackling in laughter.

He paused just outside the gates. Elias Garrett was waiting there for him and came to take his horse by the reins, looking up expectantly at the sheriff.

Tate shook his head, "Nothing there, Garrett. You have wasted my Sunday afternoon."

Elias was furious. His eyes bulged and a vein stood out on his neck. "But that bitch is breaking the law, teaching the niggers and such, getting soft with them. She needs to be taught a lesson."

"I find nothing supporting what you suggest. The plantation looks to be well run and productive and the slaves are well under control. I suggest that if you cannot abide the terms of your employment with Mrs. Lovett, then you should go elsewhere."

Elias was gone before nightfall. He came stomping back up the lane until he saw Mrs. Lovett watching him at the front steps, then cut off through the cotton field to his house. There, he told Lucy to start packing, that they were leaving immediately. When Lucy balked he began yelling at her - where had this disobedience come from? He started beating her with the butt end of his whip, but only about the arms and shoulders since she held up her hands to protect her face and head as she ran out the door - even though she knew running from him would only make it worse when he caught her.

Next thing he knew, Mrs. Lovett was there with Lucy. Julius and Jimmie were standing beside her. Lucy said she would stay, in fact, Mary wanted her to. Elias was to go. Since he had no horse of his own, he had to leave on foot.

* * * * *

With Elias gone, things calmed down. Since Mary could not go out into the fields to supervise the work herself, she would have to hire an overseer. She placed an ad in the Milledgeville newspaper and a flood of undesirables began making its way to her door. For companionship, she invited Lucy to move into one of the bedrooms in the house. Lucy's house would be needed for the new overseer anyway, so it made sense. Lucy was nervous and timid at first, but within weeks she was comfortable in the home, whether it was morning coffee with Mary in the library or dinner in the dining room. She made herself useful, enthusiastically working in the kitchen garden and tending the newly planted roses and helping Dilsie with the cooking and cleaning. (Although Dilsie still had to remind Lucy to not jump up to help her serve dinner since she was a lady of the house now.)

It was over their supper one evening that Lucy casually suggested that Mary look among her own people for her next supervisor. They already knew the land, knew the people and they knew Mary and what she wanted and expected. Mary was surprised at the idea. A Negro supervising workers was not unheard of, but had not occurred to her. After a while she asked Lucy, "Did you have anyone specific in mind?"

"Yes, ma'am, I do. It's Jimmie. He is a smart man and kind and the people know him and respect him. I think he would make a fine overseer, Mary."

Jimmie and his family moved into the manager's house. There were missteps, but Mary continued the morning meetings she had started with Elias and gently guided him as he settled into his new duties. There were a few disciplinary issues, some initial jealousies, but they were smoothed out by harvest time. Under the plan Mary had set up with Elias, Jimmie would be able to add a substantial sum to the balance under his name in Miss Mary's ledger. Mary knew the day would come when he would buy the freedom papers he so coveted for himself and his family. She planned to return the purchase price he paid for their freedom, as a leaving bonus to help them get started in a new life up north.

With things at the plantation settled, Mary's desire to contact Delilah came back even stronger than before. She asked Robert Tucker about it again the next time he came for dinner. This time, he suggested that Mary should just go on to Macon and see her. The worse Delilah could do would be to refuse to receive her. Mary decided to take Lucy along, leaving the house under Julius' supervision and the plantation under Jimmie's oversight during her absence. The drive would take them three full days by carriage, stopping overnight in Milledgeville and Gray along the way. With the trip decided, Mary found herself as excited as Lucy, who had never even been to Milledgeville, let alone Macon. An adventure lay before them.

In Macon, she showed Delilah's address, asking for directions. After three wrong turns, they found themselves at her front door. Mary raised her hand to knock, but hesitated. "I don't know if I can do this, Lucy."

Lucy reached past Mary and rapped sharply on the door with the handle of her parasol. Mary marveled at Lucy who had been so meek and mild at their first meeting. Where had this boldness come from?

She recognized the handsome woman who answered the door as Delilah. Unexpectedly, she held an infant in her arms and a toddler clung to her skirt, burying his face to hide from the strangers.

"Yes?"

"I am Mary Lovett, Richard's wife." Delilah started to close the door. "Please Delilah; I only wanted to see you, to see that you are all right. I know Richard treated you badly." Delilah glared defiantly at her, pushing the door almost shut. "I don't know why I came," she said turning to Lucy.

Lucy stuck her foot inside the door so it would be impossible for Delilah to close it.

"Shame on you, Delilah," she scolded. "Shame on you! I know you know me. You remember me, Lucy Garrett? Miss Mary only came to see you because she is the kindest woman I know and I can only say 'shame, shame, shame on you'."

Delilah smirked, "Lucy Garrett? I never would have guessed it. I can't believe Elias would have let you out of his sight."

"Oh, Elias ain't at Mercy Plantation no more, Delilah," Lucy explained. "He quit a while back and I said he couldn't make me come with him. Mary needed the house for the new overseer so she asked me to move up to the big house with her."

Delilah stood with her mouth almost hanging open at this revelation. Elias was gone? Lucy refused to go with him? Cracker girl Lucy was living in the big house?

"Jimmie's the overseer now, Delilah. They caught him and brought him back and Elias was goin' to whip him to death I think, but Mary stopped it. They is…they are living in our old house now, Jimmie and Peggie that is. You wouldn't recognize the place."

Delilah was dumbfounded for a moment. "No, I guess I wouldn't," she finally agreed. Then she opened the door widely, "Come in."

They sat visiting for the rest of the day, catching Delilah up on all the news. Mary listened as Delilah asked Lucy about each one of the people, obviously caring for them all deeply. She wondered about the baby Delilah was tending, but didn't want to ask. Maybe she was caring for it while the mother worked. She also realized the older child was blind. He functioned so well it was barely perceptible except that his eyes did not look at anything. After he grew accustomed to their voices he relaxed his hold on Delilah's skirt and contented himself by playing with the toys Delilah had for him in her small parlor.

They had tea and, finally, Mary declared it was time to go.

"Oh, but it is so late. I thought you would spend the night here. Where are you staying?" Delilah asked.

"We are guests at the Planter's Hotel. We must leave you to your evening chores, and I am sure the children's mother will be calling soon for them."

Delilah was silent.

"I am sorry," Mary said, not sure what she was apologizing for.

"I am their mother," Delilah said quietly. Mary was shocked, were these Richard's children? Mary herself was past seventy and Delilah must be close to sixty. How was this possible?

"They are not my natural-born children, but they are my children now, Miss Mary," Delilah explained. "I have adopted them."

"Oh, how wonderful!"

"No, not really. Thomas has been blind since birth. The doctor said it was syphilis, from his mother. I've only had him a year. He was abandoned behind the slave market and a neighbor brought him to me. I guess he didn't sell with his mother, since he was blind, so they left him out there in the alley overnight."

"How awful," Lucy exclaimed. Mary was unable to speak.

"I bought Jamie here at an auction. Her mother sold without the baby and she was sickly. I had a hundred dollars saved and I offered it all to the auctioneer after the auction. I probably could have paid less. They don't want to keep babies that don't sell with their mothers, especially sick ones."

Mary was silent.

"Robert Tucker helped me draw up the adoption papers and the deeds of emancipation so they are free, the same as me. He is a kind man. I don't know how I would have endured those last years at Lovett Plantation – or Mercy Plantation – without him. Even then it was he who saved me, set me up here. There is not a kinder man."

Mary was still deeply disturbed. They went back the next morning and as soon as she could after their exchanged pleasantries, she announced. "I think it's time I see a slave auction."

There was one scheduled the next day. It was to be the last day of their visit, and they would leave for home at first light the day after, but Mary insisted they attend. Ladies generally did not attend the auctions, so they were conspicuous. The auctioneer even came to ask Mary if she knew what was happening. "Of course I do. I am not that far gone, young man," she scolded. Chairs were

219

brought for Mary and Lucy to sit on. But, assuming Delilah was their maid, she was left standing until Mary insisted a third chair be brought also. The three ladies took turns holding Delilah's babies.

It was a sad and unsettling parade. Mary watched as person after person, family after family was brought forward and sold. Men were generally considered better field hands so, often, they would be sold away from their wives and children, who parted with tearful goodbyes, but seemed to be prepared for the fate. The sun rose higher, but Mary would not leave. She was riveted to the spot, unable to turn away. Around two o'clock a very dark-skinned young woman was brought on the block. She was roughly dressed and tightly held a much lighter-skinned baby in her arms. Some of the men behind Mary jostled each other, exclaiming "ain't she fresh?" and "ripe and ready for the plucking!" until Mary turned on them with a withering look. "Sorry, Ma'am," one of them said.

The auction for the woman and child began with no bidders at five hundred dollars. The auctioneer reduced it to four hundred, then three hundred fifty, and then three hundred twenty five dollars for the pair. "Sell them separate," someone yelled from the back. The woman was panicked, hugging her baby so tightly Mary wondered that it could breathe. Maybe that was what she intended; suffocate the baby so it would not be sold away from her. "Four hundred for the girl," someone called out from the rear of the crowd. The auctioneer immediately banged his hammer down, "Sold!"

The young woman was hysterical. Mary was on her feet. "I am Mary Lovett," she called out. "I am Mary Lovett of Mercy Plantation," she repeated until the crowd was silent, except for the strangled sobs of the young mother.

When she had silence, she looked directly at the girl and said slowly and deliberately so she was sure the girl understood. "I am Mary Lovett of Mercy Plantation in Hancock County and I will buy your baby."

She offered three hundred dollars, all that she had left until harvest. She would have to ask for credit at the hotel to cover their bill. She walked forward to the girl, arms out. Behind her, Lucy and Delilah stood, holding Delilah's children where the young mother could see them. The child was wailing in its mother's arms now as Mary approached.

She held out her hands and said "I am so sorry. I should have bought you both, but I didn't have the money. I will take good care of him."

"Her. My baby a girl. Her name Elisa, Miz Lovett. I am Dolly. Thank you."

And as Old Bess had done with Sukey, so many years ago, Dolly held out her baby thinking she could not let go. "I will make sure she knows about you, Dolly," Mary said gently.

"Mercy Plantation," Dolly said the words aloud, making herself remember. "It sound like heaven to me."

Lucy, who never had a child of her own, took to the baby immediately. They left Macon with promises to return and Delilah assuring that she would, indeed, come to see them. Mary promised it would be a festive reunion when she did. On the drive back Mary told all the old stories to Lucy, starting with Old Bess and everything she could remember. She realized Lucy had become a part of her family too, and now so was Elisa.

As she was leaving Delilah, she commented that she wished she could have done more, but three hundred dollars was all she had until the next cotton harvest was sold.

Delilah looked at her oddly, "Didn't you find Richard's money?" she asked.

"Yes, eight hundred and forty dollars in the hidden panel at the back of his desk. I've been making it stretch as best I could and I thought we would be fine until harvest. I will have to make arrangements for credit when I return."

"Mister Richard was a very wealthy man, Miss Mary."

"Yes, I know. I just can't understand what happened to his money. I've been over his accounts many times. I just can't figure out what he did with all of it, unless it's buried somewhere on the property."

Delilah looked around Mary to Lucy who was busy getting settled with little Elisa in the carriage. "It's not buried, Miss Mary, it's hidden in the wall behind the desk in the library. There's a little button on the paneling behind the desk. Push that button and it releases the catch. That whole panel is a door you can open. It has shelves behind it. The last time I counted it with him, before he... well, the last time I was there, he had over thirty four thousand dollars in gold in there."

* * * * *

As Mary's eightieth birthday loomed over her, she decided to move to Macon. She made the announcement at her eightieth birthday celebration at Mercy Plantation. The day had become something of a holiday with work suspended and an afternoon lunch buffet served for all the people on the veranda. Delilah made the journey from Macon with her children – six of them by then. It was something of a homecoming when she arrived. Mary's birthday was a wonderful, sunny day. After lunch she stood on the porch and explained her decision.

She first asked them to take a moment to remember the people who had moved on, both in death and those who had secured their own freedom and moved north.

Over the past ten years there had been many more in the second category. There were others, new to the plantation, who had taken their place and might make that trip one day too. She explained that she had decided to move to Macon. At her age, it was wiser to be near her doctors. She would take a house near Delilah.

Before the realization that her departure might mean the selling of Mercy Plantation she forged on. "I have decided not to sell Mercy Plantation. Lucy Garrett will remain here as long as she likes, managing this house. You all know Lucy. Like Delilah did before her, Lucy has read all the books in the library here and continues to learn. Even her knowledge of farming has amazed me. I am confident leaving Lucy in charge.

"I also want Jimmie to stay on as your manager." She waited until the patter of applause ended. "I used to think Jimmie was going to buy the freedom for himself and Peggie and his family as soon as he could and move on up north, but he seems to like it here too much to leave."

There was some laughter and a lot of smiles as Jimmie, suddenly embarrassed, curled his hat in his hands, looking at the ground. He looked up and grinned at Mary when their eyes met.

"Jimmie and I meet each morning and I know he studies everything he can on the land. He has some new ideas and we may be planting other crops in the future. Cotton just wears out the soil too much to keep on farming the same as we always have. I encourage you to listen to him and learn from him."

Before she left for Macon, Mary gave Jimmie and his family their freedom papers. He could go anywhere, but like Lucy, he understood the formula Mary had worked out for Mercy Plantation. As long as there was slavery, they would keep making a small dent in the system.

Mary assured them she would be back to visit. After all, she was only eighty years old. It wasn't like she was finished yet.

In 1837, Mercy Plantation was still in full operation. Cotton prices had collapsed and there was a banking panic that year that wiped out fortunes, but since they had diversified their crops they were not as deeply affected as their neighbors.

On her eighty-fifth birthday, Mary changed her will. The will that previously granted freedom to all her slaves at her death seemed unwise now. Giving freedom to a slave who was not prepared for it was as irresponsible as turning a child out to fend for itself. Her children and grandchildren were doing well in Louisiana, very well in fact. They did not need Mary's money. Other than bequests to Anna of the few remaining family portraits that were still in her house back in Warren County, she left the house and contents to Curley and Chloe. On her death, Mercy Plantation, in its entirety, would go to Lucy Garrett.

She bought a commodious house in Macon and Delilah and her children soon moved in with her. She loved having children around her again and it saved Delilah the cost of her monthly rent. Her house in Macon would go to Delilah.

In November, 1837, Mary attended another auction with Delilah. Slavery was still an abhorrent institution to her and she hated it with every fiber of her being, but she still went to auctions. No children were separated from their families that afternoon and Mary took it as a good sign. Maybe things were beginning to change.

They went home for a light supper and Mary went to bed early. When Delilah came to check on Mary before she went to bed, she found Mary sleeping restlessly. Delilah decided to sit with her for a while in case she woke and needed anything. Later that night, Delilah woke from a light sleep in the chair at Mary's bedside. She heard Mary's labored breathing, then Mary said one word and the breathing stopped.

That word was "Mercy."

Author's note: Listed among Mary Freeman Lovett's possessions when she died in November, 1837, in Crawford County, Georgia, were four slaves: Caroline, a girl, 13 years of age; Lucinda, a girl, 11 years old; Major, a boy 4 years old; and Haney, a girl, 2 years old.

PART THREE

ORATIO

CHAPTER NINE

Ouachita Parish, Louisiana
1830

Oratio Newman really should have been a boy, or at least that was what she told everyone the first twelve years of her life. She only stopped then because she saw how those words grieved her father. But, she still thought it even if she did not say so.

For Oratio, even her name proved that she was supposed to be a boy. It should have been Horatio instead. When she was nine and her brother Henry was eight she pinned him down behind the stables and drooled long strings of spit that almost reached his face - torturing him that way until he agreed to call her Horatio. Before long, Mama heard him, put a stop to it and punished them both. After that, he only called her Horatio to tease her.

Her sisters Amanda and Levina, who were nine and six years older, fussed over her from the first day they laid eyes on her. But her sisters fussed over everything so Oratio could never have expected anything different from them, anyway.

They fussed that their Papa's refusal to own slaves kept them from being as rich as everyone else in the county. Having no slaves also meant they had to do things for themselves that were done by servants for other girls like them. They fussed that Papa's position on slavery also meant their grandmother would leave her huge plantation to someone else. Even though his general mercantile in Monroe and his horse farm kept their husbands employed, they fussed that the horses Papa bred and sold to the wealthy planters would bring much higher prices if they lived up in Kentucky instead of down here in Louisiana.

More than anything else, her sisters fussed over Oratio. They fussed when she went out in the sunshine that her skin would be tanned and freckled. They fussed that her hair, while thin and fine, was too curly to stay in the bouncing corkscrew curls they themselves wore in fashionable clusters over their ears. They fussed that she rode - no that she _raced_ horses - with Henry, whooping like a wild Indian with her hair flying. They fussed that she rode astride with her skirts and pantalets hiked up and showing her stockings up to her knees. They even fussed that she said "Ma" and "Pa" instead of the more refined French version of Mama and Papa, even though they refused everything else French as being Creole, and they just fussed in general when there was nothing else to fuss about.

But mostly, they fussed over her eye.

By the time she was two years old, the eyelid on Oratio's right eye had started to droop. Back in Georgia, where they once lived, Mama and Papa had a doctor look at it. He said Oratio would grow out of it. Two years later another doctor said it was a lazy eye; that she could see fine with it, but was using her left eye for everything. The right one merely drifted to follow the left and that was why the lid was drooping. To fix it, he told them to keep a bandage over the good eye until the lazy eye recovered and started working. Mama made a patch that could be tied over the left eye, and Oratio had to wear it from the moment she awoke in the morning until she went to bed at night. The bandage made little Oratio so dizzy that she would reach up and pull it aside so she could see with the good eye. For months it was a battle, with Mama and Papa gently replacing the patch to cover the good eye and Oratio managing to slip it aside moments later.

After three months with no change, Papa decided they would leave off the bandage. The eye continued to droop and that was when her sisters began to fuss over it.

The thing was, Oratio had beautiful blue eyes. While all of her brothers and sisters had blue eyes, theirs were a faded blue. Oratio's eyes had an almost purple tint, making them the color of sapphires. Her "one true beauty" Amanda and Levina began saying after Oratio's twelfth birthday when she started showing the signs of becoming a woman. They started fussing again for her to at least cover her good eye when she was at home, where no one would see, to encourage the lazy eye to take over. For a while, Oratio complied, just as she let Amanda and Levina try to straighten her hair and spread their vile smelling potions on her shoulders and arms to make them pale and white.

After six months though, it was plain none of their attempts were working: her hair was still wild and untamed, her shoulders and arms were freckled and tanned, and her eye was drooping as much as ever. And besides that, her bosom had grown beyond the boundaries of good taste, something else they fussed over, especially since they sewed ruffles into their own undergarments to make theirs appear larger.

Finally, Oratio said she did not care and neither should they. She was never going to get married anyway, so they did not need to bother. With Mama's support, she kept her sisters' efforts to a minimum. But as much as she disliked being a young lady, there were times Oratio still had to follow the rules. Rules that no boy, including Henry, had to follow.

Like this afternoon, for instance. Sunday afternoons were always slow torture, and especially in this heat. While Mama went upstairs to lie down after dinner, Oratio and her sisters sat in the parlor with their embroidery. Every Sunday while their father, their husbands, and all the children went down to watch the riverboat making its way up the Ouachita River towards Monroe, Amanda and Levina relished the one time during the week when they could sit uninterrupted for an hour of casual conversation with their needlework. Amanda was happily working on another pillowcase and Levina was stitching yet another baby dress for the child she hoped to be expecting soon.

Oratio sat slightly away from them on the sofa, where the breeze from the open windows might be better - if there ever was one. She was impatiently stitching a simple square of linen napkin on an embroidery hoop. While her sisters enjoyed their afternoon of needlework, embroidery was tedious for her. She always managed to tangle and knot the silk floss more than she fed it through the fabric. She would like nothing more than to throw the entire project out the window and go watch Henry working with the new little filly he was training to take a saddle. The sound of the horse's hooves on the packed dirt of the yard and her brother talking gently as he put the horse through its paces came through the open windows on the heavy air as clearly as if he was in the room with them.

Eventually, seeing she had missed a tangle of floss on the opposite side of the napkin and would have to pull out at least a dozen stitches, she tossed the hoop down on the sofa and pulled up the hem of her skirt to fan her face, fully exposing the fancy white ruffled pantalets she had to wear on Sundays, and revealing to her sisters she had removed her smothering corset and starched petticoats as soon as they were home from church.

"Oratio!" her sisters scolded in unison. They were as shocked now as they had been earlier when Oratio came to the mid-day meal in the dining room wearing the pale blue, lightweight cotton dress that was more suited to late afternoon, with its low neckline and shortened sleeves. Even in this heat, her dutiful sisters' sleeves came down below their elbows and their white cotton matron caps, trimmed with lace, ribbon, and frills, were tied securely under their chins.

"I don't care," Oratio said, wadding the skirt at her knees and pulling up her pantalets with both hands, leaving her legs bare and uncovered to the tops of her shoes. She had removed her stockings after church too. "It is hot as blazes in here."

Even more than the shock of seeing their sister's exposed lower limbs in the parlor, the sisters were aghast at her profanity. 'Blazes', as Oratio used it, referred to the fires of Hell. Their sister might as well have said "Hell" or "Hellfire" outright. It was the same thing. It was profanity – on a Sunday too. So un-ladylike.

"Oh, I don't care," Oratio repeated, letting her skirts fall to the floor as she stood, taking up her fan and fanning her face and bare shoulders furiously. She pulled the combs from her hair and let the length of wild curls fall down her back. "You would think the two of you have never seen anyone naked before, the way you carry on."

"When have YOU seen anyone naked?" Amanda challenged before she could catch herself. Amanda and Levina were both married women, so they had been in that condition of course, but only in the privacy of their own bedrooms and only with their husbands. Oratio, only sixteen and unmarried, could not possibly have had such an encounter.

Oratio only raised an eyebrow, the one over her lazy eye, and left the question unanswered as she turned away toward the open window, fanning furiously. Raising that eyebrow always brought that eye fully open, proving to her sisters she could keep it open all the time if she really wanted to. She hoped it would distract Amanda from her current line of questioning.

"Gently, sister. Fan gently," Levina nervously reminded her. "You will only make yourself hotter fanning that way." Oratio obligingly slowed the fan. She was only moving hot air around anyway. Ouachita, Louisiana in the middle of August was like a Turkish bath, or at least what they had read a Turkish bath would be like in the books that had been shipped from Grandma Mary's library. Her sisters often fussed that they should be able to go somewhere up north like the other folks around here did during the hottest part of the summer. Even the Arkansas Mountains were not that far away and were certain to be cooler than this.

Fanning more gently now, Oratio walked around the room, holding her hair up in back while she fanned the back of her hot neck and looked up at the paintings. She settled on Great, Great, Great Aunt Charity's portrait, whom Mama said they all favored and would always simply be Aunt Charity to the family without all the 'greats' attached. Mama also said that Oratio looked the most like their great-grandmother Mercy Wainwright. Her face (without the drooping eye of course) was almost identical. It made sense. Her sisters with their pale-as-milk skin and straight, light brown hair could never be said to favor their octoroon ancestor.

"Do you think Aunt Charity ever got hot in all those clothes?" she asked her sisters, making them look up from their sewing to the portrait. "Just look at all that garb she has on. Layers and layers of it. I would fall right over in a dead faint if I had to wear all that in this heat."

"That's why they went to England," Amanda said with an air that showed just how far the family had fallen since those times. England might as well be the moon for them.

"No they didn't. They only went out to the Wainwright plantation on the river where the breezes were cooler," Oratio argued. "You are forgetting the stories, Amanda. She only went to England that one time when Mercy went to school, and then Aunt Charity died there - of pneumonia. She caught a chill in spite of always wearing everything she owned, apparently."

"You should be more reverent, Oratio," Amanda chided. "Mama did not tell you the stories just so you could be making fun of our ancestors." Beside her, Levina nodded her agreement.

"And you should have listened more carefully," Oratio replied.

"Do you remember the one about our great, great-grandmother Dove, and how she died of a broken heart?" Levina interrupted, hoping to divert an argument. "What a romantic story. It is almost like Shakespeare's 'Romeo and Juliet,' isn't it?"

"Bah!" Oratio huffed, looking up at Aunt Charity a moment longer before she turned to her sisters. "You will never catch me killing myself over a man like that. What a big baby she must have been."

"Oratio!" her sisters scolded in unison, before they saw Oratio was only teasing. Oratio had a wicked sense of humor and knew just how to get a rise out of her sisters. "Don't you ever let Mama hear you talking like that," Amanda scolded, while barely keeping the smile from her lips. Levina nodded her agreement, and the ruffled edge of her cap fluttered vigorously around her face.

Oratio sighed and moved back to the sofa, taking up her embroidery hoop to examine the damage and was wondering if she could just throw the whole thing in the kitchen stove and start over when she heard a new set of hoof beats coming up the lane from the county road. Maybe it was because of her eye, but her hearing was sharper than any one else in the family and she was the first to hear it. She turned her head toward the lane, to hear equally with both ears. Oratio knew the unique sounds of each horse on the property, and most of the neighbors' horses too. She could tell who was coming, just by hearing the cadence of the hoof beats on the gravel.

Amanda was the next to hear it, and then Levina, seeing her sisters turned to the open window, heard it too.

"Who is it?" Levina asked.

"No one we know," Oratio answered, rising from the sofa, and starting for the door.

"You can't go out there," Amanda declared. "Wait for Papa."

Oratio ignored them, already in the hall. "Take your wrap," Amanda called after her. "You can't show your shoulders this early in the day."

Oratio came back to the sofa to fetch the shawl, but she only looped the thin silk through her elbows and around her lower back, defiantly leaving her bare shoulders uncovered as she went out the front door into the hot afternoon sunshine to greet their visitor.

She stood at the top of the steps, still in the shade of the porch, as the rider came up the lane and stopped his horse at the base of the steps. He tipped his hat to her and said, "Is this the Newman place?"

"It is," she replied, too strongly Amanda would think, without smiling or any other welcoming gesture. He was a young man, surprisingly young in fact, and he was very well dressed. He was too well dressed to be from these parts or even from Monroe, she decided. He was most likely from one of the plantations down along the Mississippi River or maybe even from Natchez. Seeing him closer, Oratio guessed he was about her age.

He looked her up and down a moment, seemingly an appreciative appraisal, but Oratio would have nothing of it. "Did you want to see my Pa?" she asked.

She almost said "Papa," but at the last moment settled on the more common version that irritated her sisters, visualizing them cringing as they listened beyond the open parlor windows.

"I am Leroy Lewis Squyres, Miss Newman. My family sent me to see Samuel Newman about a horse or two."

"Are you of the South Carolina Squyres, sir?" Oratio asked him bluntly.

"Yes, ma'am," he managed, surprised at this unexpected greeting.

"John and Mary Squyres of Charleston, South Carolina, and also of Cambridgeshire, England?"

"Why...yes, I think so," he struggled to remember. "They were my father's grandparents, or maybe his great-grandparents, I think."

Oratio raised the eyebrow again for the second time that afternoon, but this time with disdain while fully showing her sapphire blue eyes to Mr. Squyres.

"Then you should also know, sir," she said, pulling the silk at her elbows up to cover her shoulders, "that your father's great-grandparents gravely insulted my dear great-grandmother, Mercy Wainwright, when she was a guest at their home in England. And I must insist that you leave this property at once."

"Oratio!" her sisters cried out in disbelief from inside the window. She heard their rapid and tiny footsteps as they jumped from their chairs, came rapidly across the parlor and through the hall to appear beside her on the porch.

"Mr. Squyres," Amanda gushed in a conciliatory tone, trying to smile while catching her breath and offering her hand at the same time she dipped in a deep curtsey. "You must forgive our little sister. Oratio just loves to play her little

Alan E Bailey

jokes, even though she knows it is sometimes unkind and gives offense. I do apologize. Won't you please come in?"

Oratio remained silent as they made their way back in the house and into the parlor, where Amanda and Levina invited him sit on the sofa and then scrambled around, picking up the litter of their afternoon. Oratio moved silently to stand beside the fireplace mantle, under Aunt Charity's portrait. There was a stirring and creaking of floorboards overhead, meaning Mama was awake and was redressing herself to join them.

Amanda and Levina settled themselves into their chairs. "Oh, do sit down, Oratio!" Amanda scolded. But rather than resuming her spot on the sofa, beside Mr. Squyres, Oratio moved away from him to sit in their mother's chair.

Amanda felt a faint flush of excitement when she realized that somehow, between the porch and the parlor, Oratio had put her hair back up, even though a few curling tendrils escaped the hastily twisted knot that was haphazardly held in place by the combs. The silk shawl was now gracefully draped to show off her shoulders and only a hint of décolletage. Amanda wished Oratio would turn slightly away from Mr. Squyres to show only the best side of her lovely face, and she wished Oratio would sit with downcast eyes and only look up at him occasionally instead of staring so boldly at him as she was doing now.

But this was the first time she could recall Oratio reacting positively to any member of the male sex. It was all she could do to not point that out to Levina, who seemed to be tongue-tied and mesmerized by their unexpected visitor.

Yes, they certainly knew of the Squyres. The Squyres brothers grew cotton down in the rich bottom lands of Catahoula Parish. Their father started the plantation back in 1814, moving his entire family of seven children, ranging in age from eighteen to four years old from Edgefield, South Carolina, where his family had lived for generations. Soon after their arrival, Leroy was born in the crowded and hastily-built frame house, followed by three more children in the next four years. As cotton prices soared, and everything related to cotton with it, their father put his profits back into the plantation, acquiring new lands and even more slaves, the process increasing their production ten-fold by some counts.

A year after the grand manor house was built, their father died in 1821. Instead of taking his inheritance and leaving his siblings with nothing, the eldest son, William, borrowed everything he could against his father's plantation and formed a consortium with his younger brothers. They sank the entire amount into land speculation.

Many easy fortunes were made in the South doing just that. Money poured across the Atlantic and into Southern banks, and was loaned out at high interest rates solely for that purpose. William Squyres and others borrowed that money to buy land they did not need and never farmed, speculating the value would continue to go up.

Rumor was that their mother had been openly against the speculation. Fearing loss of the plantation and money that had come down through at least four generations to her late husband, she engaged her own lawyers to stop them. But with the boom in land prices fueled by the cotton boom, the brothers quickly earned back the amount of the original loan, plus a handsome profit. Over the past decade, the process was repeated over and over, making them all fabulously wealthy. To appease their mother and stop her protestations, an elegant town house was built for her in nearby Natchez, on the bluff overlooking the river.

It was easy money, but Oratio's father had been skeptical. He argued that what the banks were doing was like one man loaning another man the money to bet on a horse instead of betting it himself. If it was a winning bet, the bank got its money plus interest from the winnings. If it was a losing bet, the bank still got its money plus interest. It worked for the borrower only as long as prices were going up, and nothing went up forever. "Neither a borrower nor a lender be," he would quote, closing the subject. Amanda and Levina fussed they could all be rich too, instead of just being merchants and horse farmers, if Papa wasn't so determinedly old-fashioned about money.

The Squyres now enjoyed a standard of living Amanda could only dream of, and here was the son of such an important and wealthy family in their very own parlor. If she wasn't already married herself she would definitely be pulling out all her charms. As it was, she had to use them to keep him socially engaged until Levina could find her tongue and Oratio would at least acknowledge him. If Oratio persisted in her silence, young Mr. Leroy Squyres was going to think she was slow.

"How did you find your way to Newman Farms, Mr. Squyres?" Amanda asked, silently reprimanding herself for the stupidity of her question while she shot a frantic look to Levina, beseeching her for help.

Leroy ignored the obvious. "My brother heard that your father raises the best horses in the state and he wants a new, matched team for his town carriage, so he sent me to have a look."

"You Squyres always have the finest horses," Oratio surprised them all, breaking her silence. "Our great-grandmother often fondly recalled how your great-grandparents arrived so grandly at the Charles Town port when they all sailed to England on the *Endurance*, with a team of the most beautifully matched white horses,"

"I'm afraid you know so much more about my family than I do, Miss Oratio. Perhaps you will tell me that story sometime." Leroy said with a smile, seeking to engage her. But Oratio only turned away from him for a moment with downcast eyes, signifying the discussion of that topic was finished.

"That is a portrait of her aunt, Charity Wainwright, who was a friend to the Squyres," Amanda jumped up, indicating the painting over the mantle. Then she clarified, "Our great-grandmother's aunt I mean, not Oratio's, obviously. That was painted more than a hundred years ago." Amanda wisely stopped and sat back down before she made things even worse. Levina gave a little groan of discomfort. How could they all be acting so giddily in front of their visitor? Mr. Squyres only replied with a gentle and appreciative laugh.

They lapsed into an awkward silence, punctuated only by the ticking of the clock in the hall, until Mother came down the stairs and entered the room. Oratio jumped up from the chair and said boldly, "I can show you around the stables if you like, Mr. Squyres. It may be an hour or more until our father returns." Then, acknowledging the obvious to her sisters and mother added, "I will have Henry come along with us."

Rather than argue in front of their visitor, Amanda jumped up to fetch her best parasol for Oratio to carry. Oratio, almost refused, Amanda's parasols were always so fancy they were ridiculous, but decided it would be a shield against the heat of the sun. She tramped down the front steps before Mr. Squyres could go ahead to offer her a guiding hand and then on down the lane with him trotting along behind to catch up.

"Where's the fire?" he called after her.

"What?" she stopped and turned around to face him.

"I said, 'where is the fire?' Why are you in such a hurry?"

"Oh, I am sorry if I am going too fast for you," she apologized, hoping it sounded as insincere as she meant it to be.

"Miss Newman, I apologize if my presence is so distasteful to you that you feel the need to hurry through this, but it is an exceedingly warm afternoon. Might we at least slow our pace to a rapid walk? I would be most obliged."

Oratio paused and smiled up at him in spite of herself, "I really must apologize, Mr. Squyres. I was more anxious to be out of the house than I realized. If you had not arrived, I was about to thrust a darning needle into my eye – my good eye – simply to have an excuse for my exit."

Leroy was shocked and looked at her a moment. Oratio noticed he looked at her right eye fleetingly least three times before looking away. "You should not say such things," he said quietly. "Forgive me for saying so, but it is not as bad as you make it out to be. You should not make cruel jokes about yourself."

Oratio was thoughtful and, for the first time that afternoon, she was sincerely apologetic. "I am sorry, and I do apologize that I made you uncomfortable. I suppose I make these jokes to get it out of the way. People don't know what to say at first, so I bring it up before it gets even more uncomfortable. It is what it is and I have accepted it. And you know what? I really don't care anymore. Or at least I would not care if my sisters would just leave it alone and let me be."

Henry was still working the horse as they approached the corralled area beyond the stable yard. This horse was being broke to ride and after a few more quiet sessions would be ready to be saddled for the first time. Henry would saddle the horse to let her get used to the feel of it while he exercised her. Then a while after that, he would sit on the saddle for a few days while the horse stood still and then he would start riding for short periods, training her with the bridle. He hoped to have her ready to sell in the fall.

Henry was too intent on his work to see them coming up the lane and across the stable yard. As they came closer, Oratio felt the familiar swell of pride and love for her younger brother. The two were so much younger than the rest of their siblings that they bonded from the start and had always been inseparable. Oratio could ride as well as Henry, if not better, and he secretly kept an extra shirt, breeches, and riding coat in the stable for Oratio for the times they could sneak away and race their horses across open fields and country lanes.

She watched her brother as they approached. Henry was beautiful. Oratio jealously and proudly acknowledged that the girls in Monroe were all crazy for him. He was the only one of the children with the red Newman hair, but his was a dark copper color – almost brown - and thick and curly. Oratio had teased him many times that his hair would fall naturally into the corkscrew curls their sisters so wanted for Oratio if he would just let it grow a bit longer. His eyebrows and lashes were dark brown, framing his soft blue eyes, and, unlike most redheads who burned easily in the sun, Henry's flawless skin was lightly tanned from his work outside. He was taller than Oratio, leanly muscled, and naturally graceful.

His grace was demonstrated now as he held the lead and turned in slow and endless circles, almost a dance, while his eyes carefully followed the filly around the corral. His pale tan breeches that showed the play of his muscular legs underneath were nearly spotless above his leather boots. In the heat, his white shirt was unbuttoned and the tail was pulled out all around. His Sunday jacket was hanging on the top rail of the corral fence. Had she seen that, Mama would be scolding him and saying Henry was not too old for her to cut a switch, although in all the times Oratio could remember, her mother never had done that. Mama was as charmed by Henry as every other woman.

Oratio often mused that of the two of them, Henry should have been the girl. He looked up just then, saw Oratio approaching, flashed his white and winsome smile and called out enthusiastically in his musical baritone, "I think she's almost ready for the saddle, Horatio. You will be riding this little lady in no time."

Forgetting their visitor, Oratio let down the parasol, ran to the corral fence and stepped up on the lower rung of the fence as she leaned forward looking closely at the horse trotting around the corral. "She sure is beautiful, Henry," she called out.

When Henry looked back at Oratio he saw Mr. Squyres. He gave the horse the command to slow to a walk while shortening the lunge line to require the horse to make even smaller circles. He stroked the horse's head, patting her at the neck and led her over to where his sister stood on the fence. Oratio leaned forward to run her hand down its neck, speaking softly. Her hair was coming loose and she stopped a moment, pulled away the combs and shook out the wispy curls that fell below her shoulders.

Watching her, his breath caught as Leroy realized that this sassy and unusual girl he had met only moments before was happier and more at home here on the corral fence, hugging and stroking this sweating and snorting horse, than she could ever be stitching her embroidery in a shadowed and breathless parlor. There was an exciting vitality about her out here in the hot summer sunshine, and also a look of contented happiness. This was her element and this was where she belonged.

And in that moment, Leroy Lewis Squyres realized he had fallen completely in love with Oratio Newman.

Leroy put out his hand, introducing himself and reminding Oratio of the reason she was here at the corral on a Sunday afternoon. "Leroy Squyres," he managed. His mouth had gone dry.

"Leroy _Lewis_ Squyres," Oratio mocked him from her perch on the fence, echoing the words Leroy had used to introduce himself to her. Henry could see she was back to her teasing and sassy self. He also saw that Leroy could barely look away from her to acknowledge his handshake. "His big brother sent him all the way out here to buy a team of horses from us. Do we have any old nags we can pawn off on him, Henry?"

Henry grinned, first at his sister and then at Leroy. Oratio turned to look before she stepped down from the fence and Leroy instantly put out his hand to steady her, then unexpectedly put both hands to her waist and lifted her down gently. She was light as a feather. But Oratio did not like that, not one bit; this visitor putting his hands on her like that. "I am perfectly capable of climbing down by myself, Mr. Squyres. Heck, I've been jumping from the top rung most of my life, haven't I Henry?"

Henry laughed and slapped Leroy on the shoulder. "Come on. Let's show you what we have. A carriage team is it?"

For the next two hours, Leroy was barely able to focus on the horses he was shown. Oratio's brother thoroughly described the attributes of each one. In the end, Leroy simply asked which team was the best and when Henry put forth a perfectly matched pair of grey geldings at an enormous price, Leroy simply said he would take them.

Oratio was put off by Leroy's lack of interest in the horse trading process. As the spoiled son of a large and wealthy family he obviously was used to having everything he wanted and seemed to think he could do no wrong. Unlike someone in the Newmans' position who chose a horse carefully, never bought on the first showing and argued the price down to the last penny over several visits, she could not believe Leroy simply agreed to take the first team offered and at the price named.

She supposed that even if Leroy chose unwisely or paid entirely too much it was of no real consequence in his world. But the additional amount he had paid would have bought him another colt or at least a year's worth of feed. If Leroy was any indication, all of the Squyres were a spoiled and arrogant lot and would never appreciate the fine team they had just acquired. It was no wonder Aunt Charity had hated them. Oratio turned away and started for the house.

Henry, amused by his sister's reaction to the quick sale of the team, turned to the baffled Leroy and asked him to come up to the house and have supper with them. Leroy immediately accepted, thankful for the extension of his visit.

Oratio reached the house first, finding that it had been almost transformed. Chairs were arranged for conversation on the front porch and the porch table set for tea with Aunt Charity's tea pot. Her sisters' husbands and children had been sent on home - their houses were nearby anyway - and Amanda was waiting for her, changed into her best evening dress with her matron's cap removed and her hair freshly arranged. She had even had tucked small roses into the cluster of corkscrew curls gathered at both ears, like she was a young maiden. It made Oratio laugh outright at such a fuss, angering Amanda.

"You should put forth an effort, Oratio!" she scolded. "Mama has asked, or will ask, Mr. Squyres to stay for supper. She is in the kitchen right now, with Levina helping her prepare it. Let me at least do something with your hair and pick out a more suitable dress for you to wear."

"Don't bother. I think I will take a supper tray to my room," Oratio said. "I don't think I am going to be feeling well."

"No, you most absolutely will not! I will not let Papa allow it. Now come upstairs with me. I made a bath for you and laid out your green silk and brought over one of my gowns too. We will see which one suits you best. I have some new combs that I think will keep your hair up, and I brought over some of my roses for you." She paused, screwed up her face, and tried not to cry. "Oh, Oratio, he is handsome and young and … rich. There is no crime in that. And I could see how he was watching you down at the corral."

"You were spying on us?" Oratio cried out.

"I only came down to see if you found Henry all right. I did not want him to think we would let you go out without a chaperone, even at home. Oh, Oratio, everyone is trying so hard, please just put out a little bit of effort."

Oratio put her hand on Amanda's arm before she got herself worked up into a full 'state,' as Henry called them.

"All right, Amanda. I will. But I'm telling you he is a spoiled and arrogant little bastard and I hope after this we never see him again."

At least it was a start. Amanda almost pulled Oratio all the way up the stairs to the waiting bath.

When she came downstairs and out onto the porch a half hour later, one step ahead of Amanda, she was wearing the simpler cotton dress Amanda loaned her, insisting the green silk was simply too fancy and looked ridiculous in the late afternoon. Amanda agreed the color of the second dress suited her better, but also insisted Oratio wear enough layers of petticoats so it would hang correctly. Her hair was freshly put up, but a few errant tendrils were still escaping the new combs when Oratio finally batted Amanda's fluttering hands away so they could go out the front door.

She flatly refused the roses for her hair, and was even more adamant when Amanda sought to position them at her décolletage, as if she were going to a ball. As a compromise, she carried them as a small, hastily arranged nosegay along with her fan, thinking she would set the flowers aside as soon as she settled on the porch.

Leroy was on his feet as soon as Oratio came through the front door. The other men followed his lead. Henry grinned wickedly and Oratio shot him a warning look, hoping he would delay teasing her about her "get-up" until Leroy was out of hearing.

She approached the group. Mama was pouring tea from the cherished tea pot and looked up at her approvingly. Without her really extending her hand to him, Leroy grasped it and bowed over it formally in greeting, but his eyes never left her face. "You look lovely, Miss Oratio," he drawled.

"We are not in the habit of dressing for dinner way out here in the country, Mr. Squyres," Amanda gave a little gasp, but, before she could jump in, Oratio continued in a tone that was vaguely teasing, "You must take this as a sign of being an honored guest, sir. It's usually just a bowl of beans and corn bread on the back porch for supper, I'm afraid."

While Amanda was horrified and even Mother was silent, Henry guffawed, "Oratio is just teasin' you, Leroy. Don't you listen to a word of it."

"Even beans and cornbread in such wonderful company would be a rare treat, Miss Oratio," Leroy replied with a teasing smile. So, he was not only a rich and spoiled and arrogant bastard, but he was a silver-tongued one at that. Oratio could not help smiling back at him in appreciation of his quick comeback.

Tea was served without any further faux pas and when they moved into the dining room, Oratio was surprised that Mama had arranged for one of the women who sometimes helped in the kitchen to serve the meal. The table was elegantly set, even the wine glasses had been set out for their visitor. Papa sat at the head of the table and Mama at the foot. She indicated where Mr. Squyres should sit, directly across from Oratio, where conversation would be encouraged.

For her mother's sake, Oratio behaved herself, but she only replied to Mr. Squyres direct questions and did not encourage further conversation with him. After several failed attempts by him, with everyone falling silent to see what Oratio would say, she set down her wine glass and declared, "I do hope you realize, Leroy, that you paid about twice what you had to for that team of horses this afternoon."

"Oratio!" Mama was horrified.

"No, ma'am, that's all right," Leroy grinned, pleased that Oratio had actually used his first name. "I realize that now. It's my folly, but the deal still stands"

Mama relaxed and Papa said almost absently, as he reached for another biscuit, that they thanked Leroy for his purchase.

"I am afraid I was somewhat distracted, sir," Leroy replied, his eyes never leaving Oratio's.

She blushed, and furiously. It was a blush that started at the base of her neck, worked its way down and also all the way up her face and over her scalp. Amanda took in a breath to say something in reply to Leroy, but Mama caught her eye and slightly shook her head, silencing her.

"Would anyone care for any more ham or rice before dessert?" Mama asked, diverting attention away from the young pair.

So – there was even dessert. Oratio inwardly groaned. The meal would be endless.

* * * *

Leroy left with his new horses the following morning and, although Amanda objected, Oratio hoped they had seen the last of him. There were sure to be plenty of pretty girls in Catahoula parish and even in Natchez to occupy his interest, she argued. She had been only a temporary distraction, an evening of entertainment for his trip out into the country to buy a horse or two.

Although Amanda and Levina had fussed and scolded, she did not even bother to go downstairs to say goodbye when he left. She could hear Amanda on the front porch saying that Oratio was not used to drinking wine and asked to be excused with a headache this morning. A headache over one glass of wine! Oratio caught herself before she threw open her bedroom shutters and yelled something down at Amanda over that remark.

Two weeks later, Oratio and Henry were racing down the county road when a rider approached from the other direction. Oratio was wearing Henry's extra set of breeches and shirt, and, since the weather had cooled, one of her brother's jackets. Her hair was tucked up under one of Henry's riding caps. Until they saw the rider, Oratio was winning the race. She was also riding astride instead of using a ladies' saddle. She slowed and when Henry caught up they slowed the horses down to a walk as they approached the rider.

It was Leroy. When he recognized Henry, still at some distance, he waved and called out "Hello." He could not keep the shock and surprise from his face when he recognized Oratio, dressed as a boy. She thought she detected a faint note of amusement instead of disapproval at her scandalous and sinful attire. She looked defiantly back at him and raised and waved her cap in greeting as Henry had done, shaking her hair down around her shoulders. She threw her head back and laughed as she did so. "We never see anyone on this road," she called out, as if that that explained everything.

They waited until Leroy joined them. "Did you come to buy another horse?" Henry asked him in a friendly tone.

"No," he replied, as though the thought had not occurred to him.

"Well, we don't give refunds without the returned merchandise," Oratio teased, quoting the policy from her father's mercantile.

"No, it's not that," Leroy laughed. "I…well…I've decided I have an interest in horse breeding. I would like to start an operation of my own and I thought this would be the best place I could learn about it."

"We are a working farm, Mr. Squyres, not a school," Oratio said.

"Please Oratio, I hope we are not back to that. Please call me Leroy."

"Well - Leroy - as I said we are not a school. The only thing we ever have to offer is working as a stable hand, assuming Papa would hire you, of course. You would start at the bottom."

"That sounds fine to me," Leroy agreed readily and enthusiastically.

"Do you really know what the bottom is in a stable?" Oratio asked, not quite believing him.

"Mucking out the stables all day, that's what it means," Henry added. "Shoveling horse shit and spreading out clean hay, all day long every day, seven days a week. You will only see the rear end of a horse from where you would be."

Leroy hesitated only momentarily and swallowed, "If that where I start, then that is where I start."

Oratio and Henry both laughed. "Come on," Henry said, "you would have to talk to Pa first."

Samuel was sitting in the parlor and in a bad temper when they arrived. He had just thrown down his newspaper in disgust. It looked like Andrew Jackson was going to have his way in driving all the Indians out of the South, including the Cherokees. It was in violation of every treaty and completely disregarded the Cherokee's support of the English during the Yamasee war and their efforts since then to assimilate themselves into the white man's culture. Why, a lot of white people right here in Louisiana, and across the South, had some sort of Cherokee background. Would they be also rounded up and herded west of Missouri into Indian Territory too? Where would it stop? What was going to be next?

"Yes?" he cried out angrily to the knock on the door. Henry opened it, peeking around the door to see why Papa was in such bad humor. Then he entered, followed by Oratio and Leroy. Samuel was immediately on his feet, welcoming the visitor and asking them all to sit with him. Indicating the newspaper he added, "Just a little impatient with these confounded politicians, that's all." Oratio was relieved that Leroy only nodded in agreement and did not get himself tangled in one of her father's endless discussions of politics.

Leroy laid out his proposal to Samuel. Samuel was skeptical at first – did young Mr. Squyres really want to work in the stables, just to learn about horses? Then he wisely realized the real reason behind the proposal and recalled the long-ago evening when he had used every bit of his money to pay for Anna and Mary's dinner at the hotel in Augusta. Even if Leroy had all the money in the world, he still needed to impress Oratio. Looking at his daughter, he could see she was not repulsed by the proposal, and it wouldn't hurt to have some extra help around the stables in the process. He had been thinking about expanding the operation, anyway.

"You would have to live in the house down by the stables with the other hands, doing your own cooking and washing up."

Leroy quickly agreed.

"And the pay for a stable hand is not much, not at all."

"The money is not important, sir. I only wish to learn everything I can about horse breeding operations; to start at the ground and work my way up, sir."

'And to impress and woo my daughter in the process,' Samuel thought, but did not say aloud.

"When can you start?"

"Right now, sir. That is, if you want me to."

Samuel turned to Henry, "Take Mr. Squyres down and introduce him around to the other hands and get him set up." Then to Oratio, "Tell your mother to set another place for supper. I'm sure your sisters will never forgive me if I really let Mr. Squyres fend for himself down at the bunk house, especially his first night."

It was a simple supper, even with Amanda's frantic efforts to improve the regular weekday fare. Conversation was more relaxed this time around, and when Mama invited Leroy to return and have supper with them the next evening he politely, but wisely, refused saying, "If I'm to be a stable hand, ma'am, I think I need to be eating with the other stable hands." Samuel caught a fleeting look of approval and appreciation from Oratio. Young Leroy was certainly on the right path with her.

Over time, Leroy became just another hand around the place. Even Amanda began to take his presence for granted and relaxed on the occasions when Papa insisted he join them for dinner. Oratio was receptive to him, and even started sitting on the front porch in the evenings, hoping he would drop by. He almost never disappointed her - as soon as he cleaned up after work he would walk up to the house and stand on the lawn just beyond the porch, visiting with her and anyone else who was sitting with her. Oratio came to look forward to those visits and began insisting that Leroy accompany Henry and her whenever they took horses out to ride. The other stable hands recognized he was not in the same position they were, but Leroy worked hard and won their respect, even if he was given special consideration because he was courting Miss Oratio.

It was on one of those rides, far from the house on the north edge of the property and almost six months after his arrival, that Leroy suddenly took Oratio's hand when they were watering the horses at a pool below the spring. He asked her to marry him. Oratio pulled back her hand and then turned away.

"I know this must be a surprise and I do not need an answer right now," Leroy added. "I do love you, Oratio, and I hope you will give fair consideration to my proposal."

"Oh, Leroy," Oratio turned to him. "It is true I am surprised. And I do appreciate it. But I would never fit into your world. I can only imagine what it must be like. Surely there are other girls more beautiful and refined than I, down in Natchez, who would eagerly jump at your offer."

"But I did not ask them, Oratio, I asked you. And you don't need to fit into my world. My world is built around you and you are already the center of it."

Oratio paused a moment, smiling at him. "That is very kind of you, I'm sure. But we both know it is not really true, nor can it be. Your family has wealth and position that I cannot even imagine, that I can only dream about – no, more truthfully that my sister Amanda can only dream about. Whomever you marry needs to be a good match for you in all aspects. I can never be that."

"You will be fine, Oratio."

"That is kind, and flattering even, but I can never be what you would need a wife to be, Leroy. And I could not bear to disappoint you in that way, so I must refuse your offer. I do hope we can still be friends."

"I cannot live without you, Oratio."

"How can you say that? I am sure you can – live without me, I mean. Why, you have never even kissed me, have you?"

She had not intended it as an invitation, merely to show that his proposal was premature and unfounded on reality. But Leroy moved to her, put his arms around her, and pulled her bodily to him. Even though she struggled to push him away – and just where was Henry? – his lips sought and found hers, kissing her boldly and deeply. After a moment, she no longer resisted him. It was her first kiss and she resisted the urge to let herself melt into him. When he stopped, she pushed him roughly away.

"The answer is still no!" she exclaimed, pulling her horse away from the water, and quickly mounting it to ride away.

"But your kiss said 'yes.' I will be asking you again – and often," Leroy called after her. It was only going to be a matter of time.

He wore her down, as she would later tell their children, and they were married on December 23, 1832, at his home in Catahoula. Amanda and Levina were breathless to the point that Amanda actually swooned moments before the ceremony. After her corset was loosened and she was revived with smelling salts, she regained and maintained her composure for the duration of the day.

Almost as soon as she accepted him, Oratio began having misgivings about the marriage, or more precisely, about becoming part of the huge clan on the Squyres plantation.

One afternoon when it was just the two of them in the parlor, she sweetly asked Leroy if they could just stay in Ouachita parish. He could start his horse breeding operations there just as easily. But Leroy explained that, under the terms of his oldest brother William's will, he would lose his share if he left the plantation. When she countered that she had hoped they would have a home of their own, no matter how humble, to begin married life he laughed and produced a drawing of the house that was already built for him on the plantation - one of six identical houses built along the lane to the main house. The house was larger than the Newman's house in Ouachita. There was one for each adult brother and his family. The will also dictated that his oldest surviving brother, John, and his wife, Susanna, live in the main house with their children, as well as Leroy's brothers and sisters who were not yet twenty-one or who had not yet married. It all seemed so odd, but Oratio felt better when he explained it. With their own house they should have plenty of room and privacy.

As soon as Susanna learned of their engagement, she began insisting that the wedding be held at the Squyres plantation. All of the Squyres had been married there, she explained in her letters to Leroy, although "all" at that point was only three couples including John and Susanna. Leroy assured Oratio it was not required by the will, but she could tell he wanted to follow the tradition. He assured her that the central hall of the main house would be a beautiful and commodious place for the ceremony.

He added that it would be much easier for Oratio's mother, although Oratio knew that he had not considered her mother's position on slavery and that the ease of the wedding in his family home was largely because of the household slaves who would do the work. It seemed as if he thought his offer to bring all her family to Catahoula as his guests for the wedding covered any other concerns they may have, including the slavery issue.

In spite of her misgivings, she did not want to create a rift with her new family so

Oratio agreed to have the wedding at the Squyres plantation. Susanna immediately pressed them to set a date, saying December 23 would be the best for her. As soon as that date was established, Susanna pressured Leroy's brother, Moody, and his fiancé, Frances, to be married the day before, saying it would result in substantial savings to have the two weddings at one time: the family would already be assembled at the plantation on that date and they could have one combined reception for both couples at the family home in Natchez on Christmas Eve. All of Natchez society would be included.

Moody and Frances were left with little choice but to agree. Feeling overwhelmed by the scale the event had become, a hesitant Oratio agreed to the reception plans too. She tried not to complain to Leroy about Susanna taking control, but it became more difficult with each gushing and bossy letter he received.

When Leroy shared one long letter Susanna sent complaining about the ever-increasing guest list and the resultant cost for the Natchez reception, Oratio shouted that it would have saved the entire expense if she and Leroy had just been married at her home as she first requested. Leroy was red-faced and sat in silence the rest of the evening. When he left, her mother took Oratio aside for a cautionary talk, making her understand the pressure Leroy was under to please his family as well as Oratio. What did it matter anyway? It sounded like Susanna was making plans for a wonderful party. Things would settle down for them after the wedding and when they were in their own home.

Oratio sent a note of apology to Frances, explaining as tactfully as she could (in case her words got back to Susanna) that she had not intended to interfere with her plans. She added that she so looked forward to meeting her, as well as all the Squyres, and hoped they would become good friends, as well as sisters.

Frances replied immediately saying Oratio had nothing to apologize for and was not to worry. She was happy to have Oratio as her friend, with both of them being newcomers to the family. She also was pleased that they would also be living next door to each other too. That was true; Leroy's house was next to Moody's house on the lane.

Frances added a friendly postscript that Oratio would soon learn how to manage Susanna. The best thing was to not resist Susanna's demands or she would drag you into a confrontation you could not hope to win. Just let her think she was having her way and then go ahead and do what you wanted. Half the time Susanna forgot what she had asked for anyway. "Let us just focus on and look forward to our wedding days, Oratio," she concluded. Oratio felt better after getting that letter. She could see that Frances would be an ally, both of them starting with the family at the same time and living right next door.

With the date set, Susanna sent a sketch of a wedding dress she had selected for

Oratio, saying it was an economical cut, would require minimal fittings, and would coordinate wonderfully with the dress she planned to wear for both weddings and the Natchez reception. Oratio was fit to be tied over that, ranting and tearing the letter and sketch into pieces while Mama tried to calm her down and Amanda and Levina scrambled to find all the pieces of the sketch so they could see what Oratio's dress would look like. Oratio and Frances were to be married in almost identical wedding dresses, without the slightest chance of upstaging Susanna as mistress of the plantation.

In the weeks before their wedding, Leroy shared tidbits of his late brother William's will. It was, to say the least, unusual, but also very simple when you understood that first and foremost he intended to provide for their mother and younger siblings. His brother also wanted a fair distribution of the assets to his siblings, instead of handing it all over to the eldest one, or worse yet, dividing the plantation into ten equal shares which would have destroyed it and impoverished them all.

To help with her understanding, and to prevent her from creating the annoyance of asking Leroy to explain the terms again and again, Oratio listed the terms in her diary;

> First of all, his mother, Ann, was to retain the full and exclusive use of the main plantation house, as well as the town house in Natchez, for the remainder of her life. The children who had not yet reached adulthood were to stay with her in those homes.

> The next eldest brother to succeed him was appointed as the manager of the plantation. A private home of specific measurements and design was to be built for him adjacent to the main house and facing the lane to the county road.

> Identical private homes, of the same measurements and design, would be built facing the lane for each of his brothers when they first reached the age of twenty one or were married. Profits from the plantation operations would be used to build the houses, but no more than two per year, until the required number was built.

> Each of his sisters would receive a specified cash settlement on her marriage. Should she not marry, she would be entitled to live in the main house as long as she wished. While the sisters would not share in the profits, their expenses, at a reasonable amount agreed upon by a majority vote of the brothers, would be paid for their lifetimes.

> The ownership of the plantation was placed in trust. Through the trust the brothers shared equally in the income from the plantation starting the year they married or reached the age of twenty-one, and for as long as they lived

and worked on the plantation. If a brother left the plantation, his share reverted to the trust and would be equally shared among the remaining brothers.

Work was to be assigned to each brother by the eldest brother as manager, with the assignments approved by vote by a majority of the remaining brothers. The will included a comment that the division of their duties utilizing the best of their skills in operating one plantation would result in greater earning and profits than all of them individually operating plantations of their own.

Oratio also noted the tidbits of the family Leroy revealed to her:

When the terms of the will were known, John and Susanna and their two children returned immediately from New York, where John was working as a bank clerk, to assume his rightful place as manager of the plantation. Until their new house was completed, they crowded into the main house with his mother and the Squyres children.

In all, six identical houses in the Greek style were built along the lane to the county road, three on each side, exactly spaced to allow the final two to be added by the gates when required for the youngest brothers.

The youngest sister, Maria, died in 1828 at the age of ten, deeply grieving Leroy's mother. Leroy would only say that Maria was a sweet and agreeable child, but that things had never been right with her. The one time he talked about Maria he added that it was only their mother's loving care that kept Maria alive that long. She insisted Maria lead as normal a life as possible and included her in daily life instead of shutting her away, unseen, as most would have. Oratio could see it grieved Leroy deeply, so she did not press for further details.

When Leroy's mother died in 1830, Susanna lost no time in moving into the main house, crowding the family already living there. She took over the two bedrooms next to hers, saying she needed one as a private sitting room and the other for a nursery if she had more children. Fourteen-year-old Mary Polly and her thirteen-year-old brother moved into hastily converted bedrooms in the attic. Two more rooms were taken over for Susanna's two children, so that from then on Leroy and his twin brothers, Moody and Wiley, shared a room on the ground floor across from the kitchen that had been previously used as a storeroom. They were young men by then and did not mind much. Actually, the room had its benefits: the brick floor cooled the room in the summer and they could easily come and go through the kitchen as they pleased.

There was a bitter argument between Susanna and John over the changes, but Susanna won, as always, by pointing out that William's will required only that the siblings remain in the main house, not in a specific bedroom. As soon as the changes were completed, Susanna left with her children and servants for Natchez and then New Orleans for the winter season, leaving the main house under the care of her husband, John.

Oratio also entered in the diary that she hoped she would be able to better understand Leroy's family when she went to live there, and even more so that she would be able to find her place. She added that the Squyres plantation seemed like some kind of fairy tale: an isolated kingdom presided over by an evil queen. Feeling guilty over those thoughts, she immediately tore that page from her diary and burned it in her bedroom fireplace.

Even with Susanna presiding over it, their wedding turned out to be beautiful. The only sadness of the day was that Samuel Newman had passed on that fall. He had been ill for months and while he wanted so badly to see Oratio and Leroy married, and they even considered moving the wedding date forward in spite of Susanna, it was clear by first frost that he was not going to live that long. On his death bed Samuel asked to see Oratio privately. He took her hand as she cried and told her that she had always made him proud and happy, and that he wished only that he could have lived to see her children. "Remember to tell them who they are. They will be Squyres now too. But don't let them forget they are Newman. Make sure they know your story too." Oratio promised she would. She carried his watch with her Bible on the day of her wedding, making it seem he was still a part of it.

* * * * *

Although there was a storm cloud looming on the horizon - a cloud of plummeting cotton prices and the shadows of concern it cast across the plantation system - their first year of marriage was a happy one.

Immediately after the wedding reception they boarded the elegant riverboat *Natchez* for their wedding trip or "honeymoon" some people called it. True to the term, they spent an entire moon, or month, alone and getting to know each other before beginning their domestic life together. The *Natchez,* a side wheeler, took them all the way south to New Orleans. Their cabin, located on the back of the ship, allowed access to a quiet balcony where Oratio could sit watching the river towns glide by as she had her morning coffee and wrote her correspondence; that is, as long as she was careful about the soot and cinders that fell from the steam boilers' tall smokestacks.

Arriving at the crowded docks in New Orleans, they toured the city by hired carriage before going to their hotel. They rode every morning for exercise, had their supper in a different restaurant every night, saw lively music and dancing shows that were too bawdy to be performed anywhere else, and generally fell in love with the city.

Oratio realized that her looks were not even given a second glance in the largely Creole city. When Leroy presented Oratio as an excellent horsewoman, her eye was assumed to be the result of an unfortunate riding accident. That assumption was so much more acceptable among the people they met than thinking it was something she had been born with, and Oratio found it easier to let the assumption become reality.

They returned home in time for the spring planting of 1833. Even though Leroy was turning his focus to his new horse breeding operations, building new stables and acquiring some basic breeding stock, the Squyres family was obsessively focused on increasing the cotton yield that year. Producing even more cotton was necessary to maintain their income in the face of falling cotton prices.

They had no sooner arrived home, than Susanna sent a note down the lane to Oratio that she would call that afternoon. She arrived, dressed as grandly as if she was going to Natchez; ridiculous to only come down the lane, Oratio thought as she smoothed down the day dress she had chosen for the meeting.

As Oratio offered her visitor tea, Susanna insisted that Oratio must join her and the other sisters-in-law in the afternoons at the main house. They were happily working together to stitch new seats and backs for the dining room chairs (which Oratio recognized as Susanna bullying the women into redecorating her own home) but some afternoons, Susanna added gaily, they only played whist instead.

Oratio hated whist almost as much as she hated embroidery. She opened her mouth to refuse, but remembered Frances's advice. "That sounds wonderful, and thanks for inviting me Susanna, but I am afraid I am quite hopeless with an embroidery needle."

"Oh, but surely you can do a few simple stitches. It is a complex pattern, I admit, but everyone else seems to be able to manage," Susanna insisted.

"I am not sure my household duties will allow me to attend every day," Oratio began.

"And we simply must do something about that, too. I cannot believe Leroy allows you to work your fingers to the bone keeping house for him. What is he thinking? I will tell John to have a word with him. I can have a girl or two reassigned to you, someone to cook and clean. Two girls, to start, I think," Susanna concluded.

"NO!" Oratio insisted, surprising herself more than it surprised Susanna. "I mean no, thank you. You see, I asked Leroy to allow me to do this alone for a time, so I can get to know him better. We have our dinner and supper at the main house anyway so I only have to prepare his breakfast. I am able to handle everything else. I think I have to understand his needs and how he wants things done before I can even begin to adequately supervise anyone else in those tasks."

"Well!" Susanna huffed. "That is very devoted, I suppose. Foolish, but devoted. I can see nothing to be gained by actually cooking and cleaning up after John myself."

"I will see what I can do about joining you ladies," Oratio offered. "It does sound like fun." It was a small lie. It sounded about as much fun as having a tooth pulled, but it satisfied Susanna for the time being. She would join them occasionally, but definitely not every afternoon. She also hoped that as soon as Susanna saw how dreadful she was with a needle there would be no continued pressure to join them for their embroidery afternoons anyway.

As the spring planting was completed, successful by all counts, and they settled into the summer growing season, Oratio was taken ill. The doctor was summoned and after a perfunctory examination he called Leroy into the room to give him the news. Oratio was not ill, she was pregnant. The delivery should be expected in January. The announcement excused her indefinitely from attending any more of Susanna's "afternoons."

Oratio's sisters were beside themselves with the news, and Mother replied immediately that she would come to stay before Christmas and remain until Oratio was recovered and comfortable with the baby. Leroy insisted it was going to be a boy, annoying Oratio since it could also be a girl, but otherwise the anticipation of the event was a happy one.

Cotton prices fell even more and the harvest of 1833 resulted in an enormous loss. Leroy and his brothers met and conferred for weeks about what to do. Eventually they decided to sell land they held under speculation, even though the proceeds would not be enough to fully repay the loans and the interest due. Additional mortgages were taken on next year's crop, with the slaves and other chattel property of the plantation put up as collateral. They hoped cotton prices would be better next year.

Christmas of 1833 was celebrated in the same grand style it had always been. The family crowded into the Natchez house for Christmas Eve and Christmas Day. They would stay through New Year's Day and then begin returning to the plantation in groups with John and Susanna the last to leave in mid-January. Sometimes Susanna stayed on in the Natchez house with her children until the spring planting resumed.

The Christmas celebration was much as Oratio remembered from the previous year, when they were there with the family briefly before leaving for New Orleans. Leroy marked the anniversary by presenting her with an opal and pearl-encrusted bracelet at the family's Christmas Eve dinner, and a toast was raised around the grown-ups' table to the couple.

Although she was thrilled with the gift, Oratio barely stopped herself from asking him, especially in front of his entire family, if he really should be buying her jewelry just then, what with the poor harvest and the new mortgages.

She also would have preferred for him to not give her such a personal gift with all the family around them. It would have been so much nicer if it had just been when the two of them alone where she could have kissed him warmly and let him hold her. As the ladies withdrew from the dining room after dinner, leaving the men with their brandy and cigars, she whispered those feelings of frustration to her mother, who whispered back that it was just a case of 'nerves' before having the baby. Mama always made things seem better and Oratio was glad she was there.

On the morning of January 14, 1834, Oratio woke feeling as though she was covered in a blanket of nausea. She could barely get out of bed quickly enough to make it to the basin before she vomited. Then, standing there in her night gown, her water broke in a great gushing flow that soaked the bedroom carpet. Mama, who was sleeping in the adjoining room, must have heard her because suddenly she was there helping Oratio back to the bed and calling out for help.

The babies - there were two of them - were delivered before noon. It was a quick delivery that amazed the doctor. He was surprised when Oratio kept pushing and a second head crowned. Her second daughter followed the first only minutes later. The babies had formed in one placenta, identical twins who looked more like their father than their mother. They named them Mary Ann and Sarah.

Oratio was slow to recover from the birth. She stayed in the bedroom for weeks with meals brought to her. The babies had been underweight at birth, but were rapidly catching up, either nursing or crying to nurse all the time they were awake. They did not sleep at the same time so it seemed Oratio was continually feeding one or the other. Susanna, not pleased with the slow recovery, ordered the cook to prepare foods that would help Oratio recover and produce the milk the babies needed. She insisted on sending a woman from the quarters who was nursing her own baby to help, but Oratio refused. Leroy and Oratio had a bitter argument over it, with Oratio surprising even herself by bursting into tears and Leroy slamming out of the house.

Other than Leroy's help, she would only take help from Frances who came across the garden between their two houses each morning and afternoon. The only good thing to come of her confinement was that Oratio and Frances were excused from the daily embroidery and whist sessions, as well as the sisters-in-law's quarterly shopping trip to Natchez. The group of ladies, with their personal maids, but without their children, always took the riverboat to Natchez, and stayed in the family's town house for a week to ten days while they shopped. The break from Susanna's daily visits, or 'inspections' as Oratio called them, let Oratio relax some. She did not lose any more weight that week and one of the babies almost slept through an entire night.

When the shopping party returned home, a wagon was always sent to the dock first to collect their purchases. The ladies followed at their leisure in one or two of the carriages. Oratio was standing by her window when the wagon returned. It was part of her recovery, getting up and out of bed to walk some each day. As the wagon went by, she saw that a slave girl, approximately her own age, was riding with her legs dangling over the back. One wrist was shackled and chained to the ring on the side of the wagon for that purpose. So - Susanna must have bought a new slave as part of her shopping trip.

Soon she was settled back in bed, and nursing one of the babies. Frances had finished their baths and was holding the other who was fussing to be fed. Hearing the second child, Oratio tried to not let the wave of exhaustion wash over her again. She had to get stronger. Leroy burst through the bedroom door with the girl she had seen in the wagon. Oratio was irritated at his intrusion without knocking, especially bringing a stranger into the bedroom.

"Susanna sent you a wet nurse," he said brightly.

"I have told her repeatedly that I do not want one," Oratio replied sharply. "Why is that so difficult for everyone to understand?"

"The doctor says you need help, or you will not recover, especially since the girls will not take a bottle." It was true, they immediately spit up the thinned cow's milk from the bottle. It was mostly water, but the girls still could not keep it down. After trying it for a day, Oratio insisted it be stopped. The slave girl stood behind Leroy, her hands folded and her head down. Oratio could see wet spots forming on the crude blouse she wore, just from hearing little Sara's cry, or was it Mary Ann?

Oratio took a breath and almost consented, even if just for a few minutes so the baby would stop crying, when Susanna breezed into the room. She had come immediately to the house, not stopping to change from her traveling clothes. Too cheerfully bright, she came to look at the baby Oratio was nursing, although Oratio reflexively pulled the blanket over the baby and her bared breast. "Do you ever knock, Susanna?"

The question was clearly rhetorical, but Susanna's self-satisfied face changed at Oratio's rude resistance. For a moment, Oratio thought she was going to lift the blanket to have a look anyway, so she placed her free hand firmly on her chest, making that impossible.

"Oh, good heavens!" Susanna said shaking her head, "Why are you so modest? I only wanted to see my dear niece. I think you just do that to spite me."

"Of course you would," Oratio replied. "Go have a look at the other one. You can't miss her – she is the one screaming her head off."

"Why is she crying? Did the nurse I sent you not arrive?" Susanna looked around in mock surprise as if she had not already seen the slave girl standing behind Leroy, then she said sharply to the girl, "Don't just stand there like a stupid ninny, take the baby and feed her!"

The girl moved obediently toward Frances and the second child, but Oratio stopped her, "No, Susanna. How many times have I told you I don't want a nurse? How many more times will I have to tell you before you understand me? Leroy, get her out of here and take that girl with you. I won't have it."

Leroy hesitated a moment, then he said, "Oratio, you must."

"What...do you agree with her?"

"Yes. I gave my permission. The doctor said..."

"How could you?" Oratio shouted. "How could you go behind my back?" The baby she was nursing pulled away at the shout and began fussing, unhappy with the sharp voice and the tension in her mother.

Leroy came and sat gently on the side of the bed and took her hand. She tried to snatch it away from him, but he held it firmly. "Just give it a little while. Just until the doctor says you are better. You need help with this, Oratio. It is too much for you to do alone."

Oratio, with the baby attached again, let her head fall back into the pillow. She felt like a failure and as if she had lost control of everything. Not even her body was her own any longer. She raised her head again and looked at the girl.

"What is your name?" she asked impatiently. "No one has even told me your name."

"Namie," the girl replied.

Susanna slapped her face, "Don't you dare mock your mistress, girl. I could have you whipped!"

"Not if she is mine you won't, Susanna. I am the one who decides that."

Susanna was indignant. She was used to having free reign of the plantation. If she saw that punishment was needed she ordered it. Best not to let things get out of hand, she believed. There was a pause, during which Oratio noticed there was no reaction in the girl, other than a slight tightening of the eye in reaction to the sting on that side of the face. The girl had been slapped before and knew her reaction was not allowed.

"What is your name," Oratio asked again, this time more gently.

The girl, eyes still on the floor and eyes down replied again, "Namie."

Before Susanna could draw back her hand to slap the girl again, Leroy stopped her this time, "Nor will you strike her, sister."

"Your name is Namie?" Susanna said with a sneer. "I never heard anything so ridiculous. These people are like animals, Oratio. You will have to call her something else."

"Old Master say it from the Bible when he name me, Miss 'Ratio," the girl quietly interrupted them.

"Do you mean Naomi? From the book of Ruth? That is one of my favorites. 'Whither thou goest...' Oratio stopped; she could see the girl did not know the passage. "Your name is Naomi. Na-Oh-me. We both have an 'O' in our name. My name is Oh-ratio."

Naomi, not sure what else to do, nodded her head in agreement, "Yes'm. Yes Miss Oh-ratio.

"Where is your child, Naomi?" Oratio asked, thinking someone should bring the baby to its mother. She needed to nurse. "Where is your baby?"

Naomi bit her lips together and barely shook her head.

Oratio turned on Susanna. "You bought a mother away from her baby, Susanna? How could you do that - even you?" Then she looked to her husband, "Leroy?"

"Oh, for heaven's sake, Oratio," Susanna huffed. "The child was big enough to walk, certainly too big to be nursing any more. I didn't see any reason to bring along another mouth to feed."

"Leave my house!" Oratio said, sitting fully up in bed now. Frances, holding the still wailing Mary Ann, was shocked. "I said leave my house, Susanna. Get out of here!"

As mistress of the plantation, Susanna considered all of it to be hers. She went where she liked, and when she liked. She only stopped at entering the bedrooms of her brothers-in-law at night time. They had gotten used to it, but Oratio could tolerate it no longer. If Leroy was going to do nothing to eject his sister-in-law from the room, Oratio would. She threw back the cover, exposing the nursing baby as she swung her bare legs around to sit on the side of the bed.

"Oh, for God's sake. Stay where you are, you ungrateful little witch. I will leave."

Leroy was horrified and Frances stood with her eyes wide in new admiration. But Naomi remained with her hands folded and her eyes on the floor, and the front of her blouse soaked as Mary Ann cried on.

First things first. Oratio patted the bed beside her. "Come sit by me," she said gently to Naomi. As soon as Naomi was beside her, Oratio could smell her. She definitely needed to be cleaned up, but that could wait. Oratio reached for the cloth she used to wipe her breasts before and after she fed the baby. The doctor ordered that to keep the delicate babies from infection and sickness. Naomi watched her carefully, trying not to look directly at the exposed breasts. Oratio rinsed the cloth in the basin, wrung it out and handed it to Naomi. "Can you do that?"

Naomi readily opened her blouse as if Leroy were not standing there and did the same with each nipple. Then Oratio motioned for Frances to bring her other daughter to Naomi. Naomi accepted the wailing infant eagerly, seeking relief for herself. Mary Ann started, then pushed away and struggled at the strange taste. But hunger soon prevailed and she set to nursing, although not entirely happy with it. They would have to get Naomi on the same food Oratio was eating so their milk would be more the same.

Both babies content, Oratio looked up at Leroy, motioning with her eyes for him to look away. Although Naomi was apparently not modest with the process, he did not need to watch, or at least so closely. He crossed to the window, looking out at the lane.

"What happened to her baby, Leroy?" Oratio asked him.

"Sold, most likely," he replied with a sigh. He had seen it happen before. What he did not say is that smart auctioneers would simply match a child like Naomi's with another woman, selling them as mother and child. The rare, unmatched infants and small children who were not sold were eventually abandoned. Those who survived might be picked up by orphanages. There was very little chance of finding the child now.

"Can we find out?" Oratio asked. "Can we find the child? Bring him here?"

"Her," Naomi said. "Her name Beatrice."

Oratio looked up at Leroy with such pleading in her eyes that he could not refuse. He left for Natchez on the afternoon steamer.

Although he was not even gone a week, Oratio grew less hopeful with each passing day. The longer he was gone meant the less likely it was the child would be found. He went to all of the auctioneers in Natchez, finding the ones that had sales the week Susanna bought Naomi. Their records of children sold individually did not provide even remote matches, and the names of children were rarely noted when sold with a mother.

When he came back, with no baby, Oratio went into the nursery to tell Naomi. Both the babies were asleep and Naomi was sorting through things that needed to be laundered. As soon as she entered the room, Naomi knew.

"I am so sorry, Naomi. Leroy looked everywhere. He tried his best, but no one knows where your baby is."

"Jesus know, Miss Oratio." Naomi replied before turning away to hide her own tears. She was blessed to have such a kind master and mistress. Beatrice was her third child, but the only one by the old master. All those children were somewhere. Miss Mary Ann and Miss Sarah were her babies now.

"Yes, Jesus knows." Oratio agreed, although she found it hard to believe.

She also thought that if Jesus knew, and was keeping track, His list was growing longer and more hideous each day. Some day it would be enough. She shuddered to think of the wrath that would come then.

With Oratio's acceptance of Naomi as nurse for her children, and her improved recovery, Leroy brought two women in from the fields to help Oratio as house servants, for cooking and cleaning. Oratio was furious with him again. She simply did not want slaves in her house. It had been different with Naomi, but having household servants was entirely against her beliefs. The bitter argument they had over it went on and on for several days with Frances withdrawing from her daily visits and the new girls unsure of their future in the house. It was only when Oratio realized that the bright-eyed young women, so eager to please her, would be sent back to the fields that she gave in. It made her feel like she had completely given up. Oratio's acceptance of servants would also prove Susanna right and she would miss no opportunity to point that out.

The argument took something away from their marriage. Bitterness began to creep in on both sides. Oratio realized that she was not only sharp with Leroy, but she was also constantly searching for the sarcasm in almost everything he said to her. He could ask how she was feeling and she would turn it into a criticism of her handling of the household and their children. Frances implored Oratio to forgive her husband and let bygones be bygones. Try to consider that he was only trying to do what was right and please both Oratio and his family. It had him caught in a difficult place.

"I should not have to compete with his family in my own home, should I?" she said time and again to Naomi as they sat in the nursery simultaneously nursing the babies. Naomi always agreed. It was the same way some one would pour their troubles out to a pet dog. Even if she thought differently, Naomi was in no position to contradict her mistress.

Although the doctor instructed them to occupy separate beds for at least eight weeks, presumably to give Oratio time to heal, neither Oratio nor Leroy made any move to resume their marriage relationship when the time of their imposed separation ended. Throughout the spring planting, the growing season, and even that year's harvest, they occupied separate rooms in the house. Oratio devoted herself entirely to her daughters. When the profits of the harvest were poor again that year, and Leroy scrambled with his brothers to cover their debts, Oratio knew she should go to him, to be supportive and be his helpmate, but she could not stand to even be in the same room with him by then. She began to dream of packing up herself and the babies and returning to her family home in Ouachita Parish.

There was a rare early frost that year, and it was cold enough by mid-November that they had to keep fires going all during the day. Leroy caught a cold and was miserable. Oratio could hear him coughing endlessly in his room at night, but she found herself only nagging and reminding him of the doctor's warning to keep his cold away from the children. In the state of their marriage, there was no need for the doctor to tell him to stay away from Oratio, too.

That winter, without Susanna's knowledge, and to help with the family finances, John secretly sold the house in Natchez. He returned on the next afternoon's steamer with the news and the bank draft. Susanna was furious and there was a huge argument they could hear all the way down the lane. Susanna threw John out of the main house. She even had her maids pack John's clothing in trunks and set the trunks out on the lane.

Of all the remaining houses, Oratio recognized that Leroy and she had the most room to offer him a place to stay. They had four bedrooms, same as the other five houses, but only two babies. Even with them occupying separate bedrooms and a third used for the nursery for the girls with Naomi sleeping on a low cot, there was still a spare bedroom. The other houses were crowded. One brother had ten children so twelve people were crowded into the same space Oratio and Leroy occupied.

She was sure if John moved in, not only would Susanna be coming and going as she pleased, but so would their spoiled and bratty children. Once again, Susanna had commandeered the only private place left to Leroy and Oratio. And Leroy would never have the nerve to refuse.

"I guess I am supposed to invite your brother to come and live with us now," she said to him at the supper table that night. They were dining alone while the rest of the family gathered at the main house, celebrating the rescue of the plantation for yet another year even though Susanna had locked herself away in her rooms and John was nowhere to be seen. Leroy was still not recovered fully from his cold, and the family accepted that as his excuse for their absence that evening. "Just like that, I am supposed to be your faithful and obedient wife and invite him with open arms and let his wife and children take over my house too?" It was not entirely sound logic, John would likely only sleep in the spare bedroom, but she was still angry.

"I would not dream of subjecting anyone to the hell of living with you on a daily basis," Leroy said with ice in his still-hoarse voice, making the serving staff fall silent and begin withdrawing for the argument that was sure to ensue between their master and mistress. Disagreements between the two were becoming more frequent and bitter.

Oratio only threw down her napkin and left the room in tears, crying it out privately in her bedroom, the bedroom that was hers alone now. She knew she could take no more of this family. She would have Naomi pack hers and the babies' things and they would leave for Ouachita first thing the next morning. Leroy could have his house and his entire family could move in with him if he liked.

But it was not to be. Before first light, Naomi knocked urgently on Oratio's door and then entered without waiting for permission. "Miss Mary Ann coughing bad and too hot," she cried out.

The babies had their father's cold and had been coughing now for several days. Oratio went running to the nursery and picked up her daughter, telling Naomi to turn up the lamp so she could see. Mary Ann was fussing and coughing a strange cough that almost sounded like a whistle when she caught her breath at the end. Her plump little cheeks were blotched and red with fever. Oratio quickly checked Sara, who was not coughing, but was also warm, too warm.

"How long has this been going on?" she demanded of Naomi.

"I just heard the babies coughing and went to call you as soon as I see how hot Miss Mary Ann is. I just found out, Mistress."

"Get her undressed immediately and put a cold cloth on her forehead," Oratio commanded. "We need to cool her down. Sara too."

She left Naomi with the babies and ran down the hall to Leroy's room. She did not expect the door to be locked, so she ran into it, unable to stop her momentum as she turned the knob. That infuriated her – him locking her out - so she pounded on the door with both hands, shouting his name. Leroy came sleepily to open the door, tying his dressing gown as he squinted at the light, "Oratio! What the hell? What time is it?"

"The girls are sick, Leroy. Bad sick. You have to go get the doctor. NOW!"

By the time Leroy returned with the doctor, Sara was coughing too. Sara coughed so hard it brought up her stomach, and Oratio was standing with that mess all down the front of her nightgown when the doctor entered the room. He examined the children and gave the diagnosis Oratio already expected and feared: whooping cough. The long whoop at the end of each cough took away the breath and eventually the strength of those infected.

Leroy never left their sides as Oratio and Naomi did everything the doctor commanded them to do for the babies. The doctor was there most of the time, guiding them, trying to break the fever and ease the coughing that wracked the tiny bodies. Then, as Mary Ann seemed to be over the worst of it, Sara grew worse. Sometimes she even stopped breathing a moment or two altogether after a coughing episode. Leroy would hold her upright, rub her gently and blow sharp breaths in her face until her breathing would resume. Oratio felt as if a haze settled over them as day followed night and night followed day.

As much as she fought sleep, and she was afraid Sara would slip away if she let go, she woke with a start. She was leaning against the crib, her head awkwardly cradled against it so that her neck was stiff. It was late in the night, somewhere past midnight she guessed, although she did not know what night it was. There was complete silence. The only sound in the nursery was Mary Ann's quietly rasping breath as she slept in her crib. Leroy sat, holding a silent and still little Sara to his shoulder as his tears ran.

"I am sorry, I am so, so sorry," Leroy said through his tears.

In all the things they had been through, Oratio had never seen him cry. The sight of him sitting now, holding his daughter, knowing he blamed himself for her death, and knowing that she had been the main one to make him feel that blame pierced Oratio's heart. She rose and went to her husband, kneeling at his feet. "It is not your fault," she said honestly and gently looking up at him and feeling her own tears rising. "It is not your fault."

From that point forward things were different for Leroy and Oratio. Susanna continually warned that losing a child could destroy a marriage, almost like she took some kind of delight in the prediction. But it only brought them closer together. Oratio found forgiveness in her heart for Leroy as he did for her. They still argued, and with as much passion as before, but there was love instead of hatred behind their words. For the first time, as things grew steadily worse around them, they began pulling together as one.

Oratio would also carry the conviction that little Sara had been sacrificed to save her sister, so Mary Ann could grow up with both parents. She would always carry that guilt, but she was also determined that she would not squander the second chance they had been given. Before Sara was buried, Oratio clipped a lock of Sara's hair and placed it in a special locket. She wore that locked every day for the rest of her life as a reminder of what little Sara had given them.

At John's insistence, the vacation of the plantation was entirely curtailed in 1835. Always before, at the height of the growing season, the family traveled north to cooler climates. Traditionally the entire household, including all the brothers and their wives and children, along with their personal servants, left by the middle of June and did not return until just before the harvest. Originally the practice had been adopted by the planter class to avoid malaria that was more prevalent during the summer months, but in later years the practice had also become a necessary display of status for the privileged classes, and Leroy's family was no exception.

At the height of their wealth, before Oratio arrived in Catahoula, the entire family had spent two summers in the highly fashionable Saratoga, New York, accompanied by the required jewelry, wardrobes, and luggage, of course. After their financial troubles began, about the same time Oratio came to live at the plantation, the summer vacation of the plantation was drastically reduced. In 1834, the wives and children simply went north into Arkansas, taking up residence in a new hotel in the mountains north of Little Rock, and for only six weeks. The weather had not been much cooler there and even though they still had a break from the routine of the plantation, Susanna complained bitterly at the disappointment of it all.

With John's edict, the family simply stayed at home that summer. It would mean substantial savings, but not enough to turn the tide of the disaster that was developing. No sooner than John had imposed the austere conditions, that urgent word came from Ouachita that Oratio's mother, Anna, had suffered a severe stroke and was failing rapidly. Anna was only in her fifties and had always been in robust health, so it was completely unexpected.

Leroy and Oratio left immediately, taking Mary Ann and Naomi with them. They took a light carriage and the fastest horses, but a second stroke soon followed and Anna did not survive to see her daughter and granddaughter one last time. After the funeral, Leroy took Mary Ann and Naomi home while Oratio stayed on for a while, mainly to offer her support as the family adjusted to their mother's absence and to assist in the monumental task of writing the necessary letters notifying all the family back in Georgia and South Carolina.

Amanda took it upon herself to make arrangements for Henry to continue living in the family home without his mother. She insisted on clearing out her mother's rooms, so Henry could occupy those as the new 'master of the house.' In the evenings, after Henry returned from his work, Amanda always wanted to review her newest plans with him - with Levina and Oratio in attendance, of course. Oratio could see that Henry was exhausted and was not ready for any kind of change and really cared nothing about the operation of the house. She also could see that Amanda was trying to establish some continuity for her brother to remain alone in the home. Amanda would warn that if Henry was left solely to his own devices…leaving that sentence open as if the most dire consequences were too onerous for words.

Perhaps it was because of her resentment of Susanna controlling the family at home, but Oratio found herself vocalizing a strong resistance to Amanda over a completely trivial matter. Amanda pushed back and Oratio pushed back even harder. Voices were raised with Henry entering the fray at one point, shouting that he really did not care what they decided, he would do as he liked anyway.

At that point, Levina, who had been silent, but increasingly distressed at the argument, put her palms against her temples and cried out, "Stop it. Please, all of you. Just Stop It!" Then her eyes rolled back as she went silent and collapsed back against the sofa.

Henry jumped to assist her, and Amanda quickly took Levina's wrist, slapping it sharply to revive her. Oratio crossed to the sofa, placed her hand against Levina's face, feeling no response, then pressed against her neck and found only a faint and irregular pulse. She pushed a closed eyelid up and saw no dilation of the pupil in reaction to the light. Oratio screamed out to get a doctor. Levina did not respond to their efforts to revive her.

The doctor said that he had long-advised Levina that she suffered from chronic weakness of the heart and nervous exhaustion. He had advised her to avoid nervous situations, especially when she felt the heart palpitating. Under his orders, and since it distressed her so greatly, Levina really should have removed herself from the discussion her siblings were having. She knew the risk, he insisted.

But they all felt deeply guilty, having caused Levina's death, and so soon after their mother. Her husband stayed behind to speak to them at the cemetery after the grave was filled. They were preparing themselves to walk back to the house for yet another funeral dinner with friends and neighbors. Amanda was weeping inconsolably and Henry was stony silent. As he approached, Oratio half-expected her brother-in-law to rail at them, to lecture them for causing his wife's death, and even to disclaim them as family. She steeled herself for the verbal beating she was about to take.

Instead, Edward, always as kind as Levina was gentle, only reminded them what the doctor had said, that Levina knew of her condition and since she could not change herself any more than a leopard could change its spots (he used the analogy as illustration) they were not to blame themselves in any way for what had happened. He concluded with words that pierced Oratio's heart as if he had thrust a knife through it, "She only wanted all of you to love each other and to always be happy with each other. She was the peacemaker, after all."

On those words, Amanda completely collapsed in great, gasping sobs. She hung on Edward, saying over and over that she was so sorry, that if she could only take back what she had said and that she had never meant to hurt Levina. She never even realized Levina was so upset by these things; she was always smiling and so supportive and so pleasant and accommodating. She never realized how much Levina suffered. She should have seen it. "Oh, forgive me, Levina, forgive me," she cried out toward the grave. Even Henry had tears running. Oratio was frozen in stony silence.

"She loved you all. You were her entire world. She would have said there was nothing to forgive, but I'm sure she would forgive you."

Levina might have forgiven them, even as they forgave each other that afternoon, but Oratio was not sure if she could ever forgive herself. The only thing she could do was resolve to better control her tongue and consider the consequences of the words she said before she said them. Mama always said Oratio said exactly what she thought, as though that explained and excused everything. That might have worked when she was young, but she knew she was going to have to change that.

CHAPTER TEN

Even though it was not as hot that summer as it had been in previous years, the family was not accustomed to the heat of the plantation during the summer. One hot and sticky afternoon, Oratio sat with her sisters-in-law for a light luncheon on the veranda on the shaded side of the main house. She had not been home even a week after Levina's funeral and she was still exhausted.

The brothers, including Leroy, were in a discussion in the overseer's house. The meeting had been going since early morning. Occasionally a raised voice or a shouted declaration from there came easily to them on the heavy, still air. It did nothing to improve the tense mood of the meal. Oratio was so sick of everything here and wished she had stayed in her own house with a quiet lunch tray instead.

Susanna pushed away her plate of sliced cold tomatoes and cucumbers, indicating that the course was finished. Oratio could not resist taking another defiant bite or two. The sliced tomatoes were delicious, especially when salted. Beside her, Frances silenced a giggle, but obediently set her fork beside her half-finished plate.

When all the adults dined together, John, as the eldest brother and manager of the family plantation was always seated at the head of the table, with the brothers and their wives seated in order of succession down the table, as though they were royalty waiting in line to assume the throne. When only the ladies were present, even at the smaller table on the porch, Susanna assumed John's seat and insisted the ladies remain in their seating order. It made so much more sense, and caused less confusion, she declared. ("And always reminds us of our place," Frances would quip to Oratio.)

Oratio, as the wife of the youngest married brother, occupied the lowest seat. Susanna reminded her that would change as soon as Sidney, the youngest brother, was married. She should not give up hope, Susanna said. At these luncheons, Oratio was never allowed to sit at the foot of the table opposite Susanna, either. That seat stayed vacant when the men were absent because it was solely reserved for Susanna who always seated herself opposite John when the husbands were present, at the foot of the long dining table. That also meant that Leroy and Oratio, always seated at the foot of the table and furthest from John during dinner, were also beside Susanna and hopelessly drawn into her self-absorbed dinner time conversation.

"Of course, Oratio is not as affected by this heat as we are," Susanna said, turning on Oratio with mock sweetness as the plates were cleared. Susanna had been annoyed with Oratio since her return to the plantation, almost as though it had been a desertion of her duties and Oratio had been allowed special privileges in violating John's new ban on travel. A silence fell over the table. Even the women preparing to serve the next course stopped what they were doing, waiting for Susanna's signal to continue.

"And why would that be?" Oratio asked with impertinence. She was so sick of Susanna thinking she was in charge, and her continual reminders that Oratio was at the very bottom of the ladder. They were not royalty, after all, even if Susanna thought otherwise.

"I only mean that your people are not bothered by the heat as much, that's all."

"What do you mean by my people?" Oratio shot back down the table, trying to keep her voice calm. "I am just as hot as you are right now, Susanna. I just don't complain about it every time I open my stupid mouth."

There had been talk the day before that Negroes were not as affected by the heat as white people were. It had to do with their dark skin and their African backgrounds, Susanna assured them. "Why, just look at them working away out there in the fields," she observed. "A white woman would simply faint dead away out in that sun." Oratio had bitten her tongue until she tasted blood to keep from arguing with the stupid woman over that stupid comment. She also knew from Frances that Susanna had been making veiled references to Oratio's heritage while she was away, insinuating she might actually be High Creole. What did they really know about her, after all? Oratio would be damned if she was going to remain silent today.

"Why, Oratio Newman!" Susanna said in mock surprise. "Why are you getting all he't up? I declare, I was only remembering that your family always stays up in Wa-shitta for the whole, entire summer, don't they? You and Leroy were not married yet when we used to go up north to Saratoga, so you are used to putting up with this heat all summer long, aren't you?"

"My last name is Squyres now, Susanna, the same as yours, and the parish name is pronounced Ouachita. But I have told you that so many times I have lost count now." One of the other sisters-in-law had to hide her smile behind her napkin. "And yes, with the horses and the mercantile, my family needs to be at home during the summer. I still get as hot as you, and I also think this heat is almost unbearable, but I really do try to not nag and bother Leroy about it. I think he has enough to worry about these days. Don't you?"

That shut Susanna up – at least on that line of conversation. She nagged John constantly about their imposed "exile" here in the heat of the plantation. And they were all in the same boat as far as the family finances went. But it also gave her a new line of attack. "I don't know why we (as she spread her hands to include all the sisters-in-law at the table) should be the ones to suffer these egregious economies," she lamented, then turned her face away behind her napkin as though fighting to hold back her tears. "It was not our error in judgment that got us all into this deplorable financial situation."

There was another hush of silence, broken only when Oratio said, "Are you asking me, Susanna?"

Susanna looked up, surprise to be questioned, but Oratio pressed on, "I believe my husband has been equally affected by these "egregious economies" as you call them. I also know that he has not asked me to do anything that he has not also undertaken himself."

"Oh yes," Susanna agreed with a dismissive wave of her hand, "a lesser quality of brandy and cigars, I am sure. I assure you John was brought to his knees over that one, and quite tearfully I might add." There was a titter of nervous laughter around the table.

"Leroy does not smoke and I know that he deplores brandy," Oratio countered. "These changes are for our cumulative benefit. Circumstances have changed and they are scrambling to deal with that."

"Not with any measurable degree of success. And certainly with no appreciation of our sacrifice," Susanna said with a disdainful sniff, taking another gulp of wine from her glass.

"Oh, please, Susanna. Our sacrifice? Do you not understand that the people of this plantation are going to suffer, and greatly? Having to stay home for the summer is nothing in comparison to what they will have to sacrifice if things do not improve."

"People! People? Who are you talking about, Oratio? The Negroes? I cannot be bothered with that. Not when..." there was an unexpected catch in Susanna's voice and the threat of real tears as she continued, "...not when we are facing the complete destruction of this family and the loss of the fortune of generations."

There was silence around the table and among their servants as the significance of those words, that had previously been unspoken, sank in.

Oratio cleared her throat, "I have to believe our husbands are doing the best they can, Susanna, under these circumstances."

"Yes, you would, wouldn't you?" Susanna glared at her, having recovered her composure.

"Perhaps," Oratio replied thoughtfully. "But I choose to believe Leroy when he tells me they are doing all they can do. I also try to remember my promise to him

– 'for richer or poorer.' Leroy has provided handsomely for me up until now, but if that should change and we have nothing, I will still honor those vows."

Susanna slammed down the glass, sloshing its contents, and stood to leave the table. "And that, my dear, dear sister-in-law, is why you will walk away from here with nothing. Absolutely nothing."

* * * * *

There was no relief with that year's harvest. There were more lengthy meetings of the brothers, with many slammed doors and shouted arguments. In the end, the first auction of slaves was held that year. The cash that the sale of the slaves would bring was the only way to pay what the banks demanded and get through the winter. Oratio saw that it was the beginning of the end. The reduced work force would mean a smaller harvest for the next year, which would mean less income so that even more slaves, or perhaps some of the land itself, would have to be sold. It was land that no one else wanted under the current circumstances. Along with everyone else in the family, and likely every other cotton planter across the South, she began praying for higher cotton prices the next year.

They had a slight reprieve in 1836. With careful management of the crop, timing of the sale of the cotton, and excruciating cuts to every possible expenditure, the plantation broke even for the first time in years. They had a harvest celebration of sorts at the main house, feeling a corner had been turned and profitable times might return. There was also a celebration down in the quarters since there would be no more slaves sold that year.

However, 1837 was a disaster, the likes of which had never been seen. When cotton prices started falling again after the spring planting, Dutch and English banks began recalling their funds in the United States. To comply, American banks could only call in their mortgages to raise the funds. Those who owed those mortgages generally could not repay the full amount all at once. Fearing the resulting defaults would ruin the banks, depositors began withdrawing their money. Banks closed. Even banks that were completely solvent and owed nothing to foreign investors were ruined when too many depositors began demanding the return of their deposited funds. Almost overnight, script, or paper money, became worthless with all banks refusing to convert it into gold or coin, or to even to honor it until the banking situation could be sorted. Script on a bank that was good and solvent today could become worthless paper tomorrow. Only gold and coin were secure and recognized in payment of debts.

Through their lawyers, the Squyres brothers demanded the return of their deposits from the bank they used in New York. The multiple accounts they kept with the bank were meant to receive payments for the cotton they sold abroad, and to pay their foreign agents and shippers. Although the balances were at their low point of the year, it was still a substantial combined amount. The bank closed before the transaction could be completed, taking their money with it. Minimal amounts were withdrawn from their other banks in the South before those banks froze their funds or closed altogether. There was now more gold coin on the plantation than there had ever been, hidden in various locations in case they were robbed, but it was still not enough to carry them until harvest.

Then, and unbelievably, the banks that had frozen their deposits demanded full payment of the mortgages they still held against the Squyres. Leroy and his brothers went in person to each bank, explaining their situation: that they could make some payment on the mortgages if the banks would release the frozen funds they had on deposit with them. But the banks were in the position of needing to raise even more than the frozen reserves to repay their foreign investors, so they refused. The brothers returned home knowing foreclosure was imminent.

Rather than sitting and waiting for the sheriff to arrive and post the foreclosure notice on the plantation gates, they put together a risky alternate plan. The next morning Susanna and her children went to the dock to board the riverboat to Natchez and then a second one to New Orleans. Mary Polly, the only sibling who still lived in the main house, accompanied them. To avoid arousing suspicion, even at the local dock, none of their servants accompanied them and they took only enough luggage to support the claim they were going to shop in the city - just one small valise each. If her luggage had been inspected, it would have revealed that the nervous Susanna carried only her jewelry and bags of gold coin. Otherwise, she left with only the clothing she was wearing.

Two more wives and their children boarded the next riverboat that came, this one heading north toward Monroe, and again with only one valise for each person and without their servants. When the next group arrived at the dock the following morning, the dock master commented sarcastically to his assistant that the "Panic of 1837," as it was being called in the papers, must not be as bad as everyone was letting on if all the Squyres ladies were still taking their shopping trips.

The cotton harvest was just beginning and Oratio was the only wife waiting to leave when the sheriff and his men arrived and posted the notice. Guards were posted at the gate and a firm warning was given to those who remained that the entire assets of the plantation had been impounded and no longer belonged to the family.

She had just finished hiding the gold Leroy slipped to her when the sheriff entered their house without knocking. Divided so many ways it was not a lot. She quickly stuffed the little leather bag up the chimney in her bedroom, only moments before the sheriff knocked on the door as he came through. She made an indignant show of tying the belt of her dressing gown with her back turned as he entered. Fortunately, the man was polite enough to be embarrassed and withdrew long enough that she could return to the fireplace and make sure the bag was tucked securely away before she removed the dressing gown and emerged from the room, fully dressed.

Since he had first shared the plan with her, she argued with Leroy about the
dishonesty of hiding the gold. It was in defiance of the foreclosure order and
could land them all in jail. Eventually she accepted Leroy's position that it was
not wrong, that the banks had first refused to return the money that belonged to
them, or to even offset it against what was owed. The bank seized all the
Squyres' assets. Those assets would be auctioned to pay for the debts. Their
belongings would be auctioned at much less than their actual value and the bank
would keep all the proceeds. The bank was stealing everything from them and
would leave them to starve. The gold they were hiding and spiriting away was
the only thing that would keep them alive.

They became captives in their own home, although Leroy said they should be
thankful they were allowed to stay until the property was sold. He was also
relieved the bank had decided not to pursue debtor prison, a remedy still available
in Louisiana even though it had been removed from federal law in 1833. At least
they would be free to go when the property was finally taken away from them.

For a while the plantation continued operating as before, but under the direction
of the bank trustees, who were now ensconced in the main house with the sheriff
and his deputies as their guards. Slaves were inventoried by checking them
against the meticulous plantation records. After the first counting, the slaves were
frequently re-checked against the list and warned of the dire consequences if they
decided to run to avoid being sold. Oratio knew from the comings and goings of
Naomi that an exodus had already begun. Two or three at a time crept out
through the woods each night. Several had even walked away while picking
cotton at the edge of the south fields. As few of the runaways were retrieved,
more were emboldened to run, which ultimately resulted in a total curfew in the
quarters and armed patrols being posted to enforce it. Slaves could not leave the
quarters day or night and the partly harvested cotton was left in the fields with the
gin house standing idle.

The contents of the main house were completely cataloged and tagged for the
auction. Oratio knew it was hurtful for Leroy and his brothers, but they only said
they were happy their mother was not there to witness it. There were paintings
and furniture that had been in the family for generations, some was originally
brought from England in 1700 by William and Elizabeth Squyres, who had been
friends to the parents of Aunt Charity.

The only time Oratio went to the main house, on the pretext of finding the sheriff
to insist on the issuance of her staple food supplies that had been delayed, even
more than seeing the paintings of the Squyres ancestors tagged and stacked
against the central hall walls for the sale, she was grieved to see the familiar
crystal, silver and china lined up on the dining room table and sideboards.
Generations of the family had dined from those. They had been used for

celebrations, Christmases, birthdays, weddings and anniversaries, and all would be gone without a trace. Even the wine cellar Leroy's father had so carefully built and maintained was inventoried and sealed for the auction. It looked as though every trace of the family would be erased.

That night, as they lay side by side in their darkened room, Leroy spoke softly, "One more day and you and Mary Ann would have been away from here. I am so sorry you have to go through this." Because the sheriff feared they might abscond with funds or other valuables if allowed to leave, Oratio, along with everyone else would remain on the plantation until after the auction. They were all being held as prisoners in their own homes.

"I would rather be here with you than be somewhere else and worried about you," she said.

Leroy was silent a while. "We will leave here with nothing. We will have nothing left to start over with, Oratio," his voice almost broke. "We have nothing."

"That's not true, Leroy," she said quickly. "I still have you; and we still have Mary Ann." It was obvious but needed to be said.

She was thoughtful a bit longer. "And we still know how to breed horses, Leroy. We still have that. We know how to farm, and we still have my family. We will stay with them for a while if we need to - just until we can get on our feet again. But we can, and we will, start over again, Leroy. Think of it, no debts to worry about, just us. We can get a little place somewhere and start over."

Leroy shifted to his side and put his arm across her. She whispered to him, so softly that even he could barely hear her, "I still have what you gave me. It is safely hidden."

"It's no use. We can never walk out of here with that, Oratio. I am sure they will search us to the skin on the day we finally can leave."

But Oratio had an idea. "No, we can't walk out of here with it. Not all at once."

Late the next morning, even though they were supposed to stay inside the house, Oratio walked to the stables, followed by Naomi carrying Mary Ann. It was a beautiful late September day. Oratio carried a picnic basket. She walked, uninterrupted, into the stable and told one of the surprised grooms there to help her hitch a team to the smallest, open carriage. When the team was ready, Naomi got in the back, still holding little Mary Ann. Oratio climbed up to the driver's seat and took the reins from the groom. Then she simply drove the carriage from the stable, across the yard and up the lane, passing the overseer's house. As expected, the sheriff came running out of the house, a napkin still tucked under his chin, where he had been enjoying a second breakfast, shouting at her to stop.

"Just what the holy hell do you think you are doing here, Miz Squyres?"

Oratio held up the picnic basket. "I have had enough of sitting around my house doing nothing all day long. My daughter needs some fresh air and these horses need exercise. Do you think anyone will really want to buy them if they have been let go this badly?"

"You can't go nowhere, 'specially not with them horses. It's all impounded."

"Oh come now, Sheriff," she said in an almost teasing tone. "Do you think I am trying to escape with only a picnic basket? Do you honestly think I would take out over open roads with a child and a servant and in an open carriage? I am only going to drive down to the stream on the other side of the south fields. We will have our picnic there and then we will come right back. I won't even leave the property. Come with us if you must, but since our own food seems to be so closely rationed, you will have to bring your own lunch."

He harrumphed and spat on the ground, walked around the carriage looking at it, peering over the sides at the floor and under the seat and had Naomi stand to make sure she was not sitting on anything. He even squatted down to look at the underneath side to see that nothing was hidden there. Then he examined the horses that were eager to be on their way, having been kept idle in the stables for days now. He even motioned for Oratio to open the picnic basket and with grubby hands he pawed through its contents, inspecting bread and cold meat wrapped in napkins, china and silver service for three, and three crystal water glasses. To throw him off, she packed pieces of her own china and crystal, retrieved from the inventory laid out in the dining room of the main house. The silver she packed in the picnic basket was from the family silver, heavy and elegant and generations old. She had hidden her own silver in her bedroom chimney and only moments before the contents of her own dining room and pantry were taken away to the main house to be inventoried.

"You can see the horses are eager for exercise," Oratio said, hoping to distract him from the basket to look at the prancing horses. If he inspected the basket any closer he might see the opening at the bottom of the fabric lining. If he felt around there he would surely find the four gold coins she had hidden under the fabric. It would be enough to arrest her for theft, and probably Leroy too.

"All right, go ahead," he said. "But you better be back no later than two o'clock or I will send someone to find you."

"If Mary Ann is napping I won't want to wake her," Oratio complained.

"All right then," he said, sucking a kernel of bacon from a back tooth and shaking his head. These rich women were more trouble than they were worth – having a picnic of all things and under the circumstances she was in. Didn't this little fool realize that? At least it wasn't a garden party. "Just make sure you drive back by here when you return so I know you are back or I will send someone out looking for you."

They drove along the stream looking for just the right spot for the picnic. Oratio was pleased that Naomi was included in the scheme. As soon as she was trapped with them when the foreclosure was posted, Oratio promised Naomi that she would not leave her behind. She wished she could do more for the other slaves, but even Naomi understood that was impossible. It gave Naomi a sliver of hope now that Oratio was including her in the scheme.

Finally, the perfect spot was found. It required no digging, which would leave tell-tale signs to anyone who might come later to investigate the picnic site. While Naomi stood watch, making like she was setting out the picnic lunch they had carried with them, Oratio quickly stowed the gold coins in the small wood box she took from the carriage for that purpose.

When they returned, the sheriff flagged them down, stopping the carriage. He asked for the picnic basket and looked through it to verify the silver, china and crystal – needing to be washed now - was accounted for. "Just want to make sure you warn't fixin' on stealin' these things," he explained.

Oratio gave evidence of being offended by his suggestion, "These were my wedding presents, sir." If the sheriff knew anything at all about silverware he would have known the pieces were too old for that to be true, but he did not.

But he was smug that he had been too sharp for her. "And they ain't yours no more are they? Don't think you can put one over on me. I am on to you."

Oratio showed him a bit of her anger over that, slapping the reins to drive the carriage back to the barn.

They began the routine of a daily picnic, giving Mary Ann and Naomi some air while exercising the horses. She always opened the basket to show the sheriff the contents as they left and then showed him the contents again on their return. She even defiantly insisted he inspect the basket on the days he just waved them on through, saying she did not want to be accused later of stealing her own wedding china.

When all the gold was safe in the picnic hiding place, Oratio began spiriting away her wedding silver under the basket liner. In the time before the auction she hid every last bit of it at their picnic spot. The sheriff was none the wiser.

Although she had hoped to keep Naomi with them, pleading that she was now

271

part of the family, Leroy kept trying to make Oratio see that it was impossible. Naomi was listed on the slave inventory and was included in the published auction listings. Oratio tried for days to come up with a way to save her from the auction block. Naomi, as a strong woman of child bearing years who had successfully produced children, would bring a premium price, at least eight hundred dollars. That was more than twice the amount of the gold Naomi had helped her hide away. Naomi could count and knew there was not enough money.

"You need all that money to help you start over," she told Oratio one afternoon as they were driving back from their picnic. "Don't you fret none about Naomi," she added bravely.

"I am not finished yet, Naomi. Don't you worry. I will find a way."

Oratio wrote to Henry, asking if she might possibly borrow the money. Amanda wrote back almost immediately, saying most of their cash money had been lost when the county bank closed, and they could not scrape that much together. But she promised she would see what she could do.

Although it seemed like it would never come, the day of the auction finally arrived. In the final days the gates remained firmly locked and guarded with the general public kept outside, some of them even camping along the county road. Bank representatives accompanied the more affluent buyers as they inspected the premises. Most toured the main house, the stables and had a cursory look at the slave stock and the fields under cultivation. Few expressed any appreciation of the six smaller houses along the lane. "Eyesores – the lot of them," Oratio heard one haughty browser exclaim as their carriage drove by her on their way out the front gate.

Leroy, Oratio, and Mary Ann spent their last night in the house. As Naomi requested, Mary Ann was moved to her parents' bed as soon as she drifted off to sleep instead of remaining in the nursery with Naomi. That would allow Naomi to slip out at first light and go down to the quarters to join the other slaves and prevent a traumatic farewell for Mary Ann. She added that she hoped that little Mary Ann, almost four years old now, would forget all about Naomi in time.

They were still sleeping when Oratio heard voices downstairs. It was the temporary workers, already inside the house and removing the downstairs furniture to the lawn for the auction. The crews had worked during the night emptying out the other five houses and removing the smaller contents from the upper floors of the main house. Theirs was the last house occupied and she was grateful they had been spared the indignity of being crowded in the main house with the other brothers where she would be the only woman and Mary Ann the only child. Oratio shook Leroy awake, told him it was time and rose to dress in the first light of dawn.

When they were fully dressed, they went downstairs to meet the sheriff, carrying the two valises Oratio had packed. He would inspect the bags to make sure they carried no valuables with them. While the three were dressed in their best for the auction, John had negotiated with the bank representative for all of them to be allowed a second change of clothing and their night clothes, as well as their personal toiletry items.

Rather than picking out another fancy outfit, Oratio wisely chose work clothing for Leroy and herself that would also be suitable for the kind of traveling they would begin when the auction was over. Then she had stuffed multiple dresses and underclothes for Mary Ann in her bag, hoping the Sheriff would display some kindness in not insisting those be removed for the sale. Mary Ann hid her face from the sheriff and hugged her favorite doll closely. The other toys in the nursery would be put in the sale.

"That all you're takin'?" he said, looking through the half-filled bags.

"It is what we are allowed, sir," Oratio responded before Leroy could say anything.

The sheriff grumbled something about "damned ridiculousness." He took the bags from them and stamped up the stairs. They could hear him rummaging around in the bedroom, pulling open the bureau drawers and throwing things around. Leroy, indignant at the invasion of their personal belongings, even though they no longer owned them, started to go up the stairs but Oratio put out a hand to stop him.

The Sheriff came back with their bags brimming with a jumble of clothing. He also carried the bedclothes off their bed, including the feather tick that always covered the mattress. They could make a pallet with those. There was also a jumble of toys and a set of picture books from the nursery bundled up in another sheet.

"You folks is done enough," he said, handing it all over. "Put this away in the bedroom after the boys is done. I won't let anyone come inside after that. You can stay here again tonight, but that has to be it."

"Thank you sir," Oratio said. Leroy put out his hand, offering his thanks.

Strategically, the bank representatives and the auctioneer set the order of the auction to draw the largest crowd first, to maximize their interest, and to keep the crowd there until the last item was sold.

The land would be sold first, hoping to impress the crowd with the first sale bringing a large amount, and greasing the skids, so to speak, for every item sold after that. Nothing should seem quite so expensive when people thought of how much had been paid for the land.

After that, the contents of the houses would be sold, sure to please all the ladies in attendance. When that slowed, the house auction would stop and they would move on to the livestock, especially the horses, which were bringing in buyers from the surrounding states. After that, they would return to the house and drag that out until night time. Unknown to the crowd, and the reason most were there, the auction of slaves would not begin until bright and early the second morning. They anticipated the auction of the slave stock would last all of the second day.

It was almost a carnival atmosphere. The auction of the land and buildings went quickly. A high-Creole financier from New Orleans rapidly bid the price past their best expectations and enthusiastically outbid all other eligible and interested parties. The prestige of the old-money property appealed deeply to the financier and his wife. There was a general round of applause and much excitement directed to the couple in their carriage. The woman lightly bowed in acknowledgement of the applause, but Oratio soon overheard her saying to the female companion sitting on the seat beside her that the main house would have to be completely redecorated and the six little houses down the lane, so odd and eccentric, would have to be pulled down before she would live here. That saddened Oratio, thinking the house that had been her home the past five years would be destroyed.

John was extremely agitated and excited by the amount raised by the sale of the land, thinking the debt may be satisfied before the auction was completed. A pause occurred when the family attorney, who came without being asked even though he knew he would not be paid, went into the manager's house with John and the brothers to meet with the bank representatives. The crowd could hear much shouting, but ultimately they all came out, the attorney red-faced and ranting and John resigned and dejected. The auction would continue. Leroy told Oratio the bank conceded that any excess after all debts and expenses were paid would be returned to the family. At least the attorney had negotiated that much.

The auction of the household items immediately followed. The finer furnishings, interspersed with items of lesser interest, were also bid up by the Creole couple. Oratio was happy that at least those items would remain with the house. The ancestral portraits, of no interest to the couple, were mostly parceled out to the neighbors. Leroy felt betrayed that those people, who had lived so near all his life, were so enthusiastically bidding on those paintings. At one point he had to turn and walk away to compose himself, but he was determined to remain on the premises for the entire sale. If nothing else, he owed that much to his parents and the generations before them.

At noon, the auctioneer moved on to the livestock and those were rapidly sold. Oratio had to blink away tears as she saw her favorite stallion prancing and his eyes rolling wildly as he was taken away, but she felt Leroy's hand tighten on hers in support. The saddles and tack, carriages, and even the farm wagons were taken away leaving the stable in an eerie silence.

After a break for lunch, the crowd moved back to the household items. As the auctioneer moved into the more personal items, the crowd became more somber. Oratio watched as the first of Susanna's fine wardrobe was placed on the block. The exquisite ball gown Susanna had worn for Oratio's wedding and every Christmas Eve in Natchez after that, and only because Susanna was never allowed to replace it, brought a bid of only two dollars. Then her individual dresses had no takers at the opening bid of one dollar each. They all showed the years of wear, especially in the hard sun light.

Not to be deterred, the auctioneer ordered each dress to be matched with a set of undergarments, shoes and even a hat. The young men assisting the auctioneer had no idea of how to put those things together and some of the combinations were hideous, but the groupings started bringing the required opening bid of a dollar. As much as she disliked Susanna, Oratio was glad she was not there to see her proud wardrobe deconstructed and sold for so little. It would have broken her heart.

She was numb for a while, watching the auction of the clothing her sisters-in-law had to leave behind, and tried not to remember the occasions on which those had been worn. They moved on to Oratio's wardrobe and Leroy asked if she wanted to leave for a while. Oratio shook her head. She now had a sort of perverse interest in seeing who would end up with the clothes that had been the costumes for her life on the plantation.

A large dressmaker's box was produced and opened, the tissue paper roughly pushed aside and her wedding gown was pulled out and displayed for all to see. "How about a dollar for the dress?" The auctioneer took the veil from the box and put it on his head, laughing. "How about a dollar for a used wedding dress with a veil. Anyone want a used wedding dress? How about six bits?"

There was complete silence. Through the buzzing in her head, Oratio could hear a bird singing in a faraway tree.

"This ain't right," an angry female voice shouted from the back. "This is un-Christian!" another woman insisted. "Let her keep her wedding dress," another called out. Soon there was a chorus of women's voices, even joined by several of the men, protesting the sale. There was a scream as a woman near the front of the crowd was jostled and lost her balance. The frightened auctioneer took the veil off his head and thundered his gavel repeatedly on the block for order. Two deputies beside him showed their guns, holding them high up in the air and ready to fire. The crowd was soon quiet.

"All items are to be sold, by the order of the Bankruptcy Court of the State of Louisiana!" the bank representative called out time and again until there was complete silence.

Then Oratio surprised herself, calling out in the silence. "It's all right everyone. That is my wedding dress, but my sister-in-law picked it out for me and I never did like it much."

There was general laughter, then a polite applause for her brave words, but there were no bids and the price was dropped even more. She knew if Leroy had six bits he would buy it for her, and for Mary Ann to wear one day, but he had no money now. In the end it went for six bits, or seventy-five cents. A greasy-looking cracker came forward to collect it. While he waited, the crowd watched in silence as the auctioneer's helpers re-folded the dress, wrapped it and the veil in the crumpled tissue paper and put the lid back on the box. The cracker proudly carried the box to a young woman who must have been his daughter, who accepted it with excitement, hugging the box to her. Then she looked up, apologetically to where Oratio was standing with Leroy on the porch of their empty house. Oratio smiled and nodded at her, indicating her approval, and the moment passed.

They crowd grew restless again when they began to realize the auction of the slaves would not begin until the next day. Things were agitated and spontaneous protests were shouted in unison by groups within the crowd – "Sell the niggers Now!" – until the auctioneer stopped the bidding on a small lot of assorted cooking utensils to let the bank representative speak. He announced that the auction would continue as scheduled, and for those who had no overnight accommodations the new owners would allow camping along the creek on the other side of the south field. Hearing that, Oratio had a sinking feeling. Someone would find her hidden stash of gold and silverware. If that happened, and it was turned over to the sheriff, she would have to deny ownership. There was nothing else to be done.

As the sun sank in the west, people began drifting toward the promised camp ground. The houses, except for the furnishings the Creole couple had purchased and ordered carried back indoors, were empty. Leroy and Oratio went back inside their house, found their bundle of bed clothing and valises and made a pallet by the fireplace. Mostly to occupy her time, Oratio sorted and refolded the contents of their bags, grateful for the bounty and the sheriff's generosity. She reorganized the toys in the sheet, tying it into a bundle with handles that could be more easily carried.

In the growing darkness, John came by to tell them all the brothers were going to sleep in the stable, having been locked out of the main house by the new owners who had taken up residence there for the night and would let no one else in. The slaves, all in chains now, were under guard down in the quarters, but John had insisted they be moved into the empty barns instead of spending the night in the open.

Oratio would have gone down to the barn to join the family, but she did not want Mary Ann to have the memory of that. So, instead they stayed the one final night in their little house, by the warmth and light of the fire. She made a game of it, saying it was like they were camping inside the house. There was a little flour, rice, and beans left from the provisions, but nothing to cook with, or to eat with for that matter. She managed to cook some plain flour and water biscuits in the fireplace ash, mixing the dough directly on the hearth with her bare hands. They settled down on the pallet for sleep. Oratio comforted Mary Ann while she cried for Naomi and rocked her to sleep.

In spite of being exhausted, Leroy and Oratio could not sleep. They tried not to think of the horrors that awaited them the next day.

The auctioneer's gavel was brought down completing the first sale just as the sun was beginning to light the eastern sky. Despite John's repeated requests that the slaves be sold in family groups, only individuals were brought to the block. The only exception was children aged three or less being sold with their mothers. Many were bought by traders who would take them to New Orleans for resale. When a terrified boy, who could barely be more than three, was set on the block by an auctioneer's helper, Leroy tried to lead Oratio away, but she refused. "I will not desert them," she declared vehemently.

So, while Leroy took Mary Ann back to their empty house on the pretense of giving her a nap, Oratio remained. Ladies stood in the shade and shelter of the porch of the main house. When Oratio drifted out into the crowd of men, holding her parasol high over her head, she was told firmly to go back to the porch, that it was not safe for her among the crowd.

The morning dragged on as one by one, the people of the plantation were sold. Oratio tried in vain to find Naomi in the crowd of slaves chained together and waiting for sale at the edge of the yard, but she was nowhere to be seen. She felt a faint flicker of hope when she realized that none of the personal and house servants were there. By noon, John and the family attorney were shouting again with the bank representative. Standing close to the auctioneer, John was demanding that the auction cease, that more than enough had been raised to pay the debt, the interest due and the auctioneer's fees and expenses. Beside him the attorney produced a hastily drafted paper, really of no legal significance, demanding cessation of the sale. But the bank representative prevailed, motioning to the auctioneer to continue while insisting that excess proceeds, if indeed there were any, would be distributed to the family, as previously agreed.

"For God's sake," Leroy shouted from beside Oratio on the porch. She was unaware he had returned. "Allow us to keep our personal servants at the very least. They have been with us for years and are like family."

"Some of them probably is family," a cracker yelled from the sidelines with a jeering laugh, insinuating the resentment of the interrelationships of the planter class and their lighter-skinned servants. Oratio was sickened by the cruel laughter from many of the crowd. The sale continued.

In the mid-afternoon, with much of the crowd drowsy in the warm sunshine after their mid-day meal, the last of the field hands was sold and the personal servants and household workers were brought into the yard as a group, many of them blinking in the bright sunshine. Oratio spotted Naomi and waved at her from the porch to get her attention. When Naomi nodded in recognition, Oratio pulled her own chin up high, indicating Naomi should do the same. As Naomi stood proudly and pulled back her shoulders, Oratio mouthed the words, "I...Will...Find...You."

The sale of Naomi took only moments. When the opening bid of three hundred dollars was announced there was a quick flurry of bidding, rapidly raising the price to three hundred and seventy five dollars. Then a gentleman on the opposite side of the crowd, but still standing so his hat shielded his face from Oratio's view, solemnly announced his bid, "Nine hundred and fifty dollars." There were no further bids.

In the moment before Oratio leapt down from the porch to run to Naomi, she saw the gentleman, his back still to Oratio, go to Naomi and remove the shackles from her wrists himself. He must have said something to comfort her because Naomi's face relaxed and she almost allowed herself a smile.

Oratio shoved and pushed her way through the crowd, losing her parasol and having the sleeve of her dress partially ripped away at the shoulder. When she reached the open space around the block they were gone. She pushed on through the crowd toward the manager's office where the cashier's desk was set up. She reached the lane in front of the office only in time to see the back of the man's carriage at the end of the lane, with Naomi sitting beside him on the carriage seat, cautiously looking back over her shoulder for one last look as he drove away.

She burst through the office door demanding, "Who was that? Who just bought Naomi?"

The cashier refused at first, but she slammed her hand on the table and demanded again, "Tell me who bought my Naomi. She was listed as a ladies' maid and nurse on the bill of sale and a man in a carriage just drove away with her. I just saw them leave. Who is he?"

"Even if I was allowed to tell you the names of our bidders ma'am, I could not tell you his. He did not register, he left no name and he paid cash money. Just one purchase and he paid in gold."

"You have no idea who he is? Absolutely none?"

"No, ma'am, except he is a gentleman."

Even though Naomi was lost, Oratio stubbornly remained for the rest of the auction, facing each one as they were sold, hoping they would draw some comfort from her being there for them until the very end.

There was still an hour or so of daylight left when the auction ended. They went back to their empty house to gather their things. Leroy rolled up the pallet and tied it with a thin rope, leaving enough slack in the rope that it could be carried over his shoulder. They picked up the stuffed valises and the bundle of toys. Oratio took Mary Ann by the hand and they closed the door to their house for the last time. They began their journey, on foot, back to Oratio's home. It was sixty miles, but they had no where else to go. Surely they could stay with the Newman family while they regained their footing and could decide what to do next.

Leroy knew they needed to stop at the picnic site, but they silently joined the throngs of people on foot walking down the dusty lane toward the county road. At the gates, instead of turning north toward Ouachita Parish, they turned south. Traffic was heavy as they walked the road that ran adjacent to the south field. They reached the place where the road crossed the stream that ran past the picnic spot. While others waded their way across the ford and were sometimes splashed as horses and carriages of the more affluent sped on by, others turned toward the place they had camped the night before, hoping to stay another night before continuing. Oratio was concerned someone might have already found the hidden gold, but also reasoned they would have heard about it if that had happened.

They reached the campground, surprised by the number of people starting to bed down for the night while keeping furtive watch for the plantation guards. Oratio led Leroy to her picnic spot, a little away from the crowd. The grass was not trampled; giving her hope her treasure was still intact. While Leroy spread out the pallet and gathered wood for a small fire, although they still had nothing to cook their food with, Oratio felt around inside the hiding place for the wooden box. It was still there, but she left it. She would return after dark and transfer the contents to her valise as inconspicuously as possible.

A woman close by heard Mary Ann whimper that she was hungry and came to investigate. Seeing they had nothing to cook with, she returned with a battered cooking pot and two worn spoons and said to keep them. Oratio half-filled the pot with water from the stream, added two handfuls of rice and wedged it into the fire.

As they were eating, Leroy's youngest brother Sidney happened to walk by, hand-in-hand with a young woman he introduced to them. They were to be married as soon as they could find a preacher. In defiance of her father who forbade any continuation of her association with the young Sidney Squyres when the foreclosure notice was posted on the plantation gates, she still came to those gates each day, demanding that the guards let her through. She was finally able to find Sidney the first day of the auction. She returned home that night, packed a bag and told her family she was leaving to marry Sidney, since he said he still would. She was completely cut off by her father and was bringing only with her what little she could carry.

Oratio felt a rush of emotion that the couple would never be able to occupy a house built on the lane for Sidney, and for his bride to know the family for that matter. When they parted, Leroy shook his younger brother's hand and wished him well. He invited the couple to come along to Ouachita Parish with them. Oratio echoed the invitation, but Sidney wanted to stay around these parts, hoping his future father-in-law would soften in time.

As they parted, Sidney whispered something urgent in his older brother's ear. Leroy shook his head, and then nodded as if reassuring his brother, then fiercely hugged Sidney and kissed him on the cheek. Days later Leroy would tell Oratio that Sidney had spirited away his share of the gold too. Even though it was all he had left, he offered half of it to Leroy, who of course refused. Sidney was relieved to learn Oratio and Leroy had done the same with their share of the remaining gold coins.

The next morning they simply rolled up the pallet and resumed their walk, but turned back north toward Ouachita. The road was dusty and traffic was still heavy, but mostly with people on foot. For a while an occasional broken-down wagon went by loaded with poor whites and pulled by a decrepit-looking horse or worn-out mule. The crowd thinned as people turned off the main county road. By evening the three were walking alone. They found a place to camp beside a stream. Oratio cooked more rice and then stirred up biscuits she cooked in the bottom of the pan without any grease. The next morning they were back on the road, dustier but determined. Oratio held her battered parasol overhead, trying to shield Mary Ann while she walked. Leroy carried their daughter as much as he could.

It was then that Leroy wanted to use some of the gold to buy a horse and wagon, so they could ride. Oratio argued that it was too dangerous - they were still in the county and using the gold would surely arouse suspicion. The amount they carried was barely enough to buy a horse without a wagon, anyway.

Oratio started the third day by bolting to the edge of their campsite and tossing the contents of her stomach into the tall grass. Leroy was concerned and said they should rest that day, but she felt better after breakfast. Leroy said they needed more to eat than rice and after a long discussion, they agreed he would go to the house they had passed on the road and see if he could trade one of the silver spoons for food. He came running back. The woman who opened the door had eyed him with suspicion, asked where he got the spoon and then accused him of stealing it. She produced a rifle and ordered him off the property, yelling after him that her husband was going after the sheriff.

Even though it was a very late start, they set out at a fast-paced and breathless walk, taking turns carrying Mary Ann. If they were stopped and searched and the silver and gold found, Leroy would certainly be arrested for theft, and possibly Oratio too. They barely covered three miles that day. As the sun was setting they came upon a copse of trees with a dense undergrowth of shrubs that was mostly honeysuckle. They burrowed deep into bramble, huddling together for warmth. To be safe, they stayed there all the next day, with Oratio and Mary Ann resting while Leroy found a hidden place where he could see the road and watch for any signs of the sheriff pursing them. That evening he said they had to keep going. They needed to be up and on the road at first light.

A farmer overtook them later the next morning. He stopped to ask where they were headed, looking sympathetically at the now sun-burned Oratio and Mary Ann, and offered to let them ride as far as he was going. For the next four miles they sat in the back of his wagon, luxuriating in the speed of the horse and wagon. Oratio napped even though she did not want to. They profusely thanked the farmer when he stopped and said apologetically that it was as far as he was going. He caught up with them again by evening, holding up a picnic basket covered with a clean cloth and saying his "missus" insisted he bring them a share of their dinner.

The best Oratio could reckon, they had been walking for twelve days when yet another carriage came down the road behind them. They were out of food and Oratio worried that they were lost. People with teams of horses and light carriages with thin wheels like the one coming toward them rarely even slowed down now as they passed, as if the unfortunate circumstances of the dusty and bedraggled Squyres would rub off on them. They were certainly bedraggled. All of their clothes were dusty now, even the extra ones the sheriff had crammed in the bags.

To lighten the load, they left things behind; mostly clothing that was past repair and the rest of the toys they hoped Mary Ann would not miss. Leroy had traded the set of picture books for food, cleaning himself up as much as possible before he approached the farm house where some children were playing. Oratio stood far enough back, hoping the woman who opened the door would not see how dirty she and Mary Ann were now. They were not invited in, but the trade gave them enough food to last for four days.

The driver of this carriage was whipping up his horses to increase his speed and pass them faster. Leroy swept little Mary Ann up in his arms and they all moved quickly to the side of the road and into the tall grass to let the carriage pass. Oratio stepped on the hem of her skirt and stumbled a little before catching and righting herself, but still heard the fabric rip loudly. It was her last dress. She was standing with downcast eyes, too ashamed any more to even look up as the well-dressed people passed them by, when the carriage stopped.

She heard someone jump down from the driver's seat and come running toward them. They were going to be robbed! She screamed at Leroy, "Run, run!" Instinctively she held the valise with the gold and silverware close with both arms as she turned to run after Leroy who was carrying Mary Ann across the open field. She rapidly fell behind.

The man coming so fast from behind caught her arm firmly at the elbow as she croaked out, "No!" then screamed out again at Leroy to run. She took the valise by the handles and blindly swung it around in a full circle at the man, hoping the handles would hold and the weight of the gold and silver inside would stop him, or at least make him stop long enough that she could run after Leroy. With a hoarse and animalistic shriek she landed a glancing blow on his upraised arm, but barely fazed him. She struggled to bring the bag back around again, but the man grabbed and held her arms down to her sides as she struggled against him. He was calling out her name, loudly, over and over. She stopped. The man holding her was Henry.

"Oratio! Oratio, stop. It's me. It's Henry. Oratio. Stop. Look at me. It's Henry." She realized he had been yelling those words at her from the moment he jumped down and came running after them. In her terror of being robbed she had not heard him.

Oratio stopped and stared in disbelief. They could not be home already. They had not walked that far yet. They had been so slow, what with little Mary Ann having to be carried so much and Oratio being sick and throwing up almost every morning. She was imagining this. She had lost her mind. Yes, that was what had happened. She had lost her mind. It could not really be her brother standing here in front of her.

"Henry?" she barely managed.

"Yes, Oratio. It's me. It's Henry. We have been searching everywhere for you."

"Henry?" Oratio said, laughing and crying at the same time. "It's really Henry?"

Henry was hugging her, no he was holding her up; her legs were weak and shaking and weren't doing their job any more. She looked over his shoulder. For a moment she saw that Mama was sitting there in the carriage, waving.

Maybe Oratio had died and this was heaven. But no, it was really Amanda climbing down the wheels on the side of the carriage to come running to them too. She was crying out her name, with her hand raised, and waving like she thought Oratio could not see her.

Leroy came back, carrying Mary Ann. Henry let go of Oratio to hug Leroy and Mary Ann, but no matter, Amanda was there holding onto Oratio, crying and hugging Oratio to her, brushing back her hair with her wonderfully clean handkerchief and smothering her little sister's face with kisses in between.

"We looked everywhere for you!" Amanda was saying. "Absolutely everywhere. We waited too long. It was my fault. I kept thinking we would get the money, but we never could. We started too late and when we finally got to the plantation the auction was just getting over and you weren't there any more. We asked everywhere, but we could not find you. There were so many people on the road. We have been driving up and down this road for two weeks now hoping to see you, hoping you were coming back to us. Oh, Oratio, I was so fearful we would never see you again!" Amanda burst into tears again.

Mama was there then. This must be heaven. Somehow Mama was here with them even though she wasn't supposed to be here any more. While she could still hear Amanda, whose chatter had become a buzzing in her head, her mother silently and tenderly took Oratio in her arms, hugging her close. Oratio rested her head on the soft shoulder, letting herself be enveloped in the loving presence, taking in the familiar, fresh and clean smell that was her mother. It was then, and only then, that she let herself go.

As the little group stood there, in the sunshine at the side of the road, Oratio wept. She cried out everything that was inside her, her grief for everything that was lost: their home, Leroy's family, each of her sisters-in-law - even Susanna. She cried for what this had done to all of them. She cried for the lost Naomi. She cried and she cried, Mama's hand patting and rubbing her back and encouraging her to let it all out.

When she finished, she pulled away and saw that it was actually Amanda who had been holding her all along. But she knew, and would always insist, that Mama had been there with them on the side of the road too, at least for a little while. Oratio went to Leroy, hugging him and Mary Ann as she wept afresh, with Leroy crying too. When they were finally finished, she looked up to see that even Henry had been crying.

She drew herself up, pulled up her skirt to wipe her face, and said, "Well, enough of that. Let's go home."

In the weeks that followed, Oratio realized the reason for her sickness on the road was not the lack of food and poorly cooked rice. She was pregnant. The child must have been conceived during those final weeks they spent in their little house on the plantation. It amused her that what she still thought of as "the little house" was bigger than the one they were all crowded into now. They were staying put for while. The baby would be born in her mother's house in Ouachita Parish.

Along with Mary Ann, she grieved for Naomi. Amanda explained how they had tried in vain to scrape the money together. She even wrote to the last address she had for their now-deceased grandmother, writing "current resident please open" across the front, but had heard nothing in reply. She sought to borrow individual small amounts from neighbors. She even went into Monroe and tried to sell the little jewelry they had left, but received such small offers she resisted selling her own wedding ring and some of the more precious pieces she carried, such as their mother's ring.

Henry helped; pressing to collect every account owed to the mercantile, but, in the depressed economy that followed the Panic, those collections still fell short. They left at breakneck speed the morning of the first day of the auction, driving through most of the night, only to arrive and find the auction was ending.

Oratio tried to sound sincere when she told them she was sure Naomi would be all right. She had a glimpse of the man who bought her and been reassured he was a gentleman. They could only pray now that she would be all right.

The baby was a boy and Leroy was delighted. Leroy was looking somewhat better by then, taking on some of his old duties with the horses. It was work he loved, even at the lowest level, and Oratio was happy to see some of the light return to his eyes. Mary Ann seemed none the worse for the wear of the events they had endured. Amanda assured Oratio that children were more resilient than most people thought. Mary Ann would be fine.

They were all delighted with the baby, including Mary Ann, and he was happy and healthy from the start. They named him Russell Moody. Leroy and Oratio saw him as a symbol of their new beginning.

Oratio was sitting on the front porch with Amanda one day late in 1839. Things were improving with the mercantile and a few buyers had shown up that fall asking about horses. It looked like they would be all right. Little Russell, almost a year old now, was on her shoulder fussing and working on a burp after nursing, with Oratio patting his back to help. After a resounding burp, making the sisters laugh in appreciation as he looked around at the noise, Oratio looked up to see a pitiful horse and wagon coming slowly up their lane.

A lone figure was driving and one of the wagon wheels was badly warped and slowly weaving from side to side as though it would leave the axle at any moment. Amanda followed Oratio's gaze. "Oh dear," she said. People like this showed up sometimes, down on their luck and wanting to sell the last thing they had, a broken-down old horse that really needed to be shot. "I'll go get Leroy,"

Oratio said, handing Russell to his aunt.

She went down the steps and toward the stables, but when she looked up at the approaching wagon again, she could see the driver was a colored man. An old colored man, slouched forward and wearing a battered hat. He likely wanted to collect rags, bottles, and scrap metal - a 'raggedy man' they called them. There was no need to go for Leroy. She would go instead to the bin where they set aside things for these scavengers. It had been a while since the last one, so this one was going to be richly rewarded for coming up their lane today.

She turned to go the other direction toward the bin, but looked back at the wagon. The old man smiled and waved. Oratio waved back and then motioned for him to come on down the lane, they had things for him. Then the old man stood up in the wagon, grinning ear to ear, took off his cap and waved it wildly. Oratio saw then that the raggedy old colored man was Naomi.

"Naomi," Oratio put her hand to her heart and could barely speak. "Naomi!" she cried out again but louder this time, and was running now. Naomi, still grinning, dropped the reigns and hopped down from the wagon, an easy hop since she was wearing men's trousers, and started running. The two reached each other midway, with the force of it spinning them around as they hugged and hopped and jumped up and down, laughing and crying at the same time until they finally settled into hugging each other and rocking side to side.

"Oh, but Naomi," Oratio said suddenly, pulling away, "Did you escape? Are you running?"

Naomi laughed hard at that, from deep in the gut. "Running with this old nag?" She laughed even harder, doubling over. Oratio joined her, but not quite sure she understood. When she caught her breath, Naomi said, "I am a free woman, Miss Oratio. He tol' me he set me free the day he got me. Took me all the way to Macon first to meet the lady who bought me. She a colored woman too, but she bought me and set me free. She only said she had to meet me before she gave me my 'mancipation."

That woman was Delilah, Mary Freeman's friend. The letter Amanda had sent to their grandmother eventually found its way to her. When the letter arrived in Macon there was too little time. She immediately dispatched her agent to the auction to buy Naomi.

Oratio took Naomi to the porch and introduced her to her sister, who took Naomi's hand, brought her to sit on the porch and welcomed her, saying, "Oratio has been so worried about you." Oratio presented baby Russell, saying he had been conceived those last nights on the plantation. "I'm happy something good could come out of that time," Naomi said happily. Then she asked, "Where is Miss Mary Ann? You think she remember Naomi?"

Mary Ann was napping, but Oratio went in the house and up the stairs to wake her daughter. Telling Mary Ann she had a surprise for her, she carried her back to the porch where Naomi was waiting.

When she saw the girl, Naomi's face lit up and she held out her arms. "There's my baby girl," she said softly in the same high and clear voice she always used when she talked to Mary Ann. "OMIE!" Mary Ann was delighted, running to her nurse. For the rest of the evening, Mary Ann would not allow Naomi to set her down. Naomi even had to eat supper holding Mary Ann on her lap and then sat by her bedside, leaning over to stroke the little girl's forehead, until she went to sleep.

She came back to the porch with a soft laugh, "That chil' finally asleep. She want to hear every story I ever tol' her. And some I never even 'membered telling her, too."

The adults sat on the porch long into the night in celebration of the reunion, talking and laughing and catching up on the news of the past two years. Russell woke, nursed and slept again. They paused only when Naomi insisted on tiptoeing back up the stairs to check on Mary Ann.

Leroy proudly described the horse breeding stock he was building up with his brother-in-law, Henry. Henry, shy after Naomi turned to Oratio and said in a loud whisper - "Lawd, he even more beautiful than you let on, Miss Oratio," - also shared a few additional details on the horses. Oratio brought Naomi up to date on the children, described their walk from the plantation, almost all the way to Ouachita until Henry found them walking. She even made them all laugh, now that enough time had passed, when she told them how she beat Henry half to death with her valise, thinking he was trying to steal her gold and silverware, before she saw it was him. "My sister packs a mean punch," Henry agreed, rubbing his arm like it still hurt him.

Naomi also shared her story. The moment the gentleman, Robert Tucker, bought her and removed the shackles from her wrists he told Naomi he was sent by a lady from Macon, Georgia, who was going to set her free. But the lady wanted to meet her first so he would take her to Macon.

In Macon, at Delilah's house (and Delilah knew your grandmother, Mary Freeman Lovett, did you all know that?) she interviewed Naomi, asking details of her life with the Squyres and trying to determine if Naomi was ready to be on her own.

"Delilah promise me to try to find my chil'ren, but we never could. I guess they too old now to remember they old mama anyhow. She also write letters, trying to find where you folks went. The letter Miss Amanda wrote to Miss Mary, asking for money to buy me, was sent on to Delilah with no return address for you folks, and Delilah send letters everywhere she could think of. We never heard nothing, so I finally figure you folks didn't want to see me."

"Oh, no!" Amanda exclaimed. "We never received any letters. And yes, we do want to see you. It took the longest time for little Mary Ann to stop talking about you and even a longer time before Oratio would. You can't know how much they missed you."

"Yes'm, I knows that now," Naomi grinned as Oratio took her hand. "I knows that now."

She went on to tell them that Delilah wanted her to stay with her a while, helping with Delilah's children until she would teach Naomi how to read and write. She promised that when Naomi was ready to leave, and when she was ready to be on her own, she would give Naomi a fair sum of money to help get her started. "She has money from your grandmother to do that," Naomi added, surprising them. They knew so little about their grandmother it seemed.

Finally, Delilah said Naomi was ready to leave. Naomi was determined to find the Squyres first, or to at least find what happened to them. Delilah told her it was not safe for a colored woman to travel alone, even with her emancipation papers. She could be robbed, killed, or - even worse - sold back into slavery. Finally, Delilah had an idea, and the disguise of a raggedy man was put together, even the sad old horse and wagon with a warped wheel.

Naomi, with her papers and three hundred dollars in gold hidden away, left Delilah to find her new life. Using a map Delilah gave her, she made her way across Georgia, Alabama and Mississippi, almost as though she was invisible. "Delilah right – no one bother ol' raggedy man," she laughed. In Louisiana she found her way back to the Squyres plantation and asked around, but no one knew anything of where the family had gone. Finally, she remembered Oratio was from Ouachita Parish and decided to go there.

To bring her up to date, Leroy gave a quick summary of the family and where they were now. Naomi was delighted to learn that Sidney's young lady found him and they were married. She had seen that girl hanging around the gates every day after the foreclosure notice was posted.

Leroy updated Naomi on all of them, from the youngest to the eldest, finally saying that John and Susanna and their children went to New York for a while, but their last letter said they were heading back to Louisiana soon. John was working in a bank in New York, but Susanna was no longer happy there and demanded they return.

Naomi shook her head, almost involuntarily, and clucked her tongue at the mention of Susanna's name, but said nothing.

"John tried to stop the auction that afternoon, you know," Oratio said softly. "He really did try to stop them from selling you."

"Yes'm, we saw that," Naomi said softly, remembering. "He a fine gentleman."

"Even if he was married to Susanna?" Oratio teased.

"Now, I never said that!" Naomi declared, leaning over to Oratio as she laughed out loud.

"Susanna is, and will always be Susanna," Leroy agreed. "You would not believe..." Oratio shook her head slightly and Leroy stopped, but then she continued for him.

"What Leroy was going to say was that after the auction was over and she found out there was some money that would be coming back to the family, Susanna hired her own lawyer and tried to get it all for John. Even though as one of the first to leave she had carried away the lion's share of the gold, she insisted they simply could not live in their tiny rented house, and without servants, and as the eldest son it should go to John, anyway."

"And of course, she wasted all the money she carried away with her on lawyers, and the estate had to defend against her lawsuit, so in the end there wasn't much left for anyone," Leroy added.

"I wondered 'bout that," Naomi agreed. "It seem like there should have been something left to come back. That you all should'a had something."

"We finally got four hundred and fifty dollars," Oratio said quietly. "Not much at all." They were all silent for a while, remembering those days.

Then Naomi said softly, "But we all free now. We all free."

It was true, Oratio suddenly realized. Of course, Naomi no longer belonged to the plantation. But neither did Leroy and Oratio. Nor would their children. Leroy had been held there as strongly as Naomi had been, unable to leave it. Yes, his life had been much, much better, but in a gilded cage, so to speak. All the Squyres, from Leroy and all the way back to John and Mary Squyres of Charles Town, South Carolina, had been enslaved to it. Naomi had understood that.

And now they were free. All of them. Oratio took Naomi's hand and raised it between them in understanding as she smiled over at the woman she had once owned, who was now her friend. They were free.

* * * * *

After a good, long visit, Naomi insisted it was time for her to go. Her plans were to go on to Texas. It was dangerous, but exciting. "They won't know what to do with a free colored woman and I can make good use of that," she teased.

The Newmans and Squyres all tried to talk her out of it. Her place was with them, they insisted. They tried over and over to convince her. Eventually, they had to accept it. Naomi was heading out west.

She used some of the money Delilah had given her to trade with Henry for a better horse. It was sort of a reverse trade, with Henry starting out saying he was just giving her the horse and Naomi insisting on a too-high price she was going to pay him, or she would just take her old horse with her. After days of going back and forth, they agreed on a price, spat on their palms and shook hands to seal the deal, with Naomi throwing back her head and roaring with laughter in delight at the beautiful horse that was now hers.

Henry agreed to replace the warped wheel on her wagon as part of the deal and Amanda insisted on packing the wagon with all kinds of food, pots and pans and household goods. Mary Ann had to be dragged out from under her bed to say goodbye, and then pouted and sulked so hard that Oratio had to threaten to spank her if she didn't straighten up and give Naomi a proper goodbye hug and kiss.

Finally, it came down to Oratio's turn to say goodbye. They hugged a good long while, both of them crying a little until Oratio pulled away, gave Naomi a light punch on the arm and said, "You had better write to me. I know you can now and you know where I live."

Naomi nodded. It was time for her to go.

Oratio reached in her apron pocket and brought out a bundle of freshly embroidered napkins, tied up with a satin ribbon. "Did you make these?" Naomi exclaimed. Oratio nodded. "I can do embroidery if I set my mind to it," she said defensively, but then conceded, "I still hate it, but I can do it."

"I helped her," Amanda called out from where she stood with the family on the porch.

Naomi smiled in warm appreciation of the napkins and leaned forward to give Oratio another hug. Then she felt that something else was wrapped up inside. She untied the ribbon and unrolled the napkins. There in the middle were six of the silver knives, forks and spoons. Half of what she helped Oratio hide away two years earlier. "Oh, I can't take these, Miss Oratio," she objected. "You got to pass this on to Mary Ann someday. This for your family."

Oratio suddenly could not speak and tears were stinging in her eyes. "You <u>are</u> my family, Naomi. This family is bound together with love, each of us, and you are a part of it now. You are my sister. You are my family."

The two hugged again until Leroy cleared his throat.

"And anyway, you helped me steal it or there wouldn't be any, so it's half yours anyway," Oratio said, wiping away her tears and laughing a little.

"Then I will take it. But just so I have something nice when you come visit me."

While they watched, she climbed up into the wagon bed, an easy climb since she was again dressed in her raggedy man traveling clothing. She carefully stowed the silver and napkins and climbed over the seat to take the reins. She was still standing as she slapped the reins on the horse's rump, getting him started down the lane.

"Bye, Miss Oratio," Naomi called out.

"Oratio. It's only Oratio, Naomi. Sisters don't call each other "Miss," Oratio called after her.

"They don't?" Amanda asked in mock surprise.

"No they don't, Miss Amanda," Henry added in a squeaking falsetto, making them all laugh as they stood in a group waving goodbye to Naomi as she drove away toward Texas.

CHAPTER ELEVEN

Lavaca County
South Texas,
Late winter, 1863

Silence.

Absolute silence.

At first there was silence and only silence, but then Johanna could hear the blood beating in her ears, like hammers pounding on drums right through her terror. Then she could hear her own breath in the silence, coming in irregular and ragged gasps.

For a moment she had been somewhere else. She had been in her father's parlor. Her father's parlor above his shop in Victoria. The shop he bought after he and Johanna sailed from Prussia across the sea to Galveston and then came overland to Victoria where he left her while he went to look at the land he had agreed to buy. He came back saying the land was fit for nothing but growing rattlesnakes and bought the store instead. And Johanna, as his daughter and his only living relative, lived with him in the rooms over the store.

But why Victoria? Victoria, where she freakishly stood a head taller than any man. Victoria, where rough men laughed at her and called her 'Fraulein,' and held their hands out in front of them to mock her bosom. Polite men only stared at her or looked away. The men in Victoria were tiny. She could have beaten every last one of them if she had wanted to.

If her mind had to take her away, why had she not returned to Prussia? Prussia, where she was like any other woman. Prussia, where her strength and stature were admired as evidence of the fierce northern warriors from ancient times. Prussia, where her powerful figure was perfectly suited to a dirndl. Prussia, where she had been happy and content, until the revolution of 1849 failed and the German Confederation was reestablished. With Austria once again attempting to dominate Prussia, Father decided it was time for them to leave.

Instead of Prussia, her mind had returned to the moment before Oliver asked her to marry him. He had two other girls in Victoria who would have accepted him; perfect girls with small feet and flat bosoms and so much better suited to him than Johanna. But of the three, he had asked her. She had always wondered why.

Why was it so dark? She looked around wildly and saw she was in the loft of the cabin. She could only remember sitting in the sunshine just outside the door while the baby nursed. She had a baby! And two other children too: twins, a boy and a girl. She could see their faces but could not remember their names, or even her own name for that matter. The terror had stolen that from her. She could see the loft window was open. The sunshine was bright outside, but her eyes were slow to adjust to the dim light inside.

Blood. How could there be so much blood? Pools of it were spreading across the floor and leaking through the cracks between the boards to the room below. She lifted her hands and saw they were bloody. She saw too, that her hands held an ax. It was the ax from the fireplace. She could remember picking it up before she climbed the stairs to the loft.

At her feet, one of the savages stirred. He stirred even with his skull split open from the ax blade. Johanna gripped the bloody ax in both hands, and with three guttural cries that came from some deep place that she did not know, she brought the butt end of it down in crushing blows to his temple, one...two...three times.

The words she cried, one with each blow, were in German, she realized. Her English words had left her. She could not remember how to say even those simple words now. The man was dead, the right side of his skull crushed in. Johanna reared back and kicked him. She senselessly kicked him hard with her bare foot, spattering more blood up on her skirt and across the floor.

Then the memory of it all came rushing back, a silent memory with no sounds at first. There was her husband Oliver waving as he rode away on their one horse. He was going to check their small herd of cattle set to graze north of the cabin. Then she went to the barn, if it could be called a barn with only one horse, a goat and six chickens in it. She found two eggs, brought them back to the cabin, changed the baby and took him out in the warm sunshine by the cabin door while she fed him. She looked down and saw she was still uncovered and bloody now too. Where was the baby? What had happened to the baby?

Holding the ax, coated with blood and other matter, she could only let the memory play on.

While she nursed the baby, the two other children played close by, making their happy little games. She remembered they were six years old. She could hear them laughing now. She heard herself laughing along with them. The fat baby on her lap pulled at the nipple and gurgled happily back up at her in the morning sunshine. She felt her heart swell with love for her children, more love than she had ever known, even if her spinning mind could not remember their names. She was changing the baby to the other side when she looked up at the ridge for some reason. It was the ridge that was in the opposite direction from where Oliver rode away and she saw the line of them standing there. A band of Comanche, from the looks of them, sat on their ponies. There were a dozen of them watching her in silence like she was cornered game and they were just waiting for the kill.

She hesitated a moment after she spotted them, frozen in her terror as she saw them break their line and come at a run toward the cabin, screeching out their war cries. She screamed to her children, getting them into the cabin and making the baby cry as she jostled him. Inside, she bolted the door and windows and saw that Oliver had taken their one gun with him. Holding her children to her, she waited. She waited in the silence that fell. Such an unnatural silence. Even the chickens and the goat out in the barn were silent and waiting. She realized she could no longer hear her baby's cries or her other children.

She was only aware of many soft footsteps creeping around the cabin. Stealthy steps, circling and looking for an opening. One shutter rattled after another. Then there came another long silence until she heard a bump, bump, bump and realized it was the ladder being put up to the loft window. She had not bolted the little window in the loft. Barely aware of what she was doing, she laid the baby on the bed, told the other children to stay there in such a tone she knew they would not dare move. Then she took the ax from beside the fireplace and practically flew up the ladder steps to the loft above.

When the first one poked his head through the window, peering around in the darkness inside, she was ready for him. She hit him in the forehead with the blade of the ax, killing him with a single blow. Then, with her enormous strength increased more than tenfold by her fear, she grabbed him under the arms and pulled him inside. It was as easy to drag him as it would be to drag a kitten. She threw his body to the side.

The second one, thinking the first one was still alive, stuck his head in and was killed in the same way. She struck the third, although apparently not killing him right away, and dragged him inside before the others waiting outside at the base of the ladder decided nothing was happening inside, at least nothing in their favor. While she listened and waited, there was a hushed discussion among them and moments later they remounted their ponies and rode away. Johanna saw it all now, and in the complete silence, she remembered.

"Mama?" a small voice came up the ladder.

"Stay there, Oliver. Stay on the bed. Don't come up," she called back down to her eldest, remembering his name as she spoke – the boy was named Oliver, like his father!

But her words were in German. Her son only understood his own name and called up to her again, tears threatening his brave little voice.

"Stop. Stay there." Those words came out in English, but she could still hear him rise and come to the base of the steps, crying now. "Oliver. Stop. Now."

The savages would be back. As soon as they regrouped, and added more to their numbers, they would come back. If they had not already killed Oliver, they had watched him ride away. They knew she was only a solitary woman here, alone with three small children. She had to act fast.

Without thinking further, she picked up one of the savages, amazed again at how light he was and dumped the body out the loft window. She did the same with the second, who landed with a sickening crunch of bones on the first, and finally the third. There was no time to clean up the blood, or to even wipe her hands clean. She crossed to the steps and went down the ladder, facing the ladder and holding the sides with her bloodied hands.

When she turned to face them, the girl hid her face from the blood and Oliver screamed and began crying, "No. No. No."

Johanna grabbed his shoulders and shook him to stop, but he grew more hysterical. She stopped that with a single sharp slap across his face, a slap that left a bloody handprint on the side of his sweet face.

"Stop crying!" she yelled at him in German, frightening him even more, then she knelt down and hugged him to her and managed in English. "No cry."

"I vant cry too, Oliver," she struggled to find the words. "But ve cry now, ve vill die. You must help Mami. Help me!"

Oliver squelched a sob and nodded. Her brave little man.

She knew they would not survive staying here. When the savages returned they would be ready to break down the door, or worse yet, set fire to the cabin to force them out. She could not stop them. Their only chance was to go to the neighbors, the Holts. They were almost three miles away. If the savages had not already been there, they would stand more of a chance together. Johanna could run there easily alone. She might even carry two children as she ran, but she could never carry all three.

Oliver was too small to run that far, even if she held his hand and pulled him along. The girl on the bed was frozen, her eyes shut tight since she saw the blood. She could not leave one of her children behind, even the girl, to save the other two. Something else had to be done. She considered making a sling to carry the baby on her back, but she would still have to run carrying the other two. Her progress would be slow and they would be easily caught, and all would die.

She turned to her son. "Oliver, I need you to stay inside with the baby and your sister while I run out to the barn. Can you do that for me?"

"No, Mommy – don't leave me. Don't leave."

"Oliver, ve must run to Holts, but first I need make travois. Do you remember vhat travois is? Can you help me do that?"

He nodded. He remembered a travois from his picture book. He was temporarily distracted at the thought of actually making one.

She went to the door. "Bolt this door behind me and don't open it until I tell you to. Do you understand?"

Peering outside the door, checking as much of the surrounding land as she could see from there and finding it empty, Johanna opened the door only long enough to step outside. She could hear Oliver sniffling as he slid the bolt back in place behind her. Looking around at the horizon, she ran through the silence to the barn. The barn was empty, save one lone hen sitting in the rafters, peering down and her and clucking away, telling her what had just happened. The savages had relieved them of the goat and the rest of the chickens. She found the two long poles she knew were in the shed and a length of rope and ran back to the house with them. Oliver was watching through the crack in the door and already had it unbolted and partly open when she reached it. She had not been outside even a full minute.

She threw the poles on the floor and began lashing them together with the rope, about two thirds of the way from one end. The two thirds below the crossed poles would hold a sling; the top would provide her handles to pull the travois as she ran with her children to the neighbors. She grabbed the top sheet from the bed and ripped the four corners so she could tie them easily onto the poles. It was a flimsy sling, even after she put the quilt from the bed on it. She put the baby and the girl on the sling and then positioned Oliver behind them where he could reach across them and hold onto the poles, hopefully keeping all three from bouncing out as she ran. Then she went to open the door.

"Papa. Where is Papa? What if he comes back?" Oliver cried out.

It was good, clear thinking and she was proud of him. She thought a moment, then went to the fireplace, took a burnt end of wood and went to the open door. Her English was leaving her again. What to write? She managed to scrawl across the planks of the door;

ALL SAFE
KILLED 3
GONE TO HOLTS

Oliver, who was reading some these days, nodded. At the last minute, she slammed the door shut again and scrambled back up to the loft for the bloodied axe. Even though Oliver cringed when he saw it, she slipped it beneath the quilt on the travois. It was not much defense against a band of savages, but it was better than nothing.

Pulling the travois was harder than she expected, but she knew it was better than trying to carry all three children. She looked right and left as she ran and told Oliver to watch behind, keeping him talking so she would know the children were all still there. She stumbled and fell several times, once smack into a prickly pear and alarming Oliver. She ran around mesquite, and up and down through gullies, thinking once she had completely lost her way, before she topped a small ridge and saw the Holt cabin, less than a half mile in the distance now, and ran afresh.

As she approached the door swung open and Rita Holt came out with her rifle, shoving one of her children back inside the door. She raised the rifle and pointed it, confirming to Johanna that the savages were behind her and not far away.

"Run Johanna! Run!" Rita cried out.

Turning to look behind her and seeing the line of savages on their ponies close behind her now; Johanna stumbled, flipping the travois up on its side, making the baby scream with terror. She stupidly tried to correct it, until she acknowledged Rita screaming out, "Leave it! Leave it, Johanna!"

She dragged the baby and the girl out from under the quilts and screamed for Oliver to run, "Run to Rita. Don't look back. Mami is right behind you." Then clutching her silent daughter under one arm like she was carrying a pig and the screaming baby in the other, she ran, overtaking Oliver. She grabbed him up also, two children under one arm, and ran as hard as she could.

Long ago, Rita Holt and Johanna had made a pact. It was when they were holed up together during another attack, an attack worse than this even, but before they had any children. Back then, they had pricked their fingers – Rita's idea – and made a blood pact with each other that if one of them saw that the other was about to be kilt by Injuns, or scalped, or even worse yet - carried off - she would shoot her.

She was aware of that promise now, pumping one leaden leg after the other as fast as she could. Looking at Rita, she knew that her friend remembered their promise too. If it looked like the Injuns were going to get her before she made it to Rita's door, Rita would shoot her, and then she would shoot Johanna's children too. But with relief she soon saw Rita lower the rifle and come running out to her, grabbing Oliver away from her to carry, and pulling a breathless Johanna along behind her as she ran back toward the house.

Inside, they bolted the door. Rita asked if she was hurt and if she was all right. Johanna nodded, unable to catch her breath. There was barely time for little else before they heard the whooping cry. "Ed?" Johanna asked, inquiring after Rita's husband. "Left for Victoria yesterday," Rita replied, checking the rifle.

They were on their own. Two women and five young children with one nonrepeating rifle.

The war cry stopped, followed by a long and eerie silence. It was a silence that went on an hour or longer. Rita peeked out a window and saw they were still there, a full long line of them, and even more of them than before. The savages were just playing with them, like a cat played with a captured mouse, letting the mouse think it might escape before pouncing on it again. They were going to wear them down, slowly break them without even coming close to the cabin. It was maddening and it was not fair.

Johanna saw that it would be nighttime soon. A whole day had passed since Johanna sat by her door nursing the baby. A complete day of terror had gone by in what seemed like minutes.

Unbelievably, Johanna still had the ax. So fixated had she been on it as her only defense, she had brought it along with her from the travois. Scant use it was to them now, though. Surely the savages had returned to her cabin and had seen what she had done. They would not get within range of letting her doing anything with the ax. She might as well have left it back at the cabin. But she had an idea.

Still bloodied, there had been no time or thought to wash away the blood from the morning, she rose and picked up the ax. "Open the door, Rita," she said in perfect and nearly unaccented English.

"Are you crazy, Johanna? You can't go out there. The men will be here soon. They will come and help us. You can't go out there."

"We can't count on that, they could be dead, and we can't last the night like this. Maybe I can scare them away."

Rita laughed in spite of the situation. "You – scare away all those Injuns? Have you taken complete leave of your senses, Johanna?"

"I said to open the door. I'm going out there. You remember our promise? Do you remember?"

Rita remembered, although she had always pictured that Johanna would be the last one standing. Rita would be the one captured or going to be killed or carried away, and Johanna would be the one to put a single bullet through the back of Rita's head. Then Johanna would kill her children, sending them on to heaven right after her. Then Johanna's children would be next, and finally Johanna. Rita would be the one waiting on the other side for Johanna to follow her just a few moments after she got there herself. But it looked like it was not going to be that way now.

Rita bravely nodded, picked up the rifle and came to the door with Johanna.

Johanna turned and hugged Rita. The blood on her hands and dress was still not completely dried so she left sticky smears of it on Rita. Then she turned to the door, with the ax in both hands and nodded for Rita to open it. As Johanna went out into the yard, and toward the savages, Rita stood behind her in the open door, with the rifle ready. The savages would see Rita was there too, and they would see everything that was going to happen, if it came to the worse. If there was an ounce of decency in them, which Rita doubted could be, they would stop all this and go home. If not, Rita would have to do the shooting if it came to that.

Johanna walked out into the yard as she raised and brandished the bloodied ax above her head. In the late afternoon light she let out a long, whooping cry that made Rita's blood run cold and silenced the terrified children inside the house.

"Come on, you bastards!" Johanna screamed out at them in German, although her legs were trembling now. "Come on and get me! I swear to God I will kill every last one of you. I killed three of you this morning and I am not finished yet. Come on, goddamn it. Come on and get me!"

She went on screaming and brandishing the bloodied ax and ranting at the savages for a good long while, her voice growing hoarse. So they would not see how her legs were shaking, she paced around the yard, swinging the ax high overhead and down low in long, swooping arcs in a kind of wild dance like she could not wait for them. After that, she held the ax up over her head with both hands, then lowered it and spun around a slow and sweeping circle, pointing the ax along the horizon. Her bloodied and torn dress rippled in the wind and her long hair came completely undone and blew wild, swirling in the wind like a cloud around her head and showing bright yellow and orange in the setting sun.

Finally, she raised the ax to the sky's zenith and let out a chilling cry. Then she lowered it and stood still, with her feet placed solidly apart and ax handle in her right hand and the blade resting in her left. She fell into a long, stony and glaring stare directly at their chief - or at least the one who looked to be in charge of the party.

After a long moment, the chief turned and said something to the one next to him, and turned his horse away. Unbelievably the entire war party turned and followed him. With trembling arms, Johanna raised the bloodied ax above her head one more time, the blade glinting in the setting sun as they rode away, just in case they looked back. And she repeated the three words she had cried out that morning when delivering the finishing blows to the third savage; Nicht. Meine. Kinder.

But this time the words she screamed after them were in English. "Not. My. Children."

* * * * *

Oliver was safe, they had not killed him. He came tearing up on his horse, not long after the savages left, with his rifle ready. Had he arrived any earlier when the Indians were there he would have been killed for sure.

With the three dead savages at home, they stayed overnight with the Holts. Rita made a bath for Johanna and loaned her a clean dress to wear home. Johanna sat with her children, Olive, Oliver, and Albert, the baby for a long time after they went to sleep.

Ed Holt came riding up the next morning as they were leaving for home. He had heard the news of the uprising and came racing back, riding all through the night. They could see how relieved he was when he found Rita and his children safe at home.

When they got home, the three bodies were gone, presumably carried away by the savages. A goat, not theirs but similar, was tied to the hitching post by the house and six chickens were scratching around the yard. After that, they simply went back to their lives, trying to survive and make a go of it in the harsh land of south Texas.

A month or so later, Oliver came home laughing. Ed Holt had told him a story he heard when he went to pick up the mail in Victoria. They said the Comanche were talking in reverence about the "giant, fire-hair woman" - the direct translation of the Indian name for the woman they said wielded a mighty war ax with strong medicine. She was an invincible warrior and could not be conquered, and it meant death to all who crossed her. Oliver laughed and asked Johanna if she thought they were talking about her.

Later that night, long after the children were asleep, and after he tenderly made love to the wife who stood a full head taller and could lift him off the ground if she wanted to, Oliver nestled against her and said, "I think I picked the right woman, Mrs. Bailey."

He sometimes teased Johanna that way, being so formal and mannerly in this rough land where they fought daily just to survive. Johanna sat up in bed and was about to retort with something sassy when she had a clear understanding of why she saw her father's parlor in Victoria that day she killed the three savages. Yes, Oliver had picked the right one. Those other girls with the tiny feet and small busts would have never survived it.

She plumped up her pillow before she settled back down and said, "Oliver Bailey! What makes you think that you were the one that did the picking?"

CHAPTER TWELVE

Lavaca County, Texas
Spring, 1863

Oratio leaned back and sank into the cushions of the old rocking chair. She was on the front porch of her house. With a roof over the porch and glass windows it was finally a real house now instead of a cabin. From where she sat, she could see the first hint of blue all across the low hills. The blue bonnets were late this year and she had been afraid of missing them altogether. In all these years, it was a sight she had come to love more than anything about this land of Texas. That was why she made Phinetta help her out to the porch, leaning so heavily on the poor girl and probably scaring her half to death, just so her old mother she could look at the wild flowers.

Everyone always said Oratio was tough, but this cancer was tougher. It hurt, but not more than she could stand, even if sometimes in the night she could feel it eating away at her insides. She would wake Leroy and make him promise again that he would find another woman after she was gone. The children would still need a mother and Leroy was still a good-looking man. There were more white women than ever now in the county, but they were all as tough and stringy as she was. She said he should head on over to Victoria, or maybe even Goliad or Galveston and find himself a pretty one to marry this time. Maybe even a young one who might give him another child. Leroy so loved his children.

"Did I tell you about Old Bess and Aunt Charity?" she asked Phinetta as she settled, trying to make her voice sound strong, or at least stronger than she felt. "Did I tell you all about them?"

"Yes, Mama. You did. So many times," her daughter answered impatiently while she adjusted the cushions at Oratio's back where they would cause the least amount of pain. "Now just try to rest and look at the flowers. That _is_ why you made me bring you all the way out here on the porch, ain't it?"

"Don't you sass me, young lady. You are not so big that I can't cut a switch if I have to."

That made Phinetta grin at her mother. Phinetta was only eleven years old, but Oratio could see that she was already a young woman, even if her body had not caught up yet. Her change-of-life baby, Mama would have called her, born long after she thought there would not be any more. Phinetta was just like her mother, strong-willed and determined, and would spit right in your eye if she had to. Oratio could have worn out a bucket of switches on that girl if she had ever been of a mind to.

The others were all grown up now. Mary Ann was married and had a family of her own. Russell Moody too. Then there was Lemuel, born before they left Ouachita to take the fifty acre claim in Union Parish. Phinetta was born on that homestead the same year Mary Ann got married. Mary Ann stayed behind in Louisiana when the family decided to come on out west to Texas.

Oratio laughed a little when she thought about Lemuel, so like his late Uncle Henry. That boy was on a horse almost before he was out of diapers. Lem was seventeen now and plum wild, charming all the girls in his uniform the last time he was home on leave from the war. That infernal war! She prayed every night to the Lord to keep her boys safe. She knew He would bring them home, but likely now she had seen them both for the last time.

As soon as Leroy wrote to Mary Ann about the cancer, she left her home south of Lafayette, Louisiana, went to the port and caught the next steam boat coming west from New Orleans to Port Lavaca.

From the port, Mary Ann and her children caught the overland mail coach to Victoria and then she hired a private driver who brought them the rest of the way. It was such a nice surprise, but Oratio still scolded Mary Ann that it too dangerous to travel by sea, even in the Gulf of Mexico, what with the war going on. And also the trip cost her daughter too much money, especially with Mary Ann's husband off fighting in the war too. Then seeing that her words were hurtful, she asked Mary Ann to forgive her and insisted she could not have been more pleased with the surprise.

> *Author's note: The port town on Lavaca Bay was heavily bombarded by Union forces October 31-November 1, 1862, but did not surrender. In 1863 the town was named Lavaca. Around 1887 when the town was connected by rail line to Victoria, references began showing the name as Port Lavaca, most likely to distinguish it from Lavaca County and Lavaca Bay. Although historically incorrect, I have referenced the town as Port Lavaca to provide the same distinction.*

They had a good long visit, Oratio getting to know her grandchildren again. The children teased their grandmother saying they hoped to see some wild Indians. Fortunately they were gone before the last attack where that Prussian woman had killed three of them before the rest ran off. The Comanche calmed down after that and Oratio decided she liked that woman the Indians called "Fire Hair Woman" and sent word she would like to meet her if she ever was in this part of the county.

Oratio relaxed now into the cushions, thinking it was amazing that most of the family was here in Texas now.

"Did you say something, Mama?" Phinetta asked, making her realize she had been thinking out loud again, a thing she was doing more of these days. The morphine drops the doctor gave her made her do that sometimes and that was why she tried to do without so many in the daytime. They did not make much difference lately anyway. Oratio cleared her throat and said, "I was just saying it is a wonder and a blessing that the family all seems to be gathered here now. Leroy's family and mine too."

It was true, Naomi had led the way, coming this far into the Republic of Texas before she could find a land office that would register a fourth class headright on land for a free man of color, although it was arguably required by the Republic of Texas Homestead Act of 1839.

Author's note: In response to the number of families of all classes losing their homes and property across the South as a result of the Panic of 1837 and to protect the assets of those people from their creditors as they immigrated into the Republic of Texas, The Homestead Act of 1839, recommended by Stephen F. Austin and enacted by the Republic of Texas, provided the first legal protection of the family home, including up to 50 acres, from creditors and guaranteed the uncontested passage of property to the surviving spouse and unmarried children. The act was incorporated into the Texas State Constitution in 1845, when Texas was annexed into the United States. The act was subsequently used to model many of the homestead acts of western states after 1839 and ultimately was written into United States Federal law via the National Homestead Act of 1862 that remains in effect today.

She was dressed as a man again that day, but not in her raggedy man disguise. She bought a fine new suit of men's clothes just for the occasion. She had the filing fee and her Deed of Emancipation in hand, even though the land office agents generally rejected her outright before they even looked at the paper she carried.

When the agent in Victoria examined the emancipation deed, seeing it was made out for Naomi Lovett, Naomi told him that she was Ned Lovett, Naomi's husband, and that she had brought the wrong papers. The agent scolded Ned for wasting his time; that he was a busy man what with all the claims being filed these days. He accepted the paper, but insisted that Naomi Lovett's name had to be on the deed as well, since Ned brought the wrong papers. Including the wife on the deed was meant to punish the careless Ned, but the result was that Naomi, as a head of family, became the owner of 640 acres. Since she filed after January 1, 1840 she also received an additional ten acres for cultivation.

Naomi wrote letters to Oratio, simple and almost in summary form in her painstaking block letters, but Oratio could read through the brevity to see just how much Naomi loved the new land and her pride in having her own place, the small cabin she built with her own hands, and, most of all, the seven head of cattle that was the start of her herd.

Leroy finally came to accept that the horse breeding operation he started with Henry in Union Parish was never going to make a profit. They might do better in Texas, where horses were needed and they could get a lot more land to raise them on. They decided to follow Naomi and struck out for Lavaca County.

The headright claims that Naomi received ended the last day of December, 1841. From January 1, 1845 through 1854 homesteaders could file claims for 320 acres of land. In addition, they had to live on the land three years and make improvements before the deed passed to them. In 1854 the acreage was cut back even further to 160 acres per claim, and people still came.

But in 1853, Leroy and Oratio sold the farm in Union and brought their children Russell, Lem and baby Phinetta cross country in three wagons pulled by their breeding stock of horses. Henry rode behind, leading the final two horses. They filed adjacent claims Naomi scouted out for them in Lavaca County, a total of 640 acres, and they still had access to adjacent public lands for grazing.

Oratio's eldest brother, Jonathan, and his children and grandchildren were next. They filed adjoining claims near Goliad, and then it was like the floodgates of family coming west opened. Now, in 1863, more of the Newmans and Squyres lived in these parts than had stayed back in Louisiana.

Even Leroy's eldest brother John, along with three of his four children and grandchildren, came west. Leroy's unmarried sister, Mary Polly, came with them. They settled up north in Anderson County, where they were growing cotton again, but on a much smaller scale. John had never remarried after Susanna died in 1840 and the move marked an official end to his grief of losing her so soon after losing the plantation and seeing his family scattered. His children wrote that the wide open lands of Texas seemed to give John a new life.

One way or another, many people were finding their way to Texas. A stranger came stumbling across Naomi's land on a cold February day in 1845. Naomi had ridden her horse to the north side of her property to check on her herd, set to graze out of the wind in a hollow of land. It was a rare cold snap and Naomi was bundled up in her heavy range jacket, an old hat to keep off the rain and a heavy scarf. From the back of the horse she watched him run directly toward her without ever seeing her; only her head was above the rim of the hollow. He was running hard and frequently stumbling as he looked back. He ran straight into the hollow where she was waiting, looking down the barrel of her rifle at him.

"Stop...Right...There."

He halted and put both hands in the air, panting. He was a very light-skinned black man with white man's hair and a beard that looked to be weeks old. His clothing, now in tatters, had been fine ones. The boots he wore, too big, were not.

Even with his dark brown eyes he could have easily passed for white, except for the old and faint shackle scars on his wrists, showing now as he held up his hands. She kept the gun on him, scanning the far horizon from where he just came and saw the two men on horses pursuing him.

"You runnin'?" she asked in her gruffest voice.

He hesitated, but she shoved the rifle toward him and gave him her meanest look. He could only nod. "Come on, brother," he pleaded in an educated and refined voice.

"Ain't your brother, and I won't never be," Naomi glared down at him. "Where you from?"

"Savannah, Georgia,"

"Don't lie to me, boy," she punctuated the words with her rifle. "Nobody can run that far."

"You asked me where I am from. I started running in New Orleans," he explained, more in control of his breath now. "Master lost me there in a poker game on a riverboat out of New Orleans on Christmas Eve. Soon as I got a chance I jumped and swam to shore. I took out running and been running since."

That story matched up with the length of his beard, the condition of his clothes and lack of shoes. It could still be a lie. She spat on the ground and asked, "Why didn't you go up north?"

"I am heading for Mexico." He paused, considering before he added, "I know a lady in Juarez who will help me."

He said 'Juarez' exactly like the *rancheros* she hired to help sometimes. "Hablamos Espanol?" she said to test him, readjusting her sights down the gun barrel at him. Naomi had picked up a little Mexican from her hired men.

"Si, Senor, we can speak Spanish if you prefer," his breathing was almost normal now. "Je parle aussi Français - und ein bisschen Deutch. My master rarely stayed home in Savannah."

Naomi held him there, considering what to do, and with the stranger likely thinking she had decided to simply wait until the riders behind him caught up. She could see he was looking around now, considering dodging her rifle and running, better to be shot right here than to be taken back. Without lowering her gun she asked, "Think you can jump up behind me on this horse?"

He nodded.

"Then do it," she said.

She usually rode bareback when she only went out to check the cattle, but lucky for him she had saddled the horse that morning. He could ride behind her and hang on to the saddle with his legs. With the rifle in her left hand, and her feet firmly in the stirrups, she leaned down to give him a hand up. While he got settled she rode straight into her cattle herd, yipping and chasing a few to stir them up and cover her tracks. Unless the men riding toward them were professional trackers it might buy them a few minutes. Then she took out, riding in a zigzagging route along the low ground all the way back to her cabin to keep out of sight as much as possible.

"Get inside," she commanded, stopping only a moment at her door. She put the horse in the barn, still saddled, and ran back. The stranger was standing in the middle of the room, unsure what to do.

"Get those clothes off," she ordered, crossing the room and pulling closed the sheet that curtained off her sleeping area. She rummaged around in the wooden box she kept under the bed as a trunk and brought out the suit of clothes she last wore at the land office in Victoria. She went around the curtain where he was standing, buck naked. She expected he would at least be wearing an undershirt, but his shirt, light jacket and trousers were in a jumble with the boots on the floor.

"Can you shave yourself?" she asked, trying to seem normal as she crossed to the table with her mirror. He nodded. She had a razor one of the *rancheros* left behind somewhere among the kitchen things. She quickly set out a basin, a clean towel, the razor and a precious bar of her soap. She pulled the kettle from the fireplace spit and poured hot water into the bowl. "Get to it. But put those pants on first."

While he shaved, she went behind the curtain again and pulled the one dress she had from the wooden trunk. She peeled off the rough clothes, pulled the dress over her head and put on the pair of ladies shoes that were in the bottom of the trunk. She ran the hairbrush over her closely-cropped hair and wrapped a triangle of head cloth around her head, tying and tucking in the ends at the front.

She came from behind the curtain and the stranger jumped when he saw her reflected in the mirror he was using. Fortunately he had the pants on now.

My name is Naomi. Naomi Lovett."

"Are these your husband's things?" he asked, wiping the soap residue from his face.

"Yes," Naomi lied. "His name was Ned, Ned Lovett. That be you now."

Ned nodded his understanding. As Naomi helped him into the jacket they could hear hoof beats approaching. "Bring the rifle when you come out, but don't point it. Keep it down. And you better be out there right behind me."

While Ned put on the shoes, Naomi went outside and stood by the cabin door as the two men rode into the yard. It had stopped raining. Ned came out behind her, closing the door, with the rifle in the crook of his left elbow, pointing down. Out of the corner of her eye she saw him touch the brim of his hat to the men, but he kept it on.

"You all see a runaway nigger pass through here?" the larger man asked.

Naomi shook her head, feeling her heart beating wildly in her chest.

"Did you hear me, gal?"

"She say 'No Suh'," Ned said politely, but it was in the speech pattern of a field worker. With his dark eyes under the brim of the hat and never leaving his pursuers, his voice had dropped half an octave. Turning slightly now, Naomi could see he had her hat pulled down low. Somehow, in the moments after she left him, he had blacked his face and hands, bootblack most likely, although she could still see some white behind his ears. She reached up to scratch her own ear, and tapped her index finger behind it. He gave her the faintest nod of understanding.

But the disguise could not be better. He was almost as black as Naomi. These men were looking for a soft-spoken, nearly-white and educated runaway slave with a heavy beard. Ned was anything but that.

"Mind if we have a look around then?"

"Yes, suh. I do mind," Naomi replied, "But if you must look, then go ahead."

"Who owns this place? Where are they?"

"This place belong to my husband Ned and me," Naomi answered. "Been here a little over four years now."

She could tell he did not believe her. "I go get the papers to show you."

She went back in the cabin and came back out moments later, bringing the two documents. "This our Fourth Class Headright deed," she said holding the unfolded paper up to the bigger man, still on his horse. "It say this land now belong to Ned and Naomi Lovett, dated October 25, 1840."

He made a show of examining the paper and then passed it to the other man who looked at it briefly. Naomi realized they could not read. "And this be Ned's Deed of Emancipation, dated June 15, 1838. It sign by Miss Delilah Lovett of Macon, Georgia. Ned took her last name, Lovett, when she free him."

She saw that the first man at least knew his numbers. He nodded when he recognized those numbers in the dates on the documents before he handed the papers back.

"Why you folks so dressed up?" he asked, suspicious.

"It Sunday, sir. We just fixin' to have prayer service. We may be out here among heathen Injuns, but we still have prayer meetin'. Some day folks round here is gone have a real church. You welcome to join us."

"You seem awful nervous," he said, squinting as he eyed Naomi.

"Just had Injuns ride through here a bit ago," Ned replied, much to Naomi's relief. "Most likely cotched your runaway. They whooping up a war cry, sound like. Must a cotched him."

"About a hundred of 'em, we reckon," Naomi added, nodding her agreement, "Comanche it look like."

The man scanned the horizon, "Which way?"

Naomi pointed at the horizon in the opposite direction from where these men had appeared. The riders tipped their hats and promptly rode back in the direction they just came from and away from the imaginary Comanche. The bounty on a runaway was not worth losing their scalps.

* * * * *

Instead of leaving for Mexico, Ned stayed on, with the curtain pulled firmly between them at night and Ned bedded down on a pallet by the fireplace.

He willingly helped Naomi with the cattle and fixed things, but she could see his training as a valet was better put to use inside the cabin. He mended her clothing and bedding, did her laundry to perfection, cleaned the little cabin from top to bottom, and reorganized her supplies. He kept the fire going with the sweet-smelling mesquite wood he gathered himself. He had her supper ready and waiting on the table as soon as she came in from working the cattle and cleaned herself up with the hot water and towel he had waiting for her.

Naomi kept waiting for him to leave, to go join his senorita in Juarez. But just days after Ned arrived, the United States voted to annex Texas on the twenty-ninth of December. Mexico had long warned that such an action would mean war. Following that, President Polk asserted the United States claim to land all the way to the Rio Grande, while Mexico disputed the border to instead be the Nueces River. Polk sent General Zachary Taylor to Texas and by October more armed soldiers were positioned along the Nueces. On November 10, Polk ordered Taylor and his forces to move on south to the Rio Grande, about 150 miles away. The following spring, word came that a 70 man patrol along the Rio Grande had been attacked by the Mexicans and the Mexican army was advancing north toward the Nueces River. Rumor was they would overrun all of southern Texas. Naomi and Ned made preparations to evacuate quickly in case there was a repeat of the Runaway Scrape of 1836, when the army and settlers fled overland toward Louisiana to escape an advancing Mexican army.

And through it all, Ned's senorita in Juarez seemed to have taken up residence in Naomi's house too. Ned had said nothing more about her and he gave no sign of leaving, but the exotic Mexican woman was still there, a third invisible and silent presence in the cabin. Naomi imagined her sitting at the table with her long hair, dark eyes and a low cut dress, and always ready to jump up and dance for Ned.

Naomi wondered why he did not just go ahead and leave. Even with the war it would not be impossible for him to get into Mexico, especially since he was fluent in the language. Legend was that three Spanish-speaking Texans had been spared in 1836 when the Mexican army overran the Alamo. With his coloring, Ned could easily pass for one of them - and even a member of the upper class if he wore his suit. Able to stand it no longer, Naomi finally asked him one night over supper, after insisting he sit with her at the table instead of standing to one side like he used to do with his master, watching while she ate.

He blushed, (and most charmingly, too, she would always add when she told the story) and admitted he had made up the senorita. Naomi was surprised and indignant. When she pressed him he said, "It was the best I could come up with, staring down the wrong end of your gun. I'm not even sure how to get to Mexico from here. Master and I always went by ship."

Naomi laughed out loud, and then gave him a hard time about it, calling him a liar. He laughed too, but protested, "It is no worse of a lie than you making up a husband named Ned Lovett more than four years before he shows up!"

The unspoken implication of what he had just said hung in the air between them. Naomi had been calling him Ned all along only because he would never tell her his slave name. He insisted it was to spare her the trouble of knowing a runaway slave, in case it ever came up.

Ned came around the table, went to his knees on the floor beside her and took her hand in his, "As long as you will have him, that is."

They were together almost two years, waiting for a preacher to come through, before they were really married. Finally, on Naomi's insistence, they rode down to Victoria, taking their first child with them. The preacher entered their names on the marriage certificate in the Bible Naomi insisted on buying and, with his name entered on that certificate, Ned officially became Ned Lovett, Naomi's legal husband.

In all, they would have four children, first three boys all as dark and strong-willed as their mother. Their youngest was a girl, and as light-skinned and pretty as her father. She also had Ned's straight hair that he said was from his Cherokee great-grandmother. Naomi wanted to call her Cherokee, in honor of the great-grandmother whose name was no longer known, but Ned refused. The daughter was named Victoria for the English Queen. Ned had seen the young queen riding in her coach when he was in London. Vicky, as they called their daughter, was the same age as Oratio's youngest girl, Phinetta. On the day the Squyres arrived from Louisiana, the two girls became best friends for life, just as their mothers were.

Before the cancer, they had ten good years. Sure, there was the constant threat of Indians and rattlesnakes to watch for. There was the weather that could change one moment to the next, and cattle that could drown in a sudden downpour of rain. But after a while they were used to that, same as folks got used to the problems anywhere. And as more people came there were more good things. The Lovetts and Squyres and Newmans spent their Sundays together with a shared Sunday dinner almost always followed by an afternoon of games organized by the fathers with the mothers sometimes joining in, but usually watching from the porch.

They watched their youngest daughters growing up together, sometimes acting like fussy little girls with their dolls and playing tea party, and other times whooping like wild Indians when they rode bareback, trailing behind their big brothers.

Sunday afternoon conversation was relaxed and when the children began creeping back after their games, Oratio would often tell them the stories, backed up by Naomi on some of the details. One Sunday when the girls were about eight and they were having dessert on the porch, Vicky noticed that her mother's silverware was exactly like her Aunt Oratio's. Naomi said it was because they stole it together, it was all part of one set. The girls did not believe it and listened to the story Oratio and Naomi told them together about the old days on the Squyres plantation in Louisiana where their mothers had slipped the silverware out past the sheriff, only a few pieces at a time, and hid it.

After that, the girls could not wait for a Sunday afternoon story.

It was Naomi who insisted Oratio had to see a doctor when she started having trouble with her stomach last fall. Oratio's belly had not retracted as it should after Phinetta, but that was to be expected with her age. When her belly began growing again, she thought it was just part of being almost fifty years old, but Naomi insisted it did not look right. Naomi's middle was growing too these days, especially since she had hired men who helped with the cattle and she did not ride like she used to, but she said Oratio began looking like she was pregnant. Naomi got Leroy on her side and with Oratio insisting there was nothing wrong, but that she would go along just so they would quit worrying about it, they went down to Victoria to see a doctor there.

That was last November. They waited a long time to see him. Doctors were in short supply with the war calling so many of them back east. When they finally were ushered into his office he examined her, pressing his hands to various places on her body and felt her neck and under her arms. Then he asked Naomi to sit in the waiting room while he did the full examination.

"She is my sister," Oratio said.

It was something they said over the years to tease newcomers, Oratio would introduce Naomi as her sister, adding that their maiden names had both been Newman. Others, who had the same joke pulled on them when they were new would go along with it, sometimes for weeks. It did no harm. Now the doctor just looked at Oratio without humor.

"Or at least she is like my sister. We have been together since she nursed my oldest girl, so she stays. Leroy can go, though, if you want him to."

With Naomi and Leroy standing by, Oratio was undressed to the skin and covered with a sheet while the doctor uncovered and examined every last bit of her body. When he finished, he washed his hands in a basin his nurse prepared, and motioned to Leroy to follow him. Oratio demanded that she be told at the same time. What was it?

The doctor said he suspected Oratio had a tumor of the female organs. He would need to do surgery to confirm that and to remove it. He was prepared to do it immediately.

"But it's almost Christmas. Lem is going to come home from the war if they give him leave. I don't want to spoil that for the family. No. We will come back in January. Yes. You can do it then." Oratio insisted.

"Mrs. Squyres," the doctor said gravely. "You have cancer. The tumor is advanced and must be removed immediately, today if at all possible. I do not think you will survive until Christmas otherwise."

So preparations for surgery began immediately. The surgery room the doctor kept behind his examination room was set up and Oratio was prepared.

"Stay with me, I am so scared," she said to Leroy and Naomi. Naomi stood by the operating table, holding Oratio's hand until she was fully under the chloroform. She was opened, the tumor and much of the surrounding tissue removed and the wound was closed. Unfortunately, it was too late. The cancer had spread. The doctor gave Leroy a supply of laudanum, or tincture of opium, for him and Naomi to give her as she needed it. When that was no longer effective, he could give her a stronger version of morphine.

For a time, after she was recovered from the effects of the surgery, Oratio felt fine. She was up and around for Christmas, actively participating in the preparations for Lem's visit home. Mary Ann came almost immediately when she got the news, invoking her mother's anger for coming through Port Lavaca so soon after it was shelled by Union troops. What had she been thinking? Then Oratio forgave her, and said it would be wonderful to have Mary Ann and the grandchildren with them for Christmas. How special that would be for Lem when he came home.

Oratio prohibited anyone from telling Lem until the day he left to go back. Before he left, she had him sit alone with her on the porch. She told him what had happened, and said she was only telling him because she did not want him wondering why everyone had been acting so strangely at times. She said she knew they were worried, but she was going to be fine. She felt better everyday now.

She could not see that Naomi, standing behind her and gently shaking her head, made sure that Lem knew the real truth. There were tears in his eyes when he left. He held his mother to him a long time before he rode away. When he pulled away, Oratio promised she would see him again, real soon.

After Christmas, Naomi started coming every day. She arrived by noon and stayed until suppertime, helping with things around the house. At first, she would make this excuse or that of why she came that day. Ned made such a big pot of beans they could not possibly eat it all, so she brought a share over for the Squyres to have, or she was all out of black thread and could she borrow some?

She would help Oratio, who had begun falling behind with her own housework, making Oratio sit at the table while she finished up the dishes or whatever needed to be done. Oratio was still insisting she felt fine, which the doctor told Leroy was a good sign; as long as she was resting and doing what he told her. Naomi made sure of that.

One afternoon toward the end of January, with Naomi sitting by her bed after Oratio said she thought she might lie down for a while before dinner, Oratio said, "You don't have to keep making up reasons to come by every afternoon, Naomi.

I'm glad you are here, but I don't want you neglecting your own family."

Naomi choked with unexpected tears a moment, then replied, "Ned keep house better than I ever did so it not a problem if I'm gone, Oratio. I think he prefer it, to tell you the truth. He say I always ruining his biscuits or sloshing his bean pot." They chuckled together over that. "You got yourself a good wife," Oratio teased. She often teased Naomi that way. It had been their private joke for years now. "No, I got myself a good husband, a real man," Naomi would always reply.

Naomi was a wonderful and gifted nurse. She was as strong as any man, even in Texas. Oratio had often seen Naomi rope a calf from her horse, jump to the ground, pin the calf down, and burn her brand into its hide in one fluid motion, and before the calf quite knew what hit it.

But Naomi could be gentle too, like the first time Oratio soiled herself and Naomi just cleaned her up like she was a newborn baby. She had been too weak to get out of bed that day and only realized what had happened when she smelled herself.

Naomi never batted an eye and just did what needed to be done. Then when she looked up and saw the tears of shame in Oratio's eyes she scolded, "Now why you cryin' Miss Oratio? This ain't nothing. This just the cancer. Now don't you worry, we gone get you fixed right up. You just a proud woman, that's all."

"I am not." Oratio was indignant, in spite of the situation. "I'm just not as strong as you are, Naomi, that's all."

"Bullshit!" Naomi swore, knowing it always brought a chuckle of appreciation. Naomi could cuss better than any man Oratio knew. "You forgettin' you the one walked out of Catahoula Parish and carrying that chil' and a baby inside you all the way too. I never could'a done what you did. You the strong one. I was the one that got to ride away with that rich and handsome white man in a big, fine carriage. Could'a had his way with ol' Naomi too, if he want to."

She had Oratio laughing and looking for something to throw at her by the time the bed clothes were changed. No one else knew her like Naomi. She was her best friend.

This afternoon, Naomi brought Vicky along with her. It would be good for Phinetta to have the company. Naomi was surprised to find them out on the porch, but could see immediately it had almost been too much for Oratio.

After Vicky gave her Aunt Oratio a kiss on the cheek, like she was supposed to, Oratio insisted the girls should go down to the creek for a while. It was too beautiful of a day for them to waste it sitting on this porch with a couple of old ladies, she joked. Naomi packed up a light lunch for them to take, and Oratio told

Phinetta to take her new book that came in the last mail; maybe Vicki would like to hear her read some of it. "Oh – and take your sunbonnets too," she added. The sun was getting stronger now it was spring.

As they were leaving, Phinetta came back to give her mother another kiss before she left. Oratio held her daughter an extra moment, then placed her hand against Phinetta's face and said, "Remember who you are."

It was routine. She always said it to all her children. It was something Anna always said to Oratio when she left to go somewhere and possibly her mother's mother even said it before that. It was usually a reminder to behave. But this afternoon it had a much, much deeper meaning to Oratio. Maybe Phinetta would remember that.

Together Oratio and Naomi watched the girls walk down the lane hand-in-hand, swinging the picnic basket in their sudden freedom for the afternoon. They sat together on the porch in comfortable silence for a long while before Oratio chuckled and asked, "Do you remember when Lem announced he was not going to heaven?" Oratio was smiling at the memory, and Naomi burst out laughing.

> Not that it had been a happy memory at the time. All the family had just sat down to Sunday dinner, even Ned and Naomi and their children with them, when Lem announced, "I ain't going to heaven!"

> Oratio had just settled in her chair and was busy starting to pass around the bowls of vegetables and potatoes to go with the Sunday fried chicken. She looked up in shocked surprise and insisted, "Why, honey, of course you are!"

> "No I ain't. I said I ain't and you cain't make me."

> They had been having trouble with Lem testing the boundaries and back-talking, and that had been the limit for Leroy. He jumped up from his chair, picked Lem up from his chair and carried him under one arm out to the porch, taking the shaving strap off the wall as he went.

> Oratio called after him, "Now Leroy, don't kill him." She could never stand to see her children punished. She had gone especially soft with the younger ones, so Leroy placed most of the blame on her for Lem's increasing insolence and disrespect. He knew he could get away with it, Leroy said. Oratio argued, privately of course, that it was only because Lem was too smart to just accept things without understanding why.

> They all sat in silence, unable to do anything but listen to the strap meeting Lem's bare bottom out on the porch and Lem howling. Oratio jumped a little with each crack. The children, who at first made big eyes at each

other with the unsaid gleeful words, "Lem's gonna get it," were now sitting with their eyes down and their hands clenched in their laps.

After two more whacks, Oratio stood and went to the door. "Leroy, stop it! Stop it, now!" she commanded, cutting right through Leroy's scolding words, "...sassing your mother..." he was delivering with the blows of the strap.

She went back to the table, sharply directing her own children to eat. Everyone, including Ned and Naomi, immediately took up their forks and began pushing the vegetables around on their plates, unable to eat. After a little bit, Leroy came back inside with his hand firmly on Lem's shoulder, gave him a little push and said, "Go on now."

Lem came to Oratio, eyes down and still blubbering a little and mumbled "sorry,"

"I didn't hear you," Leroy insisted.

"I am sorry," Lem still mumbled.

"I am sorry – WHAT?"

"Oh now, Leroy, stop it," Oratio scolded, "and with company here too! I never want my children to say they are sorry only when someone is making them say it. Now stop it."

She took Lem's hand and led him back to his chair, grabbing a pillow from the settee for him to sit on as she went. "Now, I'm sure you're sorry. I never heard a little boy say such a thing. Now why wouldn't you want to go to heaven? Why would you say such a thing?"

Lem, sitting with his head bowed, only shrugged.

"Lemuel!" His father warned. A shrug was no way to answer. It was not what he had been taught, and bordered on the disrespect they had been working on.

"I just ain't going, that's all," he replied. Oratio had to fight an urge to snort in laughter, both at her son's spirit and the ridiculousness of it.

Leroy stood again, but Oratio put up a hand for him to sit. Instead, she took Leroy by the hand and made him stand again, dragged his chair behind them across the room and turned it to the corner, sat him down in it and said, "You can just sit there until you change your mind, young man."

She went back to the table, took up her napkin as she looked around to see if everyone had food on their plates as if everything was a normal Sunday dinner and began eating. It was a long and mostly silent meal with Leroy fuming, Lem snuffling in the corner, and Naomi giving warning looks at her own children that they had better behave themselves.

When it was over the girls started to help clear the table and, to relieve the tension in the kitchen, Oratio said the mothers would clean up and sent the girls out to the yard where their brothers and fathers were starting a game with a thick stick and a soft leather ball. They played the game most Sundays and it was Lem's favorite, hitting the ball with the stick and then running a square track around four bases. Still, he stubbornly sat in the chair. "Well, I can be just as stubborn as you, young man," Oratio thought, "Where do you think you got it from, after all?"

Naomi and Oratio fell into a normal level of conversation over clearing the table and washing the dishes and setting the kitchen table and chairs back to rights. Naomi was sweeping the floor around the table when she stopped and caught Oratio's eye. Lem's dog, Patch, was slinking across the floor on his belly toward his owner like he expected to be beaten himself. He was a shy and nervous dog, always ready to run, and who knew what had happened to him before he found Lem.

That was just the way it was with Lem: dogs always seemed to find him. He had already had a half dozen of them over the years, sometimes two at a time, but Patch was his favorite. Patch was the only one who ever made his way inside the house. In those first weeks, as many times as Oratio put him out, he would always find his way silently back in, to sit by Lem or sleep across the foot of his bed. Oratio finally gave in – another sign, Leroy said, that she was soft with the younger children, and why they had no respect for rules. Oratio argued that it did no real harm.

Patch made his way across the floor to Lem, put his paw up on his master's thigh, and then just laid his head in his lap. Lem petted him a bit, but then Patch, instead of leaving, sat side-by-side with Lem, looking into the corner too. Oratio had to bite her lips together in silent laughter and Naomi had to go outside for a while until she could compose herself.

After another hour or so, when they were all outside on the porch, Oratio called back to ask Lem if he had changed his mind. "No, ma'am," was his reticent answer. After another half hour, the ball game ended and everyone gathered on the porch. "Mmmm, mmmm, this is sure good peach pie," Oratio called from the door. "Lem, we are having Naomi's peach pie for dessert. Have you changed your mind yet?" Regardless how many times she asked, Lem always answered back, "No, ma'am," After a while he was sitting with his elbows on his knees and his chin in his palms, but still looking at the corner.

Finally, around four o'clock, and unable to stand it any longer, Naomi went to him, gently hugged him around the shoulders and whispered to him, "I saved a piece of my peach pie for you, baby. Now do you want to tell Aunt Naomi why you don't want to go to heaven?"

Lem turned and was sobbing in Naomi's arms. Embarrassed to be almost nine years old and crying in front of everyone like a baby, he hid his face deep in her arms, soaking the front of her dress. Finally spent, he sniffled and wiped his nose on his sleeve and with streaming eyes looked up at Naomi. "Teacher (meaning his Sunday School teacher) told us that there ain't no dogs in heaven. He said that Jesus don't let them in. And if that's true and …"

"If Patch cain't go to heaven, then I ain't gonna go neither," Naomi delivered the punch line now, slapping her palm on the arm of the rocking chair, falling back with a whoop of laughter. They both laughed, good and long over the memory, with Naomi occasionally shaking her head as she wiped at her tears, adding "that boy!"

Finally, she wiped her eyes and smiled over at Oratio. Oratio was still holding Naomi's hand. "There," she said as strongly as she could, "I wanted to see you smile."

She stopped herself before she added "one more time," but Naomi had known her for too long to not know that was what she really meant.

Naomi stood over Oratio. "We best be gettin' you inside now."

"No!" Oratio protested. "Just a little while longer. Look, I think the blue bonnets have bloomed more even while we have been sitting out here. Look at how blue it is." The field was completely blue now, at least for Oratio, and all the way to where it met the sky. Then she saw that Mama was standing in the yard again, smiling at her.

Naomi looked out to the field where the blue bonnets were blooming. It might be a little more blue, but barely.

Then Naomi understood. She sat back down, but only on the edge of her chair, still facing Oratio and taking her hands. There was a new calm in Oratio's face now, the pain lines were fading, and there was a light coming up in her eyes, like she was seeing something that made her ready to break into a happy smile. "You see your Mama right now?" Naomi asked.

Oratio looked away from Mama, but only a moment. Naomi was holding her hand and searching her face with worry. "What do you think it is like, Naomi? What is it like in heaven?"

Naomi looked out to where Oratio had been looking, seeing the first haze of blue bonnets on the brown and green hills stretched out all the way to the horizon and then the big blue sky above it all. In the distance she could see Phinetta coming back home, carrying the book under her arm and swinging her sunbonnet, with Vicky right beside her.

Without looking back to Oratio she said, "I think heaven probably feel like when you first come home after being gone a long, long time. How you just so happy to be there." She paused. "But I also think heaven… I think heaven have to look like this."

Oratio was light, as light as she used to be when she was a girl and would jump from the top rail of the corral fence back in Louisiana. Back then, she convinced Henry she could fly, and now that was just how she felt. She looked at Mama, at her sweet, young and radiant face. She reached out and placed her hand against her mother's cheek, feeling the love there and in the eternity of that moment she saw the entirety of her mother's life, every moment of it, and she understood everything. Oratio drew her hand away and marveled that the hand was like it used to be, not worn and spotted any longer.

Levina was there too. Levina with her frilled matron's cap tied under her chin, looking so young and happy, smiling and forgiving. Then Oratio could see that they were all there, Grandma Mary, and all the ones she remembered.

Just beyond Grandma Mary were the ones she had never met, but who already knew her. They were all like they had been before they got old and tired. She realized she knew them all now too. She knew that the young woman behind Grandma Mary was Great-Grandmother Mercy and beyond Mercy was a young and beautiful Dove, so radiant in her white dress with her long hair flowing. Standing beside Dove was Richard Wainwright, and that had to be Aunt Charity next to them. Yes, yes it was.

And there! There was Old Bess. But not old. She was wearing a shining silk gown the color of new grass, and smiling proudly down the line to Oratio. Beside her, three young black men stood, the lost sons of Bess. Those great (so many, many times great) uncles were smiling at her, too. She could not wait to meet them and tell them how much their mother had loved them, even though they already knew it. Bess raised her arms, welcoming Oratio, as they all did. They were all there in that long line, waiting for her, so happy, and young and radiant - all of them. She could not wait to go to them.

She reached out to take Mama's hand, but first she had to tell Naomi.

She looked back to where Naomi was sitting on the porch, still holding the hand of the body Oratio had just left behind. Naomi did not know that she was gone yet. It had not even been a second since she left.

She called out to Naomi and saw that Naomi could not hear her. But she called it out again anyway. She called it out before she turned to go, "Naomi, you are right! Heaven is just like Texas!"

PART FOUR

LOUIE G

CHAPTER THIRTEEN

DeWitt County, Texas
May, 1912

With the backs of her legs still stinging, Louie stands on the wooden box by the ironing board in the kitchen of her father's house.

When her arm was finally worn out from swinging the strap, Mama Lillie set Louie roughly back on the box and hissed through clenched teeth, "Get down again before this ironing is done and I will tan you good and proper next time."

Mama Lillie did not care that Louie stopped just a little while, or that her legs ache from standing on the box since lunch time. It is Louie's chore to do the ironing - all of it and perfectly - every Tuesday and Saturday. Her sisters and brothers work in the fields. Louie stays in the house to help their new stepmother and to watch after their baby sister, Eula.

Louie tries not to think about her Mama, who has been dead a year now, and the baby sister who died along with her. Papa was sad and quiet for a long time after that. And since he married Mama Lillie and brought her home, he has been sadder and quieter than ever.

As much her stepmother's whippings hurt, Louie will never cry, but for a moment she wishes her sister Katie would just come home. Katie is ten years old and remembers their real Mama so much better than Louie. Katie can always cheer them all up, even if she is hungry, dusty and bone-tired. But that is still a long time away, there are still many more hours of sunlight left in the day.

Louie does not know why Mama Lillie hates them so much. Louie knows she is plain and dull, but everyone loves her big sisters Katie and Lillie Mae, and their baby sister Eula is sweet and beautiful with bouncing blond curls and big blue eyes. Poor little Eula has already forgotten Mama.

Eula saw the whipping and looks up at her sister with sorry and solemn eyes. Louie looks down from the ironing board at Eula and then over at their stepmother who has her back turned while she slams things around on the stove. Louie crosses her eyes and sticks out her tongue at Mama Lillie. Before Eula can laugh Louie puts a finger to her lips. Eula puts her hand over her mouth to keep quiet. She loves sharing a secret with Louie.

Louie will try to have fresh towels and a full washbasin of cool water ready for Katie and the rest of them when they come home. Since it is Saturday, she will ask Mama Lillie if she can make a big pitcher of ginger water too; cool water freshly pumped from the well with a little ginger spice and sugar stirred in. That always makes them happy, regardless how tired they may be.

And maybe if they are not too tired later on, after supper and their Saturday night baths are finished and they are all in bed, maybe Lille Mae or Katie will whisper another story for Louie tonight - one of the old time stories. That would be nice.

* * * * *

Lillie Mae Mott was almost thirty years old when her neighbor G.W. Squyres was unexpectedly widowed. His wife died in childbirth, mercifully taking the baby along with her. Merciful, Lillie's mother declared, since there were seven children already. Even though Lillie was a dyed-in-the-wool old maid by then her mother still pushed her forward, most likely hoping to get Lillie Mae out of the house. Her mother baked peach pies for Lillie to take to the funeral dinner, and then she stood behind Lillie, who held the pies like she had baked them herself, as they made the Mott family condolences to Mr. Squyres and his pitiful gaggle of children.

Lillie Mae was plain and her family was poor. They never recovered from their losses during the War of Northern Aggression. Her family hung on in South Carolina too long after the war. By the time they came out here to Texas all the best land was taken. Papa's experience with farming was only that of the gentleman farmer his father had been. Even if Papa had not lost his arm in 1862 at Sharpsburg, he still would have struggled as a dirt farmer. Lillie, the youngest of the family, was born in 1882. Her siblings were nearly all grown and scattered by the time she came along. Then Papa died when Lillie was not yet five years old, leaving her mother alone and scrambling to make a living for herself and Lillie Mae.

It might have been easier if Mama had not clung so desperately to the old ways. Their ragged and threadbare three-room house was decorated with the battered furnishings they brought west. And while she made their living doing washing, ironing, mending and sewing for people, Mama still insisted on having their Sunday afternoons of embroidery and pouring cheap tea from the old silver tea pot into chipped cups. Sometimes Lillie Mae wondered if Mama was really right in her mind – like baking those two pies to take the funeral dinner when it used all the flour and sugar they had left. Those pies were devoured by the passel of Squyres children, all of them as misbehaved as a bunch of wild Indians.

It was true they had just lost their mother, Matilda Adeline, along with the baby girl she was birthing. It was also true that Mattie, as everyone called her, had been weak and sick all during the pregnancy, no doubt why her house and her children were in the condition they were in. Before Matilda died and they would see the poor woman at church, Lillie's mother would whisper to Lillie that was what came from white women marrying colored men. It was God's judgment, plain and simple. Even though G.W. Squyres looked snow white, Mama said he was still colored. Mama could always tell.

321

Lillie and her mother hated colored people – or mostly her mother hated them and Lillie went along instead of arguing. Colored people were to blame for the war that ruined the Motts. They should have all been sent back where they came from after the war, instead of being left to pick the bones of what was left of the South. Just look at those uppity Lovetts, the whole bunch of them flaunting their land and cattle, and the sister even driving around in a fancy new motorcar, when good and decent white folks were just barely getting by. But Mama would add with a whisper that things were finally changing for the better now. Changes that would put that uppity, high-yellow Victoria Lovett back in her place. And it was about time too.

But Lillie's mother suddenly altered her prejudices against George Washington Squyres, pushing Lillie forward as if G.W. would even take notice of a plain and bitter old maid. He had seven motherless children, Mama reminded Lillie. He would need another mother to take care of them. This was Lillie's one chance. Lillie was surprised when G.W. asked her to marry so soon, but now she could see her mother was right. He only needed a mother for his children. For him, almost any woman would have done and she was the only single white woman in the three-county area he had to pick from.

Truthfully, Lillie had never wanted to be a mother and especially to another woman's children. The oldest girl, Dora, was sixteen and looked like a puff of wind could blow her away. Hopefully she should be marrying someone before long - that would take care of one of them. The boys, William and Lester, thirteen and twelve, were defiant and untamed and already becoming disgusting young men. Next after them was Katie, age ten. Katie was the only one Lillie could tolerate, except for that unnaturally curly blond hair that repulsed Lillie, almost made her skin crawl, in fact. But at least Katie tried to do something with it, pulling it back under a scarf during the week and braiding it and putting it up on Sundays, even though it was always coming loose like a fuzzy halo around her head. The girl was too optimistically cheerful. But she was somewhat polite, or at least tried to be, even though her grammar needed work.

After Katie was Lillie Mae, the sole reason Lillie had to become "Mama Lillie" since G.W. and his children would not stop calling their sister Lillie Mae. That infuriated Lillie against G.W., who should have made them change. Lillie Mae was only nine years old and they could have just as easily started calling her Belle, her middle name, or even Mae Belle, but that was not to be, regardless what Lillie's wishes were. It was simply too much for her to ask, apparently.

Then there was Louie, seven years old and full of the devil. Lillie hated that girl. Louie looked the most like G.W. Her hair was dark and curly. The girl's skin was sallow-toned and she was nothing to look at. Lillie knew she would always have to be explaining Louie's coloring, protecting Lillie's own status as not being married to a colored man with a colored family. Louie was defiant, lazy and unmannerly.

The next girl, Eula, was three. She was a quiet little thing who followed Louie around like a shadow, always getting underfoot when Louie helped Lillie in the kitchen. Lillie had to admit that Eula was pretty. However, the girl was three years old, still sucked her thumb and barely spoke a word. The girl was slow, maybe retarded even.

Lillie's work was cut out for her from the start. It seemed the girls could not say, "Yes, ma'am," and "No, thank you," no matter how many times she reminded them. Lillie had to teach them their manners if she was ever going to get them married and out of the house. She had to teach them to mind her too. She could see right away that Mattie had been way too soft with them, probably even before she was sick, and G.W. scarcely paid attention to their rudeness and lack of respect.

Her first challenge had been to get the girls to clean themselves up when they came in from the fields, all dusty and sweaty, with rings of dirt caked under their necks. Lillie continually reminded them that a lady, regardless her circumstances, always had a clean face, neck, and hands, combed hair and a fresh dress when she came to the dinner table. Even if it was only a crude table right in the middle of the kitchen, it was still dinner and young ladies should behave correctly.

The boys were past hope. By the second month after she came to live in G.W.'s house, she gave up on trying to teach them even the most basic table manners. They came up out of their chairs to reach for serving plates and bowls, never asking for things to be passed, and helping themselves to enormous amounts of food. They talked while they chewed and the napkins Lillie put by their plates went untouched. They preferred to wipe their mouths, that is if they thought to do so, on the back of their shirt sleeves, leaving stains that were up to Lillie to get out. When she tried to remind them, G.W. told Lillie to leave them be. They had worked hard all day and were hungry. He was just as bad as his sons. Lillie gave up on the boys and turned her attention to the girls instead, even if there was so little hope there too.

Even more than she did not want to be a mother, she did not want to do the disgusting things G.W. expected her to do in their bedroom. She was no ninny. She knew what would happen when she was married, but she had never been undressed, even to her underwear, in front of a man and it had all happened too fast. Then she had to lie in bed while he sweated and snored like a pig after it was over.

She had thought they would get to know each other better first, and maybe she could even sleep in another bedroom like Mama did when Papa was still alive. But the house was too crowded for that. All her stepdaughters crowded into one bedroom with only two beds and seemed not to mind it at all. They boys slept on cots in the far corner of the kitchen and the room was filled with the stench of them in the mornings when Lillie went in to start breakfast. She began telling G.W. he would have to add at least one more bedroom on the house before she had any children.

When Lillie found out she was going to be a mother herself, she almost left and went back to her own mother's house. She was sick from the start. Her feet and ankles swelled up so much she could barely put her shoes on, so she ended up going barefoot at home like a slattern. She fell behind on her housework and broke down crying in front of all of them at supper one night. Even then, G.W. barely scolded the girls - that they needed to help Mama Lillie more - while Lillie tried to convince him that she had to have help if she was going to survive. She meant she needed a hired woman, but there was no money for that. Not even enough to bring in a colored woman to do the washing and ironing.

After that she begged and pleaded for G.W. to make his Princess Dora help more in the house. The eldest girl, Dora, was already excused from the fields due to her health, and supposedly she was also too weak and delicate to lift a finger to help Lillie. She mainly sat and read books in her room all day, the room she shared with the other girls, and barely spoke to or even acknowledged Lillie, except when she needed something brought to her. If Lillie ignored her she would go all blue in the face, making a big show of doing it herself. Lillie would be damned if she would be treated like a servant to her stepdaughters in her own home.

The only solution G.W. could come up with was that Louie, too young to do much work in the fields anyway, would stay home and help Lillie. Louie would have to be the one. So Lillie got a seven year old girl instead of the hired woman she deserved. On top of everything else, Lillie had the added burden of training the ignorant little ninny, who didn't know how to do anything.

CHAPTER FOURTEEN

Gonzales County, Texas
July, 1917

When the war in Europe started, almost everyone in Texas wanted America to stay out of it. The war was really just a family squabble, started by Franz Joseph, who was the emperor of Austria and king of Hungary, and was in cahoots with Kaiser Wilhelm II of Germany. The Kaiser was fighting against his cousins, the King of England and the Tsar of Russia. The kings of Europe were all related and they had been going at it like this for centuries - like a bunch of spoiled children nursing old grievances and trying to take things away from each other that did not belong to them. Why should Americans spend their money and send their young men over there to resolve such a fuss? It was better just to stay out of it.

Those sentiments began to change a little in May, 1915. One hundred twenty-eight Americans were among those killed when the Lusitania, a British ocean liner, was sunk by German U-boats off the south coast of Ireland. Even after Germany's crime of sinking a passenger liner, killing innocent women and children, it was still not America's war.

In November of 1916, President Woodrow Wilson was elected to a second term on the simple slogan, "He kept us out of war." Those words resonated with the sympathies of most Americans, especially for the Squyres and their neighbors. America did not need to get into this war.

But all that changed in January, 1917. A secret telegram that was sent by the German foreign minister, Arthur Zimmermann, to the German Ambassador in Mexico was intercepted by the British. The British forwarded the telegram to the United States Embassy in London and from there it was sent to President Wilson. The message, officially from the German Empire, invited Mexico to join the Central Powers of Germany, Hungary, Turkey and Bulgaria in the event the United States entered the war. The telegram went on to explain that Germany planned to resume unrestricted submarine warfare and anticipated that action would draw the United States into the war. Germany offered to fully finance Mexico's participation in a war against the United States along the Rio Grande. In exchange for Mexico's support, the states of Arizona, New Mexico and Texas would be handed over to Mexico after Germany won the war.

President Wilson shared the telegram with the American press. There was a swift change in American public opinion and the president asked Congress to declare war on Germany and the Austro-Hungarian Empire. Wilson said it would be a "War to End All Wars." Fearing attack on the east coast as well as the Mexican border, Congress quickly obliged, issuing a declaration of war on April 6, 1917. Congress followed up with a Selective Service Act calling for conscription of 3 million men to assist French and English forces fighting on the Western Front.

Although Mexican president Carranza formally rejected Germany's proposal as soon as the United States declared war, the reaction in Texas against Mexico and the German Empire was still swift. With Texas promised as a trophy of war, the 36th Infantry Division was activated in July, 1917, as a part of the Texas National Guard. Rather than waiting to be drafted, thousands of young men from Texas, and even Oklahoma, volunteered to defend their homes.

Among them, Louie's brothers William and Lester had signed up. William, at eighteen, was old enough to sign up on his own. Lester, only seventeen, had to beg his father to sign for him. G.W. resisted but finally gave his permission, perhaps because Lillie's new baby turned out to be a boy and could carry on the Squyres name. Without baby Crockett, letting go of Lester could leave G.W. without a son.

Vol Bailey, the older brother of William's fiancé, Stella, joined too.

There would be a special church service for the young men the Sunday before they left for training. They would all train in Camp Bowie, up in Tarrant County near Fort Worth. From there, troop trains would carry them east to board transport ships sailing from New York City and other east coast ports directly to France.

The Squyres sat as a family that Sunday in church, taking up two pews. William, handsome in his 36th Infantry uniform, sat proudly in the first row with Stella beside him. Sitting next to Stella was Lester, also in his new uniform, and then G.W. and Mama Lillie, who was holding baby Crockett.

Louie and her four sisters sat in the row behind them. Louie was busy trying to keep two-year-old Lucy entertained and quiet during the service, but for once she was happy with the diversion and did not pass the baby off to her other sisters. It kept her from thinking about her two brothers and what might happen to them. In front of her, Stella sat holding William's hand tightly in her own, as if she could hold him in Texas that way. She only let go to dab at her eyes and nose with her handkerchief. It was odd to see Stella, who was always so happy and pleasant, fighting her tears. It was unsettling to see her so upset.

When Louie looked to the right, where the Bailey family sat across the aisle, Stella's brother Vol was always looking directly at her. He was odd, Louie thought. He never smiled. In fact, his thin little mouth and his pale blue eyes always seemed frozen, devoid of any emotion.

If this had been the first time she had ever seen him she would have thought he was solemn because he was going off to war, defending Texas from an invasion of Huns and Mexicans. But she knew he always looked like that: silent and staring. Usually he looked right through Louie, the same way he looked right through everyone else. His stare made her uncomfortable, but he was still a hero, so she gave him a small smile before Lucy demanded her attention again.

And Vol was old too! Twenty-two years old, Stella said. Ten years older than Louie. She could not help looking back again and again to see if he was still looking at her. For the entire service, he never looked away. It made her self-conscious and clumsy as she shifted the fidgeting Lucy from one side to another, trying to soothe and keep her quiet.

All the sisters had new dresses for the special service. G.W. brought home lengths of cheap and plain muslin he charged to his account at the general mercantile and told them to make new dresses. Mama Lillie, cross at the waste of the money, apportioned the fabric out, just enough for each girl, but without regard to their individual preference for color, or even which color would be best for them. Louie was old enough to hide her tears when the pale blue muslin went to Katie and a dreadful pink was put in front of Louie. Louie's skin always looked a ghastly greenish yellow when she wore pink. She drew in a breath to protest, which would get her slapped by Mama Lillie for sure, but Katie caught her eye, barely shook her head and put a finger to her lips.

When it came time to lay out the patterns and cut the fabric for their dresses, Katie quietly traded colors. Katie would look beautiful in either color and it was no real sacrifice for her, but Louie thought she could not love her big sister any more than she did at that moment. The pieces were all cut out and basted together before Mama Lillie noticed what had happened and then it was too late. She began yelling at Louie, in fact came around the table to slap Louie on the back of her head, until Katie jumped in, saying, "Mama Lillie, I wanted this pink for my dress so I made Louie trade with me. It's my fault, not hers."

Dora sewed on the new dresses all day long. The other sisters spent every free minute working on those dresses, just barely finishing them the night before the special service.

On Sunday morning, Katie brushed and braided Louie's freshly washed hair. Then she even put it up. It was the first time Louie had such a grown-up hair style and it infuriated Mama Lillie when Katie brought Louie out of the girls' bedroom. Lillie ordered her then to go back, take it down and make it as it should be. But G.W. overruled her, saying they had to go or be late. There was no time to redo Louie's hair before church.

Louie was wearing the new blue dress. Katie wove a blue ribbon into Louie's hair as she braided it that morning and said the ribbon was very pretty against the blue of the dress. But Louie would not kid herself, she was not pretty and even the dress and hair ribbons did nothing to improve on that. More than likely it was her hair that Mr. Bailey was staring at now, wondering why there was ribbon braided into it and thinking she was a silly, vain girl, trying to be pretty – just like

Mama Lillie hissed to her when she handed off little Lucy for the walk to church.

They almost always walked as a family to church. Sometimes G.W. would hitch the wagon to the family's two horses, but not during planting or harvest seasons, or when it was not too hot for the family to walk, like today. The horses needed their day of rest too, he said. So they set off as a family for the two-mile walk. The boys went on ahead, impatient to be there and likely wanting to give the county girls a chance to get a good look at their new uniforms. G.W. and Mama Lillie, carrying baby Crockett, always came next with the five sisters and little Lucy following behind them.

Katie always dragged her feet just enough to keep them far enough behind that Mama Lillie could not hear, but not so far behind that G.W. would scold them to hurry up. Katie always encouraged Dora, whose lips sometimes turned blue with the exertion of the walk, and kept Louie and Eula entertained, but not laughing too loudly on Sunday morning. They shared the carrying of Little Lucy between them, but mostly Lucy insisted that Louie be the one to carry her. Lately she had started calling Louie "Mama." That made Mama Lillie even madder than ever.

Mama Lillie could not resist getting in one more jab in at Louie's hair. Before she hurried forward to catch up with G.W., she pulled up all the sisters' chins to make sure they were adequately washed. Eula would never look directly at their stepmother, but Louie always looked right back with defiance and thinly-disguised hatred. It was a look that sometimes got her a hard slap, even on a Sunday morning, but she could not help it.

"You know, Gertrude, you look just like a little pickaninny with your hair all tied up in rags like that," Mama Lillie said sarcastically after she decided Louie had washed well enough. "Is that something you really want to show off? Shall we just give up and find you a big, strapping black buck for a husband?"

Louie hated it more than anything when her stepmother called her Gertrude, but this morning, the added comparison to a colored girl was even worse than if Mama Lillie had just slapped her. Mama Lillie's own children, Lucy and Crockett, were the same mix since it came to all of them equally through G.W., but Lillie Mott's application of the one-drop rule did not seem to extend to her own children. In fact, out of all the children it seemed to apply only to Louie.

As soon as Mama Lillie was far enough away, Eula took Louie's free arm with both hands and leaned her head against Louie's shoulder. "I think you look beautiful, Louie," Eula said softly. "I wish I could put my hair up, too." Louie laughed and pulled her arm free from Eula's grasp only to wrap it around Eula's shoulders.

"Yes," Katie agreed, walking on Louie's other side. "You look very pretty. Don't listen to one more word from Mama Lizard." Even Dora laughed at

Katie's open use of the secret name the sisters had for their stepmother.

They walked on, barefoot in the dust to keep their shoes clean for church. They always carried their shoes, with the lacings tied together and their stockings stuffed inside. When they arrived at the church they would put them on before going inside. Mama Lillie could be counted on to roll her eyes and say it was vanity, but Dora, rare to disagree with their stepmother on anything, would calmly point out that it kept the shoes from wearing out so fast. It was the same thing every Sunday. Their shoes were passed down as they outgrew them. Louie's shoes had been worn by her three older sisters before her, and she was careful to keep them as nice as possible for Eula. Poor Eula.

The preacher went on and on, railing against the Kaiser and the Huns and the evils of their empires that wanted to hand Texas over to the Mexicans, and then praising the brave men who had volunteered to go across the sea to defend Texas and their mothers and sisters. Louie let her mind wander. All she ever had to remember was the text for the sermon, and that was only if anyone remembered to ask when they were home after church. Then, of all the children except the babies, there was a one in seven chance she would be the one G.W. called on to answer the question. And even then, Katie could be counted on to silently mouth the chapter and verse across the table if Louie needed reminding.

Instead, she used the time to focus on the mental arithmetic Katie was teaching her. Since Mama Lillie rarely let Louie go to school and especially over the last year while she was expecting baby Crockett, Katie had been Louie's teacher. Katie did her best, going through the lessons, but Louie was a poor speller and a slow reader. She would never catch up now. But arithmetic was different. For some reason it just made sense to her and when Katie taught those lessons she always said Louie was smarter than she was with numbers. Now, while the preacher went on and on, she practiced the fractions Katie had been showing her.

Katie had also been the one to secretly continue the stories that their Aunt Matilda used to tell them before G.W. said he did not want the stories told any more. Texas embraced the "one-drop" rule that swept across the south, meaning that anyone with so much as one drop of colored blood was now considered colored, and should not be using facilities marked "White Only." G.W. always cussed and said his family was as white as anyone else, and they had been from way back.

Aunt Matilda, who was G.W.'s younger sister, told them how her own grandparents, Leroy Lewis Squyres and Oratio Newman had been the first ones in the family to settle here in Texas. Aunt Matilda also told them how their family went so much further back than that. It went five more generations back from their great-grandmother Oratio to the woman from Africa who was called Old Bess.

Now, as the preacher went rambling on and little Lucy slept on her lap, Louie ran through the mental calculations of it. Counting back from herself, there were eight generations from her to Old Bess. If Old Bess was one hundred percent colored, then her daughter, Dove, would be one half. Dove's daughter Mercy would be one quarter and so on. Keeping track of the generations on her fingers, Louie doubled the denominator of the fraction with each generation, coming down to a denominator of 256 for the ninth generation, representing herself, her brothers and sisters. Louie was 1/256th colored, and thus 255/256th white.

But was that still a drop?

The preacher was beginning to wind up his sermon, talking now about the everlasting fires of hell and calling for the lost to come forward and accept Jesus. It was always the same people every Sunday in their little church and Louie thought he should save that part of the sermon for a Sunday when someone new showed up. Everyone here had been baptized and were good Christian people. Well, except for Mama Lizard who was purely evil, she corrected herself and then had to fight the urge to giggle in church before she returned to her mental calculations.

So, just how much of her was actually colored? The last time they went into town G.W. let all the girls weigh themselves on the scales outside the general mercantile. Those scales were generally used for trade, weighing the cotton and peanut crops the farmers brought to town to sell, but they worked just as well for weighing people too. The last time she weighed Louie was ninety two pounds, plus a few ounces. She struggled for a moment to remember how it was that Katie showed her to apply a fraction to a measure of weight. Then she remembered. She put the 92 pounds on the top of the fraction in place of the one, and then divided the numerator into the denominator. She reckoned it was point 36 – or a little more than a third of a pound. That meant one third of a pound of her was colored.

She did not know how much blood it would take to make up a third of a pound, but looking down at her index finger she guessed it might weigh about that much. She didn't know how she could ever really weigh only her finger without cutting it off, but she knew what a pound of meat looked like and it seemed reasonable that the finger would weigh a third of a pound. So, it looked like that much of her was colored – her index finger. That was what Mama Lillie and other people were so worried about.

She decided she would keep that in mind the next time she took a drink from the "White Only" drinking fountain G.W. insisted they use outside the court house when they went into town. She might even use only that finger to turn the handle on the fountain, just to show them.

Finally the preacher finished and they were fumbling to find their hymnals and standing to sing the final hymn. A "hymn of invitation" is what it was called.

Hopefully, with the blessing of the servicemen to follow, the preacher would not hold the hymn open like he usually did, pleading and calling out for sinners to come back to Jesus. She was right, after singing only the four verses printed in the hymnal the preacher closed the invitation and called the men in uniform to come to the front of the church. The five young men from the three-county area left their pews and went forward.

With them kneeling, the pastor preached that in the olden times in the Bible, specifically in the book of Acts, Chapter 6, verse 6 – " when they had prayed they laid their hands upon them." The Bible said that before the apostle Paul sent out new believers and ministers, they would kneel before Paul and the rest of the church, bow their heads and the people of the church passed them by, putting their hands on their shoulders to bless them. It was called a "laying on of hands," and the pastor said that all the church was invited to come up front, file by the line of kneeling young men, put their hands on the tops of their heads or on their shoulders and bless them in the name of Jesus.

Row by row the filed up. Going ahead of Louie, Dora was nervous and Katie looked like she could giggle at any moment. After Katie, their sister Lillie Mae went ahead of Louie gently placing her hands on the shoulders of the young men who knelt with their heads bowed. Louie heard Lillie Mae softly say, "God bless you," or "God be with you," to each one. Louie followed her, repeating those words. Eula would follow Louie.

First was a young man Louie barely knew, then her two brothers, William and Lester. As she placed her hands on her brothers' shoulders it no longer seemed like a lark and her throat closed up like she could cry. They could be killed and not come home. All of these brave young men were willing to sacrifice their lives for everyone who was staying behind in Texas. Her words of blessing did not seem like enough.

After Lester was another young man she did not know very well, so she was able to compose herself a little as she gave him her blessing. The last was Vol Bailey, Stella's oldest brother. Louie wanted to run on by him, run out the back of the church and all the way home in fact, but if he was brave enough to go to France, she could be brave enough to bless him. She placed her hands on his shoulders and said, "God be with you."

Vol's hand came up to take hers, holding it to his shoulder a moment longer. She wanted to pull her hand away, but he looked up at her with a fleeting look of pure terror before he dropped his head again and let her hand go. Louie was surprised. The Baileys were all such brave people. One time when William brought Stella home for Sunday dinner, she told them the story of how her grandmother killed three Comanche Indians that attacked when she was alone on her claim. Stella thought it was amusing, saying if her Grandma Johanna and those children had been killed by the Indians instead, (Stella's father Albert was the baby Johanna carried when she ran to the neighbors), then Stella herself would not be here.

It was a story from long ago, from the pioneer days, but everyone knew the Baileys were strong and courageous. Their grandmother would not let them be anything else. So Louie was surprised by what she had seen in Vol's face and suddenly understood how terrified he was, and how he could tell no one, especially no one in his family.

"I will pray for you Mr. Bailey," Louie added, hoping to comfort him. "Every night."

"Thank you, Miss Gertrude," he said through barely parted lips. He was his old self, stony cold eyes and barely moving lips. He did not look up at her again.

She realized Mr. Bailey calling her by her middle name was so different from how Mama Lillie used it. Instead of making her feel worthless, when he called her that it made her feel suddenly grown up, like she was a young lady.

But Louie also wished she had not added that last part. Now she would have to remember to include him in her prayers every night until he came home from the war.

If she forgot, and he was killed, it would be her fault.

CHAPTER FIFTEEN

36th Infantry Division
Mense-Argonne Offensive
Argonne, France
September, 1918

Vol pushed his back against the mud wall and he pushed his feet against the opposite wall. He pushed as hard as he could but there was still not enough room. The rain would not stop and there was just not enough room. Mud was at his back and mud was at his feet, mud was beneath him and mud was above. He pushed as much as he could push, but there was just not enough room. But as long as this mud did not smother him it was his safety. This mud was his salvation. Before he came here he was a stranger to mud, but now it was his ally.

There was no air in this narrow trench. There was no air inside his mask, the mask that had been on his face since the alert came down, hours ago - or was it days ago? The mask saved his life and yet it stole his air from him. The mask stole his air, and even if he ripped the mask from his face there would not be enough air in this trench. The boys said the shells exploding around them stole away the oxygen. The blast of each shell shook and vibrated all the way through them. Except for the constant ringing in his ears, he could no longer hear. He could not breathe, but he had to calm himself. He had to believe, to trust that there was enough air. To think otherwise was to give in to madness.

It was also madness to look to his right. That was where Indy was. Indy was from Fort Wayne, Indiana. Indy, who had been with Vol since July when the boys of the 36th Infantry Division, all of them from Texas and Oklahoma, were thrown in with Indy's division as soon as they arrived in France. When they first met there, side-by-side in a trench, Indy called Vol "Texas." After they survived their first battle together and ended up here in Argonne, he simply shortened it to "Tex."

To look right was to see Indy. Indy - who was wearing his mask where Vol had placed it for him. Indy - who was so still. Indy - who was not feeling the mud wall, the mud beneath him, the mud in his shoes and up his legs. Indy - wearing the mask, hiding that half of his face was gone.

Last night, or maybe it was the night before, Indy stood to fire at the Huns and came down too suddenly, after a musical 'ping' lifted his helmet and blew it away. Vol took out Indy's gas mask long before the alarm sounded and covered Indy's face so Indy would be safe. Vol knew that to look to his right at Indy was to descend into the madness of this war that would never end.

Vol forced himself to breathe slowly. He made himself breathe calmly, counting the seconds between breaths. The mask had enough air, if he believed it did. If he did not believe it, like the others, and ripped it from his face, the mask could not help him any more.

He was aware of movement to his right. Movement from where Indy sat. He brought up his rifle, but he would not look, he would not see Indy.

"Soldier, look alert!" a voice called out.

Vol made ready with his gun. He was alert.

"Message relay for the rear," the voice told him.

Vol understood the command. He was next in the line. He would crawl along this mud trench with the message tucked inside his shirt, until he reached the next pair of men in the trench. There, he would join the first man he came to while the second man would take the message and carry it on. The message would be relayed that way along the trench until it finally reached the rear. Vol would have to leave Indy now. But Indy would not know.

Vol took the message. He would have to carry his rifle as he went crouching along the trench, half crawling and half running.

"Masks are off now," the voice commanded.

"Sir. I did not hear the 'all clear,' sir," Vol replied pulling off his mask and taking great gulps of the rancid air. "I did not hear."

"No problem mate. Now, on with you. It's an urgent message for the rear."

Vol started crawling, mud upon mud. Behind him he heard, "Holy Fuck!" as the voice pulled off Indy's mask. The voice understood now too.

Vol crawled and crawled. The lightning of the explosions above him showed the way. He came to the next pair of men. "Message for the rear!" he barked out.

"I'll take it," said the voice.

Vol saw his way. Indy showed him. "No sir. I take it all the way, sir. Orders!"

So they let Vol crawl over them and go on toward the rear. On and on he went, crawling over the next team and the team after that.

"Urgent Message for the Rear," he said with more authority and command each time until he reached the rear. By then, the front was overrun by the Huns. Vol joined the other soldiers at the rear as the officer called for them to retreat.

.

The urgent message and his simple lie saved Vol.

* * * * *

Four or five weeks later, somewhere in northeastern France, Vol fired his gun and ducked back down below the ruins of a stone wall. At least, he was not in a trench this time. There was no time to stop and dig as they chased the German army. As they advanced they found protection and hunkered down where they could. Between firing his gun, Vol crouched behind the stone wall. Two others had been with him, but now lay dead, their faces covered by Vol who could not stand their hideous wounds and cold, unseeing eyes.

He took two duck-like steps to the side before he came back up to fire again. That was his captain's orders; don't come up in the same spot where you just fired. The Huns watched for you to do that, ready to fire where you just ducked down. They would blow the top of your head away the moment you came back up. You took two or three steps right or left each time, but never, never in the same direction or taking the same number of steps, and never, ever following a pattern – you counted to a different number before you came back up. It was the only way Vol and the rest of them could stay alive now.

The next time Vol came up, he thought he might already be dead.

Chance, his horse, was standing there. Chance was standing across the destroyed meadow. It was a meadow framed with the scorched skeletons of ruined trees and littered with the dead and dying on both sides of this war. And it was five thousand miles from Texas.

But it was his horse, somehow here in France. He was fascinated for a moment, almost too long of a moment before he ducked back down without firing. He replayed the scene in his mind. He had moved just far enough to the right that he could see behind the crumbled rubble of a stone wall that had once been a farm house or a barn. Chance was standing there as calmly as if he was tied to the rail outside Vol's mother's house in Texas. With the chaos and utter madness all around, Chance stood there with calm and courage.

It had to be his mind playing tricks on him. Chance could not be here. Or maybe Vol was dead now too and Chance had come for him. People said that happened sometimes. The dead came back to help you cross over. But Chance, as far as he knew from Mother's last letter, was still alive and well back in Texas.

Vol checked the rifle in his hands. It was real enough. The blisters on his hands were still there and the knuckles he had skinned an hour or two earlier scrambling over some rubble were still oozing blood, his own blood mixing with the dirt. If he were dead, he reckoned he would not be bleeding like that.

He prepared to fire again, shifting even further right where he could see Chance better when he came up, if his horse really was there. He counted to twenty-three this time and then came up, keeping his helmet low and only exposing enough below the brim that he could see. This time he could see it was not Chance. The markings were almost identical, but Vol knew his horse well enough to know it was not him. He could also see the German officer, previously hidden behind the wall. The man was holding the reins in his left hand, pulling the horse's head down low. The man raised his right hand, bringing his pistol up against the horse's skull.

They had heard the Huns were doing that. Slaughtering their horses rather than leaving them behind. They were on the run, but it seemed that they would only destroy horses that could not survive the retreat. This horse looked perfect: strong and ready just like Chance would be.

Before the man could fire his pistol, Vol shot him cleanly through the temple. The man dropped, instantly dead, but his pistol still fired, shooting the horse through the neck. With a horrible scream the horse drew away, yanking the reins away from the Hun, trying to run and shaking its head to get away from the hole torn through its flesh. Vol immediately used his remaining shot to kill the horse, dropping back to his knees as soon as his shot was fired.

When he came up again, there was the horse, mercifully lying dead, but this time Vol could see that it was indeed Chance. Vol dropped back down, letting go of his gun and crouching on his haunches as he shuddered and pressed his hands to his temples while he screamed over and over for Chance. He had killed his own horse. Somehow Chance had been here with him, just across this ruined meadow on the outskirts of this village in France, and five thousand miles from Texas.

CHAPTER SIXTEEN

DeWitt County, Texas
1918

The war ended and Louie's brothers came home. They were the fortunate ones; in all nine million people died. Louie could see the war had been too terrible for her brothers to talk about. Still, they were happy and relieved to come home. Their bodies were unscathed. Their spirits would heal now they were home in Texas.

Vol Bailey did not come home – at least not to Texas. Whispered conversations said he had been injured in a different way and was being held by the army for treatment. His mother and father had been all the way to New York to see him. They were told his treatment would involve long periods of quiet rest, but Louie's brothers William and Lester knew it would be much more than that. They had seen cases of shell shock on the battlefield. It came from lesions on the brain caused by the impact of exploding shells. The Army told Vol's folks that he may have been gassed too, they were not sure. Either way, he would be in the army hospital in New York State for months, maybe years, subjected to new treatments the army was trying. In time, he might recover.

At least Louie knew her prayers had been answered. He was still alive.

* * * * *

Albert and Nannie Bailey were nearly silent during the first leg of their long train ride back from the Army hospital. It was ironic that Nannie had always wanted to ride the train, and never in her wildest dreams did she expect to go all the way to New York City on one. They had another good harvest that year and Albert said they should spend some of that money to go see Vol. There was no argument from Nannie. She would have been happy to spend every last penny of their money to go see their son.

On the way there she could afford to be excited. Vol was alive, even if he was injured somehow. She was so excited to see him again, excited at the marvelous journey, excited to be seeing the big cities of Houston, New Orleans, Memphis, Chicago, and finally New York City. They had a few brief hours in Manhattan seeing that amazing metropolis before they boarded their final train, a commuter train it was called, for the short ride to the town where the Army hospital was located. The trip had been like a holiday.

Their trip home was completely different. By then, the nation was in the first grip of the Spanish Influenza epidemic. All the windows on the train were open day and night to bring in fresh air that would kill the germs. The epidemic firmly took hold in New York during the time they visited the army hospital. When they returned to the city it was completely changed. Thousands of people were dying every day. The papers reported more than forty thousand had died in the city in one week. It was a number they simply could not comprehend: that many people all in one place, and that many of them dying in only seven days. There were not enough doctors and hospitals for the sick and dying. The government told citizens to stay inside their houses and avoid public meetings, such as schools, motion pictures and even church. The dead bodies were stacked like cord wood, waiting for ditches to be dug for the mass graves. By the time Albert and Nannie returned to the city, people were in a panic and every train leaving the city was full.

Even though they already had tickets they were still pushed and jostled to and fro while they waited in New York to board their Chicago-bound train. There were police and deputized guards stationed all along the line, wearing gauze masks and showing their clubs to keep order. Further back in their line, someone was shoved and shoved back. There was shouting and a woman screamed, temporarily drawing the guards back to the scuffle. While they were standing unprotected, a man holding a child stepped up and offered Albert two hundred dollars for their two tickets, then five hundred - all that he had. The man said his wife had died that morning and he wanted to take their child to family in Chicago. He showed them cash money and Nannie felt sorry for the child and wanted Albert to take it, but Albert refused. They could die if they stayed in the city. The man was angry and cursed at Albert as he was pushed away by the returning guards. Albert and Nannie had never seen such chaos.

That first night they sat upright in the chair car, huddled under a blanket and trying to sleep as they sped west. In Chicago, Albert switched their tickets to the last two seats on the Illinois-Central line's *Panama Limited*, paying the extra charge for the all-Pullman train because of its speed. It was expensive, but it would make the 920-mile trip to New Orleans in only 23 hours.

They could see the cities they passed through along the way beginning to hunker down as the flu epidemic was spreading and setting in. Albert told Nannie they were lucky to be ahead of the wave. He was privately concerned that the trains, an apparent source of spreading the epidemic, might be halted. Hopefully that would not happen, but if it did they would be stuck, and possibly even quarantined, in a strange city. It was best to keep pressing on toward home as long as the trains kept running. He did not want to alarm Nannie any more than she already was.

He could also see the luxury of the *Panama Limited* cheered Nannie, especially after the grim weeks they had in New York. They were scheduled to have a long layover in New Orleans while they waited for their connecting train to Houston. Their previous connection in New Orleans had been too brief to even leave the station. Albert had promised they would take advantage of the extended time on their return trip to take a tour of the city and maybe even have dinner at one of the famous restaurants. As the train approached the city, Nannie went to the ladies lounge in their car to change into her best dress, hat and gloves. In the men's room at the other end of the car, Albert shaved and put on a fresh shirt and tie and tipped the porter handsomely to brush and press the jacket, vest and pants of his suit.

But as they looked out the windows as the train pulled into the station they could sense the early stages of panic beginning to set in: a long line of taxicabs arriving at the station, people getting out of those waiting taxis to walk or run the remaining distance to the station, those people carrying only the hastily packed suitcases they could carry themselves, long and anxious cues of nervous people wanting to buy tickets, and people with tickets already lined up to board trains that would not arrive for hours. The epidemic was coming into full swing here now too.

Before they walked out the waiting room's doors into the street, Nannie quietly told Albert they could see the city another time. It did not seem right to be having a nice dinner under these circumstances, anyway. They went to stand in line for their connecting train.

The train from New Orleans to Houston was oversold, but they were among the first to board and Albert found them seats. Others further back in the line were seated in the dining car and the club car. Some ladies even sat on the sofas in the ladies' lounges, and against all regulations, the last passengers in line sat on the floor of the baggage car and the mail car. Before the train was even an hour outside New Orleans, rumor was that they may not be allowed to pull into the Houston station. Not without police and doctors boarding first, anyway, and they would quarantine the entire train if anyone showed the influenza symptoms. Some people began getting off the train before their final stop, risking being stranded at the small town depots along the way.

Things were calmer in Houston, where they connected to their final train on the Galveston, Harrisburg and San Antonio line. When that train reached the whistle-stop town of Nixon, Texas, they simply got off the train. Albert had sent a telegram from Houston and Stella and her husband were waiting in their wagon beside the small depot to take Nannie and Albert home. As they drove through the little town, Nannie marveled aloud that it looked like nothing had changed. It was as if there had been no war and no flu epidemic. A less virulent strain of the same flu had passed through earlier in the year. People were just going about their normal business, oblivious to the horrors she had just seen in the cities.

But nothing could ever be the same for Nannie and Albert. They could not put the diagnosis Vol's doctors had shared with them out of their minds: acute anxiety, fits of extreme anger, shell shock and minimal response to electric treatment. The prognosis was complete rest for an undetermined time to allow his brain lesions to heal. More upsetting than getting that news had been their visit with Vol. It was the one and only time they were allowed to actually see him during two entire weeks at the hospital.

His doctors were brutally frank in preparing them to see their son. They said Vol was found wandering near the village of St. Etienne in France after the Germans vacated it. Thought at first to be a deserter, the officer in charge their son was taken to realized that a deserter would have fled the area. Instead, Vol was wandering, dazed and without his weapon, and completely unaware of his surroundings. Had the Germans not been so busy with their retreat he surely would have been shot since he was out in the open and completely disoriented.

Following instructions in his field manual, the officer tried to snap Vol out of it with several sharp slaps to his face and then took his shoulders to give him a good shaking, but Vol remained completely unresponsive. As many as forty percent of soldiers had been similarly afflicted at the Battle of Somme and some officers believed what Vol exhibited was simply a lack of moral fiber and even cowardice. Those men were sent back to the line or treated as deserters. Fortunately this officer had read the manual. Vol was sent to the rear to be seen by medics and taken from there to England where his file was labeled "NYDN" for "Not Yet Diagnosed, Nervous." He was brought back to the United States on the next hospital ship.

When they saw him, Nannie was not sure if her son even recognized her. The words she tried to comfort him with only seemed to agitate him more as he grimaced away from her touch and rocked back and forth in muffled and frantic sobs. He did not seem to see or hear his parents and worked compulsively all during their visit at the piece work the doctors thought would be good for him, counting exactly ninety-six red-tipped safety matches and packing them into a box. Albert, in response to Nannie's sobs at the marks on their son's temples from the electric treatments he had been given, spoke sternly with the doctors who agreed to discontinue them. They were not doing any good anyway.

At the end of the two weeks, the doctors told them to go on home. Their son would heal more efficiently without them. Vol would need to be there for a long, long time.

* * * * *

Nannie Lucas Bailey knew she always held her son too closely, but she just could not help it. He was her third child, but her first two had died: little Emma in 1900 when she was only nine years old and Louis three years later, when he was only seven. After that, she held her two surviving children closer than ever. Even when the baby, Perry Howard, came along in 1910 - a complete surprise for everyone - and Nannie should have relaxed, the only thing her husband, Albert, ever scolded her for was being too soft with the children, especially the boys. His mother, Johanna, reinforced that.

Johanna was a formidable old pioneer woman and she completely scared the devil out of Nannie. From the start, Johanna scolded Nannie's children like they were her own. She scolded them when they cried, no matter what the reason was. Johanna would say they did not know what suffering, pain, and discomfort (or whatever it was they were crying about) really was. Those sorry children never would have survived the early days in Texas.

If they ever cried over a skinned knee, Johanna would tell them how she ran barefoot for three miles, with her skinned knees dripping blood, to keep from being killed by Indians. If those soft and spoiled children had been around then, they surely would have been scalped or carried off by the savages.

After a visit with Johanna, it would take Nannie days and days to get her children back to where they would sleep all night without nightmares and they could go to the outhouse alone, even in the daytime, so afraid of Indians their grandmother had made them. Nannie, raised to be quiet and gentle by her mother, was never taken seriously by her mother-in-law. If she complained, Albert just laughed and said his mother was harmless. Just don't listen to her, he told their children. He never did.

Johanna was legendary in these parts. Only a few years after she saved herself and her children from the Comanche, her husband, Oliver, up and died. It was to be expected, Johanna declared, even though Oliver was only forty-five. Johanna was his third wife, but his first in Texas. The other two wives would have never made it here, she added. Oliver had a son by his second wife who was a mama's boy and stayed behind with his mother's family in Indiana when Oliver came out to Texas. By the time he could send for the boy, the grandparents begged for him to stay, and Oliver, so weak Johanna thought, gave up his eldest son to them. If it had been up to Johanna, she would have gone back to Indiana and dragged the boy to Texas herself, the best thing that could have happened. Texas would have made a man of him.

After Oliver died, Johanna took a second husband and had a son with him. That husband died young too. Texas was a widow-maker in those days. And rather than letting her youngest son have a different last name, she simply changed it to the same name of her other children. The boy became a Bailey, even though his father had been something else. None of the rest of the Bailey family was about to argue with Johanna about it.

By contrast, Nannie's mother was quiet and gentle. Nannie was an only child. Her parents were both young when she was born. Mama was only nineteen. Her parents each came over from Louisiana with their families, then met and were married as soon as they arrived in DeWitt County. To the delight of Nannie's children, her father was a real, honest-to-goodness cowboy. He rode in the great cattle drives. Before the railroad came to Texas, those drives took herds of cattle up through Oklahoma to the railheads in Kansas and Missouri, where those cattle were shipped to the slaughterhouses in Chicago or on further east. Nannie would tell her children those stories; remembering how exciting it was when her father left for a cattle drive, even though he would be gone for months.

Nannie would remember even better when he came home and how happy Mama was. Bob Lucas would always pick up his daughter and toss her up in the air, making her squeal with laughter. Mama made up a bath for him, even if it was the middle of the week and he had a good long soak in the tub, telling Nannie stories of the drive as she sat on the other side of the curtain that Mama pulled across the corner of the kitchen. They always had a special supper after, happy around their table.

Then Bob Lucas went riding off one morning, bound for Colorado to look at some land. He never came back.

Nannie thought it might be the effects of losing her father as a young girl, having no one else but her Mama while she was growing up, and then losing the first two children when they were so young, that would not let her do anything but love her surviving children so fiercely.

The youngest boy, Perry Howard, was eight years old now and starting to push her away when she held him too long or gave him too many kisses, but she held on to him until she was finished anyway, making them both laugh.

Stella Esther married William Squyres as soon as he came back from France. Stella had a generous good humor and would be a good mother. She openly loved Nannie, hugging and kissing her when they came to visit and even more so when they had to leave. Nannie was sure William must tease Stella about it, but William was good to Nannie too. He lost his own mother, Mattie Squyres, as a boy and now he seemed to put Nannie in her place, showing her the same patience, love and generosity he would have shown to his own aging mother. Nannie could see that Stella loved him all the more for it.

Back when they were first married, Albert had been generous with Nannie's mother like that too, giving over a room in their home so she could live with them. It had been like that until her death in 1916. It had been good for the children to know their grandma Nancy in that way, so different from their other grandmother. In fact, Nancy was about as opposite as you could get from Johanna.

Grandma Nancy always doted on Vol. It was Nancy who read to the boy when he was little, patiently reading the same stories over and over, as many times as he asked for them. Even before he was two years old, little Vol would "read" the words right along with his grandmother. It was amazing what that boy could remember: numbers to no end, specific dates of the most trivial things, even names and places. Before he was five he could recite the name of every man killed at the Alamo, gaining him the rare praise of Grandma Johanna for that accomplishment, who bragged and bragged about it.

There was also something different, odd even, about Vol. The first time Nannie noticed it was when he was two. Vol's books always had to be arranged in a specific order. If something was out of place, or even out of alignment, Vol would immediately correct it. He would not do it casually; it was as if Vol was in a panic until everything was back in its rightful place.

As soon as he was big enough to sit in his own chair at the table, he would pick up and replace the dishes and silverware at his place until it was just so, measuring with his little hands the exact distance his knife, fork and spoon were from the plate until everything was perfectly aligned. Only then would he allow food to be put on his plate, but with no food ever touching and the milk glass filled to an exact level. Only then could he eat.

The most distressing thing of all was that Vol never laughed. Or at least, he never laughed at things most people would find amusing. She could not even remember him laughing as a baby. When his little sister Stella began telling her stories at the dinner table, making the family laugh with the twist she could put on words and her retellings of other stories, Vol would only stop eating and wait, his thin lips set in a straight line. He did not look at his sister with disdain; in fact he never looked directly at anyone. When she finished it was as though he was still waiting for her to finish her story. Then, when he realized Stella was finished, he solemnly resumed his methodical eating.

Vol never once lost his temper with Stella. From the day she arrived, he adored his little sister. In return Stella worshiped her big brother, and was fiercely protective of him. She had bloodied more than one nose when she thought the owner was trying to tease her brother. From the start, there was a bond that could not be cracked even by their baby brother Perry. Vol and Stella both loved Perry, but not in the same way they were devoted to each other.

In stark contrast to the lively and gay Stella, Vol rarely displayed any emotion, other than his agitation when things were out of kilter and he would have to go through his routine of taking everything apart and putting everything back into place again.

When he was five years old, Nannie and Albert took Vol to see their doctor. The doctor performed a complete examination, including a long conversation with Vol. He assured Nannie and Albert that the boy was healthy, intelligent – extremely intelligent in fact, and it was just how he was. Likely he would grow out of "it," whatever "it" was.

So Nannie held him too closely. She made things as easy as possible for him. Before his brother Louis died, Nannie and Albert gave up their bedroom so Vol could have a room of his own. From the first day, Vol kept everything in the room just so. Nannie still cleaned the room every week, knowing Vol would wipe everything down again when she was finished, remake his bed and reposition everything she had touched while dusting. But in those times, rather than being annoyed with her, he did it silently and with patience, working methodically until he was satisfied things were just right.

CHAPTER SEVENTEEN

DeWitt County Texas
1920-1921

As the calendar was turned over from 1919 to begin the new decade, George Washington Squyres realized it was the land that saved him, or more precisely, it was his hard work of the land that had been his salvation since Matilda died. If the good years continued, 1921 or maybe even 1920 would be the year he would finally accomplish his plan. He only wished his father was still alive to see it.

The past ten years had been good for Texas. Crop yields and prices were strong, and during the war it got even better with the increased demand for beef, cotton, oil and everything else that was produced in Texas.

The cities in Texas that served and supported those farm commodities also boomed. In the north, Dallas became the world's leading cotton center, as well as the insurance and financial center of Texas. In 1909, the Praetorian Insurance company proudly built the tallest skyscraper in Texas, an amazing fourteen stories tall. Houston had become the premiere deep water port for the entire area. To provide a safe port further inland, the Houston Ship Channel was built after Galveston was destroyed in the hurricane of 1900. The discovery of oil the following year at nearby Beaumont brought even more people to the city. Houston now had nearly 140,000 citizens, almost doubling in size since 1910.

But many believed the bounty was not evenly shared. Those who owned the ranches and large cotton farms saw vast increases in their wealth, not only from the increased value of their existing herds of cattle and the cotton their land produced, but also from the oil that was underneath their land. They were fabulously rich now, and it was all proportional to the amount of land owned. That inherently should be fair, but the original access to the land had not been. Some of the ranches dated back decades and had thousands and thousands of acres.

The inequities were more visible than ever after the Bolshevik revolution in Russia. The Czar and his family were deposed and the wealthy, landed classes were divested of their land. As the news of the murder of the royal family filtered back, Americans were more aware of the imbalance within their own system. Some of them worried about a similar uprising of the impoverished masses here. The only thing that seemed to divert it was the ingrained individualism of the population, especially in Texas – that you and you alone were responsible for your wealth or lack of it. If you were not rich you had no one to blame but yourself for your own misfortune.

In Texas, the strong dichotomy of land ownership went back almost as far as Texas itself. After Mexico declared independence from Spain in 1821, Moses

Austin secured the first *empresario,* or colonial land grants, from Spain. His son, Stephen Austin, led 300 American families into the area extending from the Gulf coast into central Texas. Those settlers each received a *sitio* or league of land, or 4,428 acres, for grazing. They also received another 177 acres for cultivation.

Even now in 1920, no one in Texas disputed that The Old Three Hundred deserved that land. Those people risked their lives to settle this land. In 1836, they had to flee for their lives in the Runaway Scrape, just barely ahead of the Mexican army, and running almost all the way to the Louisiana border before the Mexican General Santa Anna was captured and forced to sign the treaties of Velasco, ending the war with Mexico once and for all.

No, without The Old Three Hundred, there would be no Texas, or it would still be a part of Mexico. No one begrudged those families for those lands they still held. In fact, most Texans were very proud of them and held them, and their descendants, in high esteem.

What was the sticking point for most ordinary people was that the Republic of Texas only gave out 1,280 acre headrights of land to settlers who came after 1836. That was steadily reduced; 640 acres in 1837, 320 acres in 1845 and only 160 acres after 1854. That was almost nothing compared to the Old Three Hundred getting almost thirty times as much land. Granted, the borders of private land were less distinct in those days – you had a homestead and you had cattle, but everyone knew cattle would wander as they grazed, following the grass on the public lands. Cattle got blended in with other herds too. That was why you branded your own cattle, so you could go round them up when you needed to.

What was wrong in many of the minds of most small farmers was that the federal Morrill Act, passed in 1876, allowed the sale of the public lands to individuals. Governor John Ireland allowed individuals and even foreign investors to purchase huge tracts of land in Texas, tens of thousands of acres at a time. It was public land that should have been distributed more fairly among the people of Texas. Now, some forty years later, too much land was held by the too-privileged few. Honest, small farmers could not make a living and were being squeezed out.

Making things for small farmers even worse, when the first settlers poured across the Louisiana border into the eastern part of Texas in the 1840s, they brought the cotton plantation culture with them. In those first years cotton production increased from 58,000 bales in 1850 to more than 430,000 bales in 1860. Along with that growth, the number of slaves in the state increased from 58,000 to over 160,000 in the same period.

After those slaves were freed, their previous owners still needed farm labor, and in response, the third and lowest class of farmer emerged. Tenant farming filled the labor vacancy left by the freed slaves. These poor farmers, both black and white, did not own the land they farmed. Instead, they planted seed provided by the landlord, tended the plants, harvested the crop and brought it to market. There, they received a share of the payment for the crop, sometimes as little as a third, and never more than half. The landlord kept the rest.

Between harvests, their landlord would provide a line of credit for them to live on. That loan had to be paid back in full at harvest. The balance plus interest calculated at a rate set by the landowner was deducted from the sharecropper's portion of the harvest. Beyond that, landlords could tack on additional charges like rent for the equipment used and even rent for the shack the family lived in while they worked the land.

In general, a tenant farmer needed twenty acres of land to break even. To keep the sharecroppers tied to the land they farmed, and buried under more and more debt, unscrupulous landlords would not let one family farm any more than that. Some years, the tenant farmer could come away from the harvest even more deeply in debt, and as hopelessly and securely bound to the landlord as their predecessors had been under slavery.

As the tenant farming system flourished, more and more small farmers who could not compete were squeezed out of their land and became tenant farmers too. In 1880, more than a third of all farmers in Texas were tenant farmers. By 1900 that had increased to one half. In 1920 it was an estimated 53 percent and growing.

Although it was not known by many, G.W. Squyres was also a tenant farmer. The long-standing agreement with his landlord went back to his father. It was the farm his grandparents, Leroy and Oratio Squyres, put together when they first came to Texas. It had started with their original 640 acre claim and was added to whenever adjoining properties could be purchased. Leroy managed the land successfully and had been steadily more prosperous. Eventually the farm increased to more than 1,000 acres.

When Leroy died in 1879, the farm passed jointly to his two sons, Russell and Lemuel. The younger of the two brothers insisted on dividing the land equally.

Lemuel, the dashing officer who lost his left arm below the elbow in the war, never really wanted to farm. Like his mother Oratio's brother Henry, he was most happy working with horses, something he could still do when he returned home from the battlefield. As soon as he inherited it, Lem sold his share of the land at a premium price to a wealthy rancher who was buying up small farms. He went to Shreveport, living a comfortable life in a hotel until his money ran out. Then he made his way back to Texas, finding work with horses on a ranch near Henderson. He died there when he was only fifty.

The division of the land with Lem was devastating to Russell, both emotionally and financially. Before his father Leroy's death, Russell was running the farm anyway. It provided an adequate living for all of them and allowed Lem to spend his days working with the two horses they owned and to sit on the front porch the rest of the time. Although it seemed that Lem contributed nothing, (and Russell's wife, Catherine, complained to Russell about that frequently and bitterly), the loss of half the land had the effect of halving the family's income. Russell and Catherine and their six children struggled to survive on half of what they earned before. No matter how careful they were, their debts began to accumulate, each year adding a little more to the balance owed. The land had to be sold off bit by bit until only 200 acres remained.

The situation did not improve after the three oldest children left home. The oldest boy and his bride moved north to Brown, Texas, and the second son left for Matagorda. The oldest girl, Sarah Jane, also married and moved away. With three children gone, there were fewer to feed, but the workload shared by the youngest children also had to increase. G.W., at fifteen, worked alongside his father. They shared the work from spring planting through the harvest, but it was a losing battle against the ever-increasing load of debt on the farm.

As hard as they worked, the day finally came when Russell and Catherine saw no other solution to their situation than to sell what remained of the farm. Selling everything, lock, stock and barrel, would pay off all their debts and give them a fresh start. They would go to one of the cities, maybe up north to Dallas, or possibly back east somewhere. Russell would find work and G.W. was old enough to do a man's work and earn a man's pay. Together, and as a family, they would somehow survive.

The farm was put up for sale. That was when Victoria Lovett, the daughter of Naomi and Ned, came driving out to the Squyres farm with a proposal. She would buy their farm, but they would continue living there and in the same house the Squyres had always lived in. Instead of a fixed rent she would take half of what they produced. She would also provide half the cost of the seed and supplies, as well as the required tools and equipment to raise the crops they planted. She would pay the costs as they were incurred during the year and settle up with Russell at harvest. Compared to other tenant farmers it was an extremely generous offer.

Catherine, on her own, would have flatly refused the offer. In effect, it put the Squyres in the position of being servants to the daughter of a slave Russell's family once owned. They would be little better than slaves themselves, bound to the land they worked for its owner.

But Russell argued that the share of their crops that Victoria would take was much less than what he had been paying toward their ever-growing load of debt and the interest on it each year. They could stay in their home and go on as before, while keeping more of what they produced from their labors. There was no other way to look at Victoria's offer than generous, most likely stemming from Victoria's life-long friendship with Russell's sister, Phinetta. The two women had always been friends. In fact, Victoria was sitting by Phinetta's bedside when she died in 1880, just like their mothers had been together when Oratio died back in 1863.

So they stayed on their land as permanent tenant farmers. Catherine nearly choked every time the grandly dressed Victoria came riding in her carriage to see them. She could barely add the title "Miss" before Victoria's name, the proper salutation to the woman who owned their land now.

Before long, G.W. took over the running of the farm. He was twenty-one when his father died in 1894. By then, his sister, Matilda Oratio, was already married and his youngest brother, sixteen year old John Tobias, likely would be soon to follow. With the house emptying, Catherine encouraged her son to court a girl he liked at church. In 1895, as soon as she was eighteen, G.W. married his sweetheart, Matilda Adeline Bissett.

The only thing that changed after the wedding was that Matilda came to live with G.W. and his mother. Catherine wanted to give them the bedroom that she had shared with Russell, the bedroom that had belonged to Leroy and Oratio before that, but Matilda sweetly insisted Catherine should stay in the room. Matilda and Leroy took over the empty bedroom that had belonged to his sisters. Until he was married, John Tobias stayed in the room he had previously shared with G.W., reveling in the privacy and luxury of a space of his own.

It had been a happy time for G.W. and his gentle Matilda. They had sixteen years together, and seven children: two sons and five daughters.

Although there was little extra money, theirs was a happy home. Matilda often sang as she went about her chores. She often stopped her work to play the game they were now calling "baseball" with her children, or to carry a picnic lunch down to the creek, or to spend half the afternoon reading a favorite book with her young ones gathered around her. Her chores were never neglected because she was quick and efficient in getting the work done and the children gladly helped her.

When it came time for the spring planting, the seemingly endless hoeing or "chopping" of weeds among the young cotton plants, and then picking the cotton to take to market in the fall, Matilda would lead them all in singing as they worked in the fields. She brought ginger water to them on the hottest days and made a noontime reward of enjoying a family picnic lunch in the shade at the far side of the fields. Whenever G.W. prayed, he always included a prayer of thanksgiving for his sweet wife.

Matilda had a hard time with the youngest child, Eula. The child was born healthy enough, but Matilda did not bounce back in the same way she had with the others. As she lay in bed those first weeks, under the doctor's orders, the older girls helped their mother tend the baby and keep the house. Before he said Matilda could get out of bed, the doctor took G.W. aside to sternly warn him against Matilda having another baby. Another pregnancy would kill her, he warned G.W. and then he instructed a mortified and ashamed G.W. in what he could do to keep Matilda from getting pregnant again. G.W. was ready to swear off all such activity after that discussion, and actually did for a time as he prayed for strength, but Matilda soon won him over, convincing him she enjoyed, and now missed, their marriage bed as much as he did.

Then, as baby Eula was weaned and had her first birthday, Matilda told G.W. she wanted one more baby. Just one more, she insisted. As G.W. withdrew from her again, hoping she would see the folly of it, she grew more insistent. Eventually he returned to their bed but Matilda knew what to do, or rather she knew what to keep G.W. from doing, and as careful as he tried to be, she was pregnant again.

This pregnancy was difficult from the start. The doctor wanted to terminate it, saying it was necessary to protect Matilda. But Matilda would have nothing to do with that. She cried and threatened to leave G.W. if he insisted on it. She would go away, far away, until the baby was born, she said. By then, Matilda was almost too sick to get out of bed. The doctor said the baby was toxic. Matilda was puffy and swollen, with fingers and toes that looked like sausages. There was no way she could leave. G.W., hating himself, went along with his wife's wishes, hoping that she would miscarry and that would be the end of it. But she carried the baby almost full term and only a few hours into the labor her heart stopped, killing both Matilda and the baby she was delivering.

In 1911, when their mother died, Baby Eula was two years old and little Louie was almost six. G.W. could see it was the hardest on those two. The others seemed to handle it better. Dora, the oldest at fifteen, was still weak from having scarlet fever, but she willingly quit school and took over her mother's role the best she could. They all helped, but the load proved to be too much for Dora, and the doctor scolded G.W. for over-working the girl and ordered complete bed rest for her to recover. Anything else and G.W. would lose Dora too.

He was left with no other choice than to marry the only woman who seemed to be even vaguely interested, Lillie Mott. A step-mother, regardless how sour and plain she may be, was necessary to fill the vacancy Matilda left behind. The years that followed were dark and grim, and almost unbearable for G.W.

He could see the effects of Lillie on his children, Eula withdrawn into herself, Louie missing school and showing welts on the backs of her bare legs too often. Lillie was harsh and cold, pushed G.W. away when he reached out for her, in or out of their bedroom. He knew almost immediately he had made a grave mistake. His only happiness came when he was working in his fields with his children around him. He could almost imagine that nothing had changed – that Matilda was preparing their lunch and would come soon to join them. That she would spread out a picnic under the shade trees at the far side of the field. But instead he would see little Louie coming toward them, lugging a basket almost as big as herself, eager and excited to join them, and patient with little Eula who tottered along behind. At those times, G.W. could barely keep himself from breaking down.

In 1915, when she became pregnant, he hoped Lillie would change. A baby of her own might awaken the motherly side in her. But Lillie almost visibly cringed when the baby was placed in her arms the first time to nurse. She began handing the baby off to Louie as much as possible. Louie was ten years old by then and loved the baby. She held little Lucy in one arm while she did her chores with the other. G.W. could see she would be a tender and loving mother one day, if she was ever given the chance.

For a while, every year had been better than the one before it. G.W. felt fortunate and also a little guilty when prices soared during the Great War. His guilt would have been worse if he himself had not offered up two sons to the war. He also reasoned that the beef and cotton he raised were helping the United States and its allies win that war. In the end, he began to accept that he deserved to be rewarded for his work.

When the war was over, everyone braced themselves for a decline in prices, but the harvest of 1919 was better than ever. Cotton prices were apparently going to remain at this level. Before he had planted the 1919 cotton crop, G.W. met with Victoria Lovett about putting all the land in cotton again for one more year. Up through 1917, they had a system of rotating a portion of the cotton fields into peanuts every year. The alternate crop replenished the soil and there was an increasing demand for peanuts.

When war was declared in 1917 the peanut crop was already planted, but with the increased need for cotton for the war effort, as well as the increased price, Victoria agreed with planting the entire 120 acres in cotton for 1918. The decision paid off handsomely.

Against Lillie's protests, he gave a generous portion of the money from the 1918 harvest to his son William and his bride, Stella Bailey, to help get them started. William used all the money for a down payment on 50 acres. Then G.W. gave his daughter, Katie, and her new husband William Perry Bailey (a cousin to William's new wife, Stella) a handsome amount of cash as a wedding gift that helped them get started too. If this continued he would be able to help all his children. Other than that, his bills were paid and they would live comfortably for another year. It was a time of plenty.

G.W. and Victoria agreed to do the same again in 1919. The crop was another success. The only sadness that year was that his oldest daughter Dora died just after the harvest. The doctor said her weakened heart finally gave out. G.W. used a generous portion of his profits to buy a fine monument to mark her grave.

Now in 1920 all 120 acres were planted in cotton again. The New Orleans price for cotton that April was 42 cents a pound. If they could produce at least the same yield as 1919, it would mean that Victoria and G.W. would be splitting almost $22,000 that fall. The land had never produced that kind of profit. G.W. and Victoria agreed the next year they would begin the rotation into peanuts again. A rest for the soil was overdue.

So, once again the entire 120 acres were planted in cotton. The remainder of the 200 acre farm was taken up with the scrub wood around the creek, grazing land for the cattle, the family garden that produced most of what the family ate, the barn, outbuildings and the house. Not a single square foot of ground was wasted.

The cotton came on strong and healthy that year, surprising even G.W. It was a joy to chop away weeds and watch the plants grow. The rains came just at the right times. The blossoms were beautiful and as the blooms finished, the rounded sacks of seeds and fiber called "bolls" were healthy as they enlarged and filled. The matured bolls would be ready to pick in the fall.

G.W. began estimating his yield, conservatively calculating what the crop would sell for. He optimistically hoped for 550 pounds per acre, a new record and seemingly too optimistic until he walked the field again and saw just how bountiful the harvest was going to be. Victoria drove out every week to have a look, happy and pleased. Even Lillie was in rare good humor. They planned a special Fourth of July celebration, complete with ice cream and fireworks.

When their celebration was finished, and all the family gathered, he shared the good news. They sat patiently, then with increasing interest, as he went through his calculations and finally shared the number with them, his share of this year's harvest. It was more than they could comprehend. In 1920, when the average annual wage for the American worker was $1,236, or $103 per month, the cotton in their fields would net them a little over $15,000. None of them had ever seen that much money all at once. They were rich!

There was a spontaneous celebration, everyone toasting each other with lemonade. Even Lillie, holding two year old Walter on her lap, was smiling and happy for once. G.W. let them all celebrate and then settle down a little bit before he shared his next bit of news. When he sold the harvest that fall, he would give each of his children, including his son-in-law and daughter-in-law, a share of cash. It would be fifty dollars for each of the older children down through Eula, who was now eleven years old. The little ones, all Lillie's children, would not be left out, either. Little Lucy, now age five, Crockett age three and baby Walter, age two would each have twenty dollars for Santa Claus to spend on the toys of their choice that Christmas.

That night, Lillie Mae, Louie and Eula took the Sears and Roebuck catalog to their room. Usually it was called a 'wish book' because that was all anyone really did with a Sears and Roebuck catalog – wish for what you could not have, but they were empowered with a grand amount to spend. Lillie Mae numbered three sheets of paper and kept track of page and item number for all the things she and her sisters chose from the catalog. They dreamed over the drawings of beautiful store-bought dresses, hats and pocket books. Each girl bashfully selected things from the pages of ladies under things, lacy slips and other unmentionables they could not even imagine really wearing.

They started giggling over the pictures, trying to imagine themselves in those things and like the ladies in the drawings, standing and casually talking to each other as if they were not in their underwear. In the bedroom he shared with Lillie Mott, G.W. was happy too. He had just shared with her the rest of his plan for the harvest money - to buy back the farm, and for once Lillie did not spurn his affections. He felt empowered and alive. After harvest time he would answer to no one but himself.

Even at the going market price of $69 per acre, his share of the harvest would cover the $13,800 purchase price for the farm. He planned to have a cashier's check already made out to hand over to Victoria Lovett when they met in town. The farm would belong to the Squyres again. He was happy - happy that he could finally bring the farm back to the family, happy that Lillie finally seemed to be happy, and happy that he could provide the things his daughters were so delighted to be ordering, once the harvest came in. He told Lillie to go to the general mercantile in Nixon that Saturday and buy herself and all the girls a store-bought dress and new shoes, too. They could wear their new dresses to church on Sunday. She would buy new shirts and britches for little Crockett and Walter too. It would be on account for now, but that would be easily paid, come harvest time.

It was the same across Texas. Sharecroppers who subsisted on only a few hundred dollars a year farming twenty acres were now realizing their share of the harvest would be nearly $1,500. Even after they paid their landlords for the amounts borrowed and owed over the past year, there would still be money to spend. People began dreaming of what to buy: a radio, some new furniture, ready to wear dresses, shirts, suits and shoes. The sky seemed to be the limit. There was even a funny story going around about some farm boys who went into the mercantile and wanted to buy silk underwear for themselves, so flush with cash they would be. Everyone looked forward to harvest. The growing conditions continued to be perfect, assuring a bumper crop for all that fall.

But as July passed, a cloud appeared on the horizon. In Dallas and New Orleans, cotton brokers performing their early calculations of the estimated 1920 harvest began to realize there would be a huge surplus. Along with the bumper crop, orders were dropping, a natural - but delayed - response to the decrease in demand for cotton following the completion of the war. Without armies marching, there just was not the same worldwide need for cotton as there had been. It had just taken a while for the decrease to work its way through the system.

Then the disaster began. While the price per pound dropped some during July, everyone said it was to be expected - that during good years the price always dropped a little bit right about now. It was natural and would correct itself by the time the cotton was actually picked. But G.W. told Lillie to not charge anything else to the account at the mercantile. He still wanted to have enough to buy back the farm when he sold the harvest.

The cotton crop was still coming on strong, too strong some said, and throughout August the price continued a steady decline. After church, the area farmers talked about holding onto their harvest a while and selling it later in the fall when the price began going back up. It always happened like that, the price went down the most right when the farmers sold and then the middlemen jacked the price back up, making even more money for themselves. This time they would outsmart those peckerwoods and just keep their cotton off the market. G.W. talked to Victoria, chafing a bit that he had to share the decision with her, but she agreed to hold on to their cotton a while longer, but only until the end of October, just to see what the price did. It could not go much lower than it already had, she said.

The cotton was picked, ginned and baled. G.W.'s harvest yielded almost 150 bales of cotton, each bale weighing the standard 500 pounds. He had no place to store them, so holding onto the crop was proving to be difficult. An anxious Victoria arranged for the bales to be taken on to Houston and held in a warehouse there for 30 days. The cost of doing that was significant and would cut into their profits. Finally, at the end of November, they sold the cotton at fifteen cents a pound. After covering his share of the warehousing, G.W.'s share was just over $3,000. It was the least amount he had earned in almost a decade. Others were less lucky. In December the price declined even further to thirteen and a half cents a pound. By the following March the price had slipped to less than ten cents a pound, the lowest price for cotton in decades.

The cotton price collapse of 1920 caused an economic depression that lasted through 1921. With the devastating effect felt for two consecutive harvests, G.W. put away his plans of buying back the farm. He grew less cotton and more peanuts, and still ran cattle, but would never see the profits he had seen in the previous decade.

His son, Lester, twenty-one now, gave up the young woman he was seeing to stay home and help his father. To Louie and her sisters, it seemed like their father deflated and shrank into himself after that. He still farmed, but without enthusiasm. It reminded them of the way he had been after their mother had died, a shadow - just going through the motions. As time passed he became more distant. Mama Lillie became even more bitter, if that was possible. She would sit on the porch for hours at a time, staring off into the distance. Louie and Lillie

Mae shared the running of the house. Then Lillie Mae told Louie tearfully one night in their room that Travis Griffin had asked her to marry him.

"That's wonderful Lillie Mae!" Louie said. Travis was a handsome young man and he clearly loved Lillie Mae. She was eighteen now and could do what she wanted. She did not need Papa's permission to marry anyone, but Louie knew Papa would not object. Travis' visits were one of the few times Papa perked up and smiled, sometimes even telling Travis a joke. No, Papa and even Mama Lillie both seemed to like the young man. "But why are you crying? Don't you love him?"

"Yes, yes, I do," Lillie Mae sniffed and then blew her nose. "But I don't see how I can ever leave you and Eula here alone with that woman," she began sobbing again. "She was always so mean to you two, especially you, Louie."

"Oh, she's not as bad as she used to be," Louie said, feeling completely grown up at sixteen. "Or at least she doesn't scare me as much as she used to. And besides, I am as big as she is now. Don't you worry about us, Lillie Mae. If Travis wants to marry you then you go on and marry him."

Eula echoed Louie. "Yes, marry him, Lillie Mae, then we can come and visit you."

"Or maybe you can even come and live with us," Lillie Mae offered.

"Not when you are newlyweds we can't, Lillie Mae," Louie said. "What are you thinking? Do you think Travis would want to have his sisters-in-law around all the time like that?"

"No, I guess not. At least we won't be very far away." Lillie Mae said. The Griffin farm was just down the road and Travis' father was giving him fifty acres to get started.

"Besides, I couldn't leave little Lucy behind," Louie added. Little Lucy was now six years old. "She is almost like a daughter to me. I don't think Mama Lillie cares a fig for her. I will probably stay here until she is grown up too."

"But that is not fair to you, Louie. You should be able to marry and have your own family like me."

"There is plenty of time for that," Louie said, but not very convincingly. "Anyway, no one is exactly beating down the front door for me."

She thought it was unlikely they ever would. It was easier for Lillie Mae, who was so beautiful, and her other sisters, too. Louie was not beautiful, not even nice-looking. No one ever looked at her, except that one time Mr. Bailey looked at her in church all those years ago. Back then he was going off to the war and he had probably forgotten all about her by now. He had been injured somehow too, and was taking a long time to heal, or so she heard. No, she definitely would not be getting a proposal from him, either.

If Louie was smarter, she could go someplace and get a job. She could be one of those career girls who were living in the big cities now. She could go up to Dallas or over to Houston and have a little apartment and work in an office. Or maybe she could work as an operator for the telephone company.

She got that idea from a short film extra that played when Travis and Lillie Mae had taken Louie along when they went to see a motion picture. In the film, there were rows and rows of career girls in short dresses and silk stockings sitting on high stools in front of the big switchboards of a telephone exchange. Those girls connected telephone calls until five o'clock and then went out smoking cigarettes and dancing. The film had been intended to show the perils of city life for innocent young women, but Louie dreamed aloud about it sometimes at night, always assuring Eula she would wait until Eula was old enough too so they could go and be telephone operators together. When they left, she would have to beg Mama Lillie to let her take Little Lucy along. She could not bear to think of leaving her behind.

CHAPTER EIGHTEEN

DeWitt County Texas
1923-1937

In 1923 the Army hospital released Vol. There was a push to have cases cleared now that the war had been over for years and Vol was among the ones his doctor agreed could be sent home, if he was under careful supervision. Albert and Nannie went to New York one last time to bring him home.

Before they saw their son, they met with his doctor. They learned he was not cured, but the best thing for him now was quiet rest. The doctor thought their farm was the best place for that. Certainly it was better than the hospital in New York and anywhere else the army might send him. The doctor promised to be in touch by mail and said Vol's parents should write regularly to report on his progress. For the time being, Vol should live with them in their home and avoid situations that might make him anxious. The doctor said large crowds and loud noises, such as the backfiring of a passing automobile or someone firing a gun might bring on an attack of acute anxiety. They assured the doctor their farm was quiet. They did not own a motorcar and they would make sure no one hunted on the property. They were happy to be taking their son home, at last. Nannie cheerfully declared the best thing for Vol was to be back in Texas.

The doctor issued a mild sedative to calm Vol for the trip home. The previous week when the doctor shared the news that his parents were coming and would take him home, Vol became agitated and angry and threw his metal lunch tray across the room. The doctor had injected him with a calming drug and it had worked. The sedative was keeping him calm now and the doctor carefully instructed his parents on giving the drug, in pill form, twice a day. He promised that Vol could be weaned away from the pills as soon as he was settled at home and was in calm surroundings.

The trip home was tense, but uneventful. Even though it was an added expense, Albert arranged for them to have a private compartment on the trains. Vol could relax without feeling like people were watching him, another thing that made him nervous. Nannie and Albert kept careful watch on their son when they changed trains in Chicago, but Vol seemed fascinated with the building and the bustle of the crowd did not bother him as they anticipated it would. Albert and Nannie slept in shifts so they could keep watch, making sure Vol did not wander, or worse yet, try to get off the train at one of the stops along the way. The drugs that kept him calm also seemed to confuse him, but Albert was especially patient explaining the same things over and over, even though their son seemed to remember nothing they told him. Nannie had remembered to bring along some of the books that had been his favorites as a child, thinking it would be a nice memory for him. She discovered that reading those books to him helped calm him whenever she noticed he was growing anxious.

The exhausted trio finally reached the train station in Nixon. Their daughter Stella and her husband William would be waiting at the station for the train to take them home. Nannie could feel herself beginning to relax. Soon they would have Vol home. They could all relax.

As the train pulled in, Nannie could see others were there too. Many others, even one old soldier wearing his Civil War uniform, were waiting to welcome Vol home. They wanted to welcome him the same way they had welcomed the other soldiers who returned in 1918. Nannie had hoped to have a simple homecoming, quietly get off the train, transfer to William and Stella's waiting automobile, and take Vol home where they could have a quiet dinner and help him get adjusted to being home again. Vol's old horse, still alive after all this time, would be waiting for him to see when he was ready – the doctor said the sight of horses tended to upset him. That would have to come in time, but Nannie felt sure that seeing Chance would help heal whatever was wrong inside Vol.

The group assembled on the platform was even spilling over into the grass beside it. Dozens of farm wagons hitched to horses, and even automobiles were parked around the depot. Seemingly all of Nixon and most of Gonzales, Karnes, Lavaca and DeWitt counties had turned out. It looked like the mayor and the preacher from the Baptist Church were standing on the platform in their Sunday suits, waiting to make some kind of presentation.

Nannie knew it was too early to give Vol another pill. Hopefully, the one from this morning was still working. She quietly turned to Vol and took his hand in hers, "Honey, it looks like some people wanted to come and say hello to you. Let's just say hello and then we will go home and have a nice dinner. Daddy and I will be right here with you. Stella and William are here too."

"Stella?" Vol said hopefully. He had not seen his sister since 1917. "Stella is here?"

"Yes," Nannie said with relief, at his recognition and the surprising calm Vol was displaying. "Her husband is here too. You remember she married William Squyres. You boys used to call him Willie Squillie, I think."

Vol nodded and gave the faintest hint of a smile – so rare for him. He ran his finger around under his shirt collar, not in a nervous or fidgeting way, but as any young man would do to adjust and straighten an uncomfortable starched collar. Then he checked his tie. He looked so handsome in the new suit they had brought for him. Nannie did not want to see him in his uniform ever again. Hopefully they would all get through this fine.

As assertive as she could be and still be mannerly, Stella stood on the platform and talked to the crowd as the train approached the station, interjecting herself into the mayor's little program that afternoon. She frankly and openly told them Vol had suffered shell shock, an injury as real as any other injury. She told them the little that was known about it and that while he was much improved, he still needed things to be calm: no loud noises, no sudden movements, and no pressing of the crowd against him. Please, please just be calm and only say hello, and then only if he spoke to you first. He would know they were here. She knew that her brother, and her parents, had to be exhausted from their long journey all the way from New York. William and she would take him home where he would rest and everyone would have plenty of chances to see him again after today.

So, when the train came to a complete stop, the first one down the steps was Albert, followed by Nannie, who led her son carefully down the steps, holding his hand in her own. As he stepped off the bottom step into the sunshine, Vol looked solemnly around, then looked at the ground bashfully, but still tipped his hat to the crowd. Then Stella stepped forward, taking his hand. Vol looked up and saw his sister. For a moment, in the silence of the crowd, he looked like he might be confused, or might give in to a wave of anxiety, but instead he spoke. He spoke one word.

"Stella," he said softly in recognition.

Then he burst into tears. Stella pulled her brother to her, hugging him as he wept in great sobs, hiding his face against her shoulder, embarrassed to be crying like this. Nannie came and put her arms around her children and then Albert and William gently patted Vol's shoulders. Women in the crowd, and a few men even, dabbed at their eyes as they quietly watched the reunited family. The only sounds were the wind blowing and Vol's muffled sobs.

The train pulled away: it had a schedule to keep if it was going to arrive in San Antonio on time. Finally, Albert turned to the crowd and spoke, "Folks, Nannie and I and the rest of our family surely do want to thank you all for coming out today to welcome our Vol back home. We would like to invite you all to come out to the place and see us sometime real soon, but right now, I know Vol is real tired from his journey. It's been a long, long road home for him all the way from France back here to Nixon, but I know he's just as happy and proud as he can be to be back home in Texas. You all come on out to the place and see us real soon, now."

Stella, guiding Vol with his head still against her shoulder, led the family as they made their way to the car. The well-wishers remained where they were, silent and unmoving in respect for the returning hero who still needed time to heal. They watched as Vol got into the car, in the middle of the back seat with one parent on either side. William stood beside the front door while Stella got into the front seat, with the younger brother Perry in the middle, and then closed it for her before he walked to the front to turn the crank and start the engine. It started in one crank. Stella smiled and waved out the front window to everyone as William slipped the car in gear to drive away. It was then the crowd erupted into applause. People shouted, "Welcome home, Vol!" and "We are proud of you, son!" until the car was well out of earshot.

In the crowd, Louie and her sisters, along with their brother, Lester, who had driven them all over to Nixon in the farm wagon, cheered and waved the little American flags that had been passed around by the Nixon General Mercantile. They were told they could keep those flags as souvenirs, and even though "Nixon General Mercantile" was boldly printed on the cardboard handle, the Squyres sisters all said it would be a nice memento of the day Mr. Vol Bailey finally came home from the Great War.

* * * * *

After that afternoon at the station, Louie knew the only way she would ever see Vol Bailey again was at church. True, he was her sister-in-law Stella's brother, but even though they saw Stella often, the two families did not socialize much. The Bailey farm was in the opposite direction from the church, and even farther away from the church than the Squyres farm. She supposed it did not matter, anyway. He would probably not even remember that she had told him she would be praying for him when they had that service at the church in 1917. It was foolish to think he would remember her – or even recognize her. She was only a twelve year old girl at the time. Now she was seventeen. He was way too old for her anyway. Lillie Mae and Eula agreed with her on that.

However, Louie started putting her best foot forward after he came home. He looked so handsome in his suit and tie, with a starched collar, when he stepped off the train. She was only a face in the crowd then, he really had not looked at anyone. In times past, Mama Lillie would have scolded Louie and said she was wasting her time for taking as long as she did to get herself ready that day they went to meet Vol's train.

But Mama Lillie was still not quite herself, even though two years had passed since the collapse of cotton prices back in 1921. Lillie devoted her time almost entirely to taking care of Minnie Lee. Something wasn't right with Minnie Lee and Mama Lillie almost went completely out of her mind when that baby was born. Now, when she wasn't tending the baby she mainly sat on the porch and let Louie and Eula take care of the house, and the rest of Lillie's children. Little Lucy was eight years old now and adored Louie. Crockett was six and Walter was five. They pretty much thought of Louie as their mother, anyway.

Lillie would still hiss her hateful things to Louie, but they did not hurt so much. And once, not long ago, Lillie decided she was going to whip Lucy with the strap. No real reason, except Lucy was getting too full of herself and needed a whipping. She took the strap down from the wall and went after Lucy who was cowering and pleading, but Louie was not far behind. When Lillie's hand came up to make the first swing, Louie grabbed it and took it away. In front of Lucy and the rest of the children she made it perfectly clear to Lillie that if she ever took that strap down off the wall again, Louie would use it on her instead. Louie, as she had told her sisters, was bigger than Lillie now and could do it if she had to. Lillie could sit in her chair and glower at Louie all she wanted, but she knew she was licked.

It was not a happy home, but Louie made the best she could of it. Her cooking had improved and with Eula's, and even Lucy's adoring help, the house ran efficiently. Papa was recovering some, but was still defeated. His lot was cast. He would be a tenant farmer the rest of his life with nothing to pass on to his sons. The one change he made several months back was to give Louie a monthly allowance. When Mama Lillie protested, saying they could not afford such foolishness, G.W. overruled her. Louie was a young lady now and needed to have a little money of her own. Even though he did not want her to spend the money on anyone else, she mainly bought things the children wanted first, using anything left over on herself or saving it.

Now, with Vol Bailey back in town, Louie decided to use some of her savings for herself. With Lillie Mae and Eula helping, the next time Lester took them all to town, she went to the general mercantile where she picked out a nice ready-made, store-bought dress of the latest style, a pair of nice young ladies shoes, low cut and with only four lacing eyelets and a modest heel, two pairs of silk stockings, a fashionable new hat, gloves, and even a new pocketbook. Eula helped her put her hair up and she wore the new outfit to church the next Sunday, drawing Mama Lillie's vitriol, of course, as they set out for the walk.

"I see you will be throwing yourself at Mr. Bailey, now that he's home," Lillie observed. "It's a pity it takes someone new coming to town before you have a chance, isn't it. Even more of a pity he's such damaged goods now, isn't it?"

Louie gave Lillie a withering look as she pulled on the new gloves, but since it was Sunday morning, let it drop. Mama Lillie could say nothing to spoil her mood today.

Vol was not at church that day. Stella stopped Louie after the service to admire the new outfit. They chatted a few moments. When Louie got up her nerve to ask Stella about him, her sister-in-law said Vol still needed to rest. "But I can tell him you asked about him," Stella offered.

"Oh no!" Louie wished she had not said anything, "Don't do that. I don't think he will remember me."

"Of course Vol remembers you, Louie, you silly goose. You are my sister-in-law now. How could he not remember you?"

"Well, the last time I saw him, other than at the station I mean, was when he left for France. It was such a long, long time ago, and I was only twelve years old then." Louie felt herself begin to flush and perspire under her arms. She wished she had said nothing.

Stella stood with a slightly surprised look, realizing what was happening. "I could just tell Vol you said hello," she offered.

"Yes! Yes, if you would please. Just tell him I said hello," Louie managed. Stella was·helping her out, but it was still too much and too presumptuous. She hoped no one else was hearing her make such a complete fool of herself. She tucked the new pocketbook under her arm, took Eula's hand and said goodbye to their sister-in law.

When Lester announced over breakfast that week that he needed to go into town, Louie asked if she might go with him. Mama Lillie objected immediately, of course - just how was she supposed to get along all morning without Louie? Eula said she would do Louie's work as well as her own. G.W. said Louie could go, ending the discussion.

Although she had only worn the new dress one time, she had to buy another. That was mostly because of the preacher's sermon last Sunday morning. He titled it *The Perils of Every Modern Woman* on the new sign with changeable letters in front of the church, hoping to stir up some interest while drawing on the immensely popular serialized motion picture, *The Perils of Pauline.* But it was his same basic sermon. After reading some scripture, he launched into a diatribe about women wanting to take over the roles of men in modern society. They were unnatural women, who were still not satisfied now that they had the vote. They were unfeminine women, trying to become men and wearing drop-waist dresses that completely hid the feminine body – intended to be a thing of beauty by their creator. They were unchaste women, leaving their families without the benefit of marriage to live in dens of iniquity in the big cities, otherwise known as apartment houses. They turned away from the roles God intended for them and let the devil lead them into all sorts of unimaginable depravity.

From there he went into his usual Sunday morning admonitions against the perils of alcohol, and the mixing of the races. From the corner of her eye, Louie could see her father fold his arms across his chest as he glared at the preacher. Everyone in the county knew of the Squyres background and even though they were completely accepted as white, the preacher insisted that was not what he was preaching against, but mulattos, and the like, instead. That unwavering glare from G.W. on Sunday mornings was enough to move the preacher along to his conclusion which always contained the warning that they were living in the end of times and this may be the last Sunday they would have to turn their souls over to Jesus. When He came back it would be too late to do that then.

Until that sermon, the only depraved things Louie knew about were wearing silk dressing gowns in the daytime, drinking hard liquor and listening to Negro music on the Victrola. So when the preacher referred to the devil leading young single women in the city into "all kinds of unimaginable depravity" that was what she pictured in her mind - a young woman doing all three at one time in her big city apartment. Then in her mind, she was the young woman. Try as she might, she could not push that sinful image out of her mind.

And now, thanks to the preacher's sermon, her new dress with its dropped waist and a long-point collar that covered and minimized her bosom seemed to indicate that Louie did not want to be a woman. She had paid $2.95 for that dress and worn it only once, but now she would have to come up with something more suitable to wear to church. She especially did not want Vol to think she was trying to be un-feminine or depraved when he came to church, especially if that topic was now going to be a regular part of the Sunday sermon.

Lester enjoyed the ride to town. He propped one foot up on the wagon's buckboard and held the reins loosely. The horse knew where they would going and would likely go there even if Lester dropped the reins altogether.

"Buying another new dress today, Louie?" he teased.

Louie laughed softly and nodded her head. She loved Lester and was always good-natured about his teasing. "Apparently I need to wear something to church that is cinched in at the waist and shows my bosoms. Otherwise the preacher says I'm trying to be a man."

"I don't think anyone who could see you would accuse you of that." Lester squinted his eyes like he was examining her as he rubbed his freshly shaved chin. "You just have to remember that the preacher man knows he has to preach a good long sermon, scare the good people away from sinning and bring the required number of souls to Jesus. It's a lot easier for him to get all fired up once a week than to go back to farming and working every other day of the week like the rest of us. Besides, I don't recall seeing many men in a dress like you wore on Sunday morning, unless it was the old preacher man himself. On Sunday mornings, the preacher wore a choir robe like the small choir behind him."

Louie laughed outright at that. "Still, I think I will buy a McCall's sewing pattern and some yardage. I can make two or three dresses for what I paid for that one."

"All these new clothes all of a sudden. Are you sweet on someone, Louie?"

Louie denied it too quickly, "No! Well, no one special anyway. But I am almost eighteen now, Lester."

"Yes, and you deserve it. Although you always look beautiful anyway."

"Oh Lester," Louie scoffed. "You never were a good liar."

They argued good-naturedly back and forth a while on that. Louie challenged him by comparing herself to every girl in the three-county area who was her age. Lester declared Louie was more beautiful than every one of them. Any girl she named would bring a different response from him: "ugly as sin," "plain as mud," "could be the fat lady at the circus," and every other expression he could think of to depreciate the girl Louie brought up. When she brought up yet one more girl her age and Lester could think of no more insults he simply said, "the sister of the fat lady at the circus," making Louie laugh so hard she said she was going to fall out of the wagon if he did not stop. Lester had to be her favorite brother.

They were in good moods when they entered the Nixon General Mercantile, and the wife of the owner, realizing Louie was back and seeing another good sale, was especially attentive. Louie explained what she was doing and the woman helped Louie look at all the dresses in the ready-to-wear section, then helped her find a pattern in the pattern catalog that was closest to Louie's favorite. Fortunately, the pattern she finally selected had just arrived from McCall's, so Louie would not have to wait for it to be ordered. She bought two lengths of fabric – a soft voile and a lightweight woolen serge in a pale dove gray. The proprietor's wife assured her the material would be lovely when the dresses were made.

Louie was wearing the gray serge version of the dress on the Sunday morning Vol finally came to church. She was also wearing another new hat that went beautifully with the dress. Not even Mama Lillie could find any fault with Louie that morning, signified by her complete silence after conducting a long visual appraisal as they waited for William and Stella to come by to take them to church. These days, instead of walking, the family all piled into the one car. It was crowded, but always fun with Stella keeping them all entertained for the short drive.

Louie was standing with Lucy in the family pew as Vol and his parents approached their pew across the aisle. He could only see her from behind. He wondered who the young woman in the Squyres pew could be. He knew almost all of that family but he did not think he had seen her before. Maybe she was visiting the family. The hymn singing had already started when they arrived and the young lady was turned slightly away from the aisle as she shared the hymnal with the young girl beside her. The low brim of the stylish hat she was wearing hid her face from his view.

After the song ended, the preacher motioned for the congregation to be seated and there was a clatter of hymnals being closed and put away and a rustle of clothing and the groans of the wooden benches as everyone sat. Vol still could not see who the young lady was. The hat hid her face and she was still turned slightly away, her attention given to the young girl beside her. Maybe the young girl was her daughter. It would appear so the way the child was looking up at her.

He kept stealing glances that way, not wanting to be caught staring if she should happen to turn his way. He kept looking back again and again as the church announcements were read, and then through another hymn – the offertory. While the singing congregation remained seated, presumably so it would be easier for them to access their wallets and pocketbooks, the ushers came forward with the offering plates to pass down the rows. Vol felt in his vest pocket for the dollar his father had given him that morning - his offering. The usher was at the end of his row, handing the plate to his father when Vol turned to look again. The young woman was leaning forward to hand the offering plate back to the usher at the end of her row. As she did, she looked up at the man and smiled faintly, handing the plate forward with a smartly-gloved hand. Then something drew her attention to Vol, bringing her gaze over to rest on him.

Seeing the lovely, high cheekbones, the full lips, the smooth and lightly golden skin and the dark hazel-blue eyes beneath the brim of the hat, his breath caught. He did know her. He recognized her. It was Gertrude Squyres. The one everyone called Louie.

He had not seen her since the last morning he had been in this church, the Sunday before he left for France. Back then he had watched her across the aisle, attracted by her poise and calm as she cared for the squirming toddler in her lap. That toddler must be the young girl who looked up at her so adoringly now. Back then, Gertrude had been a gangling young girl, now she was a young woman. He could not believe the transformation. Seeing that she had caught his eye, Gertrude offered a warm and soft smile, barely bringing the dimples to her cheeks, and nodded slightly in recognition before she turned away to settle beside her sisters for the coming sermon.

Vol could not help but continue his stare, noticing a slight pink flush beginning at the base of her neck. Finally, his father firmly tapped his knee, bringing his focus away from her. Albert then pointed a single finger forward, but kept his hand down and well out of the sight of anyone else who might see it. Vol intently stared only at the preacher after that. He had to remember to behave himself if he was going to be going to church again.

The preacher was really wound up that morning, encouraged by some extra "amens" from the nearly-deaf old men seated on the front row, and preached long past twelve o'clock. The invitational hymn produced one lost soul, with the result of the preacher holding the invitation open at least eight more verses, encouraged by the results of his sermon. Louie thought about what Lester had said about the preacher, and had to bite her lips together and keep her eyes down, lest she laugh out loud.

Finally, church was over and they could make their way outside to the fresh air and sunshine. Louie and Eula always prepared the family's Sunday dinner. Stella and William were invited to join them today so there were two pies, freshly baked yesterday, potatoes already peeled and cut up in a pan of water ready to be boiled and mashed, green beans seasoned with bacon drippings, and a special treat, two fat hens already cut up and waiting to be dipped in egg, milk and flour and then fried as soon as the skillet was hot.

As Louie came down the church steps, holding Lucy's hand, she saw G.W. and Mama Lillie talking to Stella's parents, Albert and Nannie Bailey. Stella was there with them, laughing gaily over something. Even Mama Lillie was smiling at Stella. Stella's little brother Perry, (well not so little any more since he was thirteen and shooting up like a weed), was standing a bit apart from them. Boys who were becoming young men at that age did not want the girls at church to see them with their mothers for some reason. Between Perry and his parents, Vol was standing almost by himself, obviously uncomfortable and feeling a bit out of place.

Louie tucked her pocketbook under her arm, took a new grip on Lucy's hand and walked directly over to Vol, careful of her heels in the soft earth of the church yard. She stuck out her hand and said, "I bet you don't remember me. I am Louie Squyres, and this is my little sister, Lucy. She was just a baby the last time you were here."

Vol looked up at her, unsmiling for a long moment, swallowed and then managed, "Miss Gertrude."

"Anyway, I just wanted to welcome you back home, Mr. Bailey."

"Vol," he said. Then he paused, "I'd like it if you would call me Vol, Miss Gertrude."

Nannie was surprised. It was the most Vol had said to anyone outside the family since he came home. Of course, Louie was not exactly outside the family, she was Stella's sister-in-law. Vol would feel more comfortable around someone related to Stella.

"And you can just call me Gertrude, if you like, Vol," Louie replied pleasantly. "We are practically related now, aren't we, with your sister married to my brother, so you don't need to be so formal."

Mama Lillie was giving Louie a harsh stare for showing herself and being so forward. Rather than risking her stepmother making some comment, Louie stopped herself from saying more, gave a small smile and started to turn to go.

"You prayed for me," Vol said in his halting way.

"Yes. Yes, I did. We all did Vol. I am so thankful you are home now and you weren't hurt."

She was aghast. They all were. She could not have said anything worse than to bring up his injury like that. She wanted the ground to open up and swallow her right then and there. She tried to smile, but was afraid it was more of a grimace. Stella opened her mouth to say something, anything, to help Louie out, but, before she could, Vol took Louie's free hand in both his hands and said, "Thank you. I always knew you were praying. Even when I didn't, I still knew."

Louie looked back up at him. It was a beautiful thing to say. It was a beautiful thing for him to do – glazing over her horrible comment in front of everyone. She looked directly into his eyes, eyes that held hers, and smiled again.

Stella, not sure what to say, offered, "Maybe we can all come for lunch." It was not Stella's place to offer of course, and it was four more people than they had planned, but there was always plenty of food, especially on Sunday. They would have to peel a few more potatoes, cut the pies in smaller slices, put out some extra bread and butter, but Stella would help and it would be all right.

G.W. immediately agreed, and then turned to Mama Lillie to add, "There is plenty." She stupidly agreed, having no idea whether there was enough or if there was not. The girls always saw to Sunday dinner. She needed her rest. The girls always watched after baby Minnie Lee for her on Sundays, too.

With all the women working, Sunday dinner was on the table by two o'clock. Mama Lillie, intent on playing hostess to their guests, took charge of the meal although Louie and her sisters knew what to do and did it anyway, in spite of what Lillie said. The only hitch in the preparation was when Lucy dropped the cast iron lid to the skillet, making a loud bang followed by a rolling crescendo like a cymbal until the lid came to a stop on the floor. "Sorry," she apologized with contrition.

Looking through to the sitting room, Louie saw Vol cringe and clamp his hands to his ears at the clatter. She remembered what Stella had told them that day at the train station in Nixon, to avoid sudden and loud noises. Nannie went to her son, gently pulled his hands down and held them between her own hands, speaking softly to him and telling him he was all right. In less than a minute he was fine, and Nannie returned to help with the meal. Louie turned back to the work table, where she was slicing another loaf of bread for the table only to have Mama Lillie catch her eye, and raise her eyebrows in mock disbelief at what they had just seen. Louie hoped Mama Lillie would let it go.

The meal was a happy affair, all of them crowded around the table in the sitting room, with enough chairs rounded up for everyone. Eula, only a year older than Perry, sat by him at the table and urged a third and then a fourth piece of fried chicken onto his plate until Stella tactfully intervened and warned her little brother that there was peach pie coming and he needed to save room. Louie was amused that Perry would apparently still listen to his sister, but anything remotely like that from his mother would have been an insult to his budding young manhood. Texas men were always so strong and independent. It's a wonder any of them lived long enough to become real men.

Thankfully, Vol was not seated by Louie for dinner. It would have been too much for him, and also for her, but they were seated where they could steal glances at each other. Vol would look shyly across the table, wondering how the awkward young girl he remembered had grown into this lovely young woman. Louie, when he caught her eye, would give him an encouraging smile before her eyes dropped back to her plate or she turned to speak to one of her sisters.

Lester organized a baseball game after lunch, saying it was a Sunday tradition at the Squyres farm for as long as anyone could remember - likely going back to when Leroy and Oratio first came here from Louisiana. As the women gathered on the porch to watch the game, that led to the Squyres girls telling the Bailey women about their great-grandparents who came here from Louisiana and more stories even further back than that. Vol, disinclined to join the game since he did not understand the rules thoroughly, listened carefully to the stories from where he sat to one side on the porch railing. It was a comfortable and leisurely afternoon. Mama Lillie was even in a rare good mood.

At five o'clock the remains of the lunch were uncovered for supper, the leftovers having been combined and consolidated on the middle of the table and covered with a clean cloth after lunch. Louie made sandwiches of the leftover chicken and there were still a few slices of peach pie that were cut into even smaller portions and passed around. When supper was finished and the dishes were washed, Albert and Nannie said they really must be going home. Stella and William would drive them home.

After they were all situated in the Ford, with its motor running, they still lingered over goodbyes. Louie had not had another chance to speak to Vol after her unfortunate remarks at church. He looked shyly at her and then looked away. When he looked back again, Louie gave him another warm and encouraging smile. Then William protested they were burning gasoline and the drug store was closed on Sunday so he couldn't get any more, so they had better go or they would be staying the night, too. Vol looked back at Louie and all she could do was give him another understanding smile.

As soon as they were gone, Mama Lillie, who could always be counted on to point out the obvious said, "I don't care what they say, that Vol is still just not right."

Louie opened her mouth to protest, ready to say he was a war hero and deserved more respect than that, but Papa beat her to it. He turned to Mama Lillie, looking like he might hit her, but only said with disgust, "Lillie, just this one time, shut your stupid mouth."

Then he turned and walked into the house. Lillie huffed around a little while outside, sitting at first on the porch and pouting until she realized G.W. was not going to come back out and apologize. She went in the house, past G.W. where he was reading the remnants of his paper, took Minnie Lee from Lucy and went into the bedroom and slammed the door. They all heard the key turn loudly in the lock, but knew it did not matter. G.W. would be gladly spending yet another night on the sofa in the sitting room.

* * * * *

Louie married Vol in January, 1924.

At different times over the year they were courting and then were engaged it seemed that everyone, including his sister Stella, tried to talk her out of it. Louie would agree with them that she knew she did not have to marry him. She acknowledged all of their concerns. She told them she knew he still had problems, that he was not fully healed from the war. She acknowledged that he might never be.

The only thing she was stubborn about was that she loved Vol and he loved her. Eventually they all came around, except Mama Lillie who was peeved to be losing Louie when she needed her the most. Nannie told everyone that Louie was a sensible girl, would be a good mother, and was completely devoted to Vol. With her future mother-in-law's endorsement and praise, no one else could argue.

Knowing a church wedding would be too much for Vol, Louie insisted that they go to the courthouse in Nixon. They were married there by the judge with William and Stella as witnesses, then went back to the Squyres house where her sisters had cake and punch ready. After that, Vol and Louie just went home with his parents. Albert and Nannie set up a honeymoon cottage, of sorts, in what had once been a shed on their farm. It was charming, newly finished on the inside with a small kitchen and even an indoor bathroom. Vol was going to help on the farm, and Albert and Nannie would be close by if they needed anything. The tiny cottage would require little work from Louie, and she and Vol would have most of their meals with Albert and Nannie, so Louie would spend most of her days helping Nannie in the main house. Vol worked alongside his father and the methodical work of the fields seemed to be the best thing for him.

Vol was indeed different. Louie tried her best to learn what he needed and what he could and could not tolerate, but even after the first year she still struggled. He could fly into a rage over the oddest things, like a misplaced book or when Louie moved his things. She tried to explain she had to clean, but it was like he was another person while he completely tore things apart and then put them methodically back together. If he grew too agitated, Louie would run to the main house for his mother, the only person who seemed to be able to calm him at those times.

She stuck it out, determined to make it work for his sake and for her own. She could not imagine having to go back to her father's house and deal with Mama Lillie for the rest of her life. The satisfaction her stepmother would hold over her would last until the end of her days.

Sometimes, Vol seemed to be getting better. The time between his "episodes" as Nannie called them was getting longer. But even Nannie had to admit that the episodes, when they came, were worse.

At Christmas that year, Stella took Louie aside and told her she could come to live with William and herself if she wanted to leave Vol. "You can still leave him, Louie," Stella whispered.

Louie knew what her sister-in-law meant. There were no children to consider. There would only be the stigma of being a divorced woman if she left. Louie considered it, thinking she might leave now and eventually go on to Houston or Dallas. She could apply for work as a telephone operator, the old dream she used to have. Eventually she might meet someone else. Someone who did not care that she was a divorced woman.

But Vol seemed so much better after the holidays, treating Louie nicely and gently and making an effort to not be so particular about how she did things. Louie even tested him, purposely doing a few things she knew made him angry, like letting his food touch on the plate, leaving a book out of the bookcase, and hanging his shirts out of order in his closet. At those times he only looked at her, like he knew she was testing him, and quietly set things back to right. She wondered if he had heard Stella talking to her on Christmas Day, or worse yet, if Stella had said something to him about it.

It did not matter, because in April, Louie realized she could never leave Vol. She was pregnant. Louie had always been regular with her "periods" - the modern term her doctor and others now called the monthly female process. When she missed in March and again in April she knew the truth. She would have a baby that fall. She was now forever tied to Vol.

She was determined to make the best of it. Before she told anyone about the baby she did everything she could to make life as easy as possible for Vol. She kept things just the way he liked them, never let anything be out of place and made sure everything was to his liking. She kept things quiet, the way he liked them. She was determined, especially for the baby's sake, to make a happy home. It was a challenge, but not impossible, with Mama Lillie for a stepmother, she had dealt with much worse in her life.

The baby was born in November, and in the hospital in Nixon. There was really nothing that required Louie to be in the hospital, but hospital births were becoming routine. With the distance the Bailey farm was from town it would give an extra level of safety for both Louie and the baby if any complications should arise. While it was an added expense, Nannie insisted on it, even though the baby was not her first grandchild, since William and Stella already had two children.

Louie wanted to name the baby Albert after Vol's father. By rights, the middle name should have been for her father, George, but Vol wanted the middle name to be Ernest. They called him Albert.

After the baby, life settled into a routine on the farm. Louie helped Nannie and Nannie watched the baby while Louie did her own chores. Vol helped his father on the farm. His brother Perry, almost seventeen now, was showing an increased interest in the farm. Where Vol was a hard and willing worker, Louie could see that Perry grasped the management of the business side of the farm more readily. Albert was sixty-four and was beginning to slow down some. It was better for him that Perry could take over some of that responsibility.

Perry also wanted to make innovations. After the depression of 1920 and 1921, prices had shown a steady recovery and there had been some good years with bountiful harvests. Credit was easy to arrange and Perry encouraged his father to borrow to buy a gasoline powered tractor. They also leased an adjacent farm that had been abandoned when the elderly owner died and whose heirs did not want to farm it. That nearly doubled their harvest of cotton and peanuts. Times were good for the farm.

G.W. Squyres died, apparently of a heart attack, while working his fields in the summer of 1926. He had not been sick a day in his life. When he did not come home, Lester went out and found him among the cotton plants. Louie and Vol left baby Albert with Vol's parents and went to the funeral. Mama Lillie looked like she had given up. On an impulse, Louie told Vol she wanted to go stay with her stepmother for a while, mainly for the benefit of Lucy and her other half-siblings until Lillie could get back to normal, but Vol refused. He flatly said her place was with him and her own family. Lester could manage, he said.

Vol and Louie had a second child, this time a girl, in August, 1927. She was named Nannie for Vol's mother and Maureen because Louie liked it. They called her Maureen.

Albert and Maureen developed a strong bond from the start. Albert was not yet two when his sister was born, and for Louie it was like having two babies at once. Albert was calm and even-tempered and accepted the new baby as though she had always been there. He had his mother's dark complexion, curly hair and intense blue eyes, most likely the same color his great-great-grandmother Oratio's had been from the old family stories.

Maureen had brown hair and dark hazel eyes, almost brown. Louie playfully called Maureen her little Mexican when she played with the babies until one day shortly after Maureen's first birthday. Vol came in from the fields that day and overheard her. He was already tired and out of sorts and hearing that made him so angry that Louie could see he was going to strike her. She quickly put the babies in the baby bed and turned to face him, solidly protecting her children from his wrath and braced for what would come.

It was only one solid slap and she was ready for it, but it still left a bruise on the left side of her face that she could not hide. Even worse than the bruise was that that slap broke her heart. Albert, almost three now, had quickly scrambled back up to the rail of the baby bed and was standing there happily, thinking it was some kind of new game and expecting their playtime to continue. He saw his father strike his mother and screamed out. It was enough that Vol left the room without saying anything else and Louie picked little Albert up to calm him, as well as Maureen who was wailing by then, too. What broke Louie's heart is she could see the change in the way her son looked at his father after that. It could never be the same.

Billy was born in December, 1929, just weeks after the stock market crash in New York City. People were starting to get concerned. Vol's mother, Nannie, had died that summer and Vol's father seemed to give up after that. Even though he still worked on the farm every day, Louie could see he was tired of it. It was like his flame had gone out when Nannie died. Perry stepped forward in taking over most of the running of the farm. He was patient with Vol, made sure the work assigned to his older brother was level and consistent, regardless of how much work there was to do. Louie was grateful to Perry for his consideration. At nineteen, Perry was now married too, to Lily Mae Lambert and a child was on the way. Even before the market crash and all the bad news that was coming from that, Perry had his hands full.

Things completely fell apart for Louie in the spring of 1930. At sixty-eight, Albert said he wanted to retire from farming. He would still live on the farm, and would help out, but he was tired and out of ideas and wanted to turn the farm over to Perry. Perry understood that Vol was to remain on the farm as before, for as long as he wanted and Vol and Louie would remain in their house, now enlarged from two to four rooms for their growing family.

Vol fumed about his father's decision for days. He was the eldest son and the farm should be his. It was not right that Perry and Lily Mae and their child were living in his parents' house now. He would not have them "lording" it over Louie and himself. He would show them. They would all be sorry. By the end of the month, with his father, his brother Perry and even Perry's wife, Lily Mae, trying to talk him out of it, Vol packed up his family and moved them to a tenant farm at the far side of Lavaca County. They would farm a twenty acre share of a peanut farm and receive one-third of the harvest.

Louie did the best she could to clean up the little two room shack and make it livable. Vol sharply criticized everything as though it was her fault and sometimes he punctuated his words with a slap or a punch at Louie. She always made sure she was between him and the children when it looked like he was getting too wound up. She knew no one would ever come to her rescue. Some of the other farmers beat their wives, and their children too, the only way of taking out their frustrations. Louie took some comfort and assurance from the fact that Vol had never gone after his own children like that.

Her fourth child, Alton, was born in December, 1932, and it seemed things were as bad as they could possibly get. Vol's brother Perry lost the little money he had left when the bank closed and was unable to pay the mortgages on the farm. He sold the farm for what he could get and moved his family to San Antonio, hoping to find work there. Word eventually came back that he had secured a position with a natural gas company, working in their gas fields. It was hard work, but they would be all right. Louie realized that even if Vol had stayed on the farm they would be in the same fix now, living as tenant farmers. Vol's father, Albert, was heartbroken. William and Stella had taken him in, crowding their own children together to give Albert his own room in their small house. Everywhere, everyone was having their lives torn up by this thing they were calling the Great Depression.

Louie tried to have something extra for the children for Christmas that year. Albert was seven now and knew all about Santa Claus and the Baby Jesus. Maureen did too. The two little ones would not know any difference, but still, it was Christmas. Her children deserved something. Two days before Christmas, Louie scraped together the little extra money she had, asked a neighbor lady who was friendly to watch the children, and went to the little store the plantation owner operated down by the great cotton barns. Vol was doing day labor with some other men in one of those barns, but she went around the back way so he would not see her.

At the store she found a rubber ball that would be nice for Albert and the other boys. It cost ten cents, almost twice what it would have been in the store in Nixon, but she had no way to get there. She found a small baby doll for Maureen. It had only a cloth body, but a realistic looking head and hands of hard rubber. Louie could sew up a dress and diaper for the doll from the scraps she had in her rag bag. The doll was also ten cents, so she had spent half her money already. She bought four candy canes, one for each child, even though Alton was too young for it, and three oranges, one for each of the older children. With the little money left, she bought a pouch of cigarette tobacco for Vol, not his favorite brand, but one that he smoked sometimes. That would be their Christmas.

Back at home, she hid her purchases away and then brought her children home. They made chains of paper from the colored pages in the old magazines another farm wife gave her. Since there was no tree they hung those chains in the two windows of the shack. Albert and Maureen were excited, talked about Santa Claus and were sure he would find their house now since it was decorated. Vol came home, dirty and grumpy from the work, and went to bed as soon as he had supper.

Two days before Christmas, some church ladies from town drove out in a shiny Buick to bring Christmas baskets to the needy. Louie knew better than to take one. When the ladies came to her door, she lied and firmly said they already had the fixings for their Christmas dinner, but thanked them anyway. One of the ladies peered around Louie where she stood in the shacks door, seeing Albert and Maureen standing there, looking clean and dressed. They could tell there was a fire in the cook stove and could smell the beans Louie had set to boil. Satisfied things were as Louie said, they wished her a Merry Christmas and left.

Vol absolutely forbade Louie accepting anything that might be considered charity, even from another neighbor who might have extra. No one had extra these days he said, so they were lying and trying to give him charity, and he did not need it. If Louie traded something with a neighbor, she made sure Vol knew about it in advance, and for this Christmas she had already arranged to trade a pound of flour and two pounds of beans for a baking chicken. The neighbor had killed the two chickens she had kept scratching around her shack since last summer. The hens were not laying and it was better to kill them than paying to feed them. She approached Louie about the trade, her own supplies running low, and Vol had approved. Louie would first parboil the tough old hen in salt water, and then bake it in a pan with bacon drippings for flavor. The drippings would also flavor a stuffing. They still had a bag of potatoes so she would make a big bowl of mashed potatoes too. A pumpkin pie, from the last pumpkin in the garden would be dessert.

While Vol and the children slept that night, Louie stitched together the little dress for the doll and cut a square of cotton cloth for the diaper. Maureen would be delighted. The plantation owner announced some more day work, so Vol was out of the little house all day again on Christmas Eve. After lunch with the children, Louie prepared the chicken at the kitchen table while the children watched, and set it to simmer on the back of the stove. It would be ready to bake in the morning.

That night, Vol read the Christmas story from the Bible. He was quiet as the children said their prayers. He was surprised when Louie told them to put out their stockings for Santa Claus. He did not know there was anything to fill those stockings. Since they had no fireplace and no mantle to hang the stockings, Louie hammered four tacks in the sash of one window and then helped the children hang their stockings on those tacks. When Albert asked about Santa coming down the chimney, Louie said Santa would know to come in through the front door when he saw the stockings in the window.

When the children were finally asleep in the second room, Louie looked at Vol, put her finger to her lips, and brought out the stash of gifts she had hidden in the upper shelf of the beat-up Hoosier cabinet. Vol wanted to eat an orange right away, but she teasingly told him he would have to wait for Santa too, then gave him the pouch of tobacco. He was happy with that, it had been a long time since he had smoked, and he rolled a cigarette right away. Together they put an orange in each stocking, then the doll in the top of Maureen's stocking and the rubber ball in the top of Albert's with a candy cane poking out of the top of all four stockings. Louie let herself lean back into Vol as he smoked. His free hand went around her waist, pulling him to her. He kissed her neck gently when she said she had not had to charge any of it. She had saved back the money to pay cash.

The children were ecstatic on Christmas morning. Santa had not forgotten them as he had forgotten some of the children in the other shacks. While Louie prepared their Christmas dinner, Albert took Billy outside to play with the ball. Vol was getting anxious by then, being cooped up such small quarters with the excited children all morning, and had scolded Albert sharply about bouncing the ball in the house. Louie was especially careful to not let the pots and pans rattle together while she cooked, and made sure the baby was quiet. Vol sat on the battered sofa, against the wall on the opposite side of the room, squinted his eyes shut and rubbed his temples. That of itself, was not a good sign, Louie knew.

She carefully set the table, and called them all in to dinner, making sure the boys had clean hands, faces and shirts when they came to the table. Vol was silent as they all came to the table, the children growing apprehensive at their father's mood. Maureen held her new baby doll tightly as she sat silently and perfectly straight in her chair.

Louie finished setting the food on the table, looked around happily at her children who returned her warm smile and then asked Vol if he would ask the blessing. She and the children bowed their heads, but Vol did not pray. He began mumbling something, softly at first, then with increasing intensity. Almost without warning he stood, grabbed the corners of the table as he shouted at her, "I will not ask a blessing on this pile of shit," and threw the table over. As soon as he stood, Maureen ran behind Louie, clutching her doll. Albert, pulling Billy with him, scooted back from the table just in time to keep from being hit by it. Vol picked up a bowl from the mess on the floor and threw it at the wall, smashing it. Then he stormed out of the shack, slamming the door. They were left in complete silence.

After a moment, and struggling to keep her voice calm, Louie said it was all right.

Everything was all right now. She rose and put the baby back in his bed, then righted the table. She looked at the damage. Fortunately the floor was clean, she had just damp mopped it that morning. The chicken was still in one piece and she put it back on the platter. Except for the shattered serving bowl, now on the floor behind the stove, and the beans that had been in it spattered on the wall, everything else could be salvaged. There were plenty of beans still in the pot on the stove. She scooped the remaining food back into the serving bowls, reset the table, reassembled the chairs and they all sat back down. Only then did she realize she was crying.

At first, Albert came around the table to put his arms around his mother's neck, then Billy and Maureen followed, all three of them crying too. She stopped her tears and hugged all her children to her.

"I hate him," Albert declared soberly.

"No you don't, Albert. Not really. You are angry at him, but you don't hate him. He doesn't mean it. He can't help it."

"He doesn't love us, Mother. He doesn't love you."

"I love you, Albert. I love all of my children. Your Daddy loves you, but he can't show it. Remember always, though, that he loves you."

They made the best of what was left of the meal. The chicken was delicious and the stuffing too and there was plenty of mashed potatoes and brown beans for everyone. Vol was still not back when they finished and Louie went ahead with the pumpkin pie. When they were finished, she asked the children if they would like to help her prepare a plate for their father, for him to have when he came home. It helped reassure them that he would indeed be home - they knew the fathers of some of their neighbors had left their children. When the plate was ready, set at his place and covered with a clean cloth, Albert helped Louie wash the dishes. She was able to scrub most of the stain off the wall and the floor was swept and mopped again. She gathered her children to her again and by the light from the lamp read the poem, *The Night Before Christmas*. They always read it on Christmas Eve and again on Christmas night. When they used to have Christmas gifts they would open those on Christmas Eve, so it was nice to have something special again on Christmas night before they went to bed. The children had come to expect it and they seemed to be calmed by it this evening.

It was late that night, and the children had been asleep for a long time, when Louie heard Vol outside the front door. When he did not come in, she picked up his pouch of tobacco, rolling paper and a match and went to open the door. He did not turn away when the inside light fell across him and she went out, closing the door to sit beside him. She rolled a cigarette for him, then put it in her own mouth to light it and passed it to him. Vol took it, pulled a long drag, held it and exhaled.

"I am sorry, Gertrude," he said quietly. "I ruined your Christmas."

She could not remember Vol ever apologizing for anything. It gave her a glimmer of hope. She realized he was crying silently and she leaned over against him, then put her arm around his shoulder and kissed him on the cheek.

"You are a good woman, better than I deserve."

"Hush now. Hush."

They sat a while longer, looking out at the cold, clear night. The only light was the orange glow of his cigarette - the small, special luxury Louie had given him. When he finished, she asked, "Are you hungry? I saved some back for you."

Vol did not argue that the food had been on the floor. He stood and came in the house behind Louie. While she uncovered the plates at his place at the table, with the room put back in order and the stain on the wall barely showing, he went into the children's room. There he sat gently on their bed, scooped up each sleeping child to hold them tenderly to him. Louie, standing at the door, held back her tears of happiness. She would never know for sure where he had gone that afternoon or what had happened to him. But she could see that Vol did indeed, love his children. She could also see that he was trying.

It was her Christmas gift. On that Christmas night, that was enough.

* * * * *

By the next spring, William and Stella arranged for Vol and Louie to live on a farm near theirs. The owners were getting on in years and needed help. It was a larger farm and they would share half the harvest for Vol's work. In addition, the house Vol and Louie would live in had four rooms and a long, covered porch. It was the original house the settling family built, set at the back of the property, and had been kept in reasonable repair. Best of all, the house had electricity, an electric light hung from the ceiling in the middle of each room.

It was a much better arrangement, and Louie was grateful to be near William and Stella again. Their son was almost the same age as Albert and the boys, actually double cousins and as closely related as brothers would be, could keep each other company. Even Vol was appreciative of the arrangement.

They were still in the grips of the Great Depression. Farm prices were low and looked like they would stay that way. A drought was gripping most of Texas and Oklahoma, although it was not severe in their part of the state, and money was scarce. Louie became pregnant that summer and in March of 1935, another daughter was born. They named her Annie Lee.

The harvest of 1935 was not good, but Louie reminded Vol they were much better off than they had been. The house was better and they had a better share of the harvest, and more acreage to farm than before. Vol argued that it did not matter if they were only half-starving instead of completely starving. He wanted to pull up and go west, to California. He would do much better there, he said.

Stella intervened and made her brother stay put. Did he want to be on his own, and all alone out in California? As a family they would be able to survive. She and William needed him as much as Vol and Louie needed them. It was silly to think things would be better just by moving. Besides, Vol and Louie didn't have a car and William and Stella's Ford was too old to make that kind of trip. Had he thought of that?

They managed, but Vol's discontent grew. Louie did her best to make things as easy as she could for him, but Vol was getting older now, he turned forty in 1935, and the farm work was beginning to wear him down. He convinced himself he was going to die soon if things did not change.

They had a little better harvest in 1936 and enough money for a proper Christmas that year, even a gift for each child to unwrap on Christmas Eve. In February, Louie knew she was pregnant again, but Vol did not want any more children. She put off telling him as long as she could, but she finally had to tell him the baby would be born that September.

When it was time for the spring planting in 1937, Albert and Maureen, ages twelve and ten now, did a full share of work in the fields. Billy helped out too, but could not be expected to do as much. He was only eight. That summer Louie joined them, chopping cotton as much as she could. Their survival depended on the next harvest, the same as always, whether she was pregnant or not.

The summer was miserable. By mid-July the heat was intense, well over 100 degrees every day for weeks on end. Although there was little rain, the air was heavy and thick with humidity from the Gulf of Mexico. As the plants withered in the fields Vol was tense. He was even more agitated when he listened to the preacher on the radio, who claimed the heat to be just a sample of the hellfire that was coming to them, punishment for the sins of the modern world: lust, sins of the flesh, miscegenation and now the proliferation of legal alcohol, even if much of Texas remained "dry." All were signs of Satan's control over the earth. Vol would squeeze his eyes shut while he listened to the preacher, sometimes rocking back and forth as he almost silently repeated the preacher's words to himself. He gathered up what little money they had to send to the preacher to help his ministry. Louie wished at those times she could do something to get rid of the radio, or make it stop working. It was nothing but trouble to them.

By the end of July, Vol decided they needed to hoe the peanut fields again. The cotton was lost, and the peanuts were barely alive, but he decided that breaking up the baked crust on top of the soil, and removing any remaining weeds, would prepare the ground to receive the rains he asked the radio preacher to pray for. The radio preacher told Vol to prepare for the blessings of the Lord to rain down upon them. Louie knew the hoeing would only dry out the parched soil more, but did not dare argue with him. She struggled to help the first day, and, in disgust, Vol told her to go home. He said he did not want to have to carry her to the house if she decided to faint. Albert, Maureen and Billy stayed in the field, helping their father.

The morning of the second day, Albert was hoeing with a methodical and steady rhythm while keeping an eye on his father. As the morning progressed, Vol was increasingly agitated. He hoed very little actually, looking up and raising his hands as he talked to the sky, interspersed with bursts of frantic chopping that was destroying the tops of the peanut plants. Albert could not hear Vol, but he made sure he was always facing his father so he could keep an eye on him from under the brim of his hat. If his father caught him stopping or staring at him, it would mean a beating for sure.

By ten o'clock, Billy was still hoeing diligently, but had to stop to wipe the sweat that ran into his eyes. Albert stopped to help him tie a handkerchief around his head up under the brim of the hat so the sweat would not run directly into his eyes, but it was soon soaked through and nothing else could be done. They were already finished with the water Louie sent along with them that morning, a bottle for each child, tied to the belt loop of their pants with a short length of wire. They would just have to make it to lunch time somehow.

Albert went back to where he had been working and looked over to Maureen to make sure she was all right. Maureen's dress was drenched with sweat and sticking to her back and arms. The old straw hat she was wearing to keep off the sun was drooping, obviously sodden too. He caught Maureen's eye and she gave him a little wave, then leaned forward again to continue chopping.

Albert worked on, setting a goal for himself of reaching the end of the row before they stopped for lunch. It would take him past his father, who was making little progress and Vol may upbraid him for trying to show his father up, but the goal gave him something to think about. He was almost twelve years old and was able to do a man's work.

Although he was intent on his work, something drew his eye back to Maureen. She had stopped, straightened up with the hoe handle leaning against her chest, to lift her hat and wipe her forehead with the back of her hand. She looked up at the sun for a moment, most likely trying to gauge what the time was, and then put her hat back on her head. Before she resumed, she took the water bottle from her belt and brought it to her lips. From the angle, Albert could see it was empty and she was draining the last few drops. If he had any left he would share it with her. He would have to remember that after lunch when they had water again. Maureen stood still a moment longer. Albert wondered if she was dizzy. It was the first sign of a heat stroke, if he remembered right.

Then his father's movement from the corner of his eye reassured him. Vol had also seen Maureen and was walking toward her. He was walking swiftly and straight across the peanut plants, mowing them down as he walked. He would take care of Maureen. Maybe he had water to share, or would let them all rest, or maybe stop this madness completely. Moving around dried out dirt was not going to help the peanuts.

Then Albert saw that as his father crossed the field he was unbuckling his belt and yanking it from his pants. Maureen's back was turned to her father and she could not see him coming. Albert dropped his hoe and began running toward his father, screaming out to Maureen who did not hear him. As he ran, he watched his father bring the belt down across Maureen's back. The impact of it raised a small shower from the sweat on her back. Maureen's hand went up to protect herself from the unexpected sting, not sure what it was, but Vol caught her hand and twisted her around, painfully twisting the wrist.

Albert screamed out "Daddy" again and again, hoping to divert his father's attention, but Vol did not hear him. Vol brought the belt up again, but before he could bring it down again on his daughter Albert was there, grabbing his father's arm as he swung the belt and deflecting the blow. Vol was surprised by the impact and loosened his grip on Maureen enough that she wrenched her hand free.

"Run Maureen. Run home!" Albert yelled at her. Maureen turned to run and, in the moment before Vol brought the belt down on him, Albert could see Billy had already started running for home. Vol, enraged now, wildly hit Albert with the belt twice before he could leverage himself to resist. He was as tall as his father now and could fight back. He lunged forward and knocked Vol flat on his back, then grabbed the belt from his father's hand and flung it far away across the field. Only then did he start running for home himself.

Billy had sounded enough warning that Louie was down the steps and in the yard by the time Albert reached the yard. Vol had recovered and was running after him, only yards behind.

"Run and get William and Stella," Louie yelled to Albert as soon as he was close enough to hear. "Take the horse. Tell them to bring the sheriff."

Albert ran to the barn and left on the horse, riding bareback directly past his father who tried to grab him off the horse as he galloped by. Louie was back in the house, had shut and locked the door and sent Maureen with the younger children into the bedroom, telling her not to come out, no matter what happened. Vol was furious at the locked door and kicked it in. It took him four kicks before the bolt splintered through the frame. When he came into the room, and, in the moment before he slapped her face so hard she felt the jaw coming loose from her skull, she realized it was not the Vol she knew that she was facing. She had never seen the look on his face that she saw in that moment.

As she struggled with him and tried to fight back, her only thought was to protect the unborn baby. She tried to keep something between Vol and herself, usually the kitchen table, which infuriated him even more. He lunged and grabbed at her. She was not sure how long that went on, her left eye was swelling shut and there was excruciating pain in the middle of her back where he had punched her, or maybe kicked her, when she did not get away from him quickly enough. The room was in shambles and there was more and more broken glass on the floor as he picked up things to throw at her. Most of them were missing her and shattering against the walls.

After what seemed like hours but could have been only minutes, Louie was wearing down when Vol caught her and grabbed her from behind in a crushing bear hug. She tried to double forward, protecting the baby as much as she could, but his arm was around her neck. She tried to wriggle out of his grip that was taking away all her air. The floor was tilting beneath them and the room was growing dark. She tried to say his name, slapping backward at him to get his attention, to have him come back to himself, but it was no use. She realized she was going to die before William and Stella got there.

Then there was a sudden loosening of his grip on her neck. He staggered back a step and Louie, frantic, scrambled away from him, using the table to support herself as she tried to breathe in air and clear her head. She looked up to see Maureen, wide-eyed and alert and ready to spring. Against her mother's orders, she let herself out of the children's bedroom, telling Billy to keep the door closed. Seeing that her father was strangling her mother, she did the only thing she could think to do. She picked up the iron skillet from the stove and hit Vol as hard as she could with it. He did not even seem to notice so she hit him again, this time on the back of his head. It was enough for him to release his grip, but now Maureen knew she was going to be next. She hung onto the skillet, ready to swing it again.

Louie, still trying to clear her head and only her right eye seeming to function, felt around on the tabletop for what she hoped was still there. She opened and closed her jaw which seemed to go back into its socket - or at least her teeth lined up again. Her fingers finally felt the blade of her butcher knife, then felt down to the wooden handle. Her fist closed around it, keeping it hidden from Vol, and then she straightened up as much as she could and put herself between Vol and her daughter.

"Get out!" she said with more strength than she knew she had. "Get out of this house," she said again showing him the knife.

It was at that moment that William burst through the door with Stella and Albert close behind him. William crossed the room and punched Vol in the side of his head. He fell to the floor like a sack of potatoes. William straddled Vol as he lay semi-conscious on the kitchen floor and punched him another time and then a third, assuring he was completely knocked out.

The sheriff arrived moments later. Stella was helping Louie to the sofa, crying over her wounds, as she told Maureen and Albert what to do to help. Albert was to take Williams car, drive into town and bring the doctor back immediately. Albert had never driven, but had watched his uncle enough that he could work the gears and steer the car. William would have gone, but the sheriff needed him to help keep Vol restrained. Vol was coming around and was kicking and thrashing around to free his hands from the sheriff's handcuffs. William brought his fist back up and punched Vol again, subduing him. The sheriff needed William to help him load Vol into the sheriff's car so he could take him back to town and put him in jail until he calmed down.

The doctor examined Louie, dressed her wounds and said her jaw was not broken but would be sore a while. He listened to her heart with his stethoscope, then to the baby's and said he thought the baby was all right. Louie's back was bruised, but not hurting as much. The doctor said the next twenty-four hours were critical, but, as long as she did not start having labor, she and the baby would both be all right. Then he let the children put on his stethoscope and listen to their own heart.

The sheriff said there was no law in Texas against a man beating his wife; otherwise half the men in the state would be in jail. It wasn't legal though, for any man to beat a pregnant woman, even if she was his wife. If she lost the baby, Vol could be tried for murder, but it didn't look like that was going to happen, so, at the most he would be in jail for a while if Louie wanted to press charges.

William persuaded the sheriff to hold Vol until they could decide what to do. Stella stayed with Louie and her family until Louie was able to be up and around. Stella was embarrassed about what had happened and disowned her brother. She said they had always made too many allowances for him and his odd behavior. It had not helped. Instead it had led them to this.

Ultimately, with the help and encouragement of William and Stella, Louie agreed that Vol would be returned to the army hospital. If they would accept him, the army would take care of him.

Louie also had their support when she decided she would divorce him. It was a wicked thing to do, and especially against the vows she had taken to stand beside him in sickness and health. From jail, Vol wrote long letters to her reminding her of those vows, and the consequences of breaking them. She left those letters unanswered.

Her brother Lester came over from the Squyres farm with her half-brothers and harvested what was left of the crops. Albert, Maureen and Billy helped their uncles. Lester also talked to the landlord and assured him that he, and the rest of Louie's family, would make sure the crops were planted and harvested next year and the year after that. Even Mama Lillie gave an unexpected show of support, sending two peach pies for her stepdaughter and her children. She sent pies each and every time Lester went to see Louie.

A divorce was granted by the first of September. The process and the judge were sped along by the sheriff, the Squyres family minister, and especially by William, who with his Brownie camera had taken pictures of Louie's injuries, the condition of the house - even though they had mostly put things back together by then - and the welts that still showed on Maureen. The clerk at the drug store almost would not give him the photographs when she saw them, they were that awful.

The baby was born on September 11, 1937. Stella was there to help. Louie's brothers Lester and William kept the children occupied with a fishing trip to the creek and a ball game in the yard.

Louie named the baby boy Lester, after her brother. Big old Lester, as rough and tough as he liked to think he was sometimes, teared up and nearly cried when Louie told him. He knew he would never have any sons of his own now, but having a nephew named for him was the next best thing. Louie could see that her youngest would have a daddy, of sorts, in his uncle.

Vol was admitted, indefinitely, for treatment at the army hospital in Texas. Even after twenty years, they agreed it was still shell shock. He would likely never be able to live again on his own.

Louie had six children to rear by herself now. Albert was almost twelve. Maureen had just turned ten. In December, Billy would be eight and Alton would be five. Little Annie Lee was two and now there was baby Lester. Somehow, she would have to bring them up by herself.

Farming was all she knew. So for the next eighteen years - Good Lord, that would be the year 1955 and so far into the future she could not even imagine it - that was what she was going to have to do.

CHAPTER NINETEEN

San Francisco, California
May 29, 1945

Albert was at his regular station on deck beside the starboard guns as the *U.S.S. President Hayes* sailed under the Golden Gate Bridge, on its way into the San Francisco Bay. His presence there was a formality. It was unlikely they would be attacked here, especially now that Germany had surrendered and the Japs were on the run. He was happy to be up in the fresh air and sunshine, a reprieve from his regular duties as assistant quartermaster down below when they were at sea.

The early morning air promised a beautiful day ahead. He had been in San Francisco more times than he could count now. The *Hayes* always reported here before returning to Honolulu and he knew the city well enough to know it was going to be clear all day. Things had changed since the last time they were here almost three months ago. The war was still in full swing then and it was still winter. Now it was spring and VE Day, as it was being called now, had finally come. There was an evident exubcrance in the air, even here on the west coast.

They had all been on deck since oh-five-hundred-hours, almost four hours now, while the Hayes waited for a berth. San Francisco was one of the busiest war ports and was even more so now that the war in Europe was won and U.S. efforts were being directed in full force to the Pacific.

They were holding just inside the bridge. From where he stood Albert could look up at it, as long as he did so only with his eyes and did not compromise the "at ease" position. Even with the wartime shortages of rubber and strict gasoline rationing the bridge was busy. There was something comforting, exhilarating actually, in the normality of the morning traffic bustling high overhead. As they waited, a group of young women, possibly playing hooky from their final days of high school, came out on the pedestrian walkway and were waving small American flags and calling out to welcome the boys on the *Hayes* home.

Albert could not wave back; it would have him in court martial for sure. But that did not keep him from smiling and winking at the girls. One of the girls cupped her hands and boldly called something down to him, but her voice was lost in the din of traffic from the bridge and the gentle morning breeze. She fumbled around in her purse as the *Hayes* shuddered a bit and slipped forward, finally underway to its pier. The girls with her all cupped their hands and yelled out in unison, "Hey, Blue Eyes," as the girl ran along the rail until she was directly above the ship and then threw a pack of chewing gum that landed at Albert's feet. He knew when he picked it up later it would probably include her name and address or telephone number. They looked like nice girls, not like the prostitutes that hung around the military gates of the Embarcadero to meet the ships, so it was all in good fun, a little celebration.

From his vantage point on the starboard side, he watched happily as they sailed past the Presidio and the city came into view. San Francisco was so different than any other city he had ever seen. It always looked like a patchwork quilt to him, shaken and spread out, but still puffed up a little in the places where the hills were. He spotted the landmarks, one by one: the brick factory warehouses beyond the new aquatic park, a shining ribbon of the cable car rails coming down Hyde Street to the pier, then Fisherman's Wharf. As they followed the piers lined up along the Embarcadero, each one fully occupied due to the heavy traffic of ships of Pacific Fleet and the usual shipping vessels, he caught his first glimpse of Coit Tower, the firemen's memorial, on top of Telegraph Hill.

With this spectacular view of the hill and the tower his thoughts turned back to Dolores, not that they were ever far from her. The last letter he had from her caught up with him in Honolulu when the *Hayes* arrived there from Sydney. It was mailed in Missouri, hastily written on mismatched stationery, so unlike her, and posted from the train station the day she left from there with her mother and a dim-witted girl her mother agreed to let ride along with them. (That part made him laugh every time he read it - just the way Dolores described it.) They were bound for San Francisco, and weeks earlier than originally planned. In the letter, Dolores was not sure if they would even make it all the way, the way the trains were now, but she wanted to make sure he knew they were going earlier than she first said.

The baby had come early and her sister's husband had joined the army. Now - of all times, she added. She included a row of exclamation points after those last two bits of news, also so unlike her, but let him know she had written the letter at the last minute and that still gave him a rush of excitement to know that she wanted to be sure he knew she was going to be in San Francisco early. She included a brief post script that she was looking forward to being in the city again. She loved to walk there, even to the top of Telegraph Hill to look at the bay from the tower. She also wished they could do that together sometime.

As they slowed to dock in one of the even-numbered piers between the Ferry Building and the Oakland Bay Bridge, he could not help break his "at ease" posture a moment to make sure the twenty-four hour pass was still in his pocket. He had twenty-four hours in San Francisco, starting as soon as they docked and were cleared. The officer on their ship was very good about sharing those passes evenly among the men. Fairchild only had an afternoon pass this time and had to be back on board by evening mess. He teasingly tried to get Albert to trade with him - Fairchild had a girl here in the city he wanted to see, but Albert good-naturedly refused. Fairchild knew what he was up to, anyway. He knew Albert was finally going to go find this girl, Dolores. He had her address, well, actually the address of her sister, right here in the city. This was the first time they were both in the city and today he was really going to see her face to face.

When he got that letter, he wrote back immediately, but he was sure his letter was still somewhere in the sacks of mail below deck. Carrying mail was one of the things the *Hayes* had spent the four years of the war doing, along with ferrying military personnel back and forth across the Pacific, delivering military supplies and other goods and taking the wounded home. No other ship could have beat them here from Hawaii with his letter. She had no way of knowing his ship was arriving today, even if he could get that message past the censors.

They were a transport ship, but that did not mean they had not seen action. Albert had had his turn manning the guns more times than he cared to remember, once even bringing down a plane – or at least it was shot down when his and the other guns were firing at it. He would never know for sure if it was his gun that downed it. When the lone surviving Jap was fished out of the water and was paraded past the entire company of the ship standing at attention, Albert had felt sorry for the young man. It was an offense that could have meant court martial for him – for showing sympathy for the enemy - but as the pilot walked past him, defeated, Albert saw that he was just another young man, caught up in this war, who had just happened to be born in the wrong country. He realized it was easy to hate a faceless enemy far away in some another part of the world, but he could feel no hatred toward this shamed young man who had bravely done his best.

Albert and the rest of them had seen enough of war. The last time they were in Honolulu, Fairchild got into a fist fight with another serviceman (and one of the reasons he only had an afternoon pass today) who was bragging about the war. Fairchild and the others agreed that those who had seen any real action in war did not want to talk about, much less brag about it, in a public bar. They knew the man had not left his base in Hawaii during his entire time of duty. The most danger he had been in was getting a sunburn, but the schmuck kept going on and on until Fairchild took him up on it, asking exactly what action he had seen. That started a back and forth until one of Fairchild's buddies shoved him forward, sloshing his beer. The schmuck said the wrong thing and Fairchild took him down with one punch. Somehow it got back to the *Hayes* and Fairchild was now being reined in with a shortened shore leave. It was mild punishment passed down from the sympathetic, and somewhat admiring, commanding officer.

As the ship approached the pier the men sprang into action, looking like an army of white ants swarming over the decks. The ship was secured, the gangway brought alongside, and those with passes were free to go below and change from their whites to their dress blues. In Albert's case, 'dress blues' was the simple blue wool sailor uniform, with highly-shined black leather shoes and his white sailor cap. Only the officers wore the double-breasted jackets with brass buttons and gold stripes on the sleeves and the visor caps with gold braid. While ashore, Albert could fold his white cloth cap and tuck it in his belt if he liked, but changing anything else, even so much as leaving one button undone, would mean he was out of uniform, and subject to discipline. He always wore his cap anyway, unless he was indoors, where it had to be removed to show respect.

While other branches of service liked to tease the Navy about their extra wide pants, "bell-bottoms" they shouted and jeered, Albert and every other sailor knew the reason for the roomy pants was so they could be taken off over their shoes when they were in the water. When wet and in the water, those wide pant legs also could be tied off and used as a flotation device, keeping a man afloat for hours. Viewed that way - as a life saver - the silly-looking pants did not seem quite so ridiculous. Besides there were things to tease the other branches back about - like calling Marines "jar heads" and Army soldiers "dogfaces" or "grunts". Just keep it light. Everyone was fighting for the same thing.

Albert changed quickly and put everything in its rightful place for inspection. As soon as he passed inspection he would be free to go. Fairchild lounged lazily in the hammock next to Albert's, clad only in his white regulation tee shirt and boxer shorts. He smoked lazily while he flipped through a magazine. Albert chuckled when he saw it was yet another girlie magazine. On the page Fairchild was now examining the breasts of the girl, a plump brunette kneeling on a fake beach, were almost completely exposed. She was holding a beach towel up to barely cover them. Her skimpy top was on the sand beside her. Fairchild held up the magazine for Albert to see. "Looks just like Betty, don't she?"

"You dope," Albert said, tossing a half-full pack of cigarettes to Fairchild, his consolation for spending most of the day on board with nothing to do. "I could tell Dolores about that and Betty would give you the heave-ho."

Fairchild leaned languidly toward Albert in his hammock, half-closed his eyes, pursed his lips and made a long smacking noise, "Kiss your girl good for Fairchild, Bailey!" he said, making Albert laugh. "Or I guess you'd better kiss her for yourself first, hadn't you?"

Albert laughed again, "We'll see. I gotta go find her first. She could turn out to be a two-ton Tilly."

"Not that one," Fairchild said dreamily. They had seen photos of her with Betty. Fairchild said he would have made a play for her himself if he wasn't already writing to her best friend, Betty. This Dolores was completely what she said she was. Albert checked his wallet again, buttoned into his pocket. It held the four dollars he had saved. It was enough for a nice enough date to impress her. He straightened his cap and was ready.

"Hey, Blue Eyes," Fairchild said, subtly teasing Albert about the girls on the bridge earlier and clenching an unlit cigarette between his teeth while he stretched out his long legs against the hammock. He held out his hand, Albert thought it was to shake his hand for good luck - it was his first date and everything - but when he pulled his hand back there was a crisp, folded five-dollar bill tucked in it. "Dinner's on me," Fairchild said. "Take your dame someplace nice, tell her it's my treat and then make sure she writes to Betty all about it."

"You dope," Albert laughed. "Always an angle with you and the ladies, isn't there?"

It was a generous gift, even if Fairchild *could* spend all of his money on himself. As seamen second class, Fairchild and Albert were each paid $39 a month. When they made first class it would be $51 a month. Every time he was paid, Albert kept $4 for himself and sent the rest of his pay home. It wasn't difficult, the navy provided almost everything for them: food, clothing, a bed (if that's what you could call a swinging hammock) and even cigarettes. Sometimes, when he didn't spend as much on himself during the month, he could send a little more than $35, but he still didn't know how his mother managed on that little. It was nothing compared to the average $300 a month pay a civilian man was earning in 1945.

Louie worked part time now when they called her at the egg packing plant. Maureen worked full time at the drug store in town, helping fill prescriptions, tending the soda fountain and the cash register. Billy left home and joined the navy as soon as he was sixteen, but was likely spending it all on beer and dames. Louie never mentioned Billy sending her any money. Alton was almost thirteen and did odd jobs after school. In her letters, Louie insisted they were managing and for Albert not to worry about them.

With nine dollars in his pocket and feeling like he was on top of the world, Albert made his way down to the gangway and off the ship. He walked briskly along the fenced Embarcadero to the MP gate and was temporarily delayed there as he waited in line to have his leave papers checked. As the MP, or military police, looked at his paper, Albert asked him if he knew where Waller Street was. This guy had been in the city for the entire war and should know, but the MP was too busy to bother and only waved him through. The guy behind Albert in line called out for him to wait up. He said to take the streetcar all the way down Market Street. "When you get on, tell the conductor to stop at Buchanan. It's the stop before Church. Take a right. It's only a couple of blocks from there."

At the Ferry Building turnaround, Albert pushed his way into the crowded street car. Not the same as the cable cars, this bus-like vehicle ran on metal tracks down the middle of Market Street, powered by electric lines overhead. The car was loaded to maximum capacity at the Ferry Building, its first stop, and still gathered more passengers at each stop beyond that.

Half of the passengers were servicemen on leave and already in a party mood. Young women in the car openly flirted with the men, or at least smiled encouragingly. After the second stop, Albert was pressed up against a young woman in a bright yellow hat that matched her dress.

She smiled up encouragingly at him. It had to be the uniform. Before the war this kind of girl would never have given him the time of day. After she did not move away from him at any of the stops along the way, Albert leaned forward to whisper, "I'm going to see my girl, but thanks just the same, Gorgeous."

Fairchild had helped him come up with that line. It kept the girl at bay without making her feel like dog meat. The girl still wrote her name and number on the margin of the newspaper she was carrying, tore it off and tucked it in his pocket. "Just in case," she said with a knowing grin before she pushed her way through the crowded car at her stop.

Albert happened to look out the window as the car sailed past Buchanan Street without stopping, then pulled the cord and began shouting wildly to the conductor to let him off. The car stopped at Church and Market, one of those confusing five point intersections, and, as he pressed his way to the exit, another pretty girl boldly threw her arms around his neck and kissed him full on the lips, most likely on a dare from her two companions, drawing the cheers of the other servicemen and the disdain of the more respectable citizens of the car. The town had gone completely crazy since VE Day.

Albert walked back down the crowded sidewalk in the direction of Buchanan Street, but was soon completely turned around. Streets in this area along the north side of Market were positioned at forty-five degree angles instead of running straight into the street. There were odd little three-cornered squares, or just wider spaces in the sidewalks. On the other side of the street, south of Market, most of the streets ran parallel or straight into Market, but a few still ran at angles. He was no longer sure of the directions he had been given.

Instead of continuing his confused search, and knowing San Franciscans were always friendly and helpful to visitors, especially servicemen, he ducked into a drug store on Duboce Street, or at least he thought it was still Duboce, to ask directions. He remembered to wipe off the street car girl's lipstick first.

A young woman behind the counter asked with a faint southern accent how she could assist him.

She was a slender blond in her mid to late twenties, wearing a soft pink sweater pushed up at the elbows. Unlike the exuberant girls on the streetcar and the ones on the bridge earlier that morning, there was a different air about her, one of disillusion. For girls like her, the end of the war was forcing her to accept that the man she loved was not coming home again. The empty loneliness of the war years would be not be ending for her.

She parted her lips slightly and gazed languidly up through her eyelashes at him. She was very pretty.

"I am looking for Waller Street, but I think I'm lost."

She leaned forward, putting her elbows on the glass counter to point out the door, "No, honey. You are close. So close. You just walk right up this side of the street to the next corner and then you turn left on Buchanan. Walk up the hill and past the Mint building. Waller runs into it in two blocks."

"Thank you."

"Sure, any time." Her soft brown eyes stayed sad in spite of her smile. "You come on back here if you need anything else."

"Oh," he remembered, "I do need something. A box of candy maybe? Whitman's Sampler is what she said she likes, I think."

Her eyebrows raised, but only slightly at the suggestion of another woman, and she silently pointed to the candy display. Albert picked up a one pound box and brought it back to the counter. She wrapped it in red and white striped paper and tied on a bright red bow.

"Thanks," he said.

"Anytime." she replied with a sultry smile, snapping the dollar bill in the cash register's till and shoving the drawer closed, leaning into it.

It was as she said, very close. He found Waller Street. It was a neighborhood of modest row houses, all about sixty years old, and still nicely maintained in spite of the war. Number 275 was on the south side of the street and was not far from the corner.

He paused on the sidewalk at the base of the concrete steps that went up to the front door, a full story above the sidewalk. This was it! He was finally going to see her, to meet her, to actually hear her voice. He straightened his cap, climbed the stairs and rang the bell.

The door stood open behind the screen door and a little girl about four years old came to stare at him through the screen. She knit her eyebrows together and glowered up at him. "Who is it Elise?" her mother's muffled voice called from inside.

"Some man!" the girl called back loudly without turning. She continued staring at him. She reminded him so much of his own sister, Annie Lee, that it made Albert want to laugh, but he didn't dare.

In a moment, a young woman with her hair tied back in a scarf came to the door holding a baby. She was pretty without makeup, with a fresh and open face. "Yes?" she asked through the screen as she gently pushed the little girl to the side.

"I was wondering if Miss Linet might be home," he replied, feeling a flutter in his stomach. He had expected Dolores to answer the door, looking exactly like she looked in the pictures she sent him. This must be her sister, the one with the new baby and a daughter. What was her sister's name? It completely escaped him now.

"Miss Linet?" she repeated, as if she did not quite understand.

"Yes, Miss Dolores Linet. She gave me this address in her last letter. I thought she was staying here."

"Yes," she replied. "I am her sister, Carolyn, but Dolores is not here."

"Oh. Do you know when she will be back?" The woman hesitated and he realized he had not introduced himself. "I am Albert Bailey – no Ernie…I mean Ernest. My ship only got in this morning and she didn't know I was coming. I just wanted to come by and see her. I can come back."

Carolyn unhooked the lock on the screen door and pushed it open. "You had better come in, Ernest." she said. He could see there was something she was not saying. Something was wrong, terribly wrong. Then Carolyn added, "Mama and Dolores left just yesterday to go back to Missouri."

This was awful. He wanted to only be away from there now, but Dolores' sister was politely making small talk and asking him to at least come in for a cup of coffee. He followed her through the old-fashioned entry hall to the kitchen at the back of the house. Her breakfast dishes were still on the table and, still holding the baby, she started to clear the table with her free hand so they could sit down at the table.

"Here, let me help you," he offered. Carolyn was both surprised and impressed by the offer. Her husband, Loran, readily helped her, but most young men would not even consider it, especially these young servicemen, so completely full of themselves these days.

"I tell you what," Carolyn replied. "Let's have coffee in the living room. I can clean this mess up later. I have some coffee already made - at least I think I do."

"Can I do anything to help you?" Albert offered again.

"Can you hold a baby?" she said, testing him as she held out baby Marilyn. He took the infant as naturally as if she was his own. Dolores said he had a lot of younger brothers and sisters and had to help his mother. He held the baby, who looked up at him with crossed eyes, making them both laugh. "You go on out to the living room and I will have our coffee ready in a jiffy."

She was further charmed when she came into the living room that Elise was wearing his sailor cap and enjoying one of the chocolates from the box he had opened for her. He was easily balancing the baby on his lap with his free hand. "Now Elise, just one of those for now," Carolyn said.

"Sorry. I should have asked you first," Albert said.

"No, that's fine. You have a new admirer now, I hope you know." Elise already seemed enchanted with their visitor, standing so close beside him at the arm of the easy chair she was nearly standing on top of his shoes. He did not seem to mind.

They visited until lunch time. She told him a little about Dolores and her family and Albert told her a little about Texas and his family. Carolyn enjoyed the grown-up conversation, and was very impressed with this young man. She fed him lunch and after helping her wash all the dishes, both lunch and breakfast, he said he should go. He wanted to go to the USO and see if he could make a long-distance telephone call to his mother in Texas before he went back to the ship. As they said goodbye at the door, Carolyn made him promise to come and see them again any time he was in San Francisco.

She also said Dolores would be so terribly sorry she missed him. If only they had waited a couple of days more to go back home. It was the most encouraging thing he had heard for a long, long time.

CHAPTER TWENTY

Gonzales County, Texas
May, 1946

Louie put the last of the Sunday dinner dishes on the drain board for Maureen to dry and emptied the dishpans in the sink. Washing dishes was practically no effort these days, streamlined even, as they said now, with hot and cold running water right at the kitchen sink. She leaned forward to look through the little window above the sink at the back yard where the usual Sunday afternoon baseball game was underway. The baselines were beaten down dirt already, and they had lived in this house only a couple of years.

After her son Billy and all her stepbrothers either joined the army or went to work at the war plants, Louie told her brother Lester it was too much for them to try to keep both farms going. By then, Albert was sending her almost all of his navy pay, thirty-five dollars a month, and with the little she earned working herself and Maureen working now too, they could afford to rent this little house in town.

It was different living in town. Alton, Annie and Lester Ray went to school here and it was so close they could come home for their lunch. Alton was fourteen and had a job after school at the grocer, boxing up groceries and carrying them out to people's cars, or wagons, as the case may be. There were more cars than wagons, even in Nixon these days. The train came right through town twice a day – once in each direction – and they could practically set their watches by it. Everything was closer together in town, too close sometimes. Louie had to remind herself to check how she looked before she went outside and there was always the knowledge that all the other ladies on the street were watching what she and her children did. That was comforting in a way, but also could be annoying. Everything considered though, Louie enjoyed living in town.

Albert was in the front room, listening to a ball game on the radio. She was surprised that he came on home as soon as he got out of the navy in December. She half-expected to receive a letter from him in Missouri. He had certainly seemed stuck on that girl for quite a while. But as soon as he was discharged he came straight home and had not said another word about her. He got a job in the mercantile and possibly would become a manager there, which did not really mean much except that he wore a starched white shirt and a necktie when he went to work every day. He could walk to work in only a few minutes and she had given over one of the bedrooms to him, meaning the boys slept on the foldout davenport in the living room. Annie and Maureen shared the room upstairs that once had been the attic.

Hanging her dish towel on the rack to dry, Maureen said she thought she would read for a while upstairs. Louie wiped the gleaming countertop with her dishrag and then buffed it to a shine with a fresh dishtowel. After hanging that towel on the rack she poured two glasses of iced tea – an everyday treat now that she had an electric refrigerator with two ice trays in the freezer compartment at the top – and went to join Albert in the living room.

They listened to the ball game for a bit, Albert's favorite thing to do on a Sunday afternoon, visiting amicably between innings or while they waited for the next play. Finally, with his team losing, Albert snapped off the radio in disgust and then grinned when his mother teased him about it. They sat comfortably for a while, listening to the sounds of the game outside, Annie bossing and arguing with her brothers over the rules.

After a while, Louie asked Albert the question that she had been waiting for such a moment to ask. "You haven't said anything in a while about your young lady friend in Missouri, Albert," she offered as a leading opening.

"No," he replied flatly.

Louie had waited too long to discuss this and was not going to let it go at that. Finally, she got him to admit there had been a misunderstanding. She wanted to laugh when he revealed that much, but she remembered being twenty-one once too – how these things could seem like the end of the world. "Do you want to tell me about it?" she asked.

"She made it pretty plain in her last letter," was all he said. "Besides, she's in Missouri and I am not."

Pressing him further (and Louie had become known for being outspoken these days, especially since the divorce, and making it plain she did not care what anyone thought about it) she drew Albert out.

He said it all started when he mentioned in a letter that Fairchild (who was his buddy in the navy) did not deserve what Betty (who was Dolores' best friend) had done to him. Albert explained to his mother that after being Fairchild's girl all through the war, Betty sent him a "Dear John" letter as soon as the Japanese surrendered, saying she did not want to write to him anymore, that she was going to marry someone else, and even asked Fairchild to return her pictures. Even though Fairchild had other girls, Betty was the one he was going to marry after the war. Another guy, and one who was not in the service at that, had stolen his girl while he was away fighting the war.

"Did Betty know she was his girl?" Louie asked.

"How could she not know?" Albert replied.

"Did she have an engagement ring?" Then seeing the answer was to that was "no", Louie added, "Did Betty know Fairchild wanted to marry her?"

Albert shrugged his shoulders. He was not sure, but still, Fairchild was in the navy and this other guy, a slacker who sat out the war at home, had no right to steal a hero's girl.

"So you and Dolores took different sides on this."

"She got bent all out of shape. We sent several letters back and forth about it and then she finally sent me a letter, telling me off and good," he said.

"Did you write back?"

"Yes, several times."

"Did you apologize?"

"No, why should I? She was wrong. No guy should get a letter like that, especially when he is in the service. It's not forgivable. I can't believe Dolores can't see that."

"It seems to me like Betty waited until after the war was over to send her letter, at least you have to admit that was the right thing to do."

Albert grudgingly agreed

"Do you still have the letter?"

Albert hesitated and then nodded.

"I can take a look at it if you like. Maybe I will have an idea what you can say to fix it." Albert still hesitated. "I am still a woman, you know, son. You seem like you could use a woman's intuition on this."

Albert brought out the letter, and so quickly that Louie could see he knew exactly where it was. She could also see it had been wadded up, crumpled and then carefully flattened out again. Obviously it had been read many times.

The letter started out simply "Ernest." Louie had to remember that was what Albert wanted to be called now, although he would always be Albert to her.

> You have made it perfectly clear what you think of Betty. You don't need to keep sending me letters about it. Especially when I don't think she did anything wrong. I know what you think. Do you think she was supposed to wait around forever for Fairchild to give her any indication? She wanted to marry him for the longest time. She alluded to that in her letters to him, but he never responded to that in any way. I have never met him, but I have

seen his pictures and read his letters and he seems completely self-centered and arrogant to me, especially treating Betty that way and stringing her along all that time.

Betty has no one else in the world. You know she is an orphan and thinks of Mom as her own mother and of me as her sister. She cried buckets over Fairchild – buckets AND buckets. It was so hard for her to do what she did.

And you are wrong about Charley Wadlow too, Ernest. He may have been here for all of the war, but he was not at home, either. They would not let him serve because of his heart, but he DID serve. He found a way to serve and volunteered at the O'Reilly hospital here, and for almost no pay, I might add. He worked as an orderly; cleaning up after those men he worshipped as heroes. He was so down on himself by then. That's why Mom brought him home sometimes for Sunday dinner. He was so completely alone here, and away from his home.

That's why Mom did it. You can't blame her. She did not try to throw them together, as you suggested. It just happened that Betty was here most of those times too. Charley always treated Betty so kindly and expected nothing from her. Nothing! He thought she was too beautiful and too good for him, whereas I think Fairchild always thought something better was going to come along. All Charley ever did was treat Betty like she was a real girl - no like she was a beautiful woman, WHICH SHE IS!!! I could NOT be any happier for her.

And Ernest, you are also wrong in what you wrote about the heroes. Sure, every man who was at the front was a hero, but they were not the only ones. There were plenty of heroes here at home too, who helped win the war. Just take the doctors at the hospital, and even the nurses like my Mom who worked alongside them putting all those wounded men back together and trying to keep their spirits up day after day. And there were even women like your own mother, who kept their farms going by themselves, feeding all of us with the men away, and even those of us who kept our victory gardens, growing what we could to help.

And there is also Charley – another hero in my book, and always will be. He has always been friendly and happy and cheerful, always eager to serve the men in the O'Reilly hospital, even though most of them treated him like dirt because he was not in uniform.

You are so very wrong, Ernest. You and your Fairchild were not the only heroes in the war, and you need to grow up and recognize that.

She only signed it, "Dolores."

Albert expected understanding and sympathetic words from his mother. Instead, after reading the letter with her hand pressed against her mouth the entire time, she reared back in her chair and laughed. She laughed until tears ran and had to press her hand against her side. Albert was insulted, hurt even, at his mother's laughter.

Finally, Louie wiped her eyes, "I guess she told you, didn't she? I like this girl. She is not afraid to say what she thinks. And that is rare, too rare, these days, and especially among the young ladies. Most of these girls will do anything to please a man."

"But what can I do?" he asked, leaning forward with his elbows on his knees, hoping she could tell him something that would fix it. "I don't think she will even open a letter if I sent one to her."

Louie was thoughtful for a moment, considering. She could see now what this girl meant to Albert.

It had been a long time since Louie had remembered the stories. It had been a long time for all of them. The Great War, the flu epidemic, the Great Depression and the Second World War, and even just making a living and going from one day to the next had gotten in the way. No one had told the stories for a while, not even Stella. But Louie remembered all of them just now. She remembered and knew what she had to do. Just as Bess had let go of Sukey. Just as Bess had handed Sukey over to Aunt Charity to become Mercy, Louie had to do the same thing now.

She saw for the first time, that it was all part of a long, long line, coming down from Old Bess to her. It was a line of giving, giving over, and giving up. Bess had handed over her granddaughter, knowing that was best for the child. It was the worst thing for Bess, but she still did it.

It was Louie's legacy, this love. This legacy of loving the child and thinking only of the child, that Louie must follow now. Louie must hand over Albert - or Ernest as he wanted to be known - to this unknown woman who was not, and never would be, a part of Texas. Just like Bess, Louie had the power to keep him here, to make him stay. And in a way that would make Louie happy. But just like Sukey, it would not be the best thing for Albert if she did.

Louie understood now. She finally understood what it had taken for Bess to hold little Sukey out to her Aunt Charity. Louie knew, and understood, what it had meant for Bess to love someone so selflessly that she wanted the best for that person, even if losing that person would be the worst possible solution for herself. Louie finally understood now what Bess had given to Sukey, what she had handed over when she gave Sukey to Charity, for

Sukey to become Mercy. It meant that Sukey did not exist any longer, almost like Albert would become Ernest. It also meant that Ernest, like Mercy, would have a much better life.

Louie would have to hand him over. It would not be easy for her. There were still three young children at home, children who depended on her - and on Ernest - for everything.

But Louie had to hand him over. She had to hand him over to this woman he had never even met, but that he still loved. It was his destiny, just as it had been the destiny of Bess when the hood was thrown over her head, and for Dove when she lay down with Master Wainwright, and for Sukey when she became Mercy, and for Mercy when she let herself love Jean Faure instead of going back to England, and for Oratio when she came to Texas. It had been part of that line that ran down through all of them to Louie. It was all part of the plan, and the destiny, for the line that extended from Old Bess, through Louie, and now to Albert and all those who would follow him. She was a part of that plan and her part in it was to release Albert.

She had to let Albert go. Instead of holding him here, she had to let him leave to have the life he was supposed to have. She could see now that this girl, Dolores, who lived way up in Missouri, was a part of that plan.

"Then I think you have to go up to Missouri," she said. "I think you have to go find this Dolores in Missouri and apologize to her."

Albert looked at his mother, not quite believing what he was hearing.

"And then I think you have to be honest with her," she continued.

"You have to be honest and tell her that you love her. Because you, my son, are going to marry her."

Louie G

EPILOGUE

All the family went to the Greyhound stop in Nixon to see Albert off. They were there to show him they were proud of him, but they were also there for Louie, knowing how difficult this had to be for her.

Louie knew she would manage somehow. She always had. She also knew she would have to let all her children go eventually. Maureen was sweet on a young man and would probably marry him soon. If she did not marry this one, there would be someone else soon enough. Maureen was more beautiful than anyone could have ever imagined when she was a little girl. People said she looked just like Louie looked when she was the same age, but Louie did not believe it. Maureen was too beautiful.

One by one, Louie would have to let them all go. They would have the lives they were supposed to have. It would be better for her to have Albert here a while longer, at least until she could get Annie and Lester Ray raised enough that she could start working full time, but there was never going to be a perfect time. She knew that.

Something nice had happened to Louie recently though, something she had never expected. He was a good, steady and hard-working man. He treated Louie nicely, like a lady, and so much better than anyone had ever treated her before. Although she had told no one about him, she knew in her heart that some day, if he asked, she was going to marry Morris Cobb.

While they waited for the bus, Louie wished Albert had accepted her gift to him. She had scraped the money together for him to take the *Texas Special*, the train that ran from San Antonio and right through Springfield, Missouri, on its way to St. Louis. It was only a coach ticket on an old, heavy-weight train, but she wanted him to arrive on that train. She wanted those people to see that he was an important young man with a family back home who loved him. But Albert, always sensible and never caring for anything for himself, cashed in the ticket and gave the money back to her. The gesture had been enough for him. She would have to be satisfied that he had a nice suit and four white shirts to go with it.

With her help, Albert wrote a letter to Dolores, telling her that he was coming and would like to see her. He apologized for his criticism of her friend Betty. He asked if she would have dinner with him, and also if she would bring Betty and her Charley along. He would like to meet them too. There had been no refusal from Dolores, but no acknowledgement either. Louie could see the girl was not going to make it easy for him, and secretly she admired that, even though she wanted to make a long-distance telephone call and tell the girl that she would never find a more genuine and honest man than her son.

About ten minutes before the bus was scheduled to arrive, the family began

399

saying their goodbyes. William and Stella were first and Louie was sure she saw her brother press some cash into Albert's hand. "For the trip," William insisted. Stella handed him a big paper bag of sandwiches and other goodies for him to take along. Food enough for a week at least, William teased. Mama Lillie crept forward, using her cane to ease her arthritic joints. She only placed a palm against Albert's face a moment and then turned away without a word.

Even Victoria Lovett, now ninety-four years old, insisted that one of her grandnephews drive her to the station in her old Cadillac. They stood discretely off to one side as they waited. Miss Victoria had already told Albert that she could remember his great, great grandmamma Oratio Newman Squyres, a very strong woman and the first of his family to come to Texas. She said Miss Oratio would be so very proud of him.

The other aunts and uncles filed past Louie's eldest son, bidding him goodbye, then his brothers, little Annie, and finally Maureen, who hung on his neck, crying just for a moment before she pushed away and made him promise to write, and that it would be the very first thing he did when he got there.

Finally it was time for Louie. She thought fleetingly that Vol should have been there too. But he was getting the care he needed in the Veteran's hospital and he had given up this right anyway. She was the only parent for these children now, and had been for several years. She hugged her son, but she could not say anything.

The bus driver was waiting. He impatiently released the brakes with a hiss, signaling it was time to go. Albert stood before her, ready to go, but she could not say a word to him. She could not let him go.

"Remember who you are," she finally managed. "Always remember who you are."

Albert nodded. He hugged Louie one more time, then turned and bounded up the steps. The driver closed the door and Albert, now Ernest, scrambled back to his seat and leaned out the bus window as they drove away. He waved in happy anticipation as he left Texas to begin the rest of his life.

And his mother knew that it was the best gift she could ever give him.

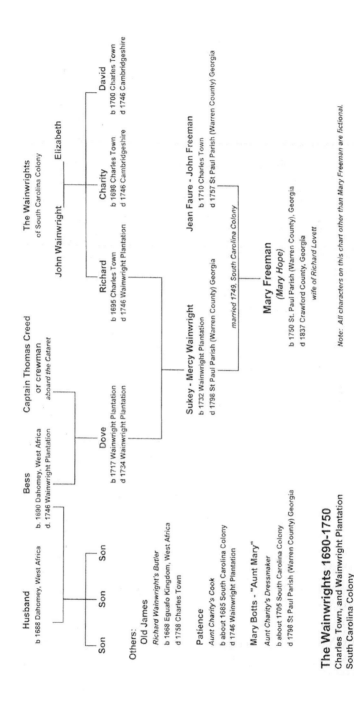

The Wainwrights of South Carolina Colony

John Wainwright — Elizabeth

David
b 1700 Charles Town
d 1746 Cambridgeshire

Charity
b 1698 Charles Town
d 1746 Cambridgeshire

Jean Faure — John Freeman
b 1710 Charles Town
d 1757 St Paul Parish (Warren County) Georgia

Richard
b 1695 Charles Town
d 1746 Wainwright Plantation

Sukey — Mercy Wainwright
b 1732 Wainwright Plantation
d 1798 St Paul Parish (Warren County) Georgia

married 1749, South Carolina Colony

Captain Thomas Creed
or crewman
aboard the Cataret

Mary Freeman
(Mary Hope)
b 1750 St. Paul Parish (Warren County), Georgia
d 1837 Crawford County, Georgia
wife of Richard Lovett

Dove
b 1717 Wainwright Plantation
d 1734 Wainwright Plantation

Bess
b 1690 Dahomey, West Africa
d. 1746 Wainwright Plantation

Note: All characters on this chart other than Mary Freeman are fictional.

Husband
b 1688 Dahomey, West Africa

Son   Son

Son

Others:

Old James
Richard Wainwright's Butler
b 1668 Eguafo Kingdom, West Africa
d 1758 Charles Town

Patience
Aunt Charity's Cook
b about 1685 South Carolina Colony
d 1746 Wainwright Plantation

Mary Botts - "Aunt Mary"
Aunt Charity's Dressmaker
b about 1705 South Carolina Colony
d 1798 St Paul Parish (Warren County) Georgia

The Wainwrights 1690-1750
Charles Town, and Wainwright Plantation
South Carolina Colony

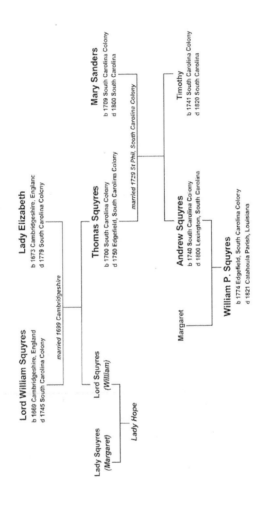

The South Carolina Squyres 1690-1780
Cambridgeshire, England and
South Carolina Colony

Lady Hope is a fictional character.

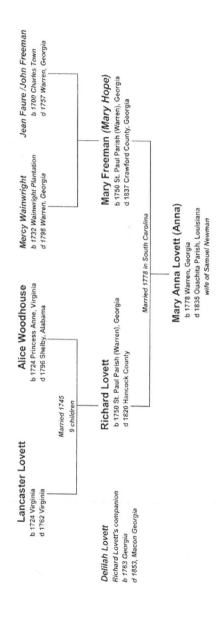

The Georgia Lovetts 1778-1795
Warren and Hancock Counties, Georgia

Names in italics are fictional characters.

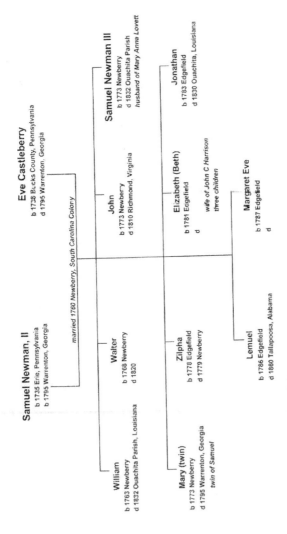

The Newmans 1730 - 1800
Newberry and Edgefield Counties, South Carolina
Warren County, Georgia

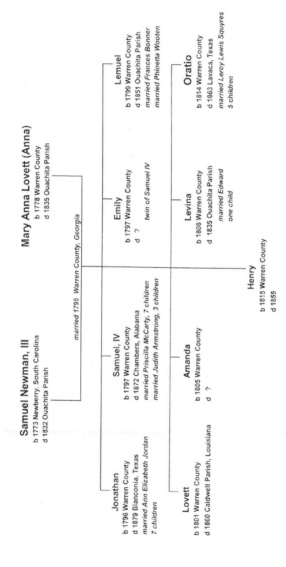

The Georgia Newmans 1795-1835
Warren County, Georgia
Ouachita Parish, Louisiana

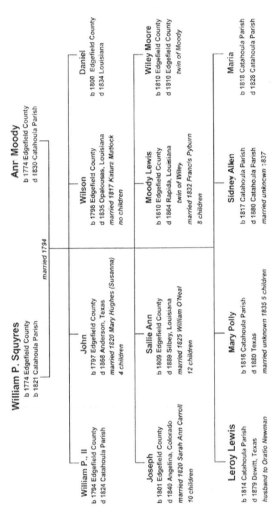

William P. Squyres
b 1774 Edgefield County
b 1821 Catahoula Parish

married 1794

Anr Moody
b 1774 Edgefield County
d 1830 Catahoula Parish

William P., II
b 1794 Edgefield County
d 1824 Catahoula Parish

Daniel
b 1800 Edgefield County
d 1834 Louisiana

John
b 1797 Edgefield County
d 1868 Anderson, Texas
married 1820 Mary Hughes (Susanna)
4 children

Wilson
b 1798 Edgefield County
d 1835 Opalousas, Louisiana
married 1817 Katura Matlock
no children

Joseph
b 1801 Edgefield County
d 1840 Angelina, Colorado
married 1820 Sarah Ann Carroll
10 children

Sallie Ann
b 1809 Edgefield County
d 1889 Silbey, Louisiana
married 1825 William O'Neal
12 children

Moody Lewis
b 1810 Edgefield County
d 1864 Rapida, Louisiana
twin of Wiley
married 1832 Francis Pyburn
8 children

Wiley Moore
b 1810 Edgefield County
d 1810 Edgefield County
twin of Moody

Leroy Lewis
b 1814 Catahoula Parish
d 1879 Dewitt, Texas
husband to Oratio Newman

Mary Polly
b 1816 Catahoula Parish
d 1880 Texas
married unknown 1835 5 children

Sidney Allen
b 1817 Catahoula Parish
d 1880 Catahoula Parish
married unknown 1837

Maria
b 1818 Catahoula Parish
d 1828 Catahoula Parish

The Louisiana Squyres 1810 - 1837
Edgefield County, South Carolina
Catahoula Parish, Louisiana

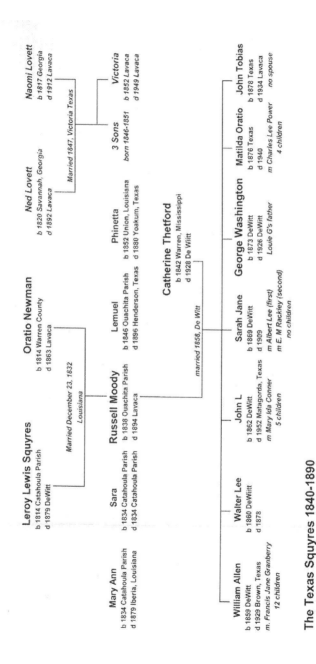

Leroy Lewis Squyres
b 1814 Catahoula Parish
d 1879 DeWitt

Oratio Newman
b 1814 Warren County
d 1863 Lavaca

Naomi Lovett
b 1817 Georgia
d 1912 Lavaca

Ned Lovett
b 1820 Savannah, Georgia
d 1892 Lavaca

Mary Ann
b 1834 Catahoula Parish
d 1879 Iberia, Louisiana

Sara
b 1834 Catahoula Parish
d 1834 Catahoula Parish

Russell Moody
b 1838 Ouachita Parish
d 1894 Lavaca

Lemuel
b 1846 Ouachita Parish
d 1896 Henderson, Texas

Phinetta
b 1852 Union, Louisiana
d 1880 Yoakum, Texas

3 Sons
born 1846-1851

Victoria
b 1852 Lavaca
d 1949 Lavaca

Married December 23, 1832
Louisiana

Married 1847, Victoria Texas

Catherine Thetford
b 1842 Warren, Mississippi
d 1928 De Witt

married 1858, De Witt

William Allen
b 1859 DeWitt
d 1929 Brown, Texas
m. Francis Jane Granberry
12 children

Walter Lee
b 1860 DeWitt
d 1878

John L
b 1862 DeWitt
d 1952 Matagorda, Texas
m Mary Ida Conner
5 children

Sarah Jane
b 1869 DeWitt
d 1909
m Albert Lee (first)
m E. M Rackley (second)
no children

George Washington
b 1873 DeWitt
d 1926 DeWitt
Louie G's father

Matilda Oratio
b 1876 Texas
d 1940
m Charles Lee Power
4 children

John Tobias
b 1878 Texas
d 1934 Texas
no spouse

Names in italics are fictional characters

The Texas Squyres 1840-1890
DeWitt and Lavaca Counties, Texas

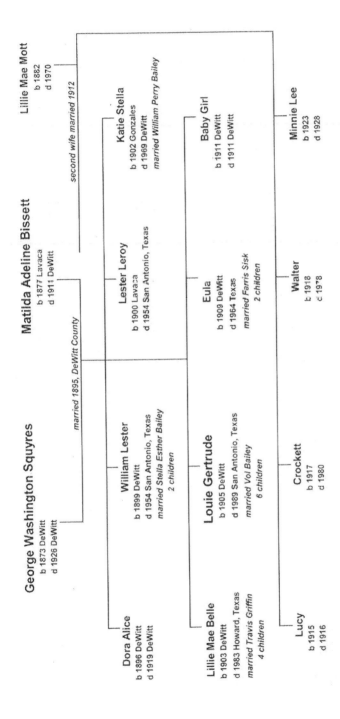

The Texas Squyres 1890-1946
DeWitt, Lavaca and Gonzales Counties, Texas

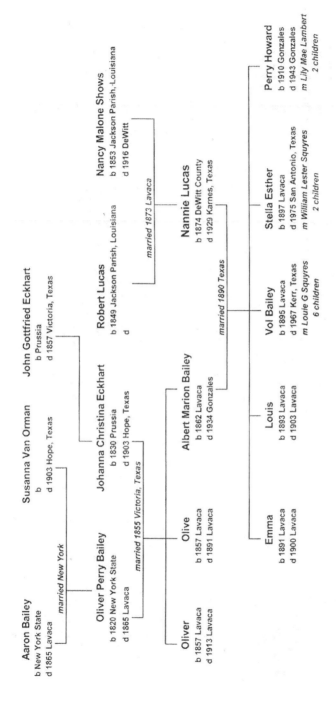

The Texas Baileys 1855-1910
DeWitt, Lavaca and Gonzales Counties, Texas

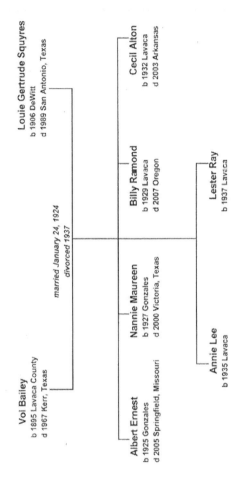

Louie G's family 1924-1946
Victoria, Gonzales and Lavaca Counties, Texas

Louie Gertrude Squyres 1906-1989
A strong Texas woman I wish I had known better.

Phinetta Squyres, about 1870
This photo inspired the book's character of
Oratio Newman Squyres who was Phinetta's mother.
(non-copyrighted photo)

Vol Bailey, age 8, about 1903

Maureen and Albert, on the Bailey farm about 1929

Brothers Albert and Billy Bailey, about 1935

Fairchild and Albert, about 1943.
Although the backdrop is fake,
they were on real shore leave in Honolulu.

Betty and Dolores - Gardening for Victory
Photo was likely taken to send to
Fairchild and Albert on the *U.S.S. President Hayes*

Albert in dress blues, 1944

Home for Christmas, Safe and Sound.
Maureen and Albert in San Antonio, December, 1945

Louie and Albert in Texas, early 1946
He returned to Texas after being released from the Navy
as Seaman First Class on December 12, 1945.

Dolores' sister, Anna Caroline (Carolyn) late 1940s
The letter Carolyn wrote to her mother, Myrtha, after Ernest arrived
in San Francisco only a few days after Dolores returned to Missouri,
opened the door for Myrtha to accept him as an eligible son-in-law.

Ernest, newly arrived in Missouri, 1946

This photograph was taken in front of the Noss home on North National, Dolores' mother, Myrtha, was newly married to Charlie Noss.

Ernest with his father, Vol, 1952

Happy at Last
Louie G. with some of her family in 1957

From left: Albert Ernest, his son Walter Gene, Louie Gertrude, Alan (the author at age 3),
Maureen's husband Louis, baby Roberta, Maureen, and Louie's husband, Morris Cobb.
Louie and Morris were happily married until his death in 1974.
Louie died in 1989 in San Antonio, at the home of her youngest daughter, Annie Lee.

Always remember who you are.

ABOUT THE AUTHOR

Louie G is the second novel in the series, *the Alexander Saga*. *Myrtha's Letters*, a supplement to *the Alexander Saga,* will be released in 2014.

The author continues work on the third and final novel in *the Alexander Saga.* A separate novel, *In Good Time,* was published in March, 2013.

Alan E Bailey is a certified public accountant and holds a master's degree from Drury University in Springfield, Missouri. He was a technical writer in accounting during much of his career. He retired in 2010 to pursue his love of travel and fiction writing on a full time basis.

When not traveling he shares his time between his home in Springfield and San Francisco.

Contact the author and see additional photos on
the Alexander Saga's Facebook page:
Myrthathebook.